The Dream of a Ridiculous Man

The Dream of a Ridiculous Man

and Other Stories

Fyodor Dostoevsky

WAKING LION PRESS

The views expressed in this book are the responsibility of the author and do not necessarily represent the position of The Editorium. The reader alone is responsible for the use of any ideas or information provided by this book.

This book is a work of fiction. The characters, places, and incidents in it are the products of the author's imagination or are represented fictitiously. Any resemblance of characters or events to actual persons or events is coincidental.

ISBN 1-60096-086-3

Published by Waking Lion Press, an imprint of The Editorium

The Editorium, LLC
West Valley City, UT 84128-3917
wakinglionpress.com
wakinglion@editorium.com

Contents

The Dream of a Ridiculous Man

Translated by Constance Garnett

I

I am a ridiculous person. Now they call me a madman. That would be a promotion if it were not that I remain as ridiculous in their eyes as before. But now I do not resent it, they are all dear to me now, even when they laugh at me—and, indeed, it is just then that they are particularly dear to me. I could join in their laughter—not exactly at myself, but through affection for them, if I did not feel so sad as I look at them. Sad because they do not know the truth and I do know it. Oh, how hard it is to be the only one who knows the truth! But they won't understand that. No, they won't understand it.

In old days I used to be miserable at seeming ridiculous. Not seeming, but being. I have always been ridiculous, and I have known it, perhaps, from the hour I was born. Perhaps from the time I was seven years old I knew I was ridiculous. Afterwards I went to school, studied at the university, and, do you know, the more I learned, the more thoroughly I understood that I was ridiculous. So that it seemed in the end as though all the sciences I studied at the university existed only to prove and make evident to me as I went more deeply into them that I was ridiculous. It was the same with life as it was with science. With every year the same consciousness of the ridiculous figure I cut in every relation grew and strengthened. Everyone always laughed at me. But not one of them knew or guessed that if there were one man on earth who knew better than anybody else that I was absurd, it was myself, and what I resented most of all was that they did not know that. But that was my own fault; I was so proud that nothing would have ever induced me to tell it to anyone. This pride grew in me with the years; and if it had happened that I allowed myself to confess to anyone that I was ridiculous, I believe that I should have blown out my brains the same evening. Oh, how I suffered in my early youth from the fear that I might give way and confess it to my schoolfellows. But since I grew to manhood, I have for some unknown reason become calmer, though I realised my awful characteristic more fully every year. I say 'unknown,' for to this day I cannot tell why it was. Perhaps it was owing to the terrible misery that was growing in my soul through something which was of more consequence than anything else about me: that something was the conviction that had come upon me that nothing in the world mattered. I had long had an inkling of it, but the full realisation came last year almost suddenly. I suddenly felt that it was all the same to me whether the world existed or whether there had never been anything at all: I began to feel with all my being that there was nothing existing. At first I fancied that many things had existed in the past, but afterwards I guessed that there never had been anything in the past either, but that it had only seemed so for some reason. Little by little I guessed that there would be nothing in the future either. Then I left off being angry with people and almost ceased to notice them. Indeed this showed itself even in the pettiest trifles: I used, for instance, to knock against people in the street. And not so much from being lost in thought: what had I to think about? I had almost given up thinking by that time; nothing mattered to me. If at least I had solved my problems! Oh, I had not settled one of them, and how many there were! But I gave up caring about anything, and all the problems disappeared.

And it was after that that I found out the truth. I learnt the truth last November—on the third of November, to be precise—and I remember every instant since. It was a gloomy evening, one of the gloomiest possible evenings. I was going home at about eleven o'clock, and I remember that I thought that the evening could not be gloomier. Even physically. Rain had been falling all day, and it had been a cold, gloomy, almost menacing rain, with, I remember, an unmistakable spite against mankind. Suddenly between ten and eleven it had stopped, and was followed by a horrible dampness, colder and damper than the rain, and a sort of steam was rising from everything, from every stone in the street, and from every by-lane if one looked down it as far as one could. A thought suddenly occurred to me, that if all the street lamps had been put out it would have been less cheerless, that the gas made one's heart sadder because it lighted it all up. I had had scarcely any dinner that day, and had been spending the evening with an engineer, and two other friends had been there also. I sat silent—I fancy I bored them. They talked of something rousing and suddenly they got excited over it. But they did not really care, I could see that, and only made a show of being excited. I suddenly said as much to them. "My friends," I said, "you really do not care one way or the other." They were not offended, but they laughed at me. That was because I spoke without any not of reproach, simply because it did not matter to me. They saw it did not, and it amused them.

As I was thinking about the gas lamps in the street I looked up at the sky. The sky was horribly dark, but one could distinctly see tattered clouds, and between them fathomless black patches. Suddenly I noticed in one of these patches a star, and began watching it intently. That was because that star had given me an idea: I decided to kill myself that night. I had firmly determined to do so two months before, and poor as I was, I bought a splendid revolver that very day, and loaded it. But two months had passed and it was still lying in my drawer; I was so utterly indifferent that I wanted to seize a moment when I would not be so indifferent—why, I don't know. And so for two months every night that I came home I thought I would shoot myself. I kept waiting for the right moment. And so now this star gave me a thought. I made up my mind that it should certainly be that night. And why the star gave me the thought I don't know.

And just as I was looking at the sky, this little girl took me by the elbow. The street was empty, and there was scarcely anyone to be seen. A cabman was sleeping in the distance in his cab. It was a child of eight with a kerchief on her head, wearing nothing but a wretched little dress all soaked with rain, but I noticed her wet broken shoes and I recall them now. They caught my eye particularly. She suddenly pulled me by the elbow and called me. She was not weeping, but was spasmodically crying out some words which could not utter properly, because she was shivering and shuddering all over. She was in terror about something, and kept crying, "Mammy, mammy!" I turned facing her, I did not say a word and went on; but she ran, pulling at me, and there was that note in her voice which in frightened children means despair. I know that sound. Though she did not articulate the words, I understood that her mother was dying, or that something of the sort was happening to them, and that she had run out to call someone, to find something to help her mother. I did not go with her; on the contrary, I had an impulse to drive her away. I told her first to go to a policeman. But clasping her hands, she ran beside me sobbing and gasping, and would not leave me. Then I stamped my foot and shouted at her. She called out "Sir! sir! . . ." but suddenly abandoned me and rushed headlong across the road. Some other passerby appeared there, and she evidently flew from me to him.

I mounted up to my fifth storey. I have a room in a flat where there are other lodgers. My room is small and poor, with a garret window in the shape of a semicircle. I have a sofa covered with American leather, a table with books on it, two chairs and a comfortable armchair, as old as old can be, but of the good old-fashioned shape. I sat down, lighted the candle, and began thinking. In the room next to mine, through the partition wall, a perfect Bedlam was going on. It had been going on for the last three days. A retired captain lived there, and he had half a dozen visitors, gentlemen of doubtful reputation, drinking vodka and playing stoss with old cards. The night before there had been a fight, and I know that two of them had been for a long time engaged in dragging each other about by the hair. The landlady wanted to complain, but she was in abject terror of the captain. There was only one other lodger in the flat, a thin little regimental lady, on a visit to Petersburg, with three little children who had been taken ill since they came into the lodgings. Both she and her children were in mortal fear of the captain, and lay trembling and crossing themselves all night, and the youngest child had a sort of fit from fright. That captain, I know for a fact, sometimes stops people in the Nevsky Prospect and begs. They won't take him into the service, but strange to say (that's why I am telling this), all this month that the captain has been here his behaviour has caused me no annoyance. I have, of course, tried to avoid his acquaintance from the very beginning, and he, too, was bored with me from the first; but I never care how much they shout the other side of the partition nor how many of them there are in there: I sit up all night and forget them so completely that I do not even hear them. I stay awake till daybreak, and have been going on like that for the last year. I sit up all night in my arm-chair at the table, doing nothing. I only read by day. I sit—don't even think; ideas of a sort wander through my mind and I let them come and go as they will. A whole candle is burnt every night. I sat down quietly at the table, took out the revolver and put it down before me. When I had put it down I asked myself, I remember, "Is that so?" and answered with complete conviction, "It is." That is, I shall shoot myself. I knew that I should shoot myself that night for certain, but how much longer I should go on sitting at the table I did not know. And no doubt I should have shot myself if it had not been for that little girl.

II

You see, though nothing mattered to me, I could feel pain, for instance. If anyone had stuck me it would have hurt me. It was the same morally: if anything very pathetic happened, I should have felt pity just as I used to do in old days when there were things in life that did matter to me. I had felt pity that evening. I should have certainly helped a child. Why, then, had I not helped the little girl? Because of an idea that occurred to me at the time: when she was calling and pulling at me, a question suddenly arose before me and I could not settle it. The question was an idle one, but I was vexed. I was vexed at the reflection that if I were going to make an end of myself that night, nothing in life ought to have mattered to me. Why was it that all at once I did not feel a strange pang, quite incongruous in my position. Really I do not know better how to convey my fleeting sensation at the moment, but the sensation persisted at home when I was sitting at the table, and I was very much irritated as I had not been for a long time past. One reflection followed another. I saw clearly that so long as I was still a human being and not nothingness, I was alive and so could suffer, be angry and feel shame at my actions. So be it. But if I am going to kill myself, in two hours, say, what is the little girl to me and what have I to do with shame or with anything else in the world? I shall turn into nothing, absolutely nothing. And can it really be true that the consciousness that I shall completely cease to exist immediately and so everything else will cease to exist, does not in the least affect my feeling of pity for the child nor the feeling of shame after a contemptible action? I stamped and shouted at the unhappy child as though to say—not only I feel no pity, but even if I behave inhumanly and contemptibly, I am free to, for in another two hours everything will be extinguished. Do you believe that that was why I shouted that? I am almost convinced of it now. I seemed clear to me that life and the world somehow depended upon me now. I may almost say that the world now seemed created for me alone: if I shot myself the world would cease to be at least for me. I say nothing of its being likely that nothing will exist for anyone when I am gone, and that as soon as my consciousness is extinguished the whole world will vanish too and become void like a phantom, as a mere appurtenance of my consciousness, for possibly all this world and all these people are only me myself. I remember that as I sat and reflected, I turned all these new questions that swarmed one after another quite the other way, and thought of something quite new. For instance, a strange reflection suddenly occurred to me, that if I had lived before on the moon or on Mars and there had committed the most disgraceful and dishonourable action and had there been put to such shame and ignominy as one can only conceive and realise in dreams, in nightmares, and if, finding myself afterwards on earth, I were able to retain the memory of what I had done on the other planet and at the same time knew that I should never, under any circumstances, return there, then looking from the earth to the moon—should I care or not? Should I feel shame for that action or not? These were idle and superfluous questions for the revolver was already lying before me, and I knew in every fibre of my being that it would happen for certain, but they excited me and I raged. I could not die now without having first settled something. In short, the child had saved me, for I put off my pistol shot for the sake of these questions. Meanwhile the clamour had begun to subside in the captain's room: they had finished their game, were settling down to sleep, and meanwhile were grumbling and languidly winding up their quarrels. At that point, I suddenly fell asleep in my chair at the table—a thing which had never happened to me before. I dropped asleep quite unawares.

Dreams, as we all know, are very queer things: some parts are presented with appalling vividness, with details worked up with the elaborate finish of jewellery, while others one gallops through, as it were, without noticing them at all, as, for instance, through space and time. Dreams seem to be spurred on not by reason but by desire, not by the head but by the heart, and yet what complicated tricks my reason has played sometimes in dreams, what utterly incomprehensible things happen to it! Mr brother died five years ago, for instance. I sometimes dream of him; he takes part in my affairs, we are very much interested, and yet all through my dream I quite know and remember that my brother is dead and buried. How is it that I am not surprised that, though he is dead, he is here beside me and working with me? Why is it that my reason fully accepts it? But enough. I will begin about my dream. Yes, I dreamed a dream, my dream of the third of November. They tease me now, telling me it was only a dream. But does it matter whether it was a dream or reality, if the dream made known to me the truth? If once one has recognized the truth and seen it, you know that it is the truth and that there is no other and there cannot be, whether you are asleep or awake. Let it be a dream, so be it, but that real life of which you make so much I had meant to extinguish by suicide, and my dream, my dream—oh, it revealed to me a different life, renewed, grand and full of power!

Listen.

III

I have mentioned that I dropped asleep unawares and even seemed to be still reflecting on the same subjects. I suddenly dreamt that I picked up the revolver and aimed it straight at my heart—my heart, and not my head; and I had determined beforehand to fire at my head, at my right temple. After aiming at my chest I waited a second or two, and suddenly my candle, my table, and the wall in front of me began moving and heaving. I made haste to pull the trigger.

In dreams you sometimes fall from a height, or are stabbed, or beaten, but you never feel pain unless, perhaps, you really bruise yourself against the bedstead, then you feel pain and almost always wake up from it. It was the same in my dream. I did not feel any pain, but it seemed as though with my shot everything within me was shaken and everything was suddenly dimmed, and it grew horribly black around me. I seemed to be blinded, and it benumbed, and I was lying on something hard, stretched on my back; I saw nothing, and could not make the slightest movement. People were walking and shouting around me, the captain bawled, the landlady shrieked—and suddenly another break and I was being carried in a closed coffin. And I felt how the coffin was shaking and reflected upon it, and for the first time the idea struck me that I was dead, utterly dead, I knew it and had no doubt of it, I could neither see nor move and yet I was feeling and reflecting. But I was soon reconciled to the position, and as one usually does in a dream, accepted the facts without disputing them.

And now I was buried in the earth. They all went away, I was left alone, utterly alone. I did not move. Whenever before I had imagined being buried the one sensation I associated with the grave was that of damp and cold. So now I felt that I was very cold, especially the tips of my toes, but I felt nothing else.

I lay still, strange to say I expected nothing, accepting without dispute that a dead man had nothing to expect. But it was damp. I don't know how long a time passed—whether an hour or several days, or many days. But all at once a drop of water fell on my closed left eye, making its way through the coffin lid; it was followed a minute later by a second, then a minute later by a third—and so on, regularly every minute. There was a sudden glow of profound indignation in my heart, and I suddenly felt in it a pang of physical pain. "That's my wound," I thought; "that's the bullet . . ." And drop after drop every minute kept falling on my closed eyelid. And all at once, not with my voice, but with my entire being, I called upon the power that was responsible for all that was happening to me:

"Whoever you may be, if you exist, and if anything more rational that what is happening here is possible, suffer it to be here now. But if you are revenging yourself upon me for my senseless suicide by the hideousness and absurdity of this subsequent existence, then let me tell you that no torture could ever equal the contempt which I shall go on dumbly feeling, though my martyrdom may last a million years!"

I made this appeal and held my peace. There was a full minute of unbroken silence and again another drop fell, but I knew with infinite unshakable certainty that everything would change immediately. And behold my grave suddenly was rent asunder, that is, I don't know whether it was opened or dug up, but I was caught up by some dark and unknown being and we found ourselves in space. I suddenly regained my sight. It was the dead of night, and never, never had there been such darkness. We were flying through space far away from the earth. I did not question the being who was taking me; I was proud and waited. I assured myself that I was not afraid, and was thrilled with ecstasy at the thought that I was not afraid. I do not know how long we were flying, I cannot imagine; it happened as it always does in dreams when you skip over space and time, and the laws of thought and existence, and only pause upon the points for which the heart yearns. I remember that I suddenly saw in the darkness a star. "Is that Sirius?" I asked impulsively, though I had not meant to ask questions.

"No, that is the star you saw between the clouds when you were coming home," the being who was carrying me replied.

I knew that it had something like a human face. Strange to say, I did not like that being, in fact I felt an intense aversion for it. I had expected complete non-existence, and that was why I had put a bullet through my heart. And here I was in the hands of a creature not human, of course, but yet living, existing. "And so there is life beyond the grave," I thought with the strange frivolity one has in dreams. But in its inmost depth my heart remained unchanged. "And if I have got to exist again," I thought, "and live once more under the control of some irresistible power, I won't be vanquished and humiliated."

"You know that I am afraid of you and despise me for that," I said suddenly to my companion, unable to refrain from the humiliating question which implied a confession, and feeling my humiliation stab my heart as with a pin. He did not answer my question, but all at once I felt that he was not even despising me, but was laughing at me and had no compassion for me, and that our journey had an unknown and mysterious object that concerned me only. Fear was growing in my heart. Something was mutely and painfully communicated to me from my silent companion, and permeated my whole being. We were flying through dark, unknown space. I had for some time lost sight of the constellations familiar to my eyes. I knew that there were stars in the heavenly spaces the light of which took thousands or millions of years to reach the earth. Perhaps we were already flying through those spaces. I expected something with a terrible anguish that tortured my heart. And suddenly I was thrilled by a familiar feeling that stirred me to the depths: I suddenly caught sight of our sun! I knew that it could not be our sun, that gave life to our earth, and that we were an infinite distance from our sun, but for some reason I knew in my whole being that it was a sun exactly like ours, a duplicate of it. A sweet, thrilling feeling resounded with ecstasy in my heart: the kindred power of the same light which had given me light stirred an echo in my heart and awakened it, and I had a sensation of life, the old life of the past for the first time since I had been in the grave.

"But if that is the sun, if that is exactly the same as our sun," I cried, "where is the earth?"

And my companion pointed to a star twinkling in the distance with an emerald light. We were flying straight towards it.

"And are such repetitions possible in the universe? Can that be the law of Nature? . . . And if that is an earth there, can it be just the same earth as ours . . . just the same, as poor, as unhappy, but precious and beloved for ever, arousing in the most ungrateful of her children the same poignant love for her that we feel for our earth?" I cried out, shaken by irresistible, ecstatic love for the old familiar earth which I had left. The image of the poor child whom I had repulsed flashed through my mind.

"You shall see it all," answered my companion, and there was a note of sorrow in his voice.

But we were rapidly approaching the planet. It was growing before my eyes; I could already distinguish the ocean, the outline of Europe; and suddenly a feeling of a great and holy jealousy glowed in my heart.

"How can it be repeated and what for? I love and can love only that earth which I have left, stained with my blood, when, in my ingratitude, I quenched my life with a bullet in my heart. But I have never, never ceased to love that earth, and perhaps on the very night I parted from it I loved it more than ever. Is there suffering upon this new earth? On our earth we can only love with suffering and through suffering. We cannot love otherwise, and we know of no other sort of love. I want suffering in order to love. I long, I thirst, this very instant, to kiss with tears the earth that I have left, and I don't want, I won't accept life on any other!"

But my companion had already left me. I suddenly, quite without noticing how, found myself on this other earth, in the bright light of a sunny day, fair as paradise. I believe I was standing on one of the islands that make up on our globe the Greek archipelago, or on the coast of the mainland facing that archipelago. Oh, everything was exactly as it is with us, only everything seemed to have a festive radiance, the splendour of some great, holy triumph attained at last. The caressing sea, green as emerald, splashed softly upon the shore and kissed it with manifest, almost conscious love. The tall, lovely trees stood in all the glory of their blossom, and their innumerable leaves greeted me, I am certain, with their soft, caressing rustle and seemed to articulate words of love. The grass glowed with bright and fragrant flowers. Birds were flying in flocks in the air, and perched fearlessly on my shoulders and arms and joyfully struck me with their darling, fluttering wings. And at last I saw and knew the people of this happy land. That came to me of themselves, they surrounded me, kissed me. The children of the sun, the children of their sun—oh, how beautiful they were! Never had I seen on our own earth such beauty in mankind. Only perhaps in our children, in their earliest years, one might find, some remote faint reflection of this beauty. The eyes of these happy people shone with a clear brightness. Their faces were radiant with the light of reason and fullness of a serenity that comes of perfect understanding, but those faces were gay; in their words and voices there was a note of childlike joy. Oh, from the first moment, from the first glance at them, I understood it all! It was the earth untarnished by the Fall; on it lived people who had not sinned. They lived just in such a paradise as that in which, according to all the legends of mankind, our first parents lived before they sinned; the only difference was that all this earth was the same paradise. These people, laughing joyfully, thronged round me and caressed me; they took me home with them, and each of them tried to reassure me. Oh, they asked me no questions, but they seemed, I fancied, to know everything without asking, and they wanted to make haste to smooth away the signs of suffering from my face.

IV

And do you know what? Well, granted that it was only a dream, yet the sensation of the love of those innocent and beautiful people has remained with me for ever, and I feel as though their love is still flowing out to me from over there. I have seen them myself, have known them and been convinced; I loved them, I suffered for them afterwards. Oh, I understood at once even at the time that in many things I could not understand them at all; as an up-to-date Russian progressive and contemptible Petersburger, it struck me as inexplicable that, knowing so much, they had, for instance, no science like our. But I soon realised that their knowledge was gained and fostered by intuitions different from those of us on earth, and that their aspirations, too, were quite different. They desired nothing and were at peace; they did not aspire to knowledge of life as we aspire to understand it, because their lives were full. But their knowledge was higher and deeper than ours; for our science seeks to explain what life is, aspires to understand it in order to teach others how to love, while they without science knew how to live; and that I understood, but I could not understand their knowledge. They showed me their trees, and I could not understand the intense love with which they looked at them; it was as though they were talking with creatures like themselves. And perhaps I shall not be mistaken if I say that they conversed with them. Yes, they had found their language, and I am convinced that the trees understood them. They looked at all Nature like that—at the animals who lived in peace with them and did not attack them, but loved them, conquered by their love. They pointed to the stars and told me something about them which I could not understand, but I am convinced that they were somehow in touch with the stars, not only in thought, but by some living channel. Oh, these people did not persist in trying to make me understand them, they loved me without that, but I knew that they would never understand me, and so I hardly spoke to them about our earth. I only kissed in their presence the earth on which they lived and mutely worshipped them themselves. And they saw that and let me worship them without being abashed at my adoration, for they themselves loved much. They were not unhappy on my account when at times I kissed their feet with tears, joyfully conscious of the love with which they would respond to mine. At times I asked myself with wonder how it was they were able never to offend a creature like me, and never once to arouse a feeling of jealousy or envy in me? Often I wondered how it could be that, boastful and untruthful as I was, I never talked to them of what I knew—of which, of course, they had no notion—that I was never tempted to do so by a desire to astonish or even to benefit them.

They were as gay and sportive as children. They wandered about their lovely woods and copses, they sang their lovely songs; their fair was light—the fruits of their trees, the honey from their woods, and the milk of the animals who loved them. The work they did for food and raiment was brief and not labourious. They loved and begot children, but I never noticed in them the impulse of that cruel sensuality which overcomes almost every man on this earth, all and each, and is the source of almost every sin of mankind on earth. They rejoiced at the arrival of children as new beings to share their happiness. There was no quarrelling, no jealousy among them, and they did not even know what the words meant. Their children were the children of all, for they all made up one family. There was scarcely any illness among them, though there was death; but their old people died peacefully, as though falling asleep, giving blessings and smiles to those who surrounded them to take their last farewell with bright and lovely smiles. I never saw grief or tears on those occasions, but only love, which reached the point of ecstasy, but a calm ecstasy, made perfect and contemplative. One might think that they were still in contact with the departed after death, and that their earthly union was not cut short by death. They scarcely understood me when I questioned them about immortality, but evidently they were so convinced of it without reasoning that it was not for them a question at all. They had no temples, but they had a real living and uninterrupted sense of oneness with the whole of the universe; they had no creed, but they had a certain knowledge that when their earthly joy had reached the limits of earthly nature, then there would come for them, for the living and for the dead, a still greater fullness of contact with the whole of the universe. They looked forward to that moment with joy, but without haste, not pining for it, but seeming to have a foretaste of it in their hearts, of which they talked to one another.

In the evening before going to sleep they liked singing in musical and harmonious chorus. In those songs they expressed all the sensations that the parting day had given them, sang its glories and took leave of it. They sang the praises of nature, of the sea, of the woods. They liked making songs about one another, and praised each other like children; they were the simplest songs, but they sprang from their hearts and went to one's heart. And not only in their songs but in all their lives they seemed to do nothing but admire one another. It was like being in love with each other, but an all-embracing, universal feeling.

Some of their songs, solemn and rapturous, I scarcely understood at all. Though I understood the words I could never fathom their full significance. It remained, as it were, beyond the grasp of my mind, yet my heart unconsciously absorbed it more and more. I often told them that I had had a presentiment of it long before, that this joy and glory had come to me on our earth in the form of a yearning melancholy that at times approached insufferable sorrow; that I had had a foreknowledge of them all and of their glory in the dreams of my heart and the visions of my mind; that often on our earth I could not look at the setting sun without tears . . . that in my hatred for the men of our earth there was always a yearning anguish: why could I not hate them without loving them? why could I not help forgiving them? and in my love for them there was a yearning grief: why could I not love them without hating them? They listened to me, and I saw they could not conceive what I was saying, but I did not regret that I had spoken to them of it: I knew that they understood the intensity of my yearning anguish over those whom I had left. But when they looked at me with their sweet eyes full of love, when I felt that in their presence my heart, too, became as innocent and just as theirs, the feeling of the fullness of life took my breath away, and I worshipped them in silence.

Oh, everyone laughs in my face now, and assures me that one cannot dream of such details as I am telling now, that I only dreamed or felt one sensation that arose in my heart in delirium and made up the details myself when I woke up. And when I told them that perhaps it really was so, my God, how they shouted with laughter in my face, and what mirth I caused! Oh, yes, of course I was overcome by the mere sensation of my dream, and that was all that was preserved in my cruelly wounded heart; but the actual forms and images of my dream, that is, the very ones I really saw at the very time of my dream, were filled with such harmony, were so lovely and enchanting and were so actual, that on awakening I was, of course, incapable of clothing them in our poor language, so that they were bound to become blurred in my mind; and so perhaps I really was forced afterwards to make up the details, and so of course to distort them in my passionate desire to convey some at least of them as quickly as I could. But on the other hand, how can I help believing that it was all true? It was perhaps a thousand times brighter, happier and more joyful than I describe it. Granted that I dreamed it, yet it must have been real. You know, I will tell you a secret: perhaps it was not a dream at all! For then something happened so awful, something so horribly true, that it could not have been imagined in a dream. My heart may have originated the dream, but would my heart alone have been capable of originating the awful event which happened to me afterwards? How could I alone have invented it or imagined it in my dream? Could my petty heart and fickle, trivial mind have risen to such a revelation of truth? Oh, judge for yourselves: hitherto I have concealed it, but now I will tell the truth. The fact is that I . . . corrupted them all!

V

Yes, yes, it ended in my corrupting them all! How it could come to pass I do not know, but I remember it clearly. The dream embraced thousands of years and left in me only a sense of the whole. I only know that I was the cause of their sin and downfall. Like a vile trichina, like a germ of the plague infecting whole kingdoms, so I contaminated all this earth, so happy and sinless before my coming. They learnt to lie, grew fond of lying, and discovered the charm of falsehood. Oh, at first perhaps it began innocently, with a jest, coquetry, with amorous play, perhaps indeed with a germ, but that germ of falsity made its way into their hearts and pleased them. Then sensuality was soon begotten, sensuality begot jealousy, jealousy—cruelty . . . Oh, I don't know, I don't remember; but soon, very soon the first blood was shed. They marvelled and were horrified, and began to be split up and divided. They formed into unions, but it was against one another. Reproaches, upbraidings followed. They came to know shame, and shame brought them to virtue. The conception of honour sprang up, and every union began waving its flags. They began torturing animals, and the animals withdrew from them into the forests and became hostile to them. They began to struggle for separation, for isolation, for individuality, for mine and thine. They began to talk in different languages. They became acquainted with sorrow and loved sorrow; they thirsted for suffering, and said that truth could only be attained through suffering. Then science appeared. As they became wicked they began talking of brotherhood and humanitarianism, and understood those ideas. As they became criminal, they invented justice and drew up whole legal codes in order to observe it, and to ensure their being kept, set up a guillotine. They hardly remembered what they had lost, in fact refused to believe that they had ever been happy and innocent. They even laughed at the possibility o this happiness in the past, and called it a dream. They could not even imagine it in definite form and shape, but, strange and wonderful to relate, though they lost all faith in their past happiness and called it a legend, they so longed to be happy and innocent once more that they succumbed to this desire like children, made an idol of it, set up temples and worshipped their own idea, their own desire; though at the same time they fully believed that it was unattainable and could not be realised, yet they bowed down to it and adored it with tears! Nevertheless, if it could have happened that they had returned to the innocent and happy condition which they had lost, and if someone had shown it to them again and had asked them whether they wanted to go back to it, they would certainly have refused. They answered me:

"We may be deceitful, wicked and unjust, we know it and weep over it, we grieve over it; we torment and punish ourselves more perhaps than that merciful Judge Who will judge us and whose Name we know not. But we have science, and by the means of it we shall find the truth and we shall arrive at it consciously. Knowledge is higher than feeling, the consciousness of life is higher than life. Science will give us wisdom, wisdom will reveal the laws, and the knowledge of the laws of happiness is higher than happiness."

That is what they said, and after saying such things everyone began to love himself better than anyone else, and indeed they could not do otherwise. All became so jealous of the rights of their own personality that they did their very utmost to curtail and destroy them in others, and made that the chief thing in their lives. Slavery followed, even voluntary slavery; the weak eagerly submitted to the strong, on condition that the latter aided them to subdue the still weaker. Then there were saints who came to these people, weeping, and talked to them of their pride, of their loss of harmony and due proportion, of their loss of shame. They were laughed at or pelted with stones. Holy blood was shed on the threshold of the temples. Then there arose men who began to think how to bring all people together again, so that everybody, while still loving himself best of all, might not interfere with others, and all might live together in something like a harmonious society. Regular wars sprang up over this idea. All the combatants at the same time firmly believed that science, wisdom and the instinct of self-preservation would force men at last to unite into a harmonious and rational society; and so, meanwhile, to hasten matters, 'the wise' endeavoured to exterminate as rapidly as possible all who were 'not wise' and did not understand their idea, that the latter might not hinder its triumph. But the instinct of self-preservation grew rapidly weaker; there arose men, haughty and sensual, who demanded all or nothing. In order to obtain everything they resorted to crime, and if they did not succeed—to suicide. There arose religions with a cult of non-existence and self-destruction for the sake of the everlasting peace of annihilation. At last these people grew weary of their meaningless toil, and signs of suffering came into their faces, and then they proclaimed that suffering was a beauty, for in suffering alone was there meaning. They glorified suffering in their songs. I moved about among them, wringing my hands and weeping over them, but I loved them perhaps more than in old days when there was no suffering in their faces and when they were innocent and so lovely. I loved the earth they had polluted even more than when it had been a paradise, if only because sorrow had come to it. Alas! I always loved sorrow and tribulation, but only for myself, for myself; but I wept over them, pitying them. I stretched out my hands to them in despair, blaming, cursing and despising myself. I told them that all this was my doing, mine alone; that it was I had brought them corruption, contamination and falsity. I besought them to crucify me; I taught them how to make a cross. I could not kill myself, I had not the strength, but I wanted to suffer at their hands. I yearned for suffering, I longed that my blood should be drained to the last drop in these agonies. But they only laughed at me, and began at last to look upon me as crazy. They justified me, they declared that they had only got what they wanted themselves, and that all that now was could not have been otherwise. At last they declared to me that I was becoming dangerous and that they should lock me up in a madhouse if I did not hold my tongue. Then such grief took possession of my soul that my heart was wrung, and I felt as though I were dying; and then . . . then I awoke.

It was morning, that is, it was not yet daylight, but about six o'clock. I woke up in the same arm-chair; my candle had burnt out; everyone was asleep in the captain's room, and there was a stillness all round, rare in our flat. First of all I leapt up in great amazement: nothing like this had ever happened to me before, not even in the most trivial detail; I had never, for instance, fallen asleep like this in my arm-chair. While I was standing and coming to myself I suddenly caught sight of my revolver lying loaded, ready—but instantly I thrust it away! Oh, now, life, life! I lifted up my hands and called upon eternal truth, not with words, but with tears; ecstasy, immeasurable ecstasy flooded my soul. Yes, life and spreading the good tidings! Oh, I at that moment resolved to spread the tidings, and resolved it, of course, for my whole life. I go to spread the tidings, I want to spread the tidings—of what? Of the truth, for I have seen it, have seen it with my own eyes, have seen it in all its glory.

And since then I have been preaching! Moreover I love all those who laugh at me more than any of the rest. Why that is so I do not know and cannot explain, but so be it. I am told that I am vague and confused, and if I am vague and confused now, what shall I be later on? It is true indeed: I am vague and confused, and perhaps as time goes on I shall be more so. And of course I shall make many blunders before I find out how to preach, that is, find out what words to say, what things to do, for it is a very difficult task. I see all that as clear as daylight, but, listen, who does not make mistakes? An yet, you know, all are making for the same goal, all are striving in the same direction anyway, from the sage to the lowest robber, only by different roads. It is an old truth, but this is what is new: I cannot go far wrong. For I have seen the truth; I have seen and I know that people can be beautiful and happy without losing the power of living on earth. I will not and cannot believe that evil is the normal condition of mankind. And it is just this faith of mine that they laugh at. But how can I help believing it? I have seen the truth—it is not as though I had invented it with my mind, I have seen it, seen it, and the living image of it has filled my soul for ever. I have seen it in such full perfection that I cannot believe that it is impossible for people to have it. And so how can I go wrong? I shall make some slips no doubt, and shall perhaps talk in second-hand language, but not for long: the living image of what I saw will always be with me and will always correct and guide me. Oh, I am full of courage and freshness, and I will go on and on if it were for a thousand years! Do you know, at first I meant to conceal the fact that I corrupted them, but that was a mistake—that was my first mistake! But truth whispered to me that I was lying, and preserved me and corrected me. But how establish paradise—I don't know, because I do not know how to put it into words. After my dream I lost command of words. All the chief words, anyway, the most necessary ones. But never mind, I shall go and I shall keep talking, I won't leave off, for anyway I have seen it with my own eyes, though I cannot describe what I saw. But the scoffers do not understand that. It was a dream, they say, delirium, hallucination. Oh! As though that meant so much! And they are so proud! A dream! What is a dream? And is not our life a dream? I will say more. Suppose that this paradise will never come to pass (that I understand), yet I shall go on preaching it. And yet how simple it is: in one day, in one hour everything could be arranged at once! The chief thing is to love others like yourself, that's the chief thing, and that's everything; nothing else is wanted—you will find out at once how to arrange it all. And yet it's an old truth which has been told and retold a billion times—but it has not formed part of our lives! The consciousness of life is higher than life, the knowledge of the laws of happiness is higher than happiness—that is what one must contend against. And I shall. If only everyone wants it, it can be arranged at once.

And I tracked down that little girl . . . and I shall go on and on!

Bobok

Translated by Constance Garnett

Semyon Ardalyonovitch said to me all of a sudden the day before yesterday: "Why, will you ever be sober, Ivan Ivanovitch? Tell me that, pray."

A strange requirement. I did not resent it, I am a timid man; but here they have actually made me out mad. An artist painted my portrait as it happened: "After all, you are a literary man," he said. I submitted, he exhibited it. I read: "Go and look at that morbid face suggesting insanity."

It may be so, but think of putting it so bluntly into print. In print everything ought to be decorous; there ought to be ideals, while instead of that . . .

Say it indirectly, at least; that's what you have style for. But no, he doesn't care to do it indirectly. Nowadays humour and a fine style have disappeared, and abuse is accepted as wit. I do not resent it: but God knows I am not enough of a literary man to go out of my mind. I have written a novel, it has not been published. I have written articles—they have been refused. Those articles I took about from one editor to another; everywhere they refused them: you have no salt they told me. "What sort of salt do you want?" I asked with a sneer. "Attic salt?"

They did not even understand, For the most part I translate from the French for the booksellers. I write advertisements for shopkeepers too: "Unique opportunity! Fine tea, from our own plantations . . ." I made a nice little sum over a panegyric on his deceased excellency Pyotr Matveyitch. I compiled the "Art of pleasing the ladies," a commission from a bookseller. I have brought out some six little works of this kind in the course of my life. I am thinking of making a collection of the bons mobs of Voltaire, but am afraid it may seem a little flat to our people. Voltaire's no good now; nowadays we want a cudgel, not Voltaire. We knock each other's last teeth out nowadays. Well, so that's the whole extent of my literary activity. Though indeed I do send round letters to the editors gratis and fully signed. I give them all sorts of counsels and admonitions, criticise and point out the true path. The letter I sent last week to an editor's office was the fortieth I had sent in the last two years. I have wasted four roubles over stamps alone for them. My temper is at the bottom of it all.

I believe that the artist who painted me did so not for the sake of literature, but for the sake of two symmetrical warts on my forehead, a natural phenomenon, he would say. They have no ideas, so now they are out for phenomena. And didn't he succeed in getting my warts in his portrait—to the life. That is what they call realism.

And as to madness, a great many people were put down as mad among us last year. And in such language! "With such original talent . . . and yet, after all, it appears" . . . "however, one ought to have foreseen it long ago." That is rather artful; so that from the point of view of pure art one may really commend it. Well, but after all, these so-called madmen have turned out cleverer than ever. So it seems the critics can call them mad, but they cannot produce anyone better.

The wisest of all, in my opinion, is he who can, if only once a month, call himself a fool—a faculty unheard of nowadays. In old days, once a year at any rate a fool would recognise that he was a fool, but nowadays not a bit of it. And they have so muddled things up that there is no telling a fool from a wise man. They have done that on purpose.

I remember a witty Spaniard saying when, two hundred and fifty years ago, the French built their first madhouses: "They have shut up all their fools in a house apart, to make sure that they are wise men themselves." Just so: you don't show your own wisdom by shutting someone else in a madhouse. "K. has gone out of his mind, means that we are sane now." No, it doesn't mean that yet.

Hang it though, why am I maundering on? I go on grumbling and grumbling. Even my maidservant is sick of me. Yesterday a friend came to see me. "Your style is changing," he said; "it is choppy: you chop and chop—and then a parenthesis, then a parenthesis in the parenthesis, then you stick in something else in brackets, then you begin chopping and chopping again."

The friend is right. Something strange is happening to me. My character is changing and my head aches. I am beginning to see and hear strange things, not voices exactly, but as though someone beside me were muttering, "bobok, bobok, bobok!"

What's the meaning of this bobok? I must divert my mind.

I went out in search of diversion, I hit upon a funeral. A distant relation—a collegiate counsellor, however. A widow and five daughters, all marriageable young ladies. What must it come to even to keep them in slippers. Their father managed it, but now there is only a little pension. They will have to eat humble pie. They have always received me ungraciously. And indeed I should not have gone to the funeral now had it not been for a peculiar circumstance. I followed the procession to the cemetery with the rest; they were stuck-up and held aloof from me. My uniform was certainly rather shabby. It's five-and-twenty years, I believe, since I was at the cemetery; what a wretched place!

To begin with the smell. There were fifteen hearses, with palls varying in expensiveness; there were actually two catafalques. One was a general's and one some lady's. There were many mourners, a great deal of feigned mourning and a great deal of open gaiety. The clergy have nothing to complain of; it brings them a good income. But the smell, the smell. I should not like to be one of the clergy here.

I kept glancing at the faces of the dead cautiously, distrusting my impressionability. Some had a mild expression, some looked unpleasant. As a rule the smiles were disagreeable, and in some cases very much so. I don't like them; they haunt one's dreams.

During the service I went out of the church into the air: it was a grey day, but dry. It was cold too, but then it was October. I walked about among the tombs. They are of different grades. The third grade cost thirty roubles; it's decent and not so very dear. The first two grades are tombs in the church and under the porch; they cost a pretty penny. On this occasion they were burying in tombs of the third grade six persons, among them the general and the lady.

I looked into the graves—and it was horrible: water and such water! Absolutely green, and . . . but there, why talk of it! The gravedigger was baling it out every minute. I went out while the service was going on and strolled outside the gates. Close by was an almshouse, and a little further off there was a restaurant. It was not a bad little restaurant: there was lunch and everything. There were lots of the mourners here. I noticed a great deal of gaiety and genuine heartiness. I had something to eat and drink.

Then I took part in the bearing of the coffin from the church to the grave. Why is it that corpses in their coffins are so heavy? They say it is due to some sort of inertia, that the body is no longer directed by its owner . . . or some nonsense of that sort, in opposition to the laws of mechanics and common sense. I don't like to hear people who have nothing but a general education venture to solve the problems that require special knowledge; and with us that's done continually. Civilians love to pass opinions about subjects that are the province of the soldier and even of the field-marshal; while men who have been educated as engineers prefer discussing philosophy and political economy.

I did not go to the requiem service. I have some pride, and if I am only received owing to some special necessity, why force myself on their dinners, even if it be a funeral dinner. The only thing I don't understand is why I stayed at the cemetery; I sat on a tombstone and sank into appropriate reflections.

I began with the Moscow exhibition and ended with reflecting upon astonishment in the abstract. My deductions about astonishment were these:

"To be surprised at everything is stupid of course, and to be astonished at nothing is a great deal more becoming and for some reason accepted as good form. But that is not really true. To my mind to be astonished at nothing is much more stupid than to be astonished at everything. And, moreover, to be astonished at nothing is almost the same as feeling respect for nothing. And indeed a stupid man is incapable of feeling respect."

"But what I desire most of all is to feel respect. I thirst to feel respect," one of my acquaintances said to me the other day.

He thirsts to feel respect! Goodness, I thought, what would happen to you if you dared to print that nowadays? At that point I sank into forgetfulness. I don't like reading the epitaphs of tombstones: they are everlastingly the same. An unfinished sandwich was lying on the tombstone near me; stupid and inappropriate. I threw it on the ground, as it was not bread but only a sandwich. Though I believe it is not a sin to throw bread on the earth, but only on the floor. I must look it up in Suvorin's calendar.

I suppose I sat there a long time-too long a time, in fact; I must have lain down on a long stone which was of the shape of a marble coffin. And how it happened I don't know, but I began to hear things of all sorts being said. At first I did not pay attention to it, but treated it with contempt. But the conversation went on. I heard muffled sounds as though the speakers' mouths were covered with a pillow, and at the same time they were distinct and very near. I came to myself, sat up and began listening attentively.

"Your Excellency, it's utterly impossible. You led hearts, I return your lead, and here you play the seven of diamonds. You ought to have given me a hint about diamonds."

"What, play by hard and fast rules? Where is the charm of that?"

"You must, your Excellency. One can't do anything without something to go upon. We must play with dummy, let one hand not be turned up."

"Well, you won't find a dummy here."

What conceited words! And it was queer and unexpected. One was such a ponderous, dignified voice, the other softly suave; I should not have believed it if I had not heard it myself. I had not been to the requiem dinner, I believe. And yet how could they be playing preference here and what general was this? That the sounds came from under the tombstones of that there could be no doubt. I bent down and read on the tomb:

"Here lies the body of Major-General Pervoyedov . . . a cavalier of such and such orders." Hm! "Passed away in August of this year . . . fifty-seven. . . . Rest, beloved ashes, till the joyful dawn!"

Hm, dash it, it really is a general! There was no monument on the grave from which the obsequious voice came, there was only a tombstone. He must have been a fresh arrival. From his voice he was a lower court councillor.

"Oh-ho-ho-ho!" I heard in a new voice a dozen yards from the general's resting-place, coming from quite a fresh grave. The voice belonged to a man and a plebeian, mawkish with its affectation of religious fervour. "Oh-ho-ho-ho!"

"Oh, here he is hiccupping again!" cried the haughty and disdainful voice of an irritated lady, apparently of the highest society. "It is an affliction to be by this shopkeeper!"

"I didn't hiccup; why, I've had nothing to eat. It's simply my nature. Really, madam, you don't seem able to get rid of your caprices here."

"Then why did you come and lie down here?"

"They put me here, my wife and little children put me here, I did not lie down here of myself. The mystery of death! And I would not have lain down beside you not for any money; I lie here as befitting my fortune, judging by the price. For we can always do that—pay for a tomb of the third grade."

"You made money, I suppose? You fleeced people?"

"Fleece you, indeed! We haven't seen the colour of your money since January. There's a little bill against you at the shop."

"Well, that's really stupid; to try and recover debts here is too stupid, to my thinking! Go to the surface. Ask my niece—she is my heiress."

"There's no asking anyone now, and no going anywhere. We have both reached our limit and, before the judgment-seat of God, are equal in our sins."

"In our sins," the lady mimicked him contemptuously. "Don't dare to speak to me."

"Oh-ho-ho-ho!"

"You see, the shopkeeper obeys the lady, your Excellency."

"Why shouldn't he?"

"Why, your Excellency, because, as we all know, things are different here."

"Different? How?"

"We are dead, so to speak, your Excellency."

"Oh, yes! But still . . ."

Well, this is an entertainment, it is a fine show, I must say! If it has come to this down here, what can one expect on the surface? But what a queer business! I went on listening, however, though with extreme indignation.

"Yes, I should like a taste of life! Yes, you know . . . I should like a taste of fife." I heard a new voice suddenly somewhere in the space between the general and the irritable lady.

"Do you hear, your Excellency, our friend is at the same game again. For three days at a time he says nothing, and then he bursts out with 'I should like a taste of life, yes, a taste of life!' And with such appetite, he-he!"

"And such frivolity."

"It gets hold of him, your Excellency, and do you know, he is growing sleepy, quite sleepy—he has been here since April; and then all of a sudden 'I should like a taste of life!'"

"It is rather dull, though," observed his Excellency.

"It is, your Excellency. Shall we tease Avdotya Ignatyevna again, he-he?"

"No, spare me, please. I can't endure that quarrelsome virago."

"And I can't endure either of you," cried the virago disdainfully. "You are both of you bores and can't tell me anything ideal. I know one little story about you, your Excellency—don't turn up your nose, please—how a manservant swept you out from under a married couple's bed one morning."

"Nasty woman," the general muttered through his teeth.

"Avdotya lgnatycvna, ma'am," the shopkeeper wailed suddenly again, "my dear lady, don't be angry, but tell me, am I going through the ordeal by torment now, or is it something else?"

"Ah, he is at it again, as I expected! For there's a smell from him which means he is turning round!"

"I am not turning round, ma'am, and there's no particular smell from me, for I've kept my body whole as it should be, while you're regularly high. For the smell is really horrible even for a place like this. I don't speak of it, merely from politeness."

"Ah, you horrid, insulting wretch. He positively stinks and talks about me."

"Oh-ho-ho-ho! If only the time for my requiem would come quickly: I should hear their tearful voices over my head, my wife's lament and my children's soft weeping! . . ."

"Well, that's a thing to fret for! They'll stuff themselves with funeral rice and go home. . . . Oh, I wish somebody would wake up!"

"Avdotya Ignatyevna," said the insinuating government clerk, "wait a bit, the new arrivals will speak."

"And are there any young people among them?"

"Yes, there are, Avdotya Ignatyevna. There are some not more than lads."

"Oh, how welcome that would be!"

"Haven't they begun yet?" inquired his Excellency.

"Even those who came the day before yesterday haven't awakened yet, your Excellency. As you know, they sometimes don't speak for a week. It's a good job that to-day and yesterday and the day before they brought a whole lot. As it is, they are all last year's for seventy feet round."

"Yes, it will be interesting."

"Yes, your Excellency, they buried Tarasevitch, the privy councillor, to-day. I knew it from the voices. I know his nephew, he helped to lower the coffin just now."

"Hm, where is he, then?"

"Five steps from you, your Excellency, on the left. . . . Almost at your feet. You should make his acquaintance, your Excellency."

"Hm, no—it's not for me to make advances."

"Oh, he will begin of himself, your Excellency. He will be flattered. Leave it to me, your Excellency, and I . . ."

"Oh, oh! . . . What is happening to me?" croaked the frightened voice of a new arrival.

"A new arrival, your Excellency, a new arrival, thank God! And how quick he's been! Sometimes they don't say a word for a week."

"Oh, I believe it's a young man!" Avdotya Ignatyevna cried shrilly.

"I . . . I . . . it was a complication, and so sudden!" faltered the young man again. "Only the evening before, Schultz said to me, 'There's a complication,' and I died suddenly before morning. Oh! oh!"

"Well, there's no help for it, young man," the general observed graciously, evidently pleased at a new arrival. "You must be comforted. You are kindly welcome to our Vale of Jehoshaphat, so to call it. We are kind-hearted people, you will come to know us and appreciate us. Major-General Vassili Vassilitch Pervoyedov, at your service."

"Oh, no, no! Certainly not! I was at Schultz's; I had a complication, you know, at first it was my chest and a cough, and then I caught a cold: my lungs and influenza . . . and all of a sudden, quite unexpectedly . . . the worst of all was its being so unexpected."

"You say it began with the chest," the government clerk put in suavely, as though he wished to reassure the new arrival.

"Yes, my chest and catarrh and then no catarrh, but still the chest, and I couldn't breathe . . . and you know . . ."

"1know, I know. But if it was the chest you ought to have gone to Ecke and not to Schultz."

"You know, I kept meaning to go to Botkin's, and all at once . . ."

"Botkin is quite prohibitive," observed the general.

"Oh, no, he is not forbidding at all; I've heard he is so attentive and foretells everything beforehand."

"His Excellency was referring to his fees," the government clerk corrected him.

"Oh, not at all, he only asks three roubles, and he makes such an examination, and gives you a prescription . . . and I was very anxious to see him, for I have been told . . . Well, gentlemen, had I better go to Ecke or to Botkin?"

"What? To whom?" The general's corpse shook with agreeable laughter. The government clerk echoed it in falsetto.

"Dear boy, dear, delightful boy, how I love you!" Avdotya Ignatyevna squealed ecstatically. "I wish they had put someone like you next to me."

No, that was too much! And these were the dead of our times! Still, I ought to listen to more and not be in too great a hurry to draw conclusions. That snivelling new arrival—I remember him just now in his coffin—had the expression of a frightened chicken, the most revolting expression in the world! However, let us wait and see.

But what happened next was such a Bedlam that I could not keep it all in my memory. For a great many woke up at once; an official—a civil councillor—woke up, and began discussing at once the project of a new sub-committee in a government department and of the probable transfer of various functionaries in connection with the subcommittee—which very greatly interested the general. I must confess I learnt a great deal that was new myself, so much so that I marvelled at the channels by which one may sometimes in the metropolis learn government news. Then an engineer half woke up, but for a long time muttered absolute nonsense, so that our friends left off worrying him and let him lie till he was ready. At last the distinguished lady who had been buried in the morning under the catafalque showed symptoms of the reanimation of the tomb. Lebeziatnikov (for the obsequious lower court councillor whom I detested and who lay beside General Pervoyedov was called, it appears, Lebeziatnikov) became much excited, and surprised that they were all waking up so soon this time. I must own I was surprised too; though some of those who woke had been buried for three days, as, for instance, a very young girl of sixteen who kept giggling . . . giggling in a horrible and predatory way.

"Your Excellency, privy councillor Tarasevitch is waking!" Lebeziatnikov announced with extreme fussiness.

"Eh? What?" the privy councillor, waking up suddenly mumbled, with a lisp of disgust. There was a note of ill-humoured peremptoriness in the sound of his voice.

I listened with curiosity—for during the last few days I had heard something about Tarasevitch—shocking and upsetting in the extreme.

"It's I, your Excellency, so far only I."

"What is your petition? What do you want?"

"Merely to inquire after your Excellency's health; in these unaccustomed surroundings everyone feels at first, as it were, oppressed. General Pervoyedov wishes to have the honour of making your Excellency's acquaintance, and hopes . . ."

"I've never heard of him."

"Surely, your Excellency! General Pervoyedov, Vassili Vassilitch . . ."

"Are you General Pervoyedov?"

"No, your Excellency, I am only the lower court councillor Lebeziatnikov, at your service, but General Pervoyedov . . ."

"Nonsense! And I beg you to leave me alone."

"Let him be." General Pervoyedov at last himself checked with dignity the disgusting officiousness of his sycophant in the grave.

"He is not fully awake, your Excellency, you must consider that; it's the novelty of it all. When he is fully awake he will take it differently."

"Let him be," repeated the general.

"Vassili Vassilitch! Hey, your Excellency!" a perfectly new voice shouted loudly and aggressively from close beside Avdotya Ignatyevna. It was a voice of gentlemanly insolence, with the languid pronunciation now fashionable and an arrogant drawl. "I've been watching you all for the last two hours. Do you remember me, Vassili Vassilitch? My name is Klinevitch, we met at the Volokonskys' where you, too, were received as a guest, I am sure I don't know why."

"What, Count Pyotr Petrovitch? . . . Can it be really you . . . and at such an early age? How sorry I am to hear it."

"Oh, I am sorry myself, though I really don't mind, and I want to amuse myself as far as I can everywhere. And I am not a count but a baron, only a baron. We are only a set of scurvy barons, risen from being flunkeys, but why I don't know and I don't care. I am only a scoundrel of the pseudo-aristocratic society, and I am regarded as 'a charming polisson.' My father is a wretched little general, and my mother was at one time received en haut lieu. With the help of the Jew Zifel I forged fifty thousand rouble notes last year and then I informed against him, while Julic Charpentier de Lusignan carried off the money to Bordeaux. And only fancy, I was engaged to be married—to a girl still at school, three months under sixteen, with a dowry of ninety thousand. Avdotya Ignatyevna, do you remember how you seduced me fifteen years ago when I was a boy of fourteen in the Corps des Pages?"

"Ah, that's you, you rascal! Well, you are a godsend, anyway, for here. . . ."

"You were mistaken in suspecting your neighbour, the business gentleman, of unpleasant fragrance. . . . I said nothing, but I laughed. The stench came from me: they had to bury me in a nailed-up coffin."

"Ugh, you horrid creature! Still, I am glad you are here; you can't imagine the lack of life and wit here."

"Quite so, quite so, and I intend to start here something original. Your Excellency—I don't mean you, Pervoyedov—your Excellency the other one, Tarasevitch, the privy councillor! Answer! I am Klinevitch, who took you to Mlle. Furie in Lent, do you hear?"

"I do, Klinevitch, and I am delighted, and trust me .

"I wouldn't trust you with a halfpenny, and I don't care. I simply want to kiss you, dear old man, but luckily I can't. Do you know, gentlemen, what this grand-pere's little game was? He died three or four days ago, and would you believe it, he left a deficit of four hundred thousand government money from the fund for widows and orphans. He was the sole person in control of it for some reason, so that his accounts were not audited for the last eight years. I can fancy what long faces they all have now, and what they call him. It's a delectable thought, isn't it? I have been wondering for the last year how a wretched old man of seventy, gouty and rheumatic, succeeded in preserving the physical energy for his debaucheries—and now the riddle is solved! Those widows and orphans—the very thought of them must have egged him on! I knew about it long ago, I was the only one who did know; it was Julie told me, and as soon as I discovered it, I attacked him in a friendly way at once in Easter week: 'Give me twenty-five thousand, if you don't they'll look into your accounts to-morrow.' And just fancy, he had only thirteen thousand left then, so it seems it was very apropos his dying now. Grand-pere, grand-pere; do you hear?"

"Cher Khnevitch, I quite agree with you, and there was no need for you . . . to go into such details. Life is so full of suffering and torment and so little to make up for it . . . that I wanted at last to be at rest, and so far as I can see I hope to get all I can from here too."

"I bet that he has already sniffed Katiche Berestoy!"

"Who? What Katiche?" There was a rapacious quiver in the old man's voice.

"A-ah, what Katiche? Why, here on the left, five paces from me and ten from you. She has been here for five days, and if only you knew, grand-pere, what a little wretch she is! Of good family and breeding and a monster, a regular monster! I did not introduce her to anyone there, I was the only one who knew her. . . . Katiche, answer!"

"He-he-he!" the girl responded with a jangling laugh, in which there was a note of something as sharp as the prick of a needle. "He-he-he!"

"And a little blonde?" the grand-pere faltered, drawling out the syllables.

"He-he-he!"

"I . . . have long . . . I have long," the old man faltered breathlessly, "cherished the dream of a little fair thing of fifteen and just in such surroundings."

"Ach, the monster!" cried Avdotya Ignatyevna.

"Enough!" Klinevitch decided. "I see there is excellent material. We shall soon arrange things better. The great thing is to spend the rest of our time cheerfully; but what time? Hey, you, government clerk, Lebeziatnikov or whatever it is, I hear that's your name!"

"Semyon Yevseitch Lebeziatnikov, lower court councillor, at your service, very, very, very much delighted to meet you."

"I don't care whether you are delighted or not, but you seem to know everything here. Tell me first of all how it is we can talk? I've been wondering ever since yesterday. We are dead and yet we are talking and seem to be moving—and yet we are not talking and not moving. What jugglery is this?"

"If you want an explanation, baron, Platon Nikolaevitch could give you one better than I."

"What Platon Nikolaevitch is that? To the point. Don't beat about the bush."

"Platon Nikolaevitch is our home-grown philosopher, scientist and Master of Arts. He has brought out several philosophical works, but for the last three months he has been getting quite drowsy, and there is no stirring him up now. Once a week he mutters something utterly irrelevant."

"To the point, to the point!"

"He explains all this by the simplest fact, namely, that when we were living on the surface we mistakenly thought that death there was death. The body revives, as it were, here, the remains of life are concentrated, but only in consciousness. I don't know how to express it, but life goes on, as it were, by inertia. In his opinion everything is concentrated somewhere in consciousness and goes on for two or three months . . . sometimes even for half a year. . . . There is one here, for instance, who is almost completely decomposed, but once every six weeks he suddenly utters one word, quite senseless of course, about some bobok, 'Bobok, bobok,' but you see that an imperceptible speck of life is still warm within him."

"It's rather stupid. Well, and how is it I have no sense of smell and yet I feel there's a stench?"

"That . . . he-he . . . Well, on that point our philosopher is a bit foggy. It's apropos of smell, he said, that the stench one perceives here is, so to speak, moral—he-he! It's the stench of the soul, he says, that in these two or three months it may have time to recover itself . . . and this is, so to speak, the last mercy. . . . Only, I think, baron, that these are mystic ravings very excusable in his position. . . .

"Enough; all the rest of it, I am sure, is nonsense. The great thing is that we have two or three months more of life and then—bobok! I propose to spend these two months as agreeably as possible, and so to arrange everything on a new basis. Gentlemen! I propose to cast aside all shame."

"Ah, let us cast aside all shame, let us!" many voices could be heard saying; and strange to say, several new voices were audible, which must have belonged to others newly awakened. The engineer, now fully awake, boomed out his agreement with peculiar delight. The girl Katiche giggled gleefully.

"Oh, how I long to cast off all shame!" Avdotya lgnatyevna exclaimed rapturously.

"I say, if Avdotya lgnatyevna wants to cast off all shame . . . "

"No, no, no, Klinevitch, I was ashamed up there all the same, but here I should like to cast off shame, I should like it awfully."

"I understand, Klinevitch," boomed the engineer, "that you want to rearrange life here on new and rational principles."

"Oh, I don't care a hang about that! For that we'll wait for Kudeyarov who was brought here yesterday. When he wakes he'll tell you all about it. He is such a personality, such a titanic personality! Tomorrow they'll bring along another natural scientist, I believe, an officer for certain, and three or four days later a journalist, and, I believe, his editor with him. But deuce take them all, there will be a little group of us anyway, and things will arrange themselves. Though meanwhile I don't want us to be telling lies. That's all I care about, for that is one thing that matters. One cannot exist on the surface without lying, for life and lying are synonymous, but here we will amuse ourselves by not lying. Hang it all, the grave has some value after all! We'll all tell our stories aloud, and we won't be ashamed of anything. First of all I'll tell you about myself. I am one of the predatory kind, you know. All that was bound and held in check by rotten cords up there on the surface. Away with cords and let us spend these two months in shameless truthfulness! Let us strip and be naked!"

"Let us be naked, let us be naked!" cried all the voices.

"I long to be naked, I long to be," Avdotya Ignatyevna shrilled.

"Ah . . . ah, I see we shall have fun here; I don't want Ecke after all."

"No, I tell you. Give me a taste of life!"

"He-he-he!" giggled Katiche.

"The great thing is that no one can interfere with us, and though I see Pervoyedov is in a temper, he can't reach me with his hand. Grand-pere, do you agree?"

"I fully agree, fully, and with the utmost satisfaction, but on condition that Katiche is the first to give us her biography."

"I protest! I protest with all my heart!" General Pervoyedov brought out firmly.

"Your Excellency!" the scoundrel Lebeziatnikov persuaded him in a murmur of fussy excitement, "your Excellency, it will be to our advantage to agree. Here, you see, there's this girl's . . . and all their little affairs."

"There's the girl, it's true, but . . ."

"It's to our advantage, your Excellency, upon my word it is! If only as an experiment, let us try it. . . ."

"Even in the grave they won't let us rest in peace."

"In the first place, General, you were playing preference in the grave, and in the second we don't care a hang about you," drawled Klinevitch.

"Sir, I beg you not to forget yourself."

"What? Why, you can't get at me, and I can tease you from here as though you were Julie's lapdog. And another thing, gentlemen, how is he a general here? He was a general there, but here is mere refuse."

"No, not mere refuse. . . . Even here. . . ."

"Here you will rot in the grave and six brass buttons will be all that will be left of you."

"Bravo, Klinevitch, ha-ha-ha!" roared voices.

"I have served my sovereign. . . . I have the sword . . ."

"Your sword is only fit to prick mice, and you never drew it even for that."

"That makes no difference; I formed a part of the whole."

"There are all sorts of parts in a whole."

"Bravo, Klinevitch, bravo! Ha-ha-ha!"

"I don't understand what the sword stands for," boomed the engineer.

"We shall run away from the Prussians like mice, they'll crush us to powder!" cried a voice in the distance that was unfamiliar to me, that was positively spluttering with glee.

"The sword, sir, is an honour," the general cried, but only I heard him. There arose a prolonged and furious roar, clamour, and hubbub, and only the hysterically impatient squeals of Avdotya Ignatyevna were audible.

"But do let us make haste! Ah, when are we going to begin to cast off all shame!"

"Oh-ho-ho! . . . The soul does in truth pass through torments!" exclaimed the voice of the plebeian, "and . . ."

And here I suddenly sneezed. It happened suddenly and unintentionally, but the effect was striking: all became as silent as one expects it to be in a churchyard, it all vanished like a dream. A real silence of the tomb set in. I don't believe they were ashamed on account of my presence: they had made up their minds to cast off all shame! I waited five minutes—not a word, not a sound. It cannot be supposed that they were afraid of my informing the police; for what could the police do to them? I must conclude that they had some secret unknown to the living, which they carefully concealed from every mortal.

"Well, my dears," I thought, "I shall visit you again." And with those words, I left the cemetery.

No, that I cannot admit; no, I really cannot! The bobok case does not trouble me (so that is what the bobok signified!)

Depravity in such a place, depravity of the last aspirations, depravity of sodden and rotten corpses—and not even sparing the last moments of consciousness! Those moments have been granted, vouchsafed to them, and . . . and, worst of all, in such a place! No, that I cannot admit.

I shall go to other tombs, I shall listen everywhere. Certainly one ought to listen everywhere and not merely at one spot in order to form an idea. Perhaps one may come across something reassuring.

But I shall certainly go back to those. They promised their biographies and anecdotes of all sorts. Tfoo! But I shall go, I shall certainly go; it is a question of conscience!

I shall take it to the Citizen; the editor there has had his portrait exhibited too. Maybe he will print it.

The Christmas Tree and the Wedding

The other day I saw a wedding. . . . But no! I would rather tell you about a Christmas tree. The wedding was superb. I liked it immensely. But the other incident was still finer. I don't know why it is that the sight of the wedding reminded me of the Christmas tree. This is the way it happened:

Exactly five years ago, on New Year's Eve, I was invited to a children's ball by a man high up in the business world, who had his connections, his circle of acquaintances, and his intrigues. So it seemed as though the children's ball was merely a pretext for the parents to come together and discuss matters of interest to themselves, quite innocently and casually.

I was an outsider, and, as I had no special matters to air, I was able to spend the evening independently of the others. There was another gentleman present who like myself had just stumbled upon this affair of domestic bliss. He was the first to attract my attention. His appearance was not that of a man of birth or high family. He was tall, rather thin, very serious, and well dressed. Apparently he had no heart for the family festivities. The instant he went off into a corner by himself the smile disappeared from his face, and his thick dark brows knitted into a frown. He knew no one except the host and showed every sign of being bored to death, though bravely sustaining the role of thorough enjoyment to the end. Later I learned that he was a provincial, had come to the capital on some important, brain-racking business, had brought a letter of recommendation to our host, and our host had taken him under his protection, not at all *con amore.* It was merely out of politeness that he had invited him to the children's ball.

They did not play cards with him, they did not offer him cigars. No one entered into conversation with him. Possibly they recognised the bird by its feathers from a distance. Thus, my gentleman, not knowing what to do with his hands, was compelled to spend the evening stroking his whiskers. His whiskers were really fine, but he stroked them so assiduously that one got the feeling that the whiskers had come into the world first and afterwards the man in order to stroke them.

There was another guest who interested me. But he was of quite a different order. He was a personage. They called him Julian Mastakovich. At first glance one could tell he was an honoured guest and stood in the same relation to the host as the host to the gentleman of the whiskers. The host and hostess said no end of amiable things to him, were most attentive, wining him, hovering over him, bringing guests up to be introduced, but never leading him to any one else. I noticed tears glisten in our host's eyes when Julian Mastakovich remarked that he had rarely spent such a pleasant evening. Somehow I began to feel uncomfortable in this personage's presence. So, after amusing myself with the children, five of whom, remarkably well-fed young persons, were our host's, I went into a little sitting-room, entirely unoccupied, and seated myself at the end that was a conservatory and took up almost half the room.

The children were charming. They absolutely refused to resemble their elders, notwithstanding the efforts of mothers and governesses. In a jiffy they had denuded the Christmas tree down to the very last sweet and had already succeeded in breaking half of their playthings before they even found out which belonged to whom.

One of them was a particularly handsome little lad, dark-eyed, curly-haired, who stubbornly persisted in aiming at me with his wooden gun. But the child that attracted the greatest attention was his sister, a girl of about eleven, lovely as a Cupid. She was quiet and thoughtful, with large, full, dreamy eyes. The children had somehow offended her, and she left them and walked into the same room that

I had withdrawn into. There she seated herself with her doll in a corner.

"Her father is an immensely wealthy business man," the guests informed each other in tones of awe. "Three hundred thousand rubles set aside for her dowry already."

As I turned to look at the group from which I heard this news item issuing, my glance met Julian Mastakovich's. He stood listening to the insipid chatter in an attitude of concentrated attention, with his hands behind his back and his head inclined to one side.

All the while I was quite lost in admiration of the shrewdness our host displayed in the dispensing of the gifts. The little maid of the many-rubied dowry received the handsomest doll, and the rest of the gifts were graded in value according to the diminishing scale of the parents' stations in life. The last child, a tiny chap of ten, thin, red-haired, freckled, came into possession of a small book of nature stories without illustrations or even head and tail pieces. He was the governess's child. She was a poor widow, and her little boy, clad in a sorry-looking little nankeen jacket, looked thoroughly crushed and intimidated. He took the book of nature stories and circled slowly about the children's toys. He would have given anything to play with them. But he did not dare to. You could tell he already knew his place.

I like to observe children. It is fascinating to watch the individuality in them struggling for self-assertion. I could see that the other children's things had tremendous charm for the red-haired boy, especially a toy theatre, in which he was so anxious to take a part that he resolved to fawn upon the other children. He smiled and began to play with them. His one and only apple he handed over to a puffy urchin whose pockets were already crammed with sweets, and he even carried another youngster pickaback—all simply that he might be allowed to stay with the theatre.

But in a few moments an impudent young person fell on him and gave him a pummeling. He did not dare even to cry. The governess came and told him to leave off interfering with the other children's games, and he crept away to the same room the little girl and I were in. She let him sit down beside her, and the two set themselves busily dressing the expensive doll.

Almost half an hour passed, and I was nearly dozing off, as I sat there in the conservatory half listening to the chatter of the red-haired boy and the dowered beauty, when Julian Mastakovich entered suddenly. He had slipped out of the drawing-room under cover of a noisy scene among the children. From my secluded corner it had not escaped my notice that a few moments before he had been eagerly conversing with the rich girl's father, to whom he had only just been introduced.

He stood still for a while reflecting and mumbling to himself, as if counting something on his fingers.

"Three hundred—three hundred—eleven—twelve—thirteen—sixteen—in five years! Let's say four per cent—five times twelve—sixty, and on these sixty—. Let us assume that in five years it will amount to—well, four hundred. Hm—hm! But the shrewd old fox isn't likely to be satisfied with four per cent. He gets eight or even ten, perhaps. Let's suppose five hundred, five hundred thousand, at least, that's sure. Anything above that for pocket money—hm—"

He blew his nose and was about to leave the room when he spied the girl and stood still. I, behind the plants, escaped his notice. He seemed to me to be quivering with excitement. It must have been his calculations that upset him so. He rubbed his hands and danced from place to place, and kept getting more and more excited. Finally, however, he conquered his emotions and came to a standstill. He cast a determined look at the future bride and wanted to move toward her, but glanced about first. Then, as if with a guilty conscience, he stepped over to the child on tip-toe, smiling, and bent down and kissed her head.

His coming was so unexpected that she uttered a shriek of alarm.

"What are you doing here, dear child?" he whispered, looking around and pinching her cheek.

"We're playing."

"What, with him?" said Julian Mastakovich with a look askance at the governess's child. "You should go into the drawing-room, my lad," he said to him.

The boy remained silent and looked up at the man with wide-open eyes. Julian Mastakovich glanced round again cautiously and bent down over the girl.

"What have you got, a doll, my dear?"

"Yes, sir." The child quailed a little, and her brow wrinkled.

"A doll? And do you know, my dear, what dolls are made of?"

"No, sir," she said weakly, and lowered her head.

"Out of rags, my dear. You, boy, you go back to the drawing-room, to the children," said Julian Mastakovich looking at the boy sternly.

The two children frowned. They caught hold of each other and would not part.

"And do you know why they gave you the doll?" asked Julian Mastakovich, dropping his voice lower and lower.

"No."

"Because you were a good, very good little girl the whole week."

Saying which, Julian Mastakovich was seized with a paroxysm of agitation. He looked round and said in a tone faint, almost inaudible with excitement and impatience:

"If I come to visit your parents will you love me, my dear?"

He tried to kiss the sweet little creature, but the red-haired boy saw that she was on the verge of tears, and he caught her hand and sobbed out loud in sympathy. That enraged the man.

"Go away! Go away! Go back to the other room, to your playmates."

"I don't want him to. I don't want him to! You go away!" cried the girl. "Let him alone! Let him alone!" She was almost weeping.

There was a sound of footsteps in the doorway. Julian Mastakovich started and straightened up his respectable body. The red-haired boy was even more alarmed. He let go the girl's hand, sidled along the wall, and escaped through the drawing-room into the dining-room.

Not to attract attention, Julian Mastakovich also made for the dining-room. He was red as a lobster. The sight of himself in a mirror seemed to embarrass him. Presumably he was annoyed at his own ardour and impatience. Without due respect to his importance and dignity, his calculations had lured and pricked him to the greedy eagerness of a boy, who makes straight for his object—though this was not as yet an object; it only would be so in five years' time. I followed the worthy man into the dining-room, where I witnessed a remarkable play.

Julian Mastakovich, all flushed with vexation, venom in his look, began to threaten the red-haired boy. The red-haired boy retreated farther and farther until there was no place left for him to retreat to, and he did not know where to turn in his fright.

"Get out of here! What are you doing here? Get out, I say, you good-for-nothing! Stealing fruit, are you? Oh, so, stealing fruit! Get out, you freckle face, go to your likes!"

The frightened child, as a last desperate resort, crawled quickly under the table. His persecutor, completely infuriated, pulled out his large linen handkerchief and used it as a lash to drive the boy out of his position.

Here I must remark that Julian Mastakovich was a somewhat corpulent man, heavy, well-fed, puffy-cheeked, with a paunch and ankles as round as nuts. He perspired and puffed and panted. So strong was his dislike (or was it jealousy?) of the child that he actually began to carry on like a madman.

I laughed heartily. Julian Mastakovich turned. He was utterly confused and for a moment, apparently, quite oblivious of his immense importance. At that moment our host appeared in the doorway opposite. The boy crawled out from under the table and wiped his knees and elbows. Julian Mastakovich hastened to carry his handkerchief, which he had been dangling by the corner, to his nose. Our host looked at the three of us rather suspiciously. But, like a man who knows the world and can readily adjust himself, he seized upon the opportunity to lay hold of his very valuable guest and get what he wanted out of him.

"Here's the boy I was talking to you about," he said, indicating the red-haired child. "I took the liberty of presuming on your goodness in his behalf."

"Oh," replied Julian Mastakovich, still not quite master of himself.

"He's my governess's son," our host continued in a beseeching tone. "She's a poor creature, the widow of an honest official. That's why, if it were possible for you—"

"Impossible, impossible!" Julian Mastakovich cried hastily. "You must excuse me, Philip Alexeyevich, I really cannot. I've made inquiries. There are no vacancies, and there is a waiting list of ten who have a greater right—I'm sorry."

"Too bad," said our host. "He's a quiet, unobtrusive child."

"A very naughty little rascal, I should say," said Julian Mastakovich, wryly. "Go away, boy. Why are you here still? Be off with you to the other children."

Unable to control himself, he gave me a sidelong glance. Nor could I control myself. I laughed straight in his face. He turned away and asked our host, in tones quite audible to me, who that odd young fellow was. They whispered to each other and left the room, disregarding me.

I shook with laughter. Then I, too, went to the drawing-room. There the great man, already surrounded by the fathers and mothers and the host and the hostess, had begun to talk eagerly with a lady to whom he had just been introduced. The lady held the rich little girl's hand. Julian Mastakovich went into fulsome praise of her. He waxed ecstatic over the dear child's beauty, her talents, her grace, her excellent breeding, plainly laying himself out to flatter the mother, who listened scarcely able to restrain tears of joy, while the father showed his delight by a gratified smile.

The joy was contagious. Everybody shared in it. Even the children were obliged to stop playing so as not to disturb the conversation. The atmosphere was surcharged with awe. I heard the mother of the important little girl, touched to her profoundest depths, ask Julian Mastakovich in the choicest language of courtesy, whether he would honour them by coming to see them. I heard Julian Mastakovich accept the invitation with unfeigned enthusiasm. Then the guests scattered decorously to different parts of the room, and I heard them, with veneration in their tones, extol the business man, the business man's wife, the business man's daughter, and, especially, Julian Mastakovich.

"Is he married?" I asked out loud of an acquaintance of mine standing beside Julian Mastakovich.

Julian Mastakovich gave me a venomous look.

"No," answered my acquaintance, profoundly shocked by my—intentional—indiscretion.

* * *

Not long ago I passed the Church of ———. I was struck by the concourse of people gathered there to witness a wedding. It was a dreary day. A drizzling rain was beginning to come down. I made my way through the throng into the church. The bridegroom was a round, well-fed, pot-bellied little man, very much dressed up. He ran and fussed about and gave orders and arranged things. Finally word was passed that the bride was coming. I pushed through the crowd, and I beheld a marvellous beauty whose first spring was scarcely commencing. But the beauty was pale and sad. She looked distracted. It seemed to me even that her eyes were red from recent weeping. The classic severity of every line of her face imparted a peculiar significance and solemnity to her beauty. But through that severity and solemnity, through the sadness, shone the innocence of a child. There was something inexpressibly naive, unsettled and young in her features, which, without words, seemed to plead for mercy.

They said she was just sixteen years old. I looked at the bridegroom carefully. Suddenly I recognised Julian Mastakovich, whom I had not seen again in all those five years. Then I looked at the bride again.—Good God! I made my way, as quickly as I could, out of the church. I heard gossiping in the crowd about the bride's wealth—about her dowry of five hundred thousand rubles—so and so much for pocket money.

"Then his calculations were correct," I thought, as I pressed out into the street.

The Grand Inquisitor

Translated by H. P. Blavatsky

The following is an extract from M. Dostoevsky's celebrated novel, The Brothers Karamazov, *the last publication from the pen of the great Russian novelist, who died a few months ago, just as the concluding chapters appeared in print. Dostoevsky is beginning to be recognized as one of the ablest and profoundest among Russian writers. His characters are invariably typical portraits drawn from various classes of Russian society, strikingly life-like and realistic to the highest degree. The following extract is a cutting satire on modern theology generally and the Roman Catholic religion in particular. The idea is that Christ revisits earth, coming to Spain at the period of the Inquisition, and is at once arrested as a heretic by the Grand Inquisitor. One of the three brothers of the story, Ivan, a rank materialist and an atheist of the new school, is supposed to throw this conception into the form of a poem, which he describes to Alyosha—the youngest of the brothers, a young Christian mystic brought up by a "saint" in a monastery—as follows.*—The Theosophist, *November 1881*

* * *

"Quite impossible, as you see, to start without an introduction," laughed Ivan. "Well, then, I mean to place the event described in the poem in the sixteenth century, an age—as you must have been told at school—when it was the great fashion among poets to make the denizens and powers of higher worlds descend on earth and mix freely with mortals. . . . In France all the notaries' clerks, and the monks in the cloisters as well, used to give grand performances, dramatic plays in which long scenes were enacted by the Madonna, the angels, the saints, Christ, and even by God Himself. In those days, everything was very artless and primitive. An instance of it may be found in Victor Hugo's drama, *Nôtre Dame de Paris,* where, at the Municipal Hall, a play called *Le Bon Jugement de la Très-sainte et Grâceuse Vierge Marie,* is enacted in honour of Louis XI, in which the Virgin appears personally to pronounce her 'good judgment.' In Moscow, during the prepetrean period, performances of nearly the same character, chosen especially from the Old Testament, were also in great favour. Apart from such plays, the world was overflooded with mystical writings, 'verses'—the heroes of which were always selected from the ranks of angels, saints and other heavenly citizens answering to the devotional purposes of the age. The recluses of our monasteries, like the Roman Catholic monks, passed their time in translating, copying, and even producing original compositions upon such subjects, and that, remember, during the Tarter period!. . . In this connection, I am reminded of a poem compiled in a convent—a translation from the Greek, of course—called, 'The Travels of the Mother of God among the Damned,' with fitting illustrations and a boldness of conception inferior nowise to that of Dante. The 'Mother of God' visits hell, in company with the archangel Michael as her cicerone to guide her through the legions of the 'damned.' She sees them all, and is witness to their multifarious tortures. Among the many other exceedingly remarkably varieties of torments—every category of sinners having its own—there is one especially worthy of notice, namely a class of the 'damned' sentenced to gradually sink in a burning lake of brimstone and fire. Those whose sins cause them to sink so low that they no longer can rise to the surface are for ever forgotten by God, i.e., they fade out from the omniscient memory, says the poem—an expression, by the way, of an extraordinary profundity of thought, when closely analysed. The Virgin is terribly shocked, and falling down upon her knees in tears before the throne of God, begs that all she has seen in hell—all, all without exception, should have their sentences remitted to them. Her dialogue with God is colossally interesting. She supplicates, she will not leave Him. And when God, pointing to the pierced hands and feet of her Son, cries, 'How can I forgive His executioners?' She then commands that all the saints, martyrs, angels and archangels, should prostrate themselves with her before the Immutable and Changeless One and implore Him to change His wrath into mercy and—forgive them all. The poem closes upon her obtaining from God a compromise, a kind of yearly respite of tortures between Good Friday and Trinity, a chorus of the 'damned' singing loud praises to God from their 'bottomless pit,' thanking and telling Him: 'Thou art right, O Lord, very right, Thou hast condemned us justly.'

"My poem is of the same character.

"In it, it is Christ who appears on the scene. True, He says nothing, but only appears and passes out of sight. Fifteen centuries have elapsed since He left the world with the distinct promise to return 'with power and great glory'; fifteen long centuries since His prophet cried, 'Prepare ye the way of the Lord!' since He Himself had foretold, while yet on earth, 'Of that day and hour knoweth no man, no, not the angels of heaven but my Father only.' But Christendom expects Him still. . . .

"It waits for Him with the same old faith and the same emotion; aye, with a far greater faith, for fifteen centuries have rolled away since the last sign from heaven was sent to man,

And blind faith remained alone
To lull the trusting heart,
As heav'n would send a sign no more.

"True, again, we have all heard of miracles being wrought ever since the 'age of miracles' passed away to return no more. We had, and still have, our saints credited with performing the most miraculous cures; and, if we can believe their biographers, there have been those among them who have been personally visited by the Queen of Heaven. But Satan sleepeth not, and the first germs of doubt, and ever-increasing unbelief in such wonders, already had begun to sprout in Christendom as early as the sixteenth century. It was just at that time that a new and terrible heresy first made its appearance in the north of Germany.* [*Luther's reform] A great star 'shining as it were a lamp . . . fell upon the fountains waters' . . . and 'they were made bitter.' This 'heresy' blasphemously denied 'miracles.' But those who had remained faithful believed all the more ardently, the tears of mankind ascended to Him as heretofore, and the Christian world was expecting Him as confidently as ever; they loved Him and hoped in Him, thirsted and hungered to suffer and die for Him just as many of them had done before. . . . So many centuries had weak, trusting humanity implored Him, crying with ardent faith and fervour: 'How long, O Lord, holy and true, dost Thou not come!' So many long centuries hath it vainly appealed to Him, that at last, in His inexhaustible compassion, He consenteth to answer the prayer. . . . He decideth that once more, if it were but for one short hour, the people—His long-suffering, tortured, fatally sinful, his loving and child-like, trusting people—shall behold Him again. The scene of action is placed by me in Spain, at Seville, during that terrible period of the Inquisition, when, for the greater glory of God, stakes were flaming all over the country.

Burning wicked heretics,
In grand auto-da-fes.

"This particular visit has, of course, nothing to do with the promised Advent, when, according to the programme, 'after the tribulation of those days,' He will appear 'coming in the clouds of heaven.' For, that 'coming of the Son of Man,' as we are informed, will take place as suddenly 'as the lightning cometh out of the east and shineth even unto the west.' No; this once, He desired to come unknown, and appear among His children, just when the bones of the heretics, sentenced to be burnt alive, had commenced crackling at the flaming stakes. Owing to His limitless mercy, He mixes once more with mortals and in the same form in which He was wont to appear fifteen centuries ago. He descends, just at the very moment when before king, courtiers, knights, cardinals, and the fairest dames of court, before the whole population of Seville, upwards of a hundred wicked heretics are being roasted, in a magnificent auto-da-fe *ad majorem Dei gloriam,* by the order of the powerful Cardinal Grand Inquisitor.

"He comes silently and unannounced; yet all—how strange—yea, all recognize Him, at once! The population rushes towards Him as if propelled by some irresistible force; it surrounds, throngs, and presses around, it follows Him. . . . Silently, and with a smile of boundless compassion upon His lips, He crosses the dense crowd, and moves softly on. The Sun of Love burns in His heart, and warm rays of Light, Wisdom and Power beam forth from His eyes, and pour down their waves upon the swarming multitudes of the rabble assembled around, making their hearts vibrate with returning love. He extends His hands over their heads, blesses them, and from mere contact with Him, aye, even with His garments, a healing power goes forth. An old man, blind from his birth, cries, 'Lord, heal me, that I may see Thee!' and the scales falling off the closed eyes, the blind man beholds Him. . . . The crowd weeps for joy, and kisses the ground upon which He treads. Children strew flowers along His path and sing to Him, 'Hosanna!' It is He, it is Himself, they say to each other, it must be He, it can be none other but He! He pauses at the portal of the old cathedral, just as a wee white coffin is carried in, with tears and great lamentations. The lid is off, and in the coffin lies the body of a fair-child, seven years old, the only child of an eminent citizen of the city. The little corpse lies buried in flowers. 'He will raise the child to life!' confidently shouts the crowd to the weeping mother. The officiating priest who had come to meet the funeral procession, looks perplexed, and frowns. A loud cry is suddenly heard, and the bereaved mother prostrates herself at His feet. 'If it be Thou, then bring back my child to life!' she cries beseechingly. The procession halts, and the little coffin is gently lowered at his feet. Divine compassion beams forth from His eyes, and as He looks at the child, His lips are heard to whisper once more, 'Talitha Cumi'—and 'straightway the damsel arose.' The child rises in her coffin. Her little hands still hold the nosegay of white roses which after death was placed in them, and, looking round with large astonished eyes she smiles sweetly . . . . The crowd is violently excited. A terrible commotion rages among them, the populace shouts and loudly weeps, when suddenly, before the cathedral door, appears the Cardinal Grand Inquisitor himself. . . . He is tall, gaunt-looking old man of nearly four-score years and ten, with a stern, withered face, and deeply sunken eyes, from the cavity of which glitter two fiery sparks. He has laid aside his gorgeous cardinal's robes in which he had appeared before the people at the auto da-fe of the enemies of the Romish Church, and is now clad in his old, rough, monkish cassock. His sullen assistants and slaves of the 'holy guard' are following at a distance. He pauses before the crowd and observes. He has seen all. He has witnessed the placing of the little coffin at His feet, the calling back to life. And now, his dark, grim face has grown still darker; his bushy grey eyebrows nearly meet, and his sunken eye flashes with sinister light. Slowly raising his finger, he commands his minions to arrest Him. . . .

"Such is his power over the well-disciplined, submissive and now trembling people, that the thick crowds immediately give way, and scattering before the guard, amid dead silence and without one breath of protest, allow them to lay their sacrilegious hands upon the stranger and lead Him away. . . . That same populace, like one man, now bows its head to the ground before the old Inquisitor, who blesses it and slowly moves onward. The guards conduct their prisoner to the ancient building of the Holy Tribunal; pushing Him into a narrow, gloomy, vaulted prison-cell, they lock Him in and retire. . . .

"The day wanes, and night—a dark, hot breathless Spanish night—creeps on and settles upon the city of Seville. The air smells of laurels and orange blossoms. In the Cimmerian darkness of the old Tribunal Hall the iron door of the cell is suddenly thrown open, and the Grand Inquisitor, holding a dark lantern, slowly stalks into the dungeon. He is alone, and, as the heavy door closes behind him, he pauses at the threshold, and, for a minute or two, silently and gloomily scrutinizes the Face before him. At last approaching with measured steps, he sets his lantern down upon the table and addresses Him in these words:

"'It is Thou! . . . Thou!' . . . Receiving no reply, he rapidly continues: 'Nay, answer not; be silent! . . . And what couldst Thou say? . . . I know but too well Thy answer. . . . Besides, Thou hast no right to add one syllable to that which was already uttered by Thee before. . . . Why shouldst Thou now return, to impede us in our work? For Thou hast come but for that only, and Thou knowest it well. But art Thou as well aware of what awaits Thee in the morning? I do not know, nor do I care to know who thou mayest be: be it Thou or only thine image, to-morrow I will condemn and burn Thee on the stake, as the most wicked of all the heretics; and that same people, who to-day were kissing Thy feet, to-morrow at one bend of my finger, will rush to add fuel to Thy funeral pile. . . . Wert Thou aware of this?' he adds, speaking as if in solemn thought, and never for one instant taking his piercing glance off the meek Face before him." . . .

"I can hardly realize the situation described—what is all this, Ivan?" suddenly interrupted Alyosha, who had remained silently listening to his brother. "Is this an extravagant fancy, or some mistake of the old man, an impossible *quid pro quo*?"

"Let it be the latter, if you like," laughed Ivan, "since modern realism has so perverted your taste that you feel unable to realize anything from the world of fancy. . . . Let it be a *quid pro quo*, if you so choose it. Again, the Inquisitor is ninety years old, and he might have easily gone mad with his one *idée fixé* of power; or, it might have as well been a delirious vision, called forth by dying fancy, overheated by the auto-da-fe of the hundred heretics in that forenoon. . . . But what matters for the poem, whether it was a *quid pro quo* or an uncontrollable fancy? The question is, that the old man has to open his heart; that he must give out his thought at last; and that the hour has come when he does speak it out, and says loudly that which for ninety years he has kept secret within his own breast."

"And his prisoner, does He never reply? Does He keep silent, looking at him, without saying a word?"

"Of course; and it could not well be otherwise," again retorted Ivan. "The Grand Inquisitor begins from his very first words by telling Him that He has no right to add one syllable to that which He had said before. To make the situation clear at once, the above preliminary monologue is intended to convey to the reader the very fundamental idea which underlies Roman Catholicism—as well as I can convey it, his words mean, in short: 'Everything was given over by Thee to the Pope, and everything now rests with him alone; Thou hast no business to return and thus hinder us in our work.' In this sense the Jesuits not only talk but write likewise.

"'Hast thou the right to divulge to us a single one of the mysteries of that world whence Thou comest?' enquires of Him my old Inquisitor, and forthwith answers for Him. 'Nay, Thou has no such right. For, that would be adding to that which was already said by Thee before; hence depriving people of that freedom for which Thou hast so stoutly stood up while yet on earth. . . . Anything new that Thou would now proclaim would have to be regarded as an attempt to interfere with that freedom of choice, as it would come as a new and a miraculous revelation superseding the old revelation of fifteen hundred years ago, when Thou didst so repeatedly tell the people: "The truth shall make you free." Behold then, Thy "free" people now!' adds the old man with sombre irony. 'Yea! . . . It has cost us dearly.' he continues, sternly looking at his victim. 'But we have at last accomplished our task, and—in Thy name. . . . For fifteen long centuries we had to toil and suffer owing to that "freedom": but now we have prevailed and our work is done, and well and strongly it is done. . . . Believest not Thou it is so very strong? . . . And why should Thou look at me so meekly as if I were not worthy even of Thy indignation? . . . Know then, that now, and only now, Thy people feel fully sure and satisfied of their freedom; and that only since they have themselves and of their own free will delivered that freedom unto our hands by placing it submissively at our feet. But then, that is what we have done. Is it that which Thou has striven for? Is this the kind of "freedom" Thou has promised them?'"

"Now again, I do not understand," interrupted Alyosha. "Does the old man mock and laugh?"

"Not in the least. He seriously regards it as a great service done by himself, his brother monks and Jesuits, to humanity, to have conquered and subjected unto their authority that freedom, and boasts that it was done but for the good of the world. 'For only now,' he says (speaking of the Inquisition) 'has it become possible to us, for the first time, to give a serious thought to human happiness. Man is born a rebel, and can rebels be ever happy? . . . Thou has been fairly warned of it, but evidently to no use, since Thou hast rejected the only means which could make mankind happy; fortunately at Thy departure Thou hast delivered the task to us. . . . Thou has promised, ratifying the pledge by Thy own words, in words giving us the right to bind and unbind . . . and surely, Thou couldst not think of depriving us of it now!'"

"But what can he mean by the words, 'Thou has been fairly warned'?" asked Alexis.

"These words give the key to what the old man has to say for his justification. . . . But listen—

"'The terrible and wise spirit, the spirit of self annihilation and non-being,' goes on the Inquisitor, 'the great spirit of negation conversed with Thee in the wilderness, and we are told that he "tempted" Thee. . . . Was it so? And if it were so, then it is impossible to utter anything more truthful than what is contained in his three offers, which Thou didst reject, and which are usually called "temptations." Yea; if ever there was on earth a genuine striking wonder produced, it was on that day of Thy three temptations, and it is precisely in these three short sentences that the marvelous miracle is contained. If it were possible that they should vanish and disappear for ever, without leaving any trace, from the record and from the memory of man, and that it should become necessary again to devise, invent, and make them reappear in Thy history once more, thinkest Thou that all the world's sages, all the legislators, initiates, philosophers and thinkers, if called upon to frame three questions which should, like these, besides answering the magnitude of the event, express in three short sentences the whole future history of this our world and of mankind—dost Thou believe, I ask Thee, that all their combined efforts could ever create anything equal in power and depth of thought to the three propositions offered Thee by the powerful and all-wise spirit in the wilderness? Judging of them by their marvelous aptness alone, one can at once perceive that they emanated not from a finite, terrestrial intellect, but indeed, from the Eternal and the Absolute. In these three offers we find, blended into one and foretold to us, the complete subsequent history of man; we are shown three images, so to say, uniting in them all the future axiomatic, insoluble problems and contradictions of human nature, the world over. In those days, the wondrous wisdom contained in them was not made so apparent as it is now, for futurity remained still veiled; but now, when fifteen centuries have elapsed, we see that everything in these three questions is so marvelously foreseen and foretold, that to add to, or to take away from, the prophecy one jot, would be absolutely impossible!

"'Decide then thyself,' sternly proceeded the Inquisitor, 'which of ye twain was right: Thou who didst reject, or he who offered? Remember the subtle meaning of question the first, which runs thus: Wouldst Thou go into the world empty-handed? Would Thou venture thither with Thy vague and undefined promise of freedom, which men, dull and unruly as they are by nature, are unable so much as to understand, which they avoid and fear?—for never was there anything more unbearable to the human race than personal freedom! Dost Thou see these stones in the desolate and glaring wilderness? Command that these stones be made bread—and mankind will run after Thee, obedient and grateful like a herd of cattle. But even then it will be ever diffident and trembling, lest Thou should take away Thy hand, and they lose thereby their bread! Thou didst refuse to accept the offer for fear of depriving men of their free choice; for where is there freedom of choice where men are bribed with bread? Man shall not live by bread alone—was Thine answer. Thou knewest not, it seems, that it was precisely in the name of that earthly bread that the terrestrial spirit would one day rise against, struggle with, and finally conquer Thee, followed by the hungry multitudes shouting: "Who is like unto that Beast, who maketh fire come down from heaven upon the earth!" Knowest Thou not that, but a few centuries hence, and the whole of mankind will have proclaimed in its wisdom and through its mouthpiece, Science, that there is no more crime, hence no more sin on earth, but only hungry people? "Feed us first and then command us to be virtuous!" will be the words written upon the banner lifted against Thee—a banner which shall destroy Thy Church to its very foundations, and in the place of Thy Temple shall raise once more the terrible Tower of Babel; and though its building be left unfinished, as was that of the first one, yet the fact will remain recorded that Thou couldst, but wouldst not, prevent the attempt to build that new tower by accepting the offer, and thus saving mankind a millennium of useless suffering on earth. And it is to us that the people will return again. They will search for us catacombs, as we shall once more be persecuted and martyred—and they will begin crying unto us: "Feed us, for they who promised us the fire from heaven have deceived us!" It is then that we will finish building their tower for them. For they alone who feed them shall finish it, and we shall feed them in Thy name, and lying to them that it is in that name. Oh, never, never, will they learn to feed themselves without our help! No science will ever give them bread so long as they remain free, so long as they refuse to lay that freedom at our feet, and say: "Enslave, but feed us!" That day must come when men will understand that freedom and daily bread enough to satisfy all are unthinkable and can never be had together, as men will never be able to fairly divide the two among themselves. And they will also learn that they can never be free, for they are weak, vicious, miserable nonentities born wicked and rebellious. Thou has promised to them the bread of life, the bread of heaven; but I ask Thee again, can that bread ever equal in the sight of the weak and the vicious, the ever ungrateful human race, their daily bread on earth? And even supposing that thousands and tens of thousands follow Thee in the name of, and for the sake of, Thy heavenly bread, what will become of the millions and hundreds of millions of human beings to weak to scorn the earthly for the sake of Thy heavenly bread? Or is it but those tens of thousands chosen among the great and the mighty, that are so dear to Thee, while the remaining millions, innumerable as the grains of sand in the seas, the weak and the loving, have to be used as material for the former? No, no! In our sight and for our purpose the weak and the lowly are the more dear to us. True, they are vicious and rebellious, but we will force them into obedience, and it is they who will admire us the most. They will regard us as gods, and feel grateful to those who have consented to lead the masses and bear their burden of freedom by ruling over them—so terrible will that freedom at last appear to men! Then we will tell them that it is in obedience to Thy will and in Thy name that we rule over them. We will deceive them once more and lie to them once again—for never, never more will we allow Thee to come among us. In this deception we will find our suffering, for we must needs lie eternally, and never cease to lie!

"'Such is the secret meaning of "temptation" the first, and that is what Thou didst reject in the wilderness for the sake of that freedom which Thou didst prize above all. Meanwhile Thy tempter's offer contained another great world-mystery. By accepting the "bread," Thou wouldst have satisfied and answered a universal craving, a ceaseless longing alive in the heart of every individual human being, lurking in the breast of collective mankind, that most perplexing problem—"whom or what shall we worship?" There exists no greater or more painful anxiety for a man who has freed himself from all religious bias, than how he shall soonest find a new object or idea to worship. But man seeks to bow before that only which is recognized by the greater majority, if not by all his fellow-men, as having a right to be worshipped; whose rights are so unquestionable that men agree unanimously to bow down to it. For the chief concern of these miserable creatures is not to find and worship the idol of their own choice, but to discover that which all others will believe in, and consent to bow down to in a mass. It is that instinctive need of having a worship in common that is the chief suffering of every man, the chief concern of mankind from the beginning of times. It is for that universality of religious worship that people destroyed each other by sword. Creating gods unto themselves, they forwith began appealing to each other: "Abandon your deities, come and bow down to ours, or death to ye and your idols!" And so will they do till the end of this world; they will do so even then, when all the gods themselves have disappeared, for then men will prostrate themselves before and worship some idea. Thou didst know, Thou couldst not be ignorant of, that mysterious fundamental principle in human nature, and still thou hast rejected the only absolute banner offered Thee, to which all the nations would remain true, and before which all would have bowed—the banner of earthly bread, rejected in the name of freedom and of "bread in the kingdom of God"! Behold, then, what Thou hast done furthermore for that "freedom's" sake! I repeat to Thee, man has no greater anxiety in life than to find some one to whom he can make over that gift of freedom with which the unfortunate creature is born. But he alone will prove capable of silencing and quieting their consciences, that shall succeed in possessing himself of the freedom of men. With "daily bread" an irresistible power was offered Thee: show a man "bread" and he will follow Thee, for what can he resist less than the attraction of bread? But if, at the same time, another succeed in possessing himself of his conscience—oh! then even Thy bread will be forgotten, and man will follow him who seduced his conscience. So far Thou wert right. For the mystery of human being does not solely rest in the desire to live, but in the problem—for what should one live at all? Without a clear perception of his reasons for living, man will never consent to live, and will rather destroy himself than tarry on earth, though he be surrounded with bread. This is the truth. But what has happened? Instead of getting hold of man's freedom, Thou has enlarged it still more! Hast Thou again forgotten that to man rest and even death are preferable to a free choice between the knowledge of Good and Evil? Nothing seems more seductive in his eyes than freedom of conscience, and nothing proves more painful. And behold! instead of laying a firm foundation whereon to rest once for all man's conscience, Thou hast chosen to stir up in him all that is abnormal, mysterious, and indefinite, all that is beyond human strength, and has acted as if Thou never hadst any love for him, and yet Thou wert He who came to "lay down His life for His friends!" Thou hast burdened man's soul with anxieties hitherto unknown to him. Thirsting for human love freely given, seeking to enable man, seduced and charmed by Thee, to follow Thy path of his own free-will, instead of the old and wise law which held him in subjection, Thou hast given him the right henceforth to choose and freely decide what is good and bad for him, guided but by Thine image in his heart. But hast Thou never dreamt of the probability, nay, of the certainty, of that same man one day rejected finally, and controverting even Thine image and Thy truth, once he would find himself laden with such a terrible burden as freedom of choice? That a time would surely come when men would exclaim that Truth and Light cannot be in Thee, for no one could have left them in a greater perplexity and mental suffering than Thou has done, lading them with so many cares and insoluble problems. Thus, it is Thyself who hast laid the foundation for the destruction of Thine own kingdom and no one but Thou is to be blamed for it.

"'Meantime, every chance of success was offered Thee. There are three Powers, three unique Forces upon earth, capable of conquering for ever by charming the conscience of these weak rebels—men—for their own good; and these Forces are: Miracle, Mystery and Authority. Thou hast rejected all the three, and thus wert the first to set them an example. When the terrible and all-wise spirit placed Thee on a pinnacle of the temple and said unto Thee, "If Thou be the son of God, cast Thyself down, for it is written, He shall give His angels charge concerning Thee: and in their hands they shall bear Thee up, lest at any time Thou dash Thy foot against a stone!"—for thus Thy faith in Thy father should have been made evident, Thou didst refuse to accept his suggestion and didst not follow it. Oh, undoubtedly, Thou didst act in this with all the magnificent pride of a god, but then men—that weak and rebel race—are they also gods, to understand Thy refusal? Of course, Thou didst well know that by taking one single step forward, by making the slightest motion to throw Thyself down, Thou wouldst have tempted "the Lord Thy God," lost suddenly all faith in Him, and dashed Thyself to atoms against that same earth which Thou camest to save, and thus wouldst have allowed the wise spirit which tempted Thee to triumph and rejoice. But, then, how many such as Thee are to be found on this globe, I ask Thee? Couldst Thou ever for a moment imagine that men would have the same strength to resist such a temptation? Is human nature calculated to reject miracle, and trust, during the most terrible moments in life, when the most momentous, painful and perplexing problems struggle within man's soul, to the free decisions of his heart for the true solution? Oh, Thou knewest well that that action of Thine would remain recorded in books for ages to come, reaching to the confines of the globe, and Thy hope was, that following Thy example, man would remain true to his God, without needing any miracle to keep his faith alive! But Thou knewest not, it seems, that no sooner would man reject miracle than he would reject God likewise, for he seeketh less God than "a sign" from Him. And thus, as it is beyond the power of man to remain without miracles, so, rather than live without, he will create for himself new wonders of his own making; and he will bow to and worship the soothsayer's miracles, the old witch's sorcery, were he a rebel, a heretic, and an atheist a hundred times over. Thy refusal to come down from the cross when people, mocking and wagging their heads were saying to Thee—"Save Thyself if Thou be the son of God, and we will believe in Thee," was due to the same determination—not to enslave man through miracle, but to obtain faith in Thee freely and apart from any miraculous influence. Thou thirstest for free and uninfluenced love, and refuses the passionate adoration of the slave before a Potency which would have subjected his will once for ever. Thou judgest of men too highly here, again, for though rebels they be, they are born slaves and nothing more. Behold, and judge of them once more, now that fifteen centuries have elapsed since that moment. Look at them, whom Thou didst try to elevate unto Thee! I swear man is weaker and lower than Thou hast ever imagined him to be! Can he ever do that which Thou art said to have accomplished? By valuing him so highly Thou hast acted as if there were no love for him in Thine heart, for Thou hast demanded of him more than he could ever give—Thou, who lovest him more than Thyself! Hadst Thou esteemed him less, less wouldst Thou have demanded of him, and that would have been more like love, for his burden would have been made thereby lighter. Man is weak and cowardly. What matters it, if he now riots and rebels throughout the world against our will and power, and prides himself upon that rebellion? It is but the petty pride and vanity of a school-boy. It is the rioting of little children, getting up a mutiny in the class-room and driving their schoolmaster out of it. But it will not last long, and when the day of their triumph is over, they will have to pay dearly for it. They will destroy the temples and raze them to the ground, flooding the earth with blood. But the foolish children will have to learn some day that, rebels though they be and riotous from nature, they are too weak to maintain the spirit of mutiny for any length of time. Suffused with idiotic tears, they will confess that He who created them rebellious undoubtedly did so but to mock them. They will pronounce these words in despair, and such blasphemous utterances will but add to their misery—for human nature cannot endure blasphemy, and takes her own revenge in the end.

"'And thus, after all Thou has suffered for mankind and its freedom, the present fate of men may be summed up in three words: Unrest, Confusion, Misery! Thy great prophet John records in his vision, that he saw, during the first resurrection of the chosen servants of God—"the number of them which were sealed" in their foreheads, "twelve thousand" of every tribe. But were they, indeed, as many? Then they must have been gods, not men. They had shared Thy Cross for long years, suffered scores of years' hunger and thirst in dreary wildernesses and deserts, feeding upon locusts and roots—and of these children of free love for Thee, and self-sacrifice in Thy name, Thou mayest well feel proud. But remember that these are but a few thousands—of gods, not men; and how about all others? And why should the weakest be held guilty for not being able to endure what the strongest have endured? Why should a soul incapable of containing such terrible gifts be punished for its weakness? Didst Thou really come to, and for, the "elect" alone? If so, then the mystery will remain for ever mysterious to our finite minds. And if a mystery, then were we right to proclaim it as one, and preach it, teaching them that neither their freely given love to Thee nor freedom of conscience were essential, but only that incomprehensible mystery which they must blindly obey even against the dictates of their conscience. Thus did we. We corrected and improved Thy teaching and based it upon "Miracle, Mystery, and Authority." And men rejoiced at finding themselves led once more like a herd of cattle, and at finding their hearts at last delivered of the terrible burden laid upon them by Thee, which caused them so much suffering. Tell me, were we right in doing as we did. Did not we show our great love for humanity, by realizing in such a humble spirit its helplessness, by so mercifully lightening its great burden, and by permitting and remitting for its weak nature every sin, provided it be committed with our authorization? For what, then, hast Thou come again to trouble us in our work? And why lookest Thou at me so penetratingly with Thy meek eyes, and in such a silence? Rather shouldst Thou feel wroth, for I need not Thy love, I reject it, and love Thee not, myself. Why should I conceal the truth from Thee? I know but too well with whom I am now talking! What I had to say was known to Thee before, I read it in Thine eye. How should I conceal from Thee our secret? If perchance Thou wouldst hear it from my own lips, then listen: We are not with Thee, but with him, and that is our secret! For centuries have we abandoned Thee to follow him, yes—eight centuries. Eight hundred years now since we accepted from him the gift rejected by Thee with indignation; that last gift which he offered Thee from the high mountain when, showing all the kingdoms of the world and the glory of them, he saith unto Thee: "All these things will I give Thee, if Thou will fall down and worship me!" We took Rome from him and the glaive of Caesar, and declared ourselves alone the kings of this earth, its sole kings, though our work is not yet fully accomplished. But who is to blame for it? Our work is but in its incipient stage, but it is nevertheless started. We may have long to wait until its culmination, and mankind have to suffer much, but we shall reach the goal some day, and become sole Caesars, and then will be the time to think of universal happiness for men.

"'Thou couldst accept the glaive of Caesar Thyself; why didst Thou reject the offer? By accepting from the powerful spirit his third offer Thou would have realized every aspiration man seeketh for himself on earth; man would have found a constant object for worship; one to deliver his conscience up to, and one that should unite all together into one common and harmonious ant-hill; for an innate necessity for universal union constitutes the third and final affliction of mankind. Humanity as a whole has ever aspired to unite itself universally. Many were, the great nations with great histories, but the greater they were, the more unhappy they felt, as they felt the stronger necessity of a universal union among men. Great conquerors, like Timoor and Tchengis-Khan, passed like a cyclone upon the face of the earth in their efforts to conquer the universe, but even they, albeit unconsciously, expressed the same aspiration towards universal and common union. In accepting the kingdom of the world and Caesar's purple, one would found a universal kingdom and secure to mankind eternal peace. And who can rule mankind better than those who have possessed themselves of man's conscience, and hold in their hand man's daily bread? Having accepted Caesar's glaive and purple, we had, of course, but to deny Thee, to henceforth follow him alone. Oh, centuries of intellectual riot and rebellious free thought are yet before us, and their science will end by anthropophagy, for having begun to build their Babylonian tower without our help they will have to end by anthropophagy. But it is precisely at that time that the Beast will crawl up to us in full submission, and lick the soles of our feet, and sprinkle them with tears of blood and we shall sit upon the scarlet-colored Beast, and lifting up high the golden cup "full of abomination and filthiness," shall show written upon it the word "Mystery"! But it is only then that men will see the beginning of a kingdom of peace and happiness. Thou art proud of Thine own elect, but Thou has none other but these elect, and we—we will give rest to all. But that is not the end. Many are those among thine elect and the laborers of Thy vineyard, who, tired of waiting for Thy coming, already have carried and will yet carry, the great fervor of their hearts and their spiritual strength into another field, and will end by lifting up against Thee Thine own banner of freedom. But it is Thyself Thou hast to thank. Under our rule and sway all will be happy, and will neither rebel nor destroy each other as they did while under Thy free banner. Oh, we will take good care to prove to them that they will become absolutely free only when they have abjured their freedom in our favor and submit to us absolutely. Thinkest Thou we shall be right or still lying? They will convince themselves of our rightness, for they will see what a depth of degrading slavery and strife that liberty of Thine has led them into. Liberty, Freedom of Thought and Conscience, and Science will lead them into such impassable chasms, place them face to face before such wonders and insoluble mysteries, that some of them—more rebellious and ferocious than the rest—will destroy themselves; others—rebellious but weak—will destroy each other; while the remainder, weak, helpless and miserable, will crawl back to our feet and cry: "'Yes; right were ye, oh Fathers of Jesus; ye alone are in possession of His mystery, and we return to you, praying that ye save us from ourselves!" Receiving their bread from us, they will clearly see that we take the bread from them, the bread made by their own hands, but to give it back to them in equal shares and that without any miracle; and having ascertained that, though we have not changed stones into bread, yet bread they have, while every other bread turned verily in their own hands into stones, they will be only to glad to have it so. Until that day, they will never be happy. And who is it that helped the most to blind them, tell me? Who separated the flock and scattered it over ways unknown if it be not Thee? But we will gather the sheep once more and subject them to our will for ever. We will prove to them their own weakness and make them humble again, whilst with Thee they have learnt but pride, for Thou hast made more of them than they ever were worth. We will give them that quiet, humble happiness, which alone benefits such weak, foolish creatures as they are, and having once had proved to them their weakness, they will become timid and obedient, and gather around us as chickens around their hen. They will wonder at and feel a superstitious admiration for us, and feel proud to be led by men so powerful and wise that a handful of them can subject a flock a thousand millions strong. Gradually men will begin to fear us. They will nervously dread our slightest anger, their intellects will weaken, their eyes become as easily accessible to tears as those of children and women; but we will teach them an easy transition from grief and tears to laughter, childish joy and mirthful song. Yes; we will make them work like slaves, but during their recreation hours they shall have an innocent child-like life, full of play and merry laughter. We will even permit them sin, for, weak and helpless, they will feel the more love for us for permitting them to indulge in it. We will tell them that every kind of sin will be remitted to them, so long as it is done with our permission; that we take all these sins upon ourselves, for we so love the world, that we are even willing to sacrifice our souls for its satisfaction. And, appearing before them in the light of their scapegoats and redeemers, we shall be adored the more for it. They will have no secrets from us. It will rest with us to permit them to live with their wives and concubines, or to forbid them, to have children or remain childless, either way depending on the degree of their obedience to us; and they will submit most joyfully to us the most agonizing secrets of their souls—all, all will they lay down at our feet, and we will authorize and remit them all in Thy name, and they will believe us and accept our mediation with rapture, as it will deliver them from their greatest anxiety and torture—that of having to decide freely for themselves. And all will be happy, all except the one or two hundred thousands of their rulers. For it is but we, we the keepers of the great Mystery who will be miserable. There will be thousands of millions of happy infants, and one hundred thousand martyrs who have taken upon themselves the curse of knowledge of good and evil. Peaceable will be their end, and peacefully will they die, in Thy name, to find behind the portals of the grave—but death. But we will keep the secret inviolate, and deceive them for their own good with the mirage of life eternal in Thy kingdom. For, were there really anything like life beyond the grave, surely it would never fall to the lot of such as they! People tell us and prophesy of Thy coming and triumphing once more on earth; of Thy appearing with the army of Thy elect, with Thy proud and mighty ones; but we will answer Thee that they have saved but themselves while we have saved all. We are also threatened with the great disgrace which awaits the whore, "Babylon the great, the mother of harlots"—who sits upon the Beast, holding in her hands the Mystery, the word written upon her forehead; and we are told that the weak ones, the lambs shall rebel against her and shall make her desolate and naked. But then will I arise, and point out to Thee the thousands of millions of happy infants free from any sin. And we who have taken their sins upon us, for their own good, shall stand before Thee and say: "Judge us if Thou canst and darest!" Know then that I fear Thee not. Know that I too have lived in the dreary wilderness, where I fed upon locusts and roots, that I too have blessed freedom with which thou hast blessed men, and that I too have once prepared to join the ranks of Thy elect, the proud and the mighty. But I awoke from my delusion and refused since then to serve insanity. I returned to join the legion of those who corrected Thy mistakes. I left the proud and returned to the really humble, and for their own happiness. What I now tell thee will come to pass, and our kingdom shall be built, I tell Thee not later than to-morrow Thou shalt see that obedient flock which at one simple motion of my hand will rush to add burning coals to Thy stake, on which I will burn Thee for having dared to come and trouble us in our work. For, if there ever was one who deserved more than any of the others our inquisitorial fires—it is Thee! To-morrow I will burn Thee. Dixi.'"

Ivan paused. He had entered into the situation and had spoken with great animation, but now he suddenly burst out laughing.

"But all that is absurd!" suddenly exclaimed Alyosha, who had hitherto listened perplexed and agitated but in profound silence. "Your poem is a glorification of Christ, not an accusation, as you, perhaps, meant to be. And who will believe you when you speak of 'freedom'? Is it thus that we Christians must understand it? It is Rome (not all Rome, for that would be unjust), but the worst of the Roman Catholics, the Inquisitors and Jesuits, that you have been exposing! Your Inquisitor is an impossible character. What are these sins they are taking upon themselves? Who are those keepers of mystery who took upon themselves a curse for the good of mankind? Who ever met them? We all know the Jesuits, and no one has a good word to say in their favor; but when were they as you depict them? Never, never! The Jesuits are merely a Romish army making ready for their future temporal kingdom, with a mitred emperor—a Roman high priest at their head. That is their ideal and object, without any mystery or elevated suffering. The most prosaic thirsting for power, for the sake of the mean and earthly pleasures of life, a desire to enslave their fellow-men, something like our late system of serfs, with themselves at the head as landed proprietors—that is all that they can be accused of. They may not believe in God, that is also possible, but your suffering Inquisitor is simply—a fancy!"

"Hold, hold!" interrupted Ivan, smiling. "Do not be so excited. A fancy, you say; be it so! Of course, it is a fancy. But stop. Do you really imagine that all this Catholic movement during the last centuries is naught but a desire for power for the mere purpose of 'mean pleasures'? Is this what your Father Paissiy taught you?"

"No, no, quite the reverse, for Father Paissiy once told me something very similar to what you yourself say, though, of course, not that—something quite different," suddenly added Alexis, blushing.

"A precious piece of information, notwithstanding your 'not that.' I ask you, why should the Inquisitors and the Jesuits of your imagination live but for the attainment of 'mean material pleasures?' Why should there not be found among them one single genuine martyr suffering under a great and holy idea and loving humanity with all his heart? Now let us suppose that among all these Jesuits thirsting and hungering but after 'mean material pleasures' there may be one, just one like my old Inquisitor, who had himself fed upon roots in the wilderness, suffered the tortures of damnation while trying to conquer flesh, in order to become free and perfect, but who had never ceased to love humanity, and who one day prophetically beheld the truth; who saw as plain as he could see that the bulk of humanity could never be happy under the old system, that it was not for them that the great Idealist had come and died and dreamt of His Universal Harmony. Having realized that truth, he returned into the world and joined—intelligent and practical people. Is this so impossible?"

"Joined whom? What intelligent and practical people?" exclaimed Alyosha quite excited. "Why should they be more intelligent than other men, and what secrets and mysteries can they have? They have neither. Atheism and infidelity is all the secret they have. Your Inquisitor does not believe in God, and that is all the Mystery there is in it!"

"It may be so. You have guessed rightly there. And it is so, and that is his whole secret; but is this not the acutest sufferings for such a man as he, who killed all his young life in asceticism in the desert, and yet could not cure himself of his love towards his fellowmen? Toward the end of his life he becomes convinced that it is only by following the advice of the great and terrible spirit that the fate of these millions of weak rebels, these 'half-finished samples of humanity created in mockery' can be made tolerable. And once convinced of it, he sees as clearly that to achieve that object, one must follow blindly the guidance of the wise spirit, the fearful spirit of death and destruction, hence accept a system of lies and deception and lead humanity consciously this time toward death and destruction, and moreover, be deceiving them all the while in order to prevent them from realizing where they are being led, and so force the miserable blind men to feel happy, at least while here on earth. And note this: a wholesale deception in the name of Him, in whose ideal the old man had so passionately, so fervently, believed during nearly his whole life! Is this no suffering? And were such a solitary exception found amidst, and at the head of, that army 'that thirsts for power but for the sake of the mean pleasures of life,' think you one such man would not suffice to bring on a tragedy? Moreover, one single man like my Inquisitor as a principal leader, would prove sufficient to discover the real guiding idea of the Romish system with all its armies of Jesuits, the greatest and chiefest conviction that the solitary type described in my poem has at no time ever disappeared from among the chief leaders of that movement. Who knows but that terrible old man, loving humanity so stubbornly and in such an original way, exists even in our days in the shape of a whole host of such solitary exceptions, whose existence is not due to mere chance, but to a well-defined association born of mutual consent, to a secret league, organized several centuries back, in order to guard the Mystery from the indiscreet eyes of the miserable and weak people, and only in view of their own happiness? And so it is; it cannot be otherwise. I suspect that even Masons have some such Mystery underlying the basis of their organization, and that it is just the reason why the Roman Catholic clergy hate them so, dreading to find in them rivals, competition, the dismemberment of the unity of the idea, for the realization of which one flock and one Shepherd are needed. However, in defending my idea, I look like an author whose production is unable to stand criticism. Enough of this."

"You are, perhaps, a Mason yourself!" exclaimed Alyosha. "You do not believe in God," he added, with a note of profound sadness in his voice. But suddenly remarking that his brother was looking at him with mockery, "How do you mean then to bring your poem to a close?" he unexpectedly enquired, casting his eyes downward, "or does it break off here?"

"My intention is to end it with the following scene: Having disburdened his heart, the Inquisitor waits for some time to hear his prisoner speak in His turn. His silence weighs upon him. He has seen that his captive has been attentively listening to him all the time, with His eyes fixed penetratingly and softly on the face of his jailer, and evidently bent upon not replying to him. The old man longs to hear His voice, to hear Him reply; better words of bitterness and scorn than His silence. Suddenly He rises; slowly and silently approaching the Inquisitor, He bends towards him and softly kisses the bloodless, four-score and-ten-year-old lips. That is all the answer. The Grand Inquisitor shudders. There is a convulsive twitch at the corner of his mouth. He goes to the door, opens it, and addressing Him, 'Go,' he says, 'go, and return no more . . . do not come again . . . never, never!' and—lets Him out into the dark night. The prisoner vanishes."

"And the old man?"

"The kiss burns his heart, but the old man remains firm in his own ideas and unbelief."

"And you, together with him? You too!" despairingly exclaimed Alyosha, while Ivan burst into a still louder fit of laughter.

The Crocodile

An Extraordinary Incident

Translated by Constance Garnett

A true story of how a gentleman of a certain age and of respectable appearance was swallowed alive by the crocodile in the Arcade, and of the consequences that followed.

Ohé Lambert! Où est Lambert?
As-tu vu Lambert?

I

On the thirteenth of January of this present year, 1865, at half-past twelve in the day, Elena Ivanovna, the wife of my cultured friend Ivan Matveitch, who is a colleague in the same department, and may be said to be a distant relation of mine, too, expressed the desire to see the crocodile now on view at a fixed charge in the Arcade. As Ivan Matveitch had already in his pocket his ticket for a tour abroad (not so much for the sake of his health as for the improvement of his mind), and was consequently free from his official duties and had nothing whatever to do that morning, he offered no objection to his wife's irresistible fancy, but was positively aflame with curiosity himself.

"A capital idea!" he said, with the utmost satisfaction. "We'll have a look at the crocodile! On the eve of visiting Europe it is as well to acquaint ourselves on the spot with its indigenous inhabitants." And with these words, taking his wife's arm, he set off with her at once for the Arcade. I joined them, as I usually do, being an intimate friend of the family. I have never seen Ivan Matveitch in a more agreeable frame of mind than he was on that memorable morning-how true it is that we know not beforehand the fate that awaits us! On entering the Arcade he was at once full of admiration for the splendours of the building and, when we reached the shop in which the monster lately arrived in Petersburg was being exhibited, he volunteered to pay the quarter-rouble for me to the crocodile owner—a thing which had never happened before. Walking into a little room, we observed that besides the crocodile there were in it parrots of the species known as cockatoo, and also a group of monkeys in a special case in a recess. Near the entrance, along the left wall stood a big tin tank that looked like a bath covered with a thin iron grating, filled with water to the depth of two inches. In this shallow pool was kept a huge crocodile, which lay like a log absolutely motionless and apparently deprived of all its faculties by our damp climate, so inhospitable to foreign visitors. This monster at first aroused no special interest in any one of us.

"So this is the crocodile!" said Elena Ivanovna, with a pathetic cadence of regret. "Why, I thought it was . . . something different."

Most probably she thought it was made of diamonds. The owner of the crocodile, a German, came out and looked at us with an air of extraordinary pride.

"He has a right to be," Ivan Matveitch whispered to me, "he knows he is the only man in Russia exhibiting a crocodile."

This quite nonsensical observation I ascribe also to the extremely good-humoured mood which had overtaken Ivan Matveitch, who was on other occasions of rather envious disposition.

"I fancy your crocodile is not alive," said Elena Ivanovna, piqued by the irresponsive stolidity of the proprietor, and addressing him with a charming smile in order to soften his churlishness—a manoeuvre so typically feminine.

"Oh, no, madam," the latter replied in broken Russian; and instantly moving the grating half off the tank, he poked the monster's head with a stick.

Then the treacherous monster, to show that it was alive, faintly stirred its paws and tail, raised its snout and emitted something like a prolonged snuffle.

"Come, don't be cross, Karlchen," said the German caressingly, gratified in his vanity.

"How horrid that crocodile is! I am really frightened," Elena Ivanovna twittered, still more coquettishly. "I know I shall dream of him now."

"But he won't bite you if you do dream of him," the German retorted gallantly, and was the first to laugh at his own jest, but none of us responded.

"Come, Semyon Semyonitch," said Elena Ivanovna, addressing me exclusively, "let us go and look at the monkeys. I am awfully fond of monkeys; they are such darlings . . . and the crocodile is horrid."

"Oh, don't be afraid, my dear!" Ivan Matveitch called after us, gallantly displaying his manly courage to his wife. "This drowsy denison of the realms of the Pharaohs will do us no harm." And he remained by the tank. What is more, he took his glove and began tickling the crocodile's nose with it, wishing, as he said afterwards, to induce him to snort. The proprietor showed his politeness to a lady by following Elena Ivanovna to the case of monkeys.

So everything was going well, and nothing could have been foreseen. Elena Ivanovna was quite skittish in her raptures over the monkeys, and seemed completely taken up with them. With shrieks of delight she was continually turning to me, as though determined not to notice the proprietor, and kept gushing with laughter at the resemblance she detected between these monkeys and her intimate friends and acquaintances. I, too, was amused, for the resemblance was unmistakable. The German did not know whether to laugh or not, and so at last was reduced to frowning. And it was at that moment that a terrible, I may say unnatural, scream set the room vibrating. Not knowing what to think, for the first moment I stood still, numb with horror, but, noticing that Elena Ivanovna was screaming too, I quickly turned round—and what did I behold! I saw—oh, heavens!—I saw the luckless Ivan Matveitch in the terrible jaws of the crocodile, held by them round the waist, lifted horizontally in the air and desperately kicking. Then—one moment, and no trace remained of him. But I must describe it in detail, for I stood all the while motionless, and had time to watch the whole process taking place before me with an attention and interest such as I never remember to have felt before. "What," I thought at that critical moment, "what if all that had happened to me instead of to Ivan Matveitch—how unpleasant it would have been for me!"

But to return to my story. The crocodile began by turning the unhappy Ivan Matveitch in his terrible jaws so that he could swallow his legs first; then bringing up Ivan Matveitch, who kept trying to jump out and clutching at the sides of the tank, sucked him down again as far as his waist. Then bringing him up again, gulped him down, and so again and again. In this way Ivan Matveitch was visibly disappearing before our eyes. At last, with a final gulp, the crocodile swallowed my cultured friend entirely, this time leaving no trace of him. From the outside of the crocodile we could see the protuberances of Ivan Matveitch's figure as he passed down the inside of the monster. I was on the point of screaming again when destiny played another treacherous trick upon us. The crocodile made a tremendous effort, probably oppressed by the magnitude of the object he had swallowed, once more opened his terrible jaws, and with a final hiccup he suddenly let the head of Ivan Matveitch pop out for a second, with an expression of despair on his face. In that brief instant the spectacles dropped off his nose to the bottom of the tank. It seemed as though that despairing countenance had only popped out to cast one last look on the objects around it, to take its last farewell of all earthly pleasures. But it had not time to carry out its intention; the crocodile made another efrort, gave a gulp and instantly it vanished again—this time for ever. This appearance and disappearance of a still living human head was so horrible, but all the same—either from its rapidity and unexpectedness or from the dropping of the spectacles—there was something so comic about it that I suddenly quite unexpectedly exploded with laughter. But pulling myself together and realising that to laugh at such a moment was not the thing for an old family friend, I turned at once to Elena Ivanovna and said with a sympathetic air:

"Now it's all over with our friend Ivan Matveitch!"

I cannot even attempt to describe how violent was the agitation of Elena Ivanovna during the whole process. After the first scream she seemed rooted to the spot, and stared at the catastrophe with apparent indifference, though her eyes looked as though they were starting out of her head; then she suddenly went off into a heart-rending wail, but I seized her hands. At this instant the proprietor, too, who had at first been also petrified by horror, suddenly elapsed his hands and cried, gazing upwards:

"Oh, my crocodile! Oh, mein allerliebster Karlchen! Mutter, Mutter, Mutter!"

A door at the rear of the room opened at this cry, and the Mutter, a rosy-cheeked, elderly but dishevelled woman in a cap made her appearance, and rushed with a shriek to her German.

A perfect Bedlam followed. Elena Ivanovna kept shrieking out the same phrase, as though in a frenzy, "Flay him! flay him!" apparently entreating them—probably in a moment of oblivion—to flay somebody for something. The proprietor and Mutter took no notice whatever of either of us; they were both bellowing like calves over the crocodile.

"He did for himself! He will burst himself at once, for he did swallow a ganz official!" cried the proprietor.

"Unser Karlchen, unser allerliebster Karlchen wird sterben," howled his wife.

"We are bereaved and without bread!" chimed in the proprietor.

"Flay him! flay him! flay him!" clamoured Elena Ivanovna, clutching at the German's coat.

"He did tease the crocodile. For what did your man tease the crocodile?" cried the German, pulling away from her. "You will, if Karlchen wird burst, therefore pay, das war mein Sohn, das war mein einziger Sohn."

I must own I was intensely indignant at the sight of such egoism in the German and the cold-heartedness of his dishevelled Mutter; at the same time Elena Ivanovna's reiterated shriek of "Flay him! flay him!" troubled me even more and absorbed at last my whole attention, positively alarming me. I may as well say straight of that I entirely misunderstood this strange exclamation: it seemed to me that Elena Ivanovna had for the moment taken leave of her senses, but nevertheless wishing to avenge the loss of her beloved Ivan Matveitch, was demanding by way of compensation that the crocodile should be severely thrashed, while she was meaning something quite different. Looking round at the door, not without embarrassment, I began to entreat Elena Ivanovna to calm herself, and above all not to use the shocking word 'flay.' For such a reactionary desire here, in the midst of the Arcade and of the most cultured society, not two paces from the hall where at this very minute Mr. Lavrov was perhaps delivering a public lecture, was not only impossible but unthinkable, and might at any moment bring upon us the hisses of culture and the caricatures of Mr. Stepanov. To my horror I was immediately proved to be correct in my alarmed suspicions: the curtain that divided the crocodile room from the little entry where the quarter-roubles were taken suddenly parted, and in the opening there appeared a figure with moustaches and beard, carrying a cap, with the upper part of its body bent a long way forward, though the feet were scrupulously held beyond the threshold of the crocodile room in order to avoid the necessity of paying the entrance money.

"Such a reactionary desire, madam," said the stranger, trying to avoid falling over in our direction and to remain standing outside the room, "does no credit to your development, and is conditioned by lack of phosphorus in your brain. You will be promptly held up to shame in the Chronicle of Progress and in our satirical prints . . ."

But he could not complete his remarks; the proprietor coming to himself, and seeing with horror that a man was talking in the crocodile room without having paid entrance money, rushed furiously at the progressive stranger and turned him out with a punch from each fist. For a moment both vanished from our sight behind a curtain, and only then I grasped that the whole uproar was about nothing. Elena Ivanovna turned out quite innocent; she had, as I have mentioned already, no idea whatever of subjecting the crocodile to a degrading corporal punishment, and had simply expressed the desire that he should be opened and her husband released from his interior.

"What! You wish that my crocodile be perished!" the proprietor yelled, running in again. "No! let your husband be perished first, before my crocodile! . . . Mein Vater showed crocodile, mein Grossvater showed crocodile, mein Sohn will show crocodile, and I will show crocodile! All will show crocodile! I am known to ganz Europa, and you are not known to ganz Europa, and you must pay me a Strafe!"

"Ja, ja," put in the vindictive German woman, "we shall not let you go, Strafe, since Karlchen is burst!"

"And, indeed, it's useless to flay the creature," I added calmly, anxious to get Elena Ivanovna away home as quickly as possible, "as our dear Ivan Matveitch is by now probably soaring somewhere in the empyrean."

"My dear"—we suddenly heard, to our intense amazement, the voice of Ivan Matveitch—"my dear, my advice is to apply direct to the superintendent's office, as without the assistance of the police the German will never be made to see reason."

These words, uttered with firmness and aplomb, and expressing an exceptional presence of mind, for the first minute so astounded us that we could not believe our ears. But, of course, we ran at once to the crocodile's tank, and with equal reverence and incredulity listened to the unhappy captive. His voice was muffled, thin and even squeaky, as though it came from a considerable distance. It reminded one of a jocose person who, covering his mouth with a pillow, shouts from an adjoining room, trying to mimic the sound of two peasants calling to one another in a deserted plain or across a wide ravine—a performance to which I once had the pleasure of listening in a friend's house at Christmas.

"Ivan Matveitch, my dear, and so you are alive!" faltered Elena Ivanovna.

"Alive and well," answered Ivan Matveitch, "and, thanks to the Almighty, swallowed without any damage whatever. I am only uneasy as to the view my superiors may take of the incident; for after getting a permit to go abroad I've got into a crocodile, which seems anything but clever."

"But, my dear, don't trouble your head about being clever; first of all we must somehow excavate you from where you are," Elena Ivanovna interrupted.

"Excavate!" cried the proprietor. "I will not let my crocodile be excavated. Now the Publicum will come many more, and I will funfzig kopecks ask and Karlchen will cease to burst."

"Gott sei Dank!" put in his wife.

"They are right," Ivan Matveitch observed tranquilly; "the principles of economics before everything."

"My dear! I will fly at once to the authorities and lodge a complaint, for I feel that we cannot settle this mess by ourselves."

"I think so too." observed Ivan Matveitch; "but in our age of industrial crisis it is not easy to rip open the belly of a crocodile without economic compensation, and meanwhile the inevitable question presents itself: What will the German take for his crocodile? And with it another: How will it be paid? For, as you know, I have no means . . ."

"Perhaps out of your salary . . ." I observed timidly, but the proprietor interrupted me at once.

"I will not the crocodile sell; I will for three thousand the crocodile sell! I will for four thousand the crocodile sell! Now the Publicum will come very many. I will for five thousand the crocodile sell!"

In fact he gave himself insufferable airs. Covetousness and a revolting greed gleamed joyfully in his eyes.

"I am going!" I cried indignantly.

"And I! I too! I shall go to Andrey Osipitch himself. I will soften him with my tears," whined Elena Ivanovna.

"Don't do that, my dear," Ivan Matveitch hastened to interpose. He had long been jealous of Andrey Osipitch on his wife's account, and he knew she would enjoy going to weep before a gentleman of refinement, for tears suited her. "And I don't advise you to do so either, my friend," he added, addressing me. "It's no good plunging headlong in that slap-dash way; there's no knowing what it may lead to. You had much better go to-day to Timofey Semyonitch, as though to pay an ordinary visit; he is an old-fashioned and by no means brilliant man, but he is trustworthy, and what matters most of all, he is straightforward. Give him my greetings and describe the circumstances of the case. And since I owe him seven roubles over our last game of cards, take the opportunity to pay him the money; that will soften the stern old man. In any case his advice may serve as a guide for us. And meanwhile take Elena Ivanovna home. . . . Calm yourself, my dear," he continued, addressing her. "I am weary of these outcries and feminine squabblings, and should like a nap. It's soft and warm in here, though I have hardly had time to look round in this unexpected haven."

"Look round! Why, is it light in there?" cried Elena Ivanovna in a tone of relief.

"I am surrounded by impenetrable night," answered the poor captive, "but I can feel and, so to speak, have a look round with my hands. . . . Good-bye; set your mind at rest and don't deny yourself recreation and diversion. Till to-morrow! And you, Semyon Semyonitch, come to me in the evening, and as you are absent-minded and may forget it, tie a knot in your handkerchief."

I confess I was glad to get away, for I was overtired and somewhat bored. Hastening to offer my arm to the disconsolate Elena Ivanovna, whose charms were only enhanced by her agitation, I hurriedly led her out of the crocodile room.

"The charge will be another quarter-rouble in the evening," the proprietor called after us.

"Oh, dear, how greedy they are!" said Elena Ivanovna, looking at herself in every mirror on the walls of the Arcade, and evidently aware that she was looking prettier than usual.

"The principles of economics," I answered with some emotion, proud that passers-by should see the lady on my arm.

"The principles of economics," she drawled in a touching little voice. "I did not in the least understand what Ivan Matveitch said about those horrid economics just now."

"I will explain to you," I answered, and began at once telling her of the beneficial effects of the introduction of foreign capital into our country, upon which I had read an article in the *Petersburg News* and the *Voice* that morning.

"How strange it is," she interrupted, after listening for some time. "But do leave off, you horrid man. What nonsense you are talking. . . . Tell me, do I look purple?"

"You look perfect, and not purple!" I observed, seizing the opportunity to pay her a compliment.

"Naughty man!" she said complacently. "Poor Ivan Matveitch," she added a minute later, putting her little head on one side coquettiswy. "I am really sorry for him. Oh, dear!" she cried suddenly, "how is he going to have his dinner . . . and . . . and . . . what will he do . . . if he wants anything?"

"An unforeseen question," I answered, perplexed in my turn. To tell the truth, it had not entered my head, so much more practical are women than we men in the solution of the problems of daily life!

"Poor dear! how could he have got into such a mess . . . nothing to amuse him, and in the dark How vexing it is that I have no photograph of him. And so now I am a sort of widow," she added, with a seductive smile, evidently interested in her new position. "Hm! . . . I am sorry for him, though."

It was, in short, the expression of the very natural and intelligible grief of a young and interesting wife for the loss of her husband. I took her home at last, soothed her, and after dining with her and drinking a cup of aromatic coffee, set off at six o'clock to Timofey Semyonitch, calculating that at that hour all married people of settled habits would be sitting or lying down at home.

Having written this first chapter in a style appropriate to the incident recorded, I intended to proceed in a language more natural though less elevated, and I beg to forewarn the reader of the fact.

II

The venerable Timofey Semyonitch met me rather nervously, as though somewhat embarrassed. He led me to his tiny study and shut the door carefully, "that the children may not hinder us," he added with evident uneasiness. There he made me sit down on a chair by the writing-table, sat down himself in an easy chair, wrapped round him the skirts of his old wadded dressing-gown, and assumed an official and even severe air, in readiness for anything, though he was not my chief nor Ivan Matveitch's, and had hitherto been reckoned as a colleague and even a friend.

"First of all," he said, "take note that I am not a person in authority, but just such a subordinate official as you and Ivan Matveitch. . . . I have nothing to do with it, and do not intend to mix myself up in the affair."

I was surprised to find that he apparently knew all about it already. In spite of that I told him the whole story over in detail. I spoke with positive excitement, for I was at that moment fulfilling the obligations of a true friend. He listened without special surprise, but with evident signs of suspicion.

"Only fancy," he said, "I always believed that this would be sure to happen to him."

"Why, Timofey Semyonitch? It is a very unusual incident in itself . . ."

"I admit it. But Ivan Matveitch's whole career in the service was leading up to this end. He was flighty-conceited indeed. It was always 'progress' and ideas of all sorts, and this is what progress brings people to!"

"But this is a most unusual incident and cannot possibly serve as a general rule for all progressives."

"Yes, indeed it can. You see, it's the effect of over-education, I assure you. For over-education leads people to poke their noses into all sorts of places, especially where they are not invited. Though perhaps you know best," he added, as though offended. "I am an old man and not of much education. I began as a soldier's son, and this year has been the jubilee of my service."

"Oh, no, Timofey Semyonitch, not at all. On the contrary, Ivan Matveitch is eager for your advice; he is eager for your guidance. He implores it, so to say, with tears."

"So to say, with tears! Hm! Those are crocodile's tears and one cannot quite believe in them. Tell me, what possessed him to want to go abroad? And how could he afford to go? Why, he has no private means!"

"He had saved the money from his last bonus," I answered plaintively. "He only wanted to go for three months—to Switzerland . . . to the land of William Tell."

"William Tell? Hm!"

"He wanted to meet the spring at Naples, to see the museums, the customs, the animals . . ."

"Hm! The animals! I think it was simply from pride. What animals? Animals, indeed! Haven't we animals enough? We have museums, menageries, camels. There are bears quite close to Petersburg! And here he's got inside a crocodile himself. . . ."

"Oh, come, Timofey Semyonitch! The man is in trouble, the man appeals to you as to a friend, as to an older relation, craves for advice—and you reproach him. Have pity at least on the unfortunate Elena Ivanovna!"

"You are speaking of his wife? A charming little lady," said Timofey Semyonitch, visibly softening and taking a pinch of snuff with relish. "Particularly prepossessing. And so plump, and always putting her pretty little head on one side. . . . Very agreeable. Andrey Osipitch was speaking of her only the other day."

"Speaking of her?"

"Yes, and in very flattering terms. Such a bust, he said, such eyes, such hair. . . . A sugar-plum, he said, not a lady—and then he laughed. He is still a young man, of course," Timofey Semyonitch blew his nose with a loud noise. "And yet, young though he is, what a career he is making for himself."

"That's quite a different thing, Timofey Semyonitch."

"Of course, of course."

"Well, what do You say then, Timofey Semyonitch?"

"Why, what can I do?"

"Give advice, guidance, as a man of experience, a relative! What are we to do? What steps are we to take? Go to the authorities and . . ."

"To the authorities? Certainly not." Timofey Semyonitch replied hurriedly. "If you ask my advice, you had better, above all, hush the matter up and act, so to speak, as a private person. It is a suspicious incident, quite unheard of. Unheard of, above all; there is no precedent for it, and it is far from creditable. . . . And so discretion above all. . . . Let him lie there a bit. We must wait and see. . . ."

"But how can we wait and see, Timofey Semyonitch? What if he is stifled there?"

"Why should he be? I think you told me that he made himself fairly comfortable there?"

I told him the whole story over again. Timofey Semyonitch pondered.

"Hm!" he said, twisting his snuff-box in his hands. "To my mind it's really a good thing he should lie there a bit, instead of going abroad. Let him reflect at his leisure. Of course he mustn't be stifled, and so he must take measures to preserve his health, avoiding a cough, for instance, and so on. . . . And as for the German, it's my personal opinion he is within his rights, and even more so than the other side, because it was the other party who got into his crocodile without asking permission, and not he who got into Ivan Matveitch's crocodile without asking permission, though, so far as I recollect, the latter has no crocodile. And a crocodile is private property, and so it is impossible to slit him open without compensation."

"For the saving of human life, Timofey Semyonitch."

"Oh, well, that's a matter for the police. You must go to them."

"But Ivan Matveitch may be needed in the department. He may be asked for."

"Ivan Matveitch needed? Ha-ha! Besides, he is on leave, so that we may ignore him—let him inspect the countries of Europe! It will be a different matter if he doesn't turn up when his leave is over. Then we shall ask for him and make inquiries."

"Three months! Timofey Semyonitch, for pity's sake!"

"It's his own fault. Nobody thrust him there. At this rate we should have to get a nurse to look after him at government expense, and that is not allowed for in the regulations. But the chief point is that the crocodile is private property, so that the principles of economics apply in this question. And the principles of economics are paramount. Only the other evening, at Luke Andreitch's, Ignaty

Prokofyitch was saying so. Do you know Ignaty Prokofyitch? A capitalist, in a big way of business, and he speaks so fluently. 'We need industrial development,' he said; 'there is very little development among us. We must create it. We must create capital, so we must create a middle-class, the so-called bourgeoisie. And as we haven't capital we must attract it from abroad. We must, in the first place, give facilities to foreign companies to buy up lands in Russia as is done now abroad. The communal holding of land is poison, is ruin.' And, you know, he spoke with such heat; well, that's all right for him—a wealthy man, and not in the service. 'With the communal system,' he said, 'there will be no improvement in industrial development or agriculture. Foreign companies,' he said, 'must as far as possible buy up the whole of our land in big lots, and then split it up, split it up, split it up, in the smallest parts possible'—and do you know he pronounced the words 'split it up' with such determination—'and then sell it as private property. Or rather, not sell it, but simply let it. When,' he said, 'all the land is in the hands of foreign companies they can fix any rent they like. And so the peasant will work three times as much for his daily bread and he can be turned out at pleasure. So that he will feel it, will be submissive and industrious, and will work three times as much for the same wages. But as it is, with the commune, what does he care? He knows he won't die of hunger, so he is lazy and drunken. And meanwhile money will be attracted into Russia, capital will be created and the bourgeoisie will spring up. The English political and literary paper, The Times, in an article the other day on our finances stated that the reason our financial position was so unsatisfactory was that we had no middle-class, no big fortunes, no accommodating proletariat.' Ignaty Prokofyitch speaks well. He is an orator. He wants to lay a report on the subject before the authorities, and then to get it published in the *News*. That's something very different from verses like Ivan Matveitch's . . ."

"But how about Ivan Matveitch?" I put in, after letting the old man babble on.

Timofey Semyonitch was sometimes fond of talking and showing that he was not behind the times, but knew all about things.

"How about Ivan Matveitch? Why, I am coming to that. Here we are, anxious to bring foreign capital into the country—and only consider: as soon as the capital of a foreigner, who has been attracted to Petersburg, has been doubled through Ivan Matveitch, instead of protecting the foreign capitalist, we are proposing to rip open the belly of his original capital—the crocodile. Is it consistent? To my mind, Ivan Matveitch, as the true son of his fatherland, ought to rejoice and to be proud that through him the value of a foreign crocodile has been doubled and possibly even trebled. That's just what is wanted to attract capital. If one man succeeds, mind you, another will come with a crocodile, and a third will bring two or three of them at once, and capital will grow up about them—there you have a bourgeoisie. It must be encouraged."

"Upon my word, Timofey Semyonitch!" I cried, "you are demanding almost supernatural self-sacrifice from poor Ivan Matveitch."

"I demand nothing, and I beg you, before everything—as I have said already—to remember that I am not a person in authority and so cannot demand anything of anyone. I am speaking as a son of the fatherland, that is, not as the Son of the Fatherland, but as a son of the fatherland. Again, what possessed him to get into the crocodile? A respectable man, a man of good grade in the service, lawfully married—and then to behave like that! Is it consistent?"

"But it was an accident."

"Who knows? And where is the money to compensate the owner to come from?"

"Perhaps out of his salary, Timofey Semyonitch?"

"Would that be enough?"

"No, it wouldn't, Timofey Semyonitch," I answered sadly. "The proprietor was at first alarmed that the crocodile would burst, but as soon as he was sure that it was all right, he began to bluster and was delighted to think that he could double the charge for entry."

"Treble and quadruple perhaps! The public will simply stampede the place now, and crocodile owners are smart people. Besides, it's not Lent yet, and people are keen on diversions, and so I say again, the great thing is that Ivan Matveitch should preserve his incognito, don't let him be in a hurry. Let everybody know, perhaps, that he is in the crocodile, but don't let them be officially informed of it. Ivan Matveitch is in particularly favourable circumstances for that, for he is reckoned to be abroad. It will be said he is in the crocodile, and we will refuse to believe it. That is how it can be managed. The great thing is that he should wait; and why should he be in a hurry?"

"Well, but if . . . "

"Don't worry, he has a good constitution."

"Well, and afterwards, when he has waited?"

"Well, I won't conceal from you that the case is exceptional in the highest degree. One doesn't know what to think of it, and the worst of it is there is no precedent. If we had a precedent we might have something to go by. But as it is, what is one to say? It will certainly take time to settle it."

A happy thought flashed upon my mind.

"Cannot we arrange," I said, "that, if he is destined to remain in the entrails of the monster and it is the will of Providence that he should remain alive, he should send in a petition to be reckoned as still serving?"

"Hm! . . . Possibly as on leave and without salary. . . ."

"But couldn't it be with salary?"

"On what grounds?"

"As sent on a special commission."

"What commission and where?"

"Why, into the entrails, the entrails of the crocodile. . . . So to speak, for exploration, for investigation of the facts on the spot. It would, of course, be a novelty, but that is progressive and would at the same time show zeal for enlightenment."

Timofey Semyonitch thought a little.

"To send a special official," he said at last, "to the inside of a crocodile to conduct a special inquiry is, in my personal opinion, an absurdity. It is not in the regulations. And what sort of special inquiry could there be there?"

"The scientific study of nature on the spot, in the living subject. The natural sciences are all the fashion nowadays, botany. . . . He could live there and report his observations. . . . For instance, concerning digestion or simply habits. For the sake of accumulating facts."

"You mean as statistics. Well, I am no great authority on that subject, indeed I am no philosopher at all. You say 'facts'-we are overwhelmed with facts as it is, and don't know what to do with them. Besides, statistics are a danger."

"In what way?"

"They are a danger. Moreover, you will admit he will report facts, so to speak, lying like a log. And, can one do one's official duties lying like a log? That would be another novelty and a dangerous one; and again, there is no precedent for it. If we had any sort of precedent for it, then, to my thinking, he might have been given the job."

"But no live crocodiles have been brought over hitherto, Timofey Semyonitch."

"Hm . . . yes," he reflected again. "Your objection is a just one, if you like, and might indeed serve as a ground for carrying the matter further; but consider again, that if with the arrival of living crocodiles government clerks begin to disappear, and then on the ground that they are warm and comfortable there, expect to receive the official sanction for their position, and then take their ease there. . . . You must admit it would be a bad example. We should have everyone trying to go the same way to get a salary for nothing."

"Do your best for him, Timofey Semyonitch. By the way, Ivan Matveitch asked me to give you seven roubles he had lost to you at cards."

"Ah, he lost that the other day at Nikifor Nikiforitch's. I remember. And how gay and amusing he was—and now!"

The old man was genuinely touched.

"Intercede for him, Timofey Semyonitch!"

"I will do my best. I will speak in my own name, as a private person, as though I were asking for information. And meanwhile, you find out indirectly, unofficially, how much would the proprietor consent to take for his crocodile?"

Timofey Semyonitch was visibly more friendly.

"Certainly," I answered. "And I will come back to you at once to report."

"And his wife . . . is she alone now? Is she depressed?"

"You should call on her, Timofey Semyonitch."

"I will. I thought of doing so before; it's a good opportunity. . . . And what on earth possessed him to go and look at the crocodile. Though, indeed, I should like to see it myself."

"Go and see the poor fellow, Timofey Semyonitch."

"I will. Of course, I don't want to raise his hopes by doing so. I shall go as a private person. . . . Well, good-bye, I am going to Nikifor Nikiforitch's again; shall you be there?"

"No, I am going to see the poor prisoner."

"Yes, now he is a prisoner! . . . Ah, that's what comes of thoughtlessness!"

I said good-bye to the old man. Ideas of all kinds were straying through my mind. A good-natured and most honest man, Timofey Semyonitch, yet, as I left him, I felt pleased at the thought that he had celebrated his fiftieth year of service, and that Timofey Semyonitchs are now a rarity among us. I flew at once, of course, to the Arcade to tell poor Ivan Matveitch all the news. And, indeed, I was moved by curiosity to know how he was getting on in the crocodile and how it was possible to live in a crocodile. And, indeed, was it possible to live in a crocodile at all? At times it really seemed to me as though it were all an outlandish, monstrous dream, especially as an outlandish monster was the chief figure in it.

III

And yet it was not a dream, but actual, indubitable fact. Should I be telling the story if it were not? But to continue.

It was late, about nine o'clock, before I reached the Arcade, and I had to go into the crocodile room by the back entrance, for the German had closed the shop earlier than usual that evening. Now in the seclusion of domesticity he was walking about in a greasy old frock-coat, but he seemed three times as pleased as he had been in the morning. It was evidently that he had no apprehensions now, and that the public had been coming "many more." The Mutter came out later, evidently to keep an eye on me. The German and the Mutter frequently whispered together. Although the shop was closed he charged me a quarter-rouble. What unnecessary exactitude!

"You will every time pay; the public will one rouble, and you one quarter pay; for you are the good friend of your good friend; and I a friend respect . . ."

"Are you alive, are you alive, my cultured friend?" I cried, as I approached the crocodile, expecting my words to reach Ivan Matveitch from a distance and to flatter his vanity.

"Alive and well," he answered, as though from a long way off or from under the bed, though I was standing close beside him. "Alive and well; but of that later. . . . How are things going?"

As though purposely not hearing the question, I was just beginning with sympathetic haste to question him how he was, what it was like in the crocodile, and what, in fact, there was inside a crocodile. Both friendship and common civility demanded this. But with capricious annoyance he interrupted me.

"How are things going?" he shouted, in a shrill and on this occasion particularly revolting voice, addressing me peremptorily as usual.

I described to him my whole conversation with Timofey Semyonitch down to the smallest detail. As I told my story I tried to show my resentment in my voice.

"The old man is right," Ivan Matveitch pronounced as abruptly as usual in his conversation with me. "I like practical people, and can't endure sentimental milk-sops. I am ready to admit, however, that your idea about a special commission is not altogether absurd. I certainly have a great deal to report, both from a scientific and from an ethical point of view. But now all this has taken a new and unexpected aspect, and it is not worth while to trouble about mere salary. Listen attentively. Are you sitting down?"

"No, I am standing up."

"Sit down on the floor if there is nothing else, and listen attentively.

Resentfully I took a chair and put it down on the floor with a bang, in my anger.

"Listen," he began dictatorially. "The public came to-day in masses. There was no room left in the evening, and the police came in to keep order. At eight o'clock, that is, earlier than usual, the proprietor thought it necessary to close the shop and end the exhibition to count the money he had taken and prepare for to-morrow more conveniently. So I know there will be a regular fair to-morrow. So we may assume that all the most cultivated people in the capital, the ladies of the best society, the foreign ambassadors, the leading lawyers and so on, will all be present. What's more, people will be flowing here from the remotest provinces of our vast and interesting empire. The upshot of it is that I am the cynosure of all eyes, and though hidden to sight, I am eminent. I shall teach the idle crowd. Taught by experience, I shall be an example of greatness and resignation to fate! I shall be, so to say, a pulpit from which to instruct mankind. The mere biological details I can furnish about the monster I am inhabiting are of priceless value. And so, far from repining at what has happened, I confidently hope for the most brilliant of careers."

"You won't find it wearisome?" I asked sarcastically.

What irritated me more than anything was the extreme pomposity of his language. Nevertheless, it all rather disconcerted me. "What on earth, what, can this frivolous blockhead find to be so cocky about?" I muttered to myself. "He ought to be crying instead of being cocky."

"No!" he answered my observation sharply, "for I am full of great ideas, only now can I at leisure ponder over the amelioration of the lot of humanity. Truth and light will come forth now from the crocodile. I shall certainly develop a new economic theory of my own and I shall be proud of it—which I have hitherto been prevented from doing by my official duties and by trivial distractions. I shall refute everything and be a new Fourier. By the way, did you give Timofey Semyonitch the seven roubles?"

"Yes, out of my own pocket," I answered, trying to emphasise that fact in my voice.

"We will settle it," he answered superciliously. "I confidently expect my salary to be raised, for who should get a rise if not I? I am of the utmost service now. But to business, My wife?"

"You are, I suppose, inquiring after Elena Ivanovna?"

"My wife?" he shouted, this time in a positive squeal.

There was no help for it! Meekly, though gnashing my teeth, I told him how I had left Elena Ivanovna. He did not even hear me out.

"I have special plans in regard to her," he began impatiently. "If I am celebrated here, I wish her to be celebrated there. Savants, poets, philosophers, foreign mineralogists, statesmen, after conversing in the morning with me, will visit her salon in the evening. From next week onwards she must have an 'At Home' every evening. With my salary doubled, we shall have the means for entertaining, and as the entertainment must not go beyond tea and hired footmen—that's settled. Both here and there they will talk of me. I have long thirsted for an opportunity for being talked about, but could not attain it, fettered by my humble position and low grade in the service. And now all this has been attained by a simple gulp on the part of the crocodile. Every word of mine will be listened to, every utterance will be thought over, repeated, printed. And I'll teach them what I am worth! They shall understand at last what abilities they have allowed to vanish in the entrails of a monster. 'This man might have been Foreign Minister or might have ruled a kingdom,' some will say. 'And that man did not rule a kingdom,' others will say. In what way am I inferior to a Garnier-Pagesishky or whatever they are called? My wife must be a worthy second—I have brains, she has beauty and charm. 'She is beautiful, and that is why she is his wife,' some will say. 'She is beautiful because she is his wife,' others will amend. To be ready for anything let Elena Ivanovna buy to-morrow the Encyclopedia edited by Andrey Kraevsky, that she may be able to converse on any topic. Above all, let her be sure to read the political leader in the *Petersburg News,* comparing it every day with the *Voice.* I imagine that the proprietor will consent to take me sometimes with the crocodile to my wife's brilliant salon. I will be in a tank in the middle of the magnificent drawing-room, and I will scintillate with witticisms which I will prepare in the morning. To the statesman I will impart my projects; to the poet I will speak in rhyme; with the ladies I can be amusing and charming without impropriety, since I shall be no danger to their husbands' peace of mind. To all the rest

I shall serve as a pattern of resignation to fate and the will of Providence. I shall make my wife a brilliant literary lady; I shall bring her forward and explain her to the public; as my wife she must be full of the most striking virtues; and if they are right in calling Andrey Alexandrovitch our Russian Alfred de Musset, they will be still more right in calling her our Russian Yevgenia Tour."

I must confess that, although this wild nonsense was rather in Ivan Matveitch's habitual style, it did occur to me that he was in a fever and delirious. It was the same, everyday Ivan Matveitch, but magnified twenty times.

"My friend," I asked him, "are you hoping for a long life? Tell me, in fact, are you well? How do you eat, how do you sleep, how do you breathe? I am your friend, and you must admit that the incident is most unnatural, and consequently my curiosity is most natural."

"Idle curiosity and nothing else," he pronounced sententiously, "but you shall be satisfied. You ask how I am managing in the entrails of the monster? To begin with, the crocodile, to my amusement, turns out to be perfectly empty. His inside consists of a sort of huge empty sack made of gutta-percha, like the elastic goods sold in the Gorohovy Street, in the Morskaya, and, if I am not mistaken, in the Voznesensky Prospect. Otherwise, if you think of it, how could I find room?"

"Is it possible?" I cried, in a surprise that may well be understood. "Can the crocodile be perfectly empty?"

"Perfectly," Ivan Matveitch maintained sternly and impressively. "And in all probability, it is so constructed by the laws of Nature. The crocodile possesses nothing but jaws furnished with sharp teeth, and besides the jaws, a tail of considerable length—that is all, properly speaking. The middle part between these two extremities is an empty space enclosed by something of the nature of gutta-percha, probably really gutta-percha."

"But the ribs, the stomach, the intestines, the liver, the heart?" I interrupted quite angrily.

"There is nothing, absolutely nothing of all that, and probably there never has been. All that is the idle fancy of frivolous travellers. As one inflates an air-cushion, I am now with my person inflating the crocodile. He is incredibly elastic. Indeed, you might, as the friend of the family, get in with me if you were generous and self-sacrificing enough—and even with you here there would be room to spare. I even think that in the last resort I might send for Elena Ivanovna. However, this void, hollow formation of the crocodile is quite in keeping with the teachings of natural science. If, for instance, one had to construct a new crocodile, the question would naturally present itself. What is the fundamental characteristic of the crocodile? The answer is clear: to swallow human beings. How is one, in constructing the crocodile, to secure that he should swallow people? The answer is clearer still: construct him hollow. It was settled by physics long ago that Nature abhors a vacuum. Hence the inside of the crocodile must be hollow so that it may abhor the vacuum, and consequently swallow and so fill itself with anything it can come across. And that is the sole rational cause why every crocodile swallows men. It is not the same in the constitution of man: the emptier a man's head is, for instance, the less he feels the thirst to fill it, and that is the one exception to the general rule. It is all as clear as day to me now. I have deduced it by my own observation and experience, being, so to say, in the very bowels of Nature, in its retort, listening to the throbbing of its pulse. Even etymology supports me, for the very word crocodile means voracity. Crocodile—crocodillo—is evidently an Italian word, dating perhaps from the Egyptian Pharaohs, and evidently derived from the French verb croquer, which means to eat, to devour, in general to absorb nourishment. All these remarks I intend to deliver as my first lecture in Elena Ivanovna's salon when they take me there in the tank."

"My friend, oughtn't you at least to take some purgative?" I cried involuntarily.

"He is in a fever, a fever, he is feverish!" I repeated to myself in alarm.

"Nonsense!" he answered contemptuously. "Besides, in my present position it would be most inconvenient. I knew, though, you would be sure to talk of taking medicine."

"But, my friend, how . . . how do you take food now? Have you dined to-day?"

"No, but I am not hungry, and most likely I shall never take food again. And that, too, is quite natural; filling the whole interior of the crocodile I make him feel always full. Now he need not be fed for some years. On the other hand, nourished by me, he will naturally impart to me all the vital juices of his body; it is the same as with some accomplished coquettes who embed themselves and their whole persons for the night in raw steak, and then, after their morning bath, are fresh, supple, buxom and fascinating. In that way nourishing the crocodile, I myself obtain nourishment from him, consequently we mutually nourish one another. But as it is difficult even for a crocodile to digest a man like me, he must, no doubt, be conscious of a certain weight in his stomach—an organ which he does not, however, possess—and that is why, to avoid causing the creature suffering, I do not often turn over, and although I could turn over I do not do so from humanitarian motives. This is the one drawback of my present position, and in an allegorical sense Timofey Semyonitch was right in saying I was lying like a log. But I will prove that even lying like a log—nay, that only lying like a log—one can revolutionise the lot of mankind. All the great ideas and movements of our newspapers and magazines have evidently been the work of men who were lying like logs; that is why they call them divorced from the realities of life—but what does it matter, their saying that! I am constructing now a complete system of my own, and you wouldn't believe how easy it is! You have only to creep into a secluded corner or into a crocodile, to shut your eyes, and you immediately devise a perfect millennium for mankind. When you went away this afternoon I set to work at once and have already invented three systems, now I am preparing the fourth. It is true that at first one must refute everything that has gone before, but from the crocodile it is so easy to refute it; besides, it all becomes clearer, seen from the inside of the crocodile. . . . There are some drawbacks, though small ones, in my position, however; it is somewhat damp here and covered with a sort of slime; moreover, there is rather a smell of india-rubber exactly like the smell of my old galoshes. That is all, there are no other drawbacks."

"Ivan Matveitch," I interrupted, "all this is a miracle in which I can scarcely believe. And can you, can you intend never to dine again?"

"What trivial nonsense you are troubling about, you thoughtless, frivolous creature! I talk to you about great ideas, and you . . . Understand that I am sufficiently nourished by the great ideas which light up the darkness in which I am enveloped. The good-natured proprietor has, however, after consulting the kindly Mutter, decided with her that they will every morning insert into the monster's jaws a bent metal tube, something like a whistle pipe, by means of which I can absorb coffee or broth with bread soaked in it. The pipe has already been bespoken in the neighbourhood, but I think this is superfluous luxury. I hope to live at least a thousand years, if it is true that crocodiles live so long, which, by the way—good thing I thought of it—you had better look up in some natural history to-morrow and tell me, for I may have been mistaken and have mixed it up with some excavated monster. There is only one reflection rather troubles me: as I am dressed in cloth and have boots on, the crocodile can obviously not digest me. Besides, I am alive, and so am opposing the process of digestion with my whole will power; for you can understand that I do not wish to be turned into what all nourishment turns into, for that would be too humiliating for me. But there is one thing I am afraid of: in a thousand years the cloth of my coat, unfortunately of Russian make, may decay, and then, left without clothing, I might perhaps, in spite of my indignation, begin to be digested; and though by day nothing would induce me to allow it, at night, in my sleep, when a man's will deserts him, I may be overtaken by the humiliating destiny of a potato, a pancake, or veal. Such an idea reduces me to fury. This alone is an argument for the revision of the tariff and the encouragement of the importation of English cloth, which is stronger and so will withstand Nature longer when one is swallowed by a crocodile. At the first opportunity I will impart this idea to some statesman and at the same time to the political writers on our Petersburg dailies. Let them publish it abroad. I trust this will not be the only idea they will borrow from me. I foresee that every morning a regular crowd of them, provided with quarter-roubles from the editorial office, will be flocking round me to seize my ideas on the telegrams of the previous day. In brief, the future presents itself to me in the rosiest light."

"Fever, fever!" I whispered to myself.

"My friend, and freedom?" I asked, wishing to learn his views thoroughly. "You are, so to speak, in prison, while every man has a right to the enjoyment of freedom."

"You are a fool," he answered. "Savages love independence, wise men love order; and if there is no order.

"Ivan Matveitch, spare me, please!"

"Hold your tongue and listen!" he squealed, vexed at my interrupting him. "Never has my spirit soared as now. In my narrow refuge there is only one thing that I dread—the literary criticisms of the monthlies and the lies of our satirical papers. I am afraid that thoughtless visitors, stupid and envious people and nihilists in general, may turn me into ridicule. But I will take measures. I am impatiently awaiting the response of the public to-morrow, and especially the opinion of the newspapers. You must tell me about the papers to-morrow."

"Very good; to-morrow I will bring a perfect pile of papers with me."

"To-morrow it is too soon to expect reports in the newspapers, for it will take four days for it to be advertised. But from to-day come to me every evening by the back way through the yard. I am intending to employ you as my secretary. You shall read the newspapers and magazines to me, and I will dictate to you my ideas and give you commissions. Be particularly careful not to forget the foreign telegrams. Let all the European telegrams be here every day. But enough; most likely you are sleepy by now. Go home, and do not think of what I said just now about criticisms: I am not afraid of it, for the critics themselves are in a critical position. One has only to be wise and virtuous and one will certainly get on to a pedestal. If not Socrates, then Diogenes, or perhaps both of them together-that is my future role among mankind."

So frivolously and boastfully did Ivan Matveitch hasten to express himself before me, like feverish weak-willed women who, as we are told by the proverb, cannot keep a secret. All that he told me about the crocodile struck me as most suspicious. How was it possible that the crocodile was absolutely hollow? I don't mind betting that he was bragging from vanity and partly to humiliate me. It is true that he was an invalid and one must make allowances for invalids; but I must frankly confess, I never could endure Ivan Matveitch. I have been trying all my life, from a child up, to escape from his tutelage and have not been able to! A thousand times over I have been tempted to break with him altogether, and every time I have been drawn to him again, as though I were still hoping to prove something to him or to revenge myself on him. A strange thing, this friendship! I can positively assert that nine-tenths of my friendship for him was made up of malice. On this occasion, however, we parted with genuine feeling.

"Your friend a very clever man!" the German said to me in an undertone as he moved to see me out; he had been listening all the time attentively to our conversation.

"Apropos," I said, "while I think of it: how much would you ask for your crocodile in case anyone wanted to buy it?"

Ivan Matveitch, who heard the question, was waiting with curiosity for the answer; it was evident that he did not want the German to ask too little; anyway, he cleared his throat in a peculiar way on hearing my question.

At first the German would not listen—was positively angry.

"No one will dare my own crocodile to buy!" he cried furiously, and turned as red as a boiled lobster. "Me not want to sell the crocodile! I would not for the crocodile a million thalers take. I took a hundred and thirty thalers from the public to-day, and I shall to-morrow ten thousand take, and then a hundred thousand every day I shall take. I will not him sell."

Ivan Matveitch positively chuckled with satisfaction. Controlling myself—for I felt it was a duty to my friend—I hinted coolly and reasonably to the crazy German that his calculations were not quite correct, that if he makes a hundred thousand every day, all Petersburg will have visited him in four days, and then there will be no one left to bring him roubles, that life and death are in God's hands, that the crocodile may burst or Ivan Matveitch may fall ill and die, and so on and so on.

The German grew pensive.

"I will him drops from the chemist's get," he said, after pondering, "and will save your friend that he die not."

"Drops are all very well," I answered, "but consider, too, that the thing may get into the law courts. Ivan Matveitch's wife may demand the restitution of her lawful spouse. You are intending to get rich, but do you intend to give Elena Ivanovna a pension?"

"No, me not intend," said the German in stern decision.

"No, we not intend," said the Mutter, with positive malignancy.

"And so would it not be better for you to accept something now, at once, a secure and solid though moderate sum, than to leave things to chance? I ought to tell you that I am inquiring simply from curiosity."

The German drew the Mutter aside to consult with her in a corner where there stood a case with the largest and ugliest monkey of his collection.

"Well, you will see!" said Ivan Matveitch.

As for me, I was at that moment burning with the desire, first, to give the German a thrashing, next, to give the Mutter an even sounder one, and, thirdly, to give Ivan Matveitch the soundest thrashing of all for his boundless vanity. But all this paled beside the answer of the rapacious German.

After consultation with the Mutter he demanded for his crocodile fifty thousand roubles in bonds of the last Russian loan with lottery voucher attached, a brick house in Gorohovy Street with a chemist's shop attached, and in addition the rank of Russian colonel.

"You see!" Ivan Matveitch cried triumphantly. "I told you so! Apart from this last senseless desire for the rank of a colonel, he is perfectly right, for he fully understands the present value of the monster he is exhibiting. The economic principle before everything!"

"Upon my word!" I cried furiously to the German. "But what should you be made a colonel for? What exploit have you performed? What service have you done? In what way have you gained military glory? You are really crazy!"

"Crazy!" cried the German, offended. "No, a person very sensible, but you very stupid! I have a colonel deserved for that I have a crocodile shown and in him a live Hofrath sitting! And a Russian can a crocodile not show and a live Hofrath in him sitting! Me extremely clever man and much wish colonel to be!"

"Well, good-bye, then, Ivan Matveitch!" I cried, shaking with fury, and I went out of the crocodile room almost at a run.

I felt that in another minute I could not have answered for myself. The unnatural expectations of these two blockheads were insupportable. The cold air refreshed me and somewhat moderated my indignation. At last, after spitting vigorously fifteen times on each side, I took a cab, got home, undressed and flung myself into bed. What vexed me more than anything was my having become his secretary. Now I was to die of boredom there every evening, doing the duty of a true friend! I was ready to beat myself for it, and I did, in fact, after putting out the candle and pulling up the bedclothes, punch myself several times on the head and various parts of my body. That somewhat relieved me, and at last I fell asleep fairly soundly, in fact, for I was very tired. All night long I could dream of nothing but monkeys, but towards morning I dreamt of Elena Ivanovna.

IV

The monkeys I dreamed about, I suppose, because they were shut up in the case at the German's; but Elena Ivanovna was a different story.

I may as well say at once, I loved the lady, but I make haste—posthaste—to make a qualification. I loved her as a father, neither more nor less. I judge that because I often felt an irresistible desire to kiss her little head or her rosy cheek. And though I never carried out this inclination, I would not have refused even to kiss her lips. And not merely her lips, but her teeth, which always gleamed so charmingly like two rows of pretty, well-matched pearls when she laughed. She laughed extraordinarily often. Ivan Matveitch in demonstrative moments used to call her his "darling absurdity"—a name extremely happy and appropriate. She was a perfect sugarplum, and that was all one could say of her. Therefore I am utterly at a loss to understand what possessed Ivan Matveitch to imagine his wife as a Russian Yevgenia Tour? Anyway, my dream, with the exception of the monkeys, left a most pleasant impression upon me, and going over all the incidents of the previous day as I drank my morning cup of tea, I resolved to go and see Elena Ivanovna at once on my way to the office—which, indeed, I was bound to do as the friend of the family.

In a tiny little room out of the bedroom—the so-called little drawing-room, though their big drawing-room was little too—Elena Ivanovna was sitting, in some half-transparent morning wrapper, on a smart little sofa before a little tea-table, drinking coffee out of a little cup in which she was dipping a minute biscuit. She was ravishingly pretty, but struck me as being at the same time rather pensive.

"Ah, that's you, naughty man!" she said, greeting me with an absent-minded smile. "Sit down, feather-head, have some coffee. Well, what were you doing yesterday? Were you at the masquerade?"

"Why, were you? I don't go, you know. Besides, yesterday I was visiting our captive. . . . I sighed and assumed a pious expression as I took the coffee.

"Whom? . . . What captive? . . . Oh, yes! Poor fellow! Well, how is he—bored? Do you know . . . I wanted to ask you . . . I suppose I can ask for a divorce now?"

"A divorce!" I cried in indignation and almost spilled the coffee. "It's that swarthy fellow," I thought to myself bitterly.

There was a certain swarthy gentleman with little moustaches who was something in the architectural fine, and who came far too often to see them, and was extremely skilful in amusing Elena Ivanovna. I must confess I hated him and there was no doubt that he had succeeded in seeing Elena Ivanovna yesterday either at the masquerade or even here, and putting all sorts of nonsense into her head.

"Why," Elena Ivanovna rattled off hurriedly, as though it were a lesson she had learnt, "if he is going to stay on in the crocodile, perhaps not come back all his life, while I sit waiting for him here! A husband ought to live at home, and not in a crocodile. . . ."

"But this was an unforeseen occurrence," I was beginning, in very comprehensible agitation.

"Oh, no, don't talk to me, I won't listen, I won't listen," she cried, suddenly getting quite cross. "You are always against me, you wretch! There's no doing anything with you, you will never give me any advice! Other people tell me that I can get a divorce because Ivan Matveitch will not get his salary now."

"Elena Ivanovna! is it you I hear!" I exclaimed pathetically. "What villain could have put such an idea into your head? And divorce on such a trivial ground as a salary is quite impossible. And poor Ivan Matveitch, poor Ivan Matveitch is, so to speak, burning with love for you even in the bowels of the monster. What's more, he is melting away with love like a lump of sugar. Yesterday while you were enjoying yourself at the masquerade, he was saying that he might in the last resort send for you as his lawful spouse to join him in the entrails of the monster, especially as it appears the crocodile is exceedingly roomy, not only able to accommodate two but even three persons. . . ."

And then I told her all that interesting part of my conversation the night before with Ivan Matveitch.

"What, what!" she cried, in surprise. "You want me to get into the monster too, to be with Ivan Matveitch? What an idea! And how am I to get in there, in my hat and crinoline? Heavens, what foolishness! And what should I look like while I was getting into it, and very likely there would be someone there to see me! It's absurd! And what should I have to eat there? And . . . and . . . and what should I do there when . . . Oh, my goodness, what will they think of next? . . . And what should I have to amuse me there? . . . You say there's a smell of gutta-percha? And what should I do if we quarrelled—should we have to go on staying there side by side? Foo, how horrid!"

"I agree, I agree with all those arguments, my sweet Elena Ivanovna," I interrupted, striving to express myself with that natural enthusiasm which always overtakes a man when he feels the truth is on his side. "But one thing you have not appreciated in all this, you have not realised that he cannot live without you if he is inviting you there; that is a proof of love, passionate, faithful, ardent love. . . . You have thought too little of his love, dear Elena Ivanovna!"

"I won't, I won't, I won't hear anything about it!" waving me off with her pretty little hand with glistening pink nails that had just been washed and polished. "Horrid man! You will reduce me to tears! Get into it yourself, if you like the prospect. You are his friend, get in and keep him company, and spend your life discussing some tedious science. . . ."

"You are wrong to laugh at this suggestion"—I checked the frivolous woman with dignity—"lvan Matveitch has invited me as it is. You, of course, are summoned there by duty; for me, it would be an act of generosity. But when Ivan Matveitch described to me last night the elasticity of the crocodile, he hinted very plainly that there would be room not only for you two, but for me also as a friend of the family, especially if I wished to join you, and therefore . . ."

"How so, the three of us?" cried Elena Ivanovna, looking at me in surprise. "Why, how should we . . . are we going to be all three there together? Ha-ha-ha! How silly you both are! Ha-ha-ha 1I shall certainly pinch you all the time, you wretch! Ha-ha-ha! Ha-ha-ha!"

And falling back on the sofa, she laughed till she cried. All this—the tears and the laughter-were so fascinating that I could not resist rushing eagerly to kiss her hand, which she did not oppose, though she did pinch my cars lightly as a sign of reconciliation.

Then we both grew very cheerful, and I described to her in detail all Ivan Matveitch's plans. The thought of her evening receptions and her salon pleased her very much.

"Only I should need a great many new dresses," she observed, "and so Ivan Matveitch must send me as much of his salary as possible and as soon as possible. Only . . . only I don't know about that," she added thoughtfully. "How can he be brought here in the tank? That's very absurd. I don't want my husband to be carried about in a tank. I should feel quite ashamed for my visitors to see it. . . . I don't want that, no, I don't."

"By the way, while I think of it, was Timofey Semyonitch here yesterday?"

"Oh, yes, he was; he came to comfort me, and do you know, we played cards all the time. He played for sweetmeats, and if I lost he was to kiss my hands. What a wretch he is! And only fancy, he almost came to the masquerade with me, really!"

"He was carried away by his feelings!" I observed. "And who would not be with you, you charmer?"

"Oh, get along with your compliments! Stay, I'll give you a pinch as a parting present. I've learnt to pinch awfully well lately. Well, what do you say to that? By the way, you say Ivan Matveitch spoke several times of me yesterday?"

"N-no, not exactly. . . . I must say he is thinking more now of the fate of humanity, and wants . . ."

"Oh, let him! You needn't go on! I am sure it's fearfully boring. I'll go and see him some time. I shall certainly go tomorrow. Only not to-day; I've got a headache, and besides, there will be such a lot of people there to-day. . . . They'll say, 'That's his wife,' and I shall feel ashamed. . . . Good-bye. You will be . . . there this evening, won't you?"

"To see him, yes. He asked me to go and take him the papers."

"That's capital. Go and read to him. But don't come and see me to-day. I am not well, and perhaps I may go and see someone. Good-bye, you naughty man."

"It's that swarthy fellow is going to see her this evening," I thought.

At the office, of course, I gave no sign of being consumed by these cares and anxieties. But soon I noticed some of the most progressive papers seemed to be passing particularly rapidly from hand to hand among my colleagues, and were being read with an extremely serious expression of face. The first one that reached me was the *News-sheet,* a paper of no particular party but humanitarian in general, for which it was regarded with contempt among us, though it was read. Not without surprise I read in it the following paragraph:

"Yesterday strange rumours were circulating among the spacious ways and sumptuous buildings of our vast metropolis. A certain well-known bon-vivant of the highest society, probably weary of the cuisine at Borel's and at the X Club, went into the Arcade, into the place where an immense crocodile recently brought to the metropolis is being exhibited, and insisted on its being prepared for his dinner. After bargaining with the proprietor he at once set to work to devour him (that is, not the proprietor, a very meek and punctilious German, but his crocodile), cutting juicy morsels with his penknife from the living animal, and swallowing them with extraordinary rapidity. By degrees the whole crocodile disappeared into the vast recesses of his stomach, so that he was even on the point of attacking an ichneumon, a constant companion of the crocodile, probably imagining that the latter would be as savoury. We are by no means opposed to that new article of diet with which foreign gourmands have long been familiar. We have, indeed, predicted that it would come. English lords and travellers make up regular parties for catching crocodiles in Egypt, and consume the back of the monster cooked like beef-steak, with mustard, onions and potatoes. The French followed in the train of Lesseps prefer the paws baked in hot ashes, which they do, however, in opposition to the English, who laugh at them. Probably both ways would be appreciated among us. For our part, we are delighted at a new branch of industry, of which our great and varied fatherland stands pre-eminently in need. Probably before a year is out crocodiles will be brought in hundreds to replace this first one, lost in the stomach of a Petersburg gourmand. And why should not the crocodile be acclimatised among us in Russia? If the water of the Neva is too cold for these interesting strangers, there are ponds in the capital and rivers and lakes outside it. Why not breed crocodiles at Pargolovo, for instance, or at Pavlovsk, in the Presnensky Ponds and in Samoteka in Moscow? While providing agreeable, wholesome nourishment for our fastidious gourmands, they might at the same time entertain the ladies who walk about these ponds and instruct the children in natural history. The crocodile skin might be used for making jewel-cases, boxes, cigar-cases, pocket-books, and possibly more than one thousand saved up in the greasy notes that are peculiarly beloved of merchants might be laid by in crocodile skin. We hope to return more than once to this interesting topic."

Though I had foreseen something of the sort, yet the reckless inaccuracy of the paragraph overwhelmed me. Finding no one with whom to share my impression, I turned to Prohor Savvitch who was sitting opposite to me, and noticed that the latter had been watching me for some time, while in his hand he held the *Voice* as though he were on the point of passing it to me. Without a word he took the *News-sheet* from me, and as he handed me the *Voice* he drew a line with his nail against an article to which he probably wished to call my attention. This Prohor Savvitch was a very queer man: a taciturn old bachelor, he was not on intimate terms with any of us, scarcely spoke to anyone in the office, always had an opinion of his own about everything, but could not bear to impart it to anyone. He lived alone. Hardly anyone among us had ever been in his lodging.

This was what I read in the *Voice*.

"Everyone knows that we are progressive and humanitarian and want to be on a level with Europe in this respect. But in spite of all our exertions and the efforts of our paper we are still far from maturity, as may be judged from the shocking incident which took place yesterday in the Arcade and which we predicted long ago. A foreigner arrives in the capital bringing with him a crocodile which he begins exhibiting in the Arcade. We immediately hasten to welcome a new branch of useful industry such as our powerful and varied fatherland stands in great need of. Suddenly yesterday at four o'clock in the afternoon a gentleman of exceptional stoutness enters the foreigner's shop in an intoxicated condition, pays his entrance money, and immediately without any warning leaps into the jaws of the crocodile, who was forced, of course, to swallow him, if only from an instinct of self-preservation, to avoid being crushed. Tumbling into the inside of the crocodile, the stranger at once dropped asleep. Neither the shouts of the foreign proprietor, nor the lamentations of his terrified family, nor threats to send for the police made the slightest impression. Within the crocodile was heard nothing but laughter and a promise to flay him, though the poor mammal, compelled to swallow such a mass, was vainly shedding tears. An uninvited guest is worse than a Tartar. But in spite of the proverb the insolent visitor would not leave. We do not know how to explain such barbarous incidents which prove our lack of culture and disgrace us in the eyes of foreigners. The recklessness of the Russian temperament has found a fresh outlet. It may be asked what was the object of the uninvited visitor? A warm and comfortable abode? But there are many excellent houses in the capital with very cheap and comfortable lodgings, with the Neva water laid on, and a staircase lighted by gas, frequently with a hall-porter maintained by the proprietor. We would call our readers' attention to the barbarous treatment of domestic animals: it is difficult, of course, for the crocodile to digest such a mass all at once, and now he lies swollen out to the size of a mountain, awaiting death in insufferable agonies. In Europe persons guilty of inhumanity towards domestic animals have long been punished by law. But in spite of our European enlightenment, in spite of our European pavements, in spite of the European architecture of our houses, we are still far from shaking off our time-honoured traditions.

"Though the houses are new, the conventions are old."

And, indeed, the houses are not new, at least the staircases in them are not. We have more than once in our paper alluded to the fact that in the Petersburg Side in the house of the merchant Lukyanov the steps of the wooden staircase have decayed, fallen away, and have long been a danger for Afimya Skapidarov, a soldier's wife who works in the house, and is often obliged to go up the stairs with water or armfuls of wood. At last our predictions have come true: yesterday evening at half-past eight Afimya Skapidarov fell down with a basin of soup and broke her leg. We do not know whether Lukyanov will mend his staircase now, Russians are often wise after the event, but the victim of Russian carelessness has by now been taken to the hospital. In the same way we shall never cease to maintain that the house-porters who clear away the mud from the wooden pavement in the Viborgsky Side ought not to spatter the legs of passers-by, but should throw the mud up into heaps as is done in Europe," and so on, and so on.

"What's this?" I asked in some perplexity, looking at Prohor Savvitch. "What's the meaning of it?"

"How do you mean?"

"Why, upon my word! Instead of pitying Ivan Matveitch, they pity the crocodile!"

"What of it? They have pity even for a beast, a mammal. We must be up to Europe, mustn't we? They have a very warm feeling for crocodiles there too. He-he-he!"

Saying this, queer old Prohor Savvitch dived into his papers and would not utter another word.

I stuffed the *Voice* and the *News-sheet* into my pocket and collected as many old copies of the newspapers as I could find for Ivan Matveitch's diversion in the evening, and though the evening was far off, yet on this occasion I slipped away from the office early to go to the Arcade and look, if only from a distance, at what was going on there, and to listen to the various remarks and currents of opinion. I foresaw that there would be a regular crush there, and turned up the collar of my coat to meet it. I somehow felt rather shy—so unaccustomed are we to publicity. But I feel that I have no right to report my own prosaic feelings when faced with this remarkable and original incident.

Notes from Underground

Part I: Underground

The author of the diary and the diary itself are, of course, imaginary. Nevertheless it is clear that such persons as the writer of these notes not only may, but positively must, exist in our society, when we consider the circumstances in the midst of which our society is formed. I have tried to expose to the view of the public more distinctly than is commonly done, one of the characters of the recent past. He is one of the representatives of a generation still living. In this fragment, entitled "Underground," this person introduces himself and his views, and, as it were, tries to explain the causes owing to which he has made his appearance and was bound to make his appearance in our midst. In the second fragment there are added the actual notes of this person concerning certain events in his life.—AUTHOR'S NOTE.

* * *

I

I am a sick man. . . . I am a spiteful man. I am an unattractive man. I believe my liver is diseased. However, I know nothing at all about my disease, and do not know for certain what ails me. I don't consult a doctor for it, and never have, though I have a respect for medicine and doctors. Besides, I am extremely superstitious, sufficiently so to respect medicine, anyway (I am well-educated enough not to be superstitious, but I am superstitious). No, I refuse to consult a doctor from spite. That you probably will not understand. Well, I understand it, though. Of course, I can't explain who it is precisely that I am mortifying in this case by my spite: I am perfectly well aware that I cannot "pay out" the doctors by not consulting them; I know better than anyone that by all this I am only injuring myself and no one else. But still, if I don't consult a doctor it is from spite. My liver is bad, well—let it get worse!

I have been going on like that for a long time—twenty years. Now I am forty. I used to be in the government service, but am no longer. I was a spiteful official. I was rude and took pleasure in being so. I did not take bribes, you see, so I was bound to find a recompense in that, at least. (A poor jest, but I will not scratch it out. I wrote it thinking it would sound very witty; but now that I have seen myself that I only wanted to show off in a despicable way, I will not scratch it out on purpose!)

When petitioners used to come for information to the table at which I sat, I used to grind my teeth at them, and felt intense enjoyment when I succeeded in making anybody unhappy. I almost did succeed. For the most part they were all timid people—of course, they were petitioners. But of the uppish ones there was one officer in particular I could not endure. He simply would not be humble, and clanked his sword in a disgusting way. I carried on a feud with him for eighteen months over that sword. At last I got the better of him. He left off clanking it. That happened in my youth, though. But do you know, gentlemen, what was the chief point about my spite? Why, the whole point, the real sting of it lay in the fact that continually, even in the moment of the acutest spleen, I was inwardly conscious with shame that I was not only not a spiteful but not even an embittered man, that I was simply scaring sparrows at random and amusing myself by it. I might foam at the mouth, but bring me a doll to play with, give me a cup of tea with sugar in it, and maybe I should be appeased. I might even be genuinely touched, though probably I should grind my teeth at myself afterwards and lie awake at night with shame for months after. That was my way.

I was lying when I said just now that I was a spiteful official. I was lying from spite. I was simply amusing myself with the petitioners and with the officer, and in reality I never could become spiteful. I was conscious every moment in myself of many, very many elements absolutely opposite to that. I felt them positively swarming in me, these opposite elements. I knew that they had been swarming in me all my life and craving some outlet from me, but I would not let them, would not let them, purposely would not let them come out. They tormented me till I was ashamed: they drove me to convulsions and—sickened me, at last, how they sickened me! Now, are not you fancying, gentlemen, that I am expressing remorse for something now, that I am asking your forgiveness for something? I am sure you are fancying that. . . . However, I assure you I do not care if you are. . . .

It was not only that I could not become spiteful, I did not know how to become anything; neither spiteful nor kind, neither a rascal nor an honest man, neither a hero nor an insect. Now, I am living out my life in my corner, taunting myself with the spiteful and useless consolation that an intelligent man cannot become anything seriously, and it is only the fool who becomes anything. Yes, a man in the nineteenth century must and morally ought to be pre-eminently a characterless creature; a man of character, an active man is preeminently a limited creature. That is my conviction of forty years. I am forty years old now, and you know forty years is a whole lifetime; you know it is extreme old age. To live longer than forty years is bad manners, is vulgar, immoral. Who does live beyond forty? Answer that, sincerely and honestly I will tell you who do: fools and worthless fellows. I tell all old men that to their face, all these venerable old men, all these silver-haired and reverend seniors! I tell the whole world that to its face! I have a right to say so, for I shall go on living to sixty myself. To seventy! To eighty! . . . Stay, let me take breath . . .

You imagine no doubt, gentlemen, that I want to amuse you. You are mistaken in that, too. I am by no means such a mirthful person as you imagine, or as you may imagine; however, irritated by all this babble (and I feel that you are irritated) you think fit to ask me who I am—then my answer is, I am a collegiate assessor. I was in the service that I might have something to eat (and solely for that reason), and when last year a distant relation left me six thousand roubles in his will I immediately retired from the service and settled down in my corner. I used to live in this corner before, but now I have settled down in it. My room is a wretched, horrid one in the outskirts of the town. My servant is an old country-woman, ill-natured from stupidity, and, moreover, there is always a nasty smell about her. I am told that the Petersburg climate is bad for me, and that with my small means it is very expensive to live in Petersburg. I know all that better than all these sage and experienced counsellors and monitors. . . . But I am remaining in Petersburg; I am not going away from Petersburg! I am not going away because . . . ech! Why, it is absolutely no matter whether I am going away or not going away.

But what can a decent man speak of with most pleasure?

Answer: Of himself.

Well, so I will talk about myself.

II

I want now to tell you, gentlemen, whether you care to hear it or not, why I could not even become an insect. I tell you solemnly, that I have many times tried to become an insect. But I was not equal even to that. I swear, gentlemen, that to be too conscious is an illness—a real thorough-going illness. For man's everyday needs, it would have been quite enough to have the ordinary human consciousness, that is, half or a quarter of the amount which falls to the lot of a cultivated man of our unhappy nineteenth century, especially one who has the fatal ill-luck to inhabit Petersburg, the most theoretical and intentional town on the whole terrestrial globe. (There are intentional and unintentional towns.) It would have been quite enough, for instance, to have the consciousness by which all so-called direct persons and men of action live. I bet you think I am writing all this from affectation, to be witty at the expense of men of action; and what is more, that from ill-bred affectation, I am clanking a sword like my officer. But, gentlemen, whoever can pride himself on his diseases and even swagger over them?

Though, after all, everyone does do that; people do pride themselves on their diseases, and I do, may be, more than anyone. We will not dispute it; my contention was absurd. But yet I am firmly persuaded that a great deal of consciousness, every sort of consciousness, in fact, is a disease. I stick to that. Let us leave that, too, for a minute. Tell me this: why does it happen that at the very, yes, at the very moments when I am most capable of feeling every refinement of all that is "sublime and beautiful," as they used to say at one time, it would, as though of design, happen to me not only to feel but to do such ugly things, such that . . . Well, in short, actions that all, perhaps, commit; but which, as though purposely, occurred to me at the very time when I was most conscious that they ought not to be committed. The more conscious I was of goodness and of all that was "sublime and beautiful," the more deeply I sank into my mire and the more ready I was to sink in it altogether. But the chief point was that all this was, as it were, not accidental in me, but as though it were bound to be so. It was as though it were my most normal condition, and not in the least disease or depravity, so that at last all desire in me to struggle against this depravity passed. It ended by my almost believing (perhaps actually believing) that this was perhaps my normal condition. But at first, in the beginning, what agonies I endured in that struggle! I did not believe it was the same with other people, and all my life I hid this fact about myself as a secret. I was ashamed (even now, perhaps, I am ashamed): I got to the point of feeling a sort of secret abnormal, despicable enjoyment in returning home to my corner on some disgusting Petersburg night, acutely conscious that that day I had committed a loathsome action again, that what was done could never be undone, and secretly, inwardly gnawing, gnawing at myself for it, tearing and consuming myself till at last the bitterness turned into a sort of shameful accursed sweetness, and at last—into positive real enjoyment! Yes, into enjoyment, into enjoyment! I insist upon that. I have spoken of this because I keep wanting to know for a fact whether other people feel such enjoyment? I will explain; the enjoyment was just from the too intense consciousness of one's own degradation; it was from feeling oneself that one had reached the last barrier, that it was horrible, but that it could not be otherwise; that there was no escape for you; that you never could become a different man; that even if time and faith were still left you to change into something different you would most likely not wish to change; or if you did wish to, even then you would do nothing; because perhaps in reality there was nothing for you to change into.

And the worst of it was, and the root of it all, that it was all in accord with the normal fundamental laws of over-acute consciousness, and with the inertia that was the direct result of those laws, and that consequently one was not only unable to change but could do absolutely nothing. Thus it would follow, as the result of acute consciousness, that one is not to blame in being a scoundrel; as though that were any consolation to the scoundrel once he has come to realise that he actually is a scoundrel. But enough. . . . Ech, I have talked a lot of nonsense, but what have I explained? How is enjoyment in this to be explained? But I will explain it. I will get to the bottom of it! That is why I have taken up my pen. . . .

I, for instance, have a great deal of *amour propre*. I am as suspicious and prone to take offence as a humpback or a dwarf. But upon my word I sometimes have had moments when if I had happened to be slapped in the face I should, perhaps, have been positively glad of it. I say, in earnest, that I should probably have been able to discover even in that a peculiar sort of enjoyment—the enjoyment, of course, of despair; but in despair there are the most intense enjoyments, especially when one is very acutely conscious of the hopelessness of one's position. And when one is slapped in the face—why then the consciousness of being rubbed into a pulp would positively overwhelm one. The worst of it is, look at it which way one will, it still turns out that I was always the most to blame in everything. And what is most humiliating of all, to blame for no fault of my own but, so to say, through the laws of nature. In the first place, to blame because I am cleverer than any of the people surrounding me. (I have always considered myself cleverer than any of the people surrounding me, and sometimes, would you believe it, have been positively ashamed of it. At any rate, I have all my life, as it were, turned my eyes away and never could look people straight in the face.)

To blame, finally, because even if I had had magnanimity, I should only have had more suffering from the sense of its uselessness. I should certainly have never been able to do anything from being magnanimous—neither to forgive, for my assailant would perhaps have slapped me from the laws of nature, and one cannot forgive the laws of nature; nor to forget, for even if it were owing to the laws of nature, it is insulting all the same. Finally, even if I had wanted to be anything but magnanimous, had desired on the contrary to revenge myself on my assailant, I could not have revenged myself on any one for anything because I should certainly never have made up my mind to do anything, even if I had been able to. Why should I not have made up my mind? About that in particular I want to say a few words.

III

With people who know how to revenge themselves and to stand up for themselves in general, how is it done? Why, when they are possessed, let us suppose, by the feeling of revenge, then for the time there is nothing else but that feeling left in their whole being. Such a gentleman simply dashes straight for his object like an infuriated bull with its horns down, and nothing but a wall will stop him. (By the way: facing the wall, such gentlemen—that is, the "direct" persons and men of action—are genuinely nonplussed. For them a wall is not an evasion, as for us people who think and consequently do nothing; it is not an excuse for turning aside, an excuse for which we are always very glad, though we scarcely believe in it ourselves, as a rule. No, they are nonplussed in all sincerity. The wall has for them something tranquillising, morally soothing, final—maybe even something mysterious . . . but of the wall later.)

Well, such a direct person I regard as the real normal man, as his tender mother nature wished to see him when she graciously brought him into being on the earth. I envy such a man till I am green in the face. He is stupid. I am not disputing that, but perhaps the normal man should be stupid, how do you know? Perhaps it is very beautiful, in fact. And I am the more persuaded of that suspicion, if one can call it so, by the fact that if you take, for instance, the antithesis of the normal man, that is, the man of acute consciousness, who has come, of course, not out of the lap of nature but out of a retort (this is almost mysticism, gentlemen, but I suspect this, too), this retort-made man is sometimes so nonplussed in the presence of his antithesis that with all his exaggerated consciousness he genuinely thinks of himself as a mouse and not a man. It may be an acutely conscious mouse, yet it is a mouse, while the other is a man, and therefore, et caetera, et caetera. And the worst of it is, he himself, his very own self, looks on himself as a mouse; no one asks him to do so; and that is an important point. Now let us look at this mouse in action. Let us suppose, for instance, that it feels insulted, too (and it almost always does feel insulted), and wants to revenge itself, too. There may even be a greater accumulation of spite in it than in *l'homme de la nature et de la verité.* The base and nasty desire to vent that spite on its assailant rankles perhaps even more nastily in it than in *l'homme de la nature et de la verité.* For through his innate stupidity the latter looks upon his revenge as justice pure and simple; while in consequence of his acute consciousness the mouse does not believe in the justice of it. To come at last to the deed itself, to the very act of revenge. Apart from the one fundamental nastiness the luckless mouse succeeds in creating around it so many other nastinesses in the form of doubts and questions, adds to the one question so many unsettled questions that there inevitably works up around it a sort of fatal brew, a stinking mess, made up of its doubts, emotions, and of the contempt spat upon it by the direct men of action who stand solemnly about it as judges and arbitrators, laughing at it till their healthy sides ache. Of course the only thing left for it is to dismiss all that with a wave of its paw, and, with a smile of assumed contempt in which it does not even itself believe, creep ignominiously into its mouse-hole. There in its nasty, stinking, underground home our insulted, crushed and ridiculed mouse promptly becomes absorbed in cold, malignant and, above all, everlasting spite. For forty years together it will remember its injury down to the smallest, most ignominious details, and every time will add, of itself, details still more ignominious, spitefully teasing and tormenting itself with its own imagination. It will itself be ashamed of its imaginings, but yet it will recall it all, it will go over and over every detail, it will invent unheard of things against itself, pretending that those things might happen, and will forgive nothing. Maybe it will begin to revenge itself, too, but, as it were, piecemeal, in trivial ways, from behind the stove, incognito, without believing either in its own right to vengeance, or in the success of its revenge, knowing that from all its efforts at revenge it will suffer a hundred times more than he on whom it revenges itself, while he, I daresay, will not even scratch himself. On its deathbed it will recall it all over again, with interest accumulated over all the years and . . .

But it is just in that cold, abominable half despair, half belief, in that conscious burying oneself alive for grief in the underworld for forty years, in that acutely recognised and yet partly doubtful hopelessness of one's position, in that hell of unsatisfied desires turned inward, in that fever of oscillations, of resolutions determined for ever and repented of again a minute later—that the savour of that strange enjoyment of which I have spoken lies. It is so subtle, so difficult of analysis, that persons who are a little limited, or even simply persons of strong nerves, will not understand a single atom of it. "Possibly," you will add on your own account with a grin, "people will not understand it either who have never received a slap in the face," and in that way you will politely hint to me that I, too, perhaps, have had the experience of a slap in the face in my life, and so I speak as one who knows. I bet that you are thinking that. But set your minds at rest, gentlemen, I have not received a slap in the face, though it is absolutely a matter of indifference to me what you may think about it. Possibly, I even regret, myself, that I have given so few slaps in the face during my life. But enough . . . not another word on that subject of such extreme interest to you.

I will continue calmly concerning persons with strong nerves who do not understand a certain refinement of enjoyment. Though in certain circumstances these gentlemen bellow their loudest like bulls, though this, let us suppose, does them the greatest credit, yet, as I have said already, confronted with the impossible they subside at once. The impossible means the stone wall! What stone wall? Why, of course, the laws of nature, the deductions of natural science, mathematics. As soon as they prove to you, for instance, that you are descended from a monkey, then it is no use scowling, accept it for a fact. When they prove to you that in reality one drop of your own fat must be dearer to you than a hundred thousand of your fellow-creatures, and that this conclusion is the final solution of all so-called virtues and duties and all such prejudices and fancies, then you have just to accept it, there is no help for it, for twice two is a law of mathematics. Just try refuting it.

"Upon my word, they will shout at you, it is no use protesting: it is a case of twice two makes four! Nature does not ask your permission, she has nothing to do with your wishes, and whether you like her laws or dislike them, you are bound to accept her as she is, and consequently all her conclusions. A wall, you see, is a wall . . . and so on, and so on."

Merciful Heavens! but what do I care for the laws of nature and arithmetic, when, for some reason I dislike those laws and the fact that twice two makes four? Of course I cannot break through the wall by battering my head against it if I really have not the strength to knock it down, but I am not going to be reconciled to it simply because it is a stone wall and I have not the strength.

As though such a stone wall really were a consolation, and really did contain some word of conciliation, simply because it is as true as twice two makes four. Oh, absurdity of absurdities! How much better it is to understand it all, to recognise it all, all the impossibilities and the stone wall; not to be reconciled to one of those impossibilities and stone walls if it disgusts you to be reconciled to it; by the way of the most inevitable, logical combinations to reach the most revolting conclusions on the everlasting theme, that even for the stone wall you are yourself somehow to blame, though again it is as clear as day you are not to blame in the least, and therefore grinding your teeth in silent impotence to sink into luxurious inertia, brooding on the fact that there is no one even for you to feel vindictive against, that you have not, and perhaps never will have, an object for your spite, that it is a sleight of hand, a bit of juggling, a card-sharper's trick, that it is simply a mess, no knowing what and no knowing who, but in spite of all these uncertainties and jugglings, still there is an ache in you, and the more you do not know, the worse the ache.

IV

"Ha, ha, ha! You will be finding enjoyment in toothache next," you cry, with a laugh.

"Well, even in toothache there is enjoyment," I answer. I had toothache for a whole month and I know there is. In that case, of course, people are not spiteful in silence, but moan; but they are not candid moans, they are malignant moans, and the malignancy is the whole point. The enjoyment of the sufferer finds expression in those moans; if he did not feel enjoyment in them he would not moan. It is a good example, gentlemen, and I will develop it. Those moans express in the first place all the aimlessness of your pain, which is so humiliating to your consciousness; the whole legal system of nature on which you spit disdainfully, of course, but from which you suffer all the same while she does not. They express the consciousness that you have no enemy to punish, but that you have pain; the consciousness that in spite of all possible Wagenheims you are in complete slavery to your teeth; that if someone wishes it, your teeth will leave off aching, and if he does not, they will go on aching another three months; and that finally if you are still contumacious and still protest, all that is left you for your own gratification is to thrash yourself or beat your wall with your fist as hard as you can, and absolutely nothing more. Well, these mortal insults, these jeers on the part of someone unknown, end at last in an enjoyment which sometimes reaches the highest degree of voluptuousness. I ask you, gentlemen, listen sometimes to the moans of an educated man of the nineteenth century suffering from toothache, on the second or third day of the attack, when he is beginning to moan, not as he moaned on the first day, that is, not simply because he has toothache, not just as any coarse peasant, but as a man affected by progress and European civilisation, a man who is "divorced from the soil and the national elements," as they express it now-a-days. His moans become nasty, disgustingly malignant, and go on for whole days and nights. And of course he knows himself that he is doing himself no sort of good with his moans; he knows better than anyone that he is only lacerating and harassing himself and others for nothing; he knows that even the audience before whom he is making his efforts, and his whole family, listen to him with loathing, do not put a ha'porth of faith in him, and inwardly understand that he might moan differently, more simply, without trills and flourishes, and that he is only amusing himself like that from ill-humour, from malignancy. Well, in all these recognitions and disgraces it is that there lies a voluptuous pleasure. As though he would say: "I am worrying you, I am lacerating your hearts, I am keeping everyone in the house awake. Well, stay awake then, you, too, feel every minute that I have toothache. I am not a hero to you now, as I tried to seem before, but simply a nasty person, an impostor. Well, so be it, then! I am very glad that you see through me. It is nasty for you to hear my despicable moans: well, let it be nasty; here I will let you have a nastier flourish in a minute. . . ." You do not understand even now, gentlemen? No, it seems our development and our consciousness must go further to understand all the intricacies of this pleasure. You laugh? Delighted. My jests, gentlemen, are of course in bad taste, jerky, involved, lacking self-confidence. But of course that is because I do not respect myself. Can a man of perception respect himself at all?

V

Come, can a man who attempts to find enjoyment in the very feeling of his own degradation possibly have a spark of respect for himself? I am not saying this now from any mawkish kind of remorse. And, indeed, I could never endure saying, "Forgive me, Papa, I won't do it again," not because I am incapable of saying that—on the contrary, perhaps just because I have been too capable of it, and in what a way, too. As though of design I used to get into trouble in cases when I was not to blame in any way. That was the nastiest part of it. At the same time I was genuinely touched and penitent, I used to shed tears and, of course, deceived myself, though I was not acting in the least and there was a sick feeling in my heart at the time. . . . For that one could not blame even the laws of nature, though the laws of nature have continually all my life offended me more than anything. It is loathsome to remember it all, but it was loathsome even then. Of course, a minute or so later I would realise wrathfully that it was all a lie, a revolting lie, an affected lie, that is, all this penitence, this emotion, these vows of reform. You will ask why did I worry myself with such antics: answer, because it was very dull to sit with one's hands folded, and so one began cutting capers. That is really it. Observe yourselves more carefully, gentlemen, then you will understand that it is so. I invented adventures for myself and made up a life, so as at least to live in some way. How many times it has happened to me—well, for instance, to take offence simply on purpose, for nothing; and one knows oneself, of course, that one is offended at nothing; that one is putting it on, but yet one brings oneself at last to the point of being really offended. All my life I have had an impulse to play such pranks, so that in the end I could not control it in myself. Another time, twice, in fact, I tried hard to be in love. I suffered, too, gentlemen, I assure you. In the depth of my heart there was no faith in my suffering, only a faint stir of mockery, but yet I did suffer, and in the real, orthodox way; I was jealous, beside myself . . . and it was all from *ennui,* gentlemen, all from *ennui;* inertia overcame me. You know the direct, legitimate fruit of consciousness is inertia, that is, conscious sitting-with-the-hands-folded. I have referred to this already. I repeat, I repeat with emphasis: all "direct" persons and men of action are active just because they are stupid and limited. How explain that? I will tell you: in consequence of their limitation they take immediate and secondary causes for primary ones, and in that way persuade themselves more quickly and easily than other people do that they have found an infallible foundation for their activity, and their minds are at ease and you know that is the chief thing. To begin to act, you know, you must first have your mind completely at ease and no trace of doubt left in it. Why, how am I, for example, to set my mind at rest? Where are the primary causes on which I am to build? Where are my foundations? Where am I to get them from?

I exercise myself in reflection, and consequently with me every primary cause at once draws after itself another still more primary, and so on to infinity. That is just the essence of every sort of consciousness and reflection. It must be a case of the laws of nature again. What is the result of it in the end? Why, just the same. Remember I spoke just now of vengeance. (I am sure you did not take it in.) I said that a man revenges himself because he sees justice in it. Therefore he has found a primary cause, that is, justice. And so he is at rest on all sides, and consequently he carries out his revenge calmly and successfully, being persuaded that he is doing a just and honest thing. But I see no justice in it, I find no sort of virtue in it either, and consequently if I attempt to revenge myself, it is only out of spite. Spite, of course, might overcome everything, all my doubts, and so might serve quite successfully in place of a primary cause, precisely because it is not a cause. But what is to be done if I have not even spite (I began with that just now, you know). In consequence again of those accursed laws of consciousness, anger in me is subject to chemical disintegration. You look into it, the object flies off into air, your reasons evaporate, the criminal is not to be found, the wrong becomes not a wrong but a phantom, something like the toothache, for which no one is to blame, and consequently there is only the same outlet left again—that is, to beat the wall as hard as you can. So you give it up with a wave of the hand because you have not found a fundamental cause. And try letting yourself be carried away by your feelings, blindly, without reflection, without a primary cause, repelling consciousness at least for a time; hate or love, if only not to sit with your hands folded. The day after tomorrow, at the latest, you will begin despising yourself for having knowingly deceived yourself. Result: a soap-bubble and inertia. Oh, gentlemen, do you know, perhaps I consider myself an intelligent man, only because all my life I have been able neither to begin nor to finish anything. Granted I am a babbler, a harmless vexatious babbler, like all of us. But what is to be done if the direct and sole vocation of every intelligent man is babble, that is, the intentional pouring of water through a sieve?

VI

Oh, if I had done nothing simply from laziness! Heavens, how I should have respected myself, then. I should have respected myself because I should at least have been capable of being lazy; there would at least have been one quality, as it were, positive in me, in which I could have believed myself. Question: What is he? Answer: A sluggard; how very pleasant it would have been to hear that of oneself! It would mean that I was positively defined, it would mean that there was something to say about me. "Sluggard"—why, it is a calling and vocation, it is a career. Do not jest, it is so. I should then be a member of the best club by right, and should find my occupation in continually respecting myself. I knew a gentleman who prided himself all his life on being a connoisseur of Lafitte. He considered this as his positive virtue, and never doubted himself. He died, not simply with a tranquil, but with a triumphant conscience, and he was quite right, too. Then I should have chosen a career for myself, I should have been a sluggard and a glutton, not a simple one, but, for instance, one with sympathies for everything sublime and beautiful. How do you like that? I have long had visions of it. That "sublime and beautiful" weighs heavily on my mind at forty But that is at forty; then—oh, then it would have been different! I should have found for myself a form of activity in keeping with it, to be precise, drinking to the health of everything "sublime and beautiful." I should have snatched at every opportunity to drop a tear into my glass and then to drain it to all that is "sublime and beautiful." I should then have turned everything into the sublime and the beautiful; in the nastiest, unquestionable trash, I should have sought out the sublime and the beautiful. I should have exuded tears like a wet sponge. An artist, for instance, paints a picture worthy of Gay. At once I drink to the health of the artist who painted the picture worthy of Gay, because I love all that is "sublime and beautiful." An author has written *as you will*: at once I drink to the health of "anyone you will" because I love all that is "sublime and beautiful."

I should claim respect for doing so. I should persecute anyone who would not show me respect. I should live at ease, I should die with dignity, why, it is charming, perfectly charming! And what a good round belly I should have grown, what a treble chin I should have established, what a ruby nose I should have coloured for myself, so that everyone would have said, looking at me: "Here is an asset! Here is something real and solid!" And, say what you like, it is very agreeable to hear such remarks about oneself in this negative age.

VII

But these are all golden dreams. Oh, tell me, who was it first announced, who was it first proclaimed, that man only does nasty things because he does not know his own interests; and that if he were enlightened, if his eyes were opened to his real normal interests, man would at once cease to do nasty things, would at once become good and noble because, being enlightened and understanding his real advantage, he would see his own advantage in the good and nothing else, and we all know that not one man can, consciously, act against his own interests, consequently, so to say, through necessity, he would begin doing good? Oh, the babe! Oh, the pure, innocent child! Why, in the first place, when in all these thousands of years has there been a time when man has acted only from his own interest? What is to be done with the millions of facts that bear witness that men, *consciously*, that is fully understanding their real interests, have left them in the background and have rushed headlong on another path, to meet peril and danger, compelled to this course by nobody and by nothing, but, as it were, simply disliking the beaten track, and have obstinately, wilfully, struck out another difficult, absurd way, seeking it almost in the darkness. So, I suppose, this obstinacy and perversity were pleasanter to them than any advantage. . . . Advantage! What is advantage? And will you take it upon yourself to define with perfect accuracy in what the advantage of man consists? And what if it so happens that a man's advantage, *sometimes*, not only may, but even must, consist in his desiring in certain cases what is harmful to himself and not advantageous. And if so, if there can be such a case, the whole principle falls into dust. What do you think—are there such cases? You laugh; laugh away, gentlemen, but only answer me: have man's advantages been reckoned up with perfect certainty? Are there not some which not only have not been included but cannot possibly be included under any classification? You see, you gentlemen have, to the best of my knowledge, taken your whole register of human advantages from the averages of statistical figures and politico-economical formulas. Your advantages are prosperity, wealth, freedom, peace—and so on, and so on. So that the man who should, for instance, go openly and knowingly in opposition to all that list would to your thinking, and indeed mine, too, of course, be an obscurantist or an absolute madman: would not he? But, you know, this is what is surprising: why does it so happen that all these statisticians, sages and lovers of humanity, when they reckon up human advantages invariably leave out one? They don't even take it into their reckoning in the form in which it should be taken, and the whole reckoning depends upon that. It would be no greater matter, they would simply have to take it, this advantage, and add it to the list. But the trouble is, that this strange advantage does not fall under any classification and is not in place in any list. I have a friend for instance . . . Ech! gentlemen, but of course he is your friend, too; and indeed there is no one, no one to whom he is not a friend! When he prepares for any undertaking this gentleman immediately explains to you, elegantly and clearly, exactly how he must act in accordance with the laws of reason and truth. What is more, he will talk to you with excitement and passion of the true normal interests of man; with irony he will upbraid the short-sighted fools who do not understand their own interests, nor the true significance of virtue; and, within a quarter of an hour, without any sudden outside provocation, but simply through something inside him which is stronger than all his interests, he will go off on quite a different tack—that is, act in direct opposition to what he has just been saying about himself, in opposition to the laws of reason, in opposition to his own advantage, in fact in opposition to everything . . . I warn you that my friend is a compound personality and therefore it is difficult to blame him as an individual. The fact is, gentlemen, it seems there must really exist something that is dearer to almost every man than his greatest advantages, or (not to be illogical) there is a most advantageous advantage (the very one omitted of which we spoke just now) which is more important and more advantageous than all other advantages, for the sake of which a man if necessary is ready to act in opposition to all laws; that is, in opposition to reason, honour, peace, prosperity—in fact, in opposition to all those excellent and useful things if only he can attain that fundamental, most advantageous advantage which is dearer to him than all. "Yes, but it's advantage all the same," you will retort. But excuse me, I'll make the point clear, and it is not a case of playing upon words. What matters is, that this advantage is remarkable from the very fact that it breaks down all our classifications, and continually shatters every system constructed by lovers of mankind for the benefit of mankind. In fact, it upsets everything. But before I mention this advantage to you, I want to compromise myself personally, and therefore I boldly declare that all these fine systems, all these theories for explaining to mankind their real normal interests, in order that inevitably striving to pursue these interests they may at once become good and noble—are, in my opinion, so far, mere logical exercises! Yes, logical exercises. Why, to maintain this theory of the regeneration of mankind by means of the pursuit of his own advantage is to my mind almost the same thing . . . as to affirm, for instance, following Buckle, that through civilisation mankind becomes softer, and consequently less bloodthirsty and less fitted for warfare. Logically it does seem to follow from his arguments. But man has such a predilection for systems and abstract deductions that he is ready to distort the truth intentionally, he is ready to deny the evidence of his senses only to justify his logic. I take this example because it is the most glaring instance of it. Only look about you: blood is being spilt in streams, and in the merriest way, as though it were champagne. Take the whole of the nineteenth century in which Buckle lived. Take Napoleon—the Great and also the present one. Take North America—the eternal union. Take the farce of Schleswig-Holstein. . . . And what is it that civilisation softens in us? The only gain of civilisation for mankind is the greater capacity for variety of sensations—and absolutely nothing more. And through the development of this many-sidedness man may come to finding enjoyment in bloodshed. In fact, this has already happened to him. Have you noticed that it is the most civilised gentlemen who have been the subtlest slaughterers, to whom the Attilas and Stenka Razins could not hold a candle, and if they are not so conspicuous as the Attilas and Stenka Razins it is simply because they are so often met with, are so ordinary and have become so familiar to us. In any case civilisation has made mankind if not more bloodthirsty, at least more vilely, more loathsomely bloodthirsty. In old days he saw justice in bloodshed and with his conscience at peace exterminated those he thought proper. Now we do think bloodshed abominable and yet we engage in this abomination, and with more energy than ever. Which is worse? Decide that for yourselves. They say that Cleopatra (excuse an instance from Roman history) was fond of sticking gold pins into her slave-girls' breasts and derived gratification from their screams and writhings. You will say that that was in the comparatively barbarous times; that these are barbarous times too, because also, comparatively speaking, pins are stuck in even now; that though man has now learned to see more clearly than in barbarous ages, he is still far from having learnt to act as reason and science would dictate. But yet you are fully convinced that he will be sure to learn when he gets rid of certain old bad habits, and when common sense and science have completely re-educated human nature and turned it in a normal direction. You are confident that then man will cease from *intentional* error and will, so to say, be compelled not to want to set his will against his normal interests. That is not all; then, you say, science itself will teach man (though to my mind it's a superfluous luxury) that he never has really had any caprice or will of his own, and that he himself is something of the nature of a piano-key or the stop of an organ, and that there are, besides, things called the laws of nature; so that everything he does is not done by his willing it, but is done of itself, by the laws of nature. Consequently we have only to discover these laws of nature, and man will no longer have to answer for his actions and life will become exceedingly easy for him. All human actions will then, of course, be tabulated according to these laws, mathematically, like tables of logarithms up to 108,000, and entered in an index; or, better still, there would be published certain edifying works of the nature of encyclopaedic lexicons, in which everything will be so clearly calculated and explained that there will be no more incidents or adventures in the world.

Then—this is all what you say—new economic relations will be established, all ready-made and worked out with mathematical exactitude, so that every possible question will vanish in the twinkling of an eye, simply because every possible answer to it will be provided. Then the "Palace of Crystal" will be built. Then . . . In fact, those will be halcyon days. Of course there is no guaranteeing (this is my comment) that it will not be, for instance, frightfully dull then (for what will one have to do when everything will be calculated and tabulated), but on the other hand everything will be extraordinarily rational. Of course boredom may lead you to anything. It is boredom sets one sticking golden pins into people, but all that would not matter. What is bad (this is my comment again) is that I dare say people will be thankful for the gold pins then. Man is stupid, you know, phenomenally stupid; or rather he is not at all stupid, but he is so ungrateful that you could not find another like him in all creation. I, for instance, would not be in the least surprised if all of a sudden, *à propos* of nothing, in the midst of general prosperity a gentleman with an ignoble, or rather with a reactionary and ironical, countenance were to arise and, putting his arms akimbo, say to us all: "I say, gentleman, hadn't we better kick over the whole show and scatter rationalism to the winds, simply to send these logarithms to the devil, and to enable us to live once more at our own sweet foolish will!" That again would not matter, but what is annoying is that he would be sure to find followers—such is the nature of man. And all that for the most foolish reason, which, one would think, was hardly worth mentioning: that is, that man everywhere and at all times, whoever he may be, has preferred to act as he chose and not in the least as his reason and advantage dictated. And one may choose what is contrary to one's own interests, and sometimes one *positively ought* (that is my idea). One's own free unfettered choice, one's own caprice, however wild it may be, one's own fancy worked up at times to frenzy—is that very "most advantageous advantage" which we have overlooked, which comes under no classification and against which all systems and theories are continually being shattered to atoms. And how do these wiseacres know that man wants a normal, a virtuous choice? What has made them conceive that man must want a rationally advantageous choice? What man wants is simply *independent* choice, whatever that independence may cost and wherever it may lead. And choice, of course, the devil only knows what choice.

VIII

"Ha! ha! ha! But you know there is no such thing as choice in reality, say what you like," you will interpose with a chuckle. "Science has succeeded in so far analysing man that we know already that choice and what is called freedom of will is nothing else than—"

Stay, gentlemen, I meant to begin with that myself I confess, I was rather frightened. I was just going to say that the devil only knows what choice depends on, and that perhaps that was a very good thing, but I remembered the teaching of science . . . and pulled myself up. And here you have begun upon it. Indeed, if there really is some day discovered a formula for all our desires and caprices—that is, an explanation of what they depend upon, by what laws they arise, how they develop, what they are aiming at in one case and in another and so on, that is a real mathematical formula—then, most likely, man will at once cease to feel desire, indeed, he will be certain to. For who would want to choose by rule? Besides, he will at once be transformed from a human being into an organ-stop or something of the sort; for what is a man without desires, without free will and without choice, if not a stop in an organ? What do you think? Let us reckon the chances—can such a thing happen or not?

"H'm!" you decide. "Our choice is usually mistaken from a false view of our advantage. We sometimes choose absolute nonsense because in our foolishness we see in that nonsense the easiest means for attaining a supposed advantage. But when all that is explained and worked out on paper (which is perfectly possible, for it is contemptible and senseless to suppose that some laws of nature man will never understand), then certainly so-called desires will no longer exist. For if a desire should come into conflict with reason we shall then reason and not desire, because it will be impossible retaining our reason to be *senseless* in our desires, and in that way knowingly act against reason and desire to injure ourselves. And as all choice and reasoning can be really calculated—because there will some day be discovered the laws of our so-called free will—so, joking apart, there may one day be something like a table constructed of them, so that we really shall choose in accordance with it. If, for instance, some day they calculate and prove to me that I made a long nose at someone because I could not help making a long nose at him and that I had to do it in that particular way, what *freedom* is left me, especially if I am a learned man and have taken my degree somewhere? Then I should be able to calculate my whole life for thirty years beforehand. In short, if this could be arranged there would be nothing left for us to do; anyway, we should have to understand that. And, in fact, we ought unwearyingly to repeat to ourselves that at such and such a time and in such and such circumstances nature does not ask our leave; that we have got to take her as she is and not fashion her to suit our fancy, and if we really aspire to formulas and tables of rules, and well, even . . . to the chemical retort, there's no help for it, we must accept the retort too, or else it will be accepted without our consent. . . ."

Yes, but here I come to a stop! Gentlemen, you must excuse me for being over-philosophical; it's the result of forty years underground! Allow me to indulge my fancy. You see, gentlemen, reason is an excellent thing, there's no disputing that, but reason is nothing but reason and satisfies only the rational side of man's nature, while will is a manifestation of the whole life, that is, of the whole human life including reason and all the impulses. And although our life, in this manifestation of it, is often worthless, yet it is life and not simply extracting square roots. Here I, for instance, quite naturally want to live, in order to satisfy all my capacities for life, and not simply my capacity for reasoning, that is, not simply one twentieth of my capacity for life. What does reason know? Reason only knows what it has succeeded in learning (some things, perhaps, it will never learn; this is a poor comfort, but why not say so frankly?) and human nature acts as a whole, with everything that is in it, consciously or unconsciously, and, even if it goes wrong, it lives. I suspect, gentlemen, that you are looking at me with compassion; you tell me again that an enlightened and developed man, such, in short, as the future man will be, cannot consciously desire anything disadvantageous to himself, that that can be proved mathematically. I thoroughly agree, it can—by mathematics. But I repeat for the hundredth time, there is one case, one only, when man may consciously, purposely, desire what is injurious to himself, what is stupid, very stupid—simply in order to have the right to desire for himself even what is very stupid and not to be bound by an obligation to desire only what is sensible. Of course, this very stupid thing, this caprice of ours, may be in reality, gentlemen, more advantageous for us than anything else on earth, especially in certain cases. And in particular it may be more advantageous than any advantage even when it does us obvious harm, and contradicts the soundest conclusions of our reason concerning our advantage—for in any circumstances it preserves for us what is most precious and most important—that is, our personality, our individuality. Some, you see, maintain that this really is the most precious thing for mankind; choice can, of course, if it chooses, be in agreement with reason; and especially if this be not abused but kept within bounds. It is profitable and sometimes even praiseworthy. But very often, and even most often, choice is utterly and stubbornly opposed to reason . . . and . . . and . . . do you know that that, too, is profitable, sometimes even praiseworthy? Gentlemen, let us suppose that man is not stupid. (Indeed one cannot refuse to suppose that, if only from the one consideration, that, if man is stupid, then who is wise?) But if he is not stupid, he is monstrously ungrateful! Phenomenally ungrateful. In fact, I believe that the best definition of man is the ungrateful biped. But that is not all, that is not his worst defect; his worst defect is his perpetual moral obliquity, perpetual—from the days of the Flood to the Schleswig-Holstein period. Moral obliquity and consequently lack of good sense; for it has long been accepted that lack of good sense is due to no other cause than moral obliquity. Put it to the test and cast your eyes upon the history of mankind. What will you see? Is it a grand spectacle? Grand, if you like. Take the Colossus of Rhodes, for instance, that's worth something. With good reason Mr. Anaevsky testifies of it that some say that it is the work of man's hands, while others maintain that it has been created by nature herself. Is it many-coloured? May be it is many-coloured, too: if one takes the dress uniforms, military and civilian, of all peoples in all ages—that alone is worth something, and if you take the undress uniforms you will never get to the end of it; no historian would be equal to the job. Is it monotonous? May be it's monotonous too: it's fighting and fighting; they are fighting now, they fought first and they fought last—you will admit, that it is almost too monotonous. In short, one may say anything about the history of the world—anything that might enter the most disordered imagination. The only thing one can't say is that it's rational. The very word sticks in one's throat. And, indeed, this is the odd thing that is continually happening: there are continually turning up in life moral and rational persons, sages and lovers of humanity who make it their object to live all their lives as morally and rationally as possible, to be, so to speak, a light to their neighbours simply in order to show them that it is possible to live morally and rationally in this world. And yet we all know that those very people sooner or later have been false to themselves, playing some queer trick, often a most unseemly one. Now I ask you: what can be expected of man since he is a being endowed with strange qualities? Shower upon him every earthly blessing, drown him in a sea of happiness, so that nothing but bubbles of bliss can be seen on the surface; give him economic prosperity, such that he should have nothing else to do but sleep, eat cakes and busy himself with the continuation of his species, and even then out of sheer ingratitude, sheer spite, man would play you some nasty trick. He would even risk his cakes and would deliberately desire the most fatal rubbish, the most uneconomical absurdity, simply to introduce into all this positive good sense his fatal fantastic element. It is just his fantastic dreams, his vulgar folly that he will desire to retain, simply in order to prove to himself—as though that were so necessary—that men still are men and not the keys of a piano, which the laws of nature threaten to control so completely that soon one will be able to desire nothing but by the calendar. And that is not all: even if man really were nothing but a piano-key, even if this were proved to him by natural science and mathematics, even then he would not become reasonable, but would purposely do something perverse out of simple ingratitude, simply to gain his point. And if he does not find means he will contrive destruction and chaos, will contrive sufferings of all sorts, only to gain his point! He will launch a curse upon the world, and as only man can curse (it is his privilege, the primary distinction between him and other animals), may be by his curse alone he will attain his object—that is, convince himself that he is a man and not a piano-key! If you say that all this, too, can be calculated and tabulated—chaos and darkness and curses, so that the mere possibility of calculating it all beforehand would stop it all, and reason would reassert itself, then man would purposely go mad in order to be rid of reason and gain his point! I believe in it, I answer for it, for the whole work of man really seems to consist in nothing but proving to himself every minute that he is a man and not a piano-key! It may be at the cost of his skin, it may be by cannibalism! And this being so, can one help being tempted to rejoice that it has not yet come off, and that desire still depends on something we don't know?

You will scream at me (that is, if you condescend to do so) that no one is touching my free will, that all they are concerned with is that my will should of itself, of its own free will, coincide with my own normal interests, with the laws of nature and arithmetic.

Good heavens, gentlemen, what sort of free will is left when we come to tabulation and arithmetic, when it will all be a case of twice two make four? Twice two makes four without my will. As if free will meant that!

IX

Gentlemen, I am joking, and I know myself that my jokes are not brilliant,but you know one can take everything as a joke. I am, perhaps, jesting against the grain. Gentlemen, I am tormented by questions;

answer them for me. You, for instance, want to cure men of their old habits and reform their will in accordance with science and good sense. But how do you know, not only that it is possible, but also that it is *desirable* to reform man in that way? And what leads you to the conclusion that man's inclinations *need* reforming? In short, how do you know that such a reformation will be a benefit to man? And to go to the root of the matter, why are you so positively convinced that not to act against his real normal interests guaranteed by the conclusions of reason and arithmetic is certainly always advantageous for man and must always be a law for mankind? So far, you know, this is only your supposition. It may be the law of logic, but not the law of humanity. You think, gentlemen, perhaps that I am mad? Allow me to defend myself. I agree that man is pre-eminently a creative animal, predestined to strive consciously for an object and to engage in engineering—that is, incessantly and eternally to make new roads, *wherever they may lead*. But the reason why he wants sometimes to go off at a tangent may just be that he is *predestined* to make the road, and perhaps, too, that however stupid the "direct" practical man may be, the thought sometimes will occur to him that the road almost always does lead *somewhere*, and that the destination it leads to is less important than the process of making it, and that the chief thing is to save the well-conducted child from despising engineering, and so giving way to the fatal idleness, which, as we all know, is the mother of all the vices. Man likes to make roads and to create, that is a fact beyond dispute. But why has he such a passionate love for destruction and chaos also? Tell me that! But on that point I want to say a couple of words myself. May it not be that he loves chaos and destruction (there can be no disputing that he does sometimes love it) because he is instinctively afraid of attaining his object and completing the edifice he is constructing? Who knows, perhaps he only loves that edifice from a distance, and is by no means in love with it at close quarters; perhaps he only loves building it and does not want to live in it, but will leave it, when completed, for the use of *les animaux domestiques*—such as the ants, the sheep, and so on. Now the ants have quite a different taste. They have a marvellous edifice of that pattern which endures for ever—the ant-heap.

With the ant-heap the respectable race of ants began and with the ant-heap they will probably end, which does the greatest credit to their perseverance and good sense. But man is a frivolous and incongruous creature, and perhaps, like a chess player, loves the process of the game, not the end of it. And who knows (there is no saying with certainty), perhaps the only goal on earth to which mankind is striving lies in this incessant process of attaining, in other words, in life itself, and not in the thing to be attained, which must always be expressed as a formula, as positive as twice two makes four, and such positiveness is not life, gentlemen, but is the beginning of death. Anyway, man has always been afraid of this mathematical certainty, and I am afraid of it now. Granted that man does nothing but seek that mathematical certainty, he traverses oceans, sacrifices his life in the quest, but to succeed, really to find it, dreads, I assure you. He feels that when he has found it there will be nothing for him to look for. When workmen have finished their work they do at least receive their pay, they go to the tavern, then they are taken to the police-station—and there is occupation for a week. But where can man go? Anyway, one can observe a certain awkwardness about him when he has attained such objects. He loves the process of attaining, but does not quite like to have attained, and that, of course, is very absurd. In fact, man is a comical creature; there seems to be a kind of jest in it all. But yet mathematical certainty is after all, something insufferable. Twice two makes four seems to me simply a piece of insolence. Twice two makes four is a pert coxcomb who stands with arms akimbo barring your path and spitting. I admit that twice two makes four is an excellent thing, but if we are to give everything its due, twice two makes five is sometimes a very charming thing too.

And why are you so firmly, so triumphantly, convinced that only the normal and the positive—in other words, only what is conducive to welfare—is for the advantage of man? Is not reason in error as regards advantage? Does not man, perhaps, love something besides well-being? Perhaps he is just as fond of suffering? Perhaps suffering is just as great a benefit to him as well-being? Man is sometimes extraordinarily, passionately, in love with suffering, and that is a fact. There is no need to appeal to universal history to prove that; only ask yourself, if you are a man and have lived at all. As far as my personal opinion is concerned, to care only for well-being seems to me positively ill-bred. Whether it's good or bad, it is sometimes very pleasant, too, to smash things. I hold no brief for suffering nor for well-being either. I am standing for . . . my caprice, and for its being guaranteed to me when necessary. Suffering would be out of place in vaudevilles, for instance; I know that. In the "Palace of Crystal" it is unthinkable; suffering means doubt, negation, and what would be the good of a "palace of crystal" if there could be any doubt about it? And yet I think man will never renounce real suffering, that is, destruction and chaos. Why, suffering is the sole origin of consciousness. Though I did lay it down at the beginning that consciousness is the greatest misfortune for man, yet I know man prizes it and would not give it up for any satisfaction. Consciousness, for instance, is infinitely superior to twice two makes four. Once you have mathematical certainty there is nothing left to do or to understand. There will be nothing left but to bottle up your five senses and plunge into contemplation. While if you stick to consciousness, even though the same result is attained, you can at least flog yourself at times, and that will, at any rate, liven you up. Reactionary as it is, corporal punishment is better than nothing.

X

You believe in a palace of crystal that can never be destroyed—a palace at which one will not be able to put out one's tongue or make a long nose on the sly. And perhaps that is just why I am afraid of this edifice, that it is of crystal and can never be destroyed and that one cannot put one's tongue out at it even on the sly.

You see, if it were not a palace, but a hen-house, I might creep into it to avoid getting wet, and yet I would not call the hen-house a palace out of gratitude to it for keeping me dry. You laugh and say that in such circumstances a hen-house is as good as a mansion. Yes, I answer, if one had to live simply to keep out of the rain.

But what is to be done if I have taken it into my head that that is not the only object in life, and that if one must live one had better live in a mansion? That is my choice, my desire. You will only eradicate it when you have changed my preference. Well, do change it, allure me with something else, give me another ideal. But meanwhile I will not take a hen-house for a mansion. The palace of crystal may be an idle dream, it may be that it is inconsistent with the laws of nature and that I have invented it only through my own stupidity, through the old-fashioned irrational habits of my generation. But what does it matter to me that it is inconsistent? That makes no difference since it exists in my desires, or rather exists as long as my desires exist. Perhaps you are laughing again? Laugh away; I will put up with any mockery rather than pretend that I am satisfied when I am hungry. I know, anyway, that I will not be put off with a compromise, with a recurring zero, simply because it is consistent with the laws of nature and actually exists. I will not accept as the crown of my desires a block of buildings with tenements for the poor on a lease of a thousand years, and perhaps with a sign-board of a dentist hanging out. Destroy my desires, eradicate my ideals, show me something better, and I will follow you. You will say, perhaps, that it is not worth your trouble; but in that case I can give you the same answer. We are discussing things seriously; but if you won't deign to give me your attention, I will drop your acquaintance. I can retreat into my underground hole.

But while I am alive and have desires I would rather my hand were withered off than bring one brick to such a building! Don't remind me that I have just rejected the palace of crystal for the sole reason that one cannot put out one's tongue at it. I did not say because I am so fond of putting my tongue out. Perhaps the thing I resented was, that of all your edifices there has not been one at which one could not put out one's tongue. On the contrary, I would let my tongue be cut off out of gratitude if things could be so arranged that I should lose all desire to put it out. It is not my fault that things cannot be so arranged, and that one must be satisfied with model flats. Then why am I made with such desires? Can I have been constructed simply in order to come to the conclusion that all my construction is a cheat? Can this be my whole purpose? I do not believe it.

But do you know what: I am convinced that we underground folk ought to be kept on a curb. Though we may sit forty years underground without speaking, when we do come out into the light of day and break out we talk and talk and talk. . . .

XI

The long and the short of it is, gentlemen, that it is better to do nothing! Better conscious inertia! And so hurrah for underground! Though I have said that I envy the normal man to the last drop of my bile, yet I should not care to be in his place such as he is now (though I shall not cease envying him). No, no; anyway the underground life is more advantageous. There, at any rate, one can. . . . Oh, but even now I am lying! I am lying because I know myself that it is not underground that is better, but something different, quite different, for which I am thirsting, but which I cannot find! Damn underground!

I will tell you another thing that would be better, and that is, if I myself believed in anything of what I have just written. I swear to you, gentlemen, there is not one thing, not one word of what I have written that I really believe. That is, I believe it, perhaps, but at the same time I feel and suspect that I am lying like a cobbler.

"Then why have you written all this?" you will say to me. "I ought to put you underground for forty years without anything to do and then come to you in your cellar, to find out what stage you have reached! How can a man be left with nothing to do for forty years?"

"Isn't that shameful, isn't that humiliating?" you will say, perhaps, wagging your heads contemptuously. "You thirst for life and try to settle the problems of life by a logical tangle. And how persistent, how insolent are your sallies, and at the same time what a scare you are in! You talk nonsense and are pleased with it; you say impudent things and are in continual alarm and apologising for them. You declare that you are afraid of nothing and at the same time try to ingratiate yourself in our good opinion. You declare that you are gnashing your teeth and at the same time you try to be witty so as to amuse us. You know that your witticisms are not witty, but you are evidently well satisfied with their literary value. You may, perhaps, have really suffered, but you have no respect for your own suffering. You may have sincerity, but you have no modesty; out of the pettiest vanity you expose your sincerity to publicity and ignominy. You doubtlessly mean to say something, but hide your last word through fear, because you have not the resolution to utter it, and only have a cowardly impudence. You boast of consciousness, but you are not sure of your ground, for though your mind works, yet your heart is darkened and corrupt, and you cannot have a full, genuine consciousness without a pure heart. And how intrusive you are, how you insist and grimace! Lies, lies, lies!"

Of course I have myself made up all the things you say. That, too, is from underground. I have been for forty years listening to you through a crack under the floor. I have invented them myself, there was nothing else I could invent. It is no wonder that I have learned it by heart and it has taken a literary form. . . .

But can you really be so credulous as to think that I will print all this and give it to you to read too? And another problem: why do I call you "gentlemen," why do I address you as though you really were my readers? Such confessions as I intend to make are never printed nor given to other people to read. Anyway, I am not strong-minded enough for that, and I don't see why I should be. But you see a fancy has occurred to me and I want to realise it at all costs. Let me explain.

Every man has reminiscences which he would not tell to everyone, but only to his friends. He has other matters in his mind which he would not reveal even to his friends, but only to himself, and that in secret. But there are other things which a man is afraid to tell even to himself, and every decent man has a number of such things stored away in his mind. The more decent he is, the greater the number of such things in his mind. Anyway, I have only lately determined to remember some of my early adventures. Till now I have always avoided them, even with a certain uneasiness. Now, when I am not only recalling them, but have actually decided to write an account of them, I want to try the experiment whether one can, even with oneself, be perfectly open and not take fright at the whole truth. I will observe, in parenthesis, that Heine says that a true autobiography is almost an impossibility, and that man is bound to lie about himself. He considers that Rousseau certainly told lies about himself in his confessions, and even intentionally lied, out of vanity. I am convinced that Heine is right; I quite understand how sometimes one may, out of sheer vanity, attribute regular crimes to oneself, and indeed I can very well conceive that kind of vanity. But Heine judged of people who made their confessions to the public. I write only for myself, and I wish to declare once and for all that if I write as though I were addressing readers, that is simply because it is easier for me to write in that form. It is a form, an empty form—I shall never have readers. I have made this plain already. . . .

I don't wish to be hampered by any restrictions in the compilation of my notes. I shall not attempt any system or method. I will jot things down as I remember them.

But here, perhaps, someone will catch at the word and ask me: if you really don't reckon on readers, why do you make such compacts with yourself—and on paper too—that is, that you won't attempt any system or method, that you jot things down as you remember them, and so on, and so on? Why are you explaining? Why do you apologise?

Well, there it is, I answer.

There is a whole psychology in all this, though. Perhaps it is simply that I am a coward. And perhaps that I purposely imagine an audience before me in order that I may be more dignified while I write. There are perhaps thousands of reasons. Again, what is my object precisely in writing? If it is not for the benefit of the public why should I not simply recall these incidents in my own mind without putting them on paper?

Quite so; but yet it is more imposing on paper. There is something more impressive in it; I shall be better able to criticise myself and improve my style. Besides, I shall perhaps obtain actual relief from writing. Today, for instance, I am particularly oppressed by one memory of a distant past. It came back vividly to my mind a few days ago, and has remained haunting me like an annoying tune that one cannot get rid of. And yet I must get rid of it somehow. I have hundreds of such reminiscences; but at times some one stands out from the hundred and oppresses me. For some reason I believe that if I write it down I should get rid of it. Why not try?

Besides, I am bored, and I never have anything to do. Writing will be a sort of work. They say work makes man kind-hearted and honest. Well, here is a chance for me, anyway.

Snow is falling today, yellow and dingy. It fell yesterday, too, and a few days ago. I fancy it is the wet snow that has reminded me of that incident which I cannot shake off now. And so let it be a story *à propos* of the falling snow.

Part II: A Propos of the Wet Snow

When from dark error's subjugation
My words of passionate exhortation
Had wrenched thy fainting spirit free;
And writhing prone in thine affliction
Thou didst recall with malediction
The vice that had encompassed thee:
And when thy slumbering conscience, fretting
By recollection's torturing flame,
Thou didst reveal the hideous setting
Of thy life's current ere I came:
When suddenly I saw thee sicken,
And weeping, hide thine anguished face,
Revolted, maddened, horror-stricken,
At memories of foul disgrace.

—Nekrassov (translated by Juliet Soskice)

I

At that time I was only twenty-four. My life was even then gloomy, ill-regulated, and as solitary as that of a savage. I made friends with no one and positively avoided talking, and buried myself more and more in my hole. At work in the office I never looked at anyone, and was perfectly well aware that my companions looked upon me, not only as a queer fellow, but even looked upon me—I always fancied this—with a sort of loathing. I sometimes wondered why it was that nobody except me fancied that he was looked upon with aversion? One of the clerks had a most repulsive, pock-marked face, which looked positively villainous. I believe I should not have dared to look at anyone with such an unsightly countenance. Another had such a very dirty old uniform that there was an unpleasant odour in his proximity. Yet not one of these gentlemen showed the slightest self-consciousness—either about their clothes or their countenance or their character in any way. Neither of them ever imagined that they were looked at with repulsion; if they had imagined it they would not have minded—so long as their superiors did not look at them in that way. It is clear to me now that, owing to my unbounded vanity and to the high standard I set for myself, I often looked at myself with furious discontent, which verged on loathing, and so I inwardly attributed the same feeling to everyone. I hated my face, for instance: I thought it disgusting, and even suspected that there was something base in my expression, and so every day when I turned up at the office I tried to behave as independently as possible, and to assume a lofty expression, so that I might not be suspected of being abject. "My face may be ugly," I thought, "but let it be lofty, expressive, and, above all, *extremely* intelligent." But I was positively and painfully certain that it was impossible for my countenance ever to express those qualities. And what was worst of all, I thought it actually stupid looking, and I would have been quite satisfied if I could have looked intelligent. In fact, I would even have put up with looking base if, at the same time, my face could have been thought strikingly intelligent.

Of course, I hated my fellow clerks one and all, and I despised them all, yet at the same time I was, as it were, afraid of them. In fact, it happened at times that I thought more highly of them than of myself. It somehow happened quite suddenly that I alternated between despising them and thinking them superior to myself. A cultivated and decent man cannot be vain without setting a fearfully high standard for himself, and without despising and almost hating himself at certain moments. But whether I despised them or thought them superior I dropped my eyes almost every time I met anyone. I even made experiments whether I could face so and so's looking at me, and I was always the first to drop my eyes. This worried me to distraction. I had a sickly dread, too, of being ridiculous, and so had a slavish passion for the conventional in everything external. I loved to fall into the common rut, and had a whole-hearted terror of any kind of eccentricity in myself. But how could I live up to it? I was morbidly sensitive as a man of our age should be. They were all stupid, and as like one another as so many sheep. Perhaps I was the only one in the office who fancied that I was a coward and a slave, and I fancied it just because I was more highly developed. But it was not only that I fancied it, it really was so. I was a coward and a slave. I say this without the slightest embarrassment. Every decent man of our age must be a coward and a slave. That is his normal condition. Of that I am firmly persuaded. He is made and constructed to that very end. And not only at the present time owing to some casual circumstances, but always, at all times, a decent man is bound to be a coward and a slave. It is the law of nature for all decent people all over the earth. If anyone of them happens to be valiant about something, he need not be comforted nor carried away by that; he would show the white feather just the same before something else. That is how it invariably and inevitably ends. Only donkeys and mules are valiant, and they only till they are pushed up to the wall. It is not worth while to pay attention to them for they really are of no consequence.

Another circumstance, too, worried me in those days: that there was no one like me and I was unlike anyone else. "I am alone and they are *everyone*," I thought—and pondered.

From that it is evident that I was still a youngster.

The very opposite sometimes happened. It was loathsome sometimes to go to the office; things reached such a point that I often came home ill. But all at once, *à propos* of nothing, there would come a phase of scepticism and indifference (everything happened in phases to me), and I would laugh myself at my intolerance and fastidiousness, I would reproach myself with being *romantic*. At one time I was unwilling to speak to anyone, while at other times I would not only talk, but go to the length of contemplating making friends with them. All my fastidiousness would suddenly, for no rhyme or reason, vanish. Who knows, perhaps I never had really had it, and it had simply been affected, and got out of books. I have not decided that question even now. Once I quite made friends with them, visited their homes, played preference, drank vodka, talked of promotions. . . . But here let me make a digression.

We Russians, speaking generally, have never had those foolish transcendental "romantics"—German, and still more French—on whom nothing produces any effect; if there were an earthquake, if all France perished at the barricades, they would still be the same, they would not even have the decency to affect a change, but would still go on singing their transcendental songs to the hour of their death, because they are fools. We, in Russia, have no fools; that is well known. That is what distinguishes us from foreign lands. Consequently these transcendental natures are not found amongst us in their pure form. The idea that they are is due to our "realistic" journalists and critics of that day, always on the look out for Kostanzhoglos and Uncle Pyotr Ivanitchs and foolishly accepting them as our ideal; they have slandered our romantics, taking them for the same transcendental sort as in Germany or France. On the contrary, the characteristics of our "romantics" are absolutely and directly opposed to the transcendental European type, and no European standard can be applied to them. (Allow me to make use of this word "romantic"—an old-fashioned and much respected word which has done good service and is familiar to all.) The characteristics of our romantic are to understand everything, *to see everything and to see it often incomparably more clearly than our most realistic minds see it*; to refuse to accept anyone or anything, but at the same time not to despise anything; to give way, to yield, from policy; never to lose sight of a useful practical object (such as rent-free quarters at the government expense, pensions, decorations), to keep their eye on that object through all the enthusiasms and volumes of lyrical poems, and at the same time to preserve "the sublime and the beautiful" inviolate within them to the hour of their death, and to preserve themselves also, incidentally, like some precious jewel wrapped in cotton wool if only for the benefit of "the sublime and the beautiful." Our "romantic" is a man of great breadth and the greatest rogue of all our rogues, I assure you. . . . I can assure you from experience, indeed. Of course, that is, if he is intelligent. But what am I saying! The romantic is always intelligent, and I only meant to observe that although we have had foolish romantics they don't count, and they were only so because in the flower of their youth they degenerated into Germans, and to preserve their precious jewel more comfortably, settled somewhere out there—by preference in Weimar or the Black Forest.

I, for instance, genuinely despised my official work and did not openly abuse it simply because I was in it myself and got a salary for it. Anyway, take note, I did not openly abuse it. Our romantic would rather go out of his mind—a thing, however, which very rarely happens—than take to open abuse, unless he had some other career in view; and he is never kicked out. At most, they would take him to the lunatic asylum as "the King of Spain" if he should go very mad. But it is only the thin, fair people who go out of their minds in Russia. Innumerable "romantics" attain later in life to considerable rank in the service. Their many-sidedness is remarkable! And what a faculty they have for the most contradictory sensations! I was comforted by this thought even in those days, and I am of the same opinion now. That is why there are so many "broad natures" among us who never lose their ideal even in the depths of degradation; and though they never stir a finger for their ideal, though they are arrant thieves and knaves, yet they tearfully cherish their first ideal and are extraordinarily honest at heart. Yes, it is only among us that the most incorrigible rogue can be absolutely and loftily honest at heart without in the least ceasing to be a rogue. I repeat, our romantics, frequently, become such accomplished rascals (I use the term "rascals" affectionately), suddenly display such a sense of reality and practical knowledge that their bewildered superiors and the public generally can only ejaculate in amazement.

Their many-sidedness is really amazing, and goodness knows what it may develop into later on, and what the future has in store for us. It is not a poor material! I do not say this from any foolish or boastful patriotism. But I feel sure that you are again imagining that I am joking. Or perhaps it's just the contrary and you are convinced that I really think so. Anyway, gentlemen, I shall welcome both views as an honour and a special favour. And do forgive my digression.

I did not, of course, maintain friendly relations with my comrades and soon was at loggerheads with them, and in my youth and inexperience I even gave up bowing to them, as though I had cut off all relations. That, however, only happened to me once. As a rule, I was always alone.

In the first place I spent most of my time at home, reading. I tried to stifle all that was continually seething within me by means of external impressions. And the only external means I had was reading. Reading, of course, was a great help—exciting me, giving me pleasure and pain. But at times it bored me fearfully. One longed for movement in spite of everything, and I plunged all at once into dark, underground, loathsome vice of the pettiest kind. My wretched passions were acute, smarting, from my continual, sickly irritability I had hysterical impulses, with tears and convulsions. I had no resource except reading, that is, there was nothing in my surroundings which I could respect and which attracted me. I was overwhelmed with depression, too; I had an hysterical craving for incongruity and for contrast, and so I took to vice. I have not said all this to justify myself. . . . But, no! I am lying. I did want to justify myself. I make that little observation for my own benefit, gentlemen. I don't want to lie. I vowed to myself I would not.

And so, furtively, timidly, in solitude, at night, I indulged in filthy vice, with a feeling of shame which never deserted me, even at the most loathsome moments, and which at such moments nearly made me curse. Already even then I had my underground world in my soul. I was fearfully afraid of being seen, of being met, of being recognised. I visited various obscure haunts.

One night as I was passing a tavern I saw through a lighted window some gentlemen fighting with billiard cues, and saw one of them thrown out of the window. At other times I should have felt very much disgusted, but I was in such a mood at the time, that I actually envied the gentleman thrown out of the window—and I envied him so much that I even went into the tavern and into the billiard-room. "Perhaps," I thought, "I'll have a fight, too, and they'll throw me out of the window."

I was not drunk—but what is one to do—depression will drive a man to such a pitch of hysteria? But nothing happened. It seemed that I was not even equal to being thrown out of the window and I went away without having my fight.

An officer put me in my place from the first moment.

I was standing by the billiard-table and in my ignorance blocking up the way, and he wanted to pass; he took me by the shoulders and without a word—without a warning or explanation—moved me from where I was standing to another spot and passed by as though he had not noticed me. I could have forgiven blows, but I could not forgive his having moved me without noticing me.

Devil knows what I would have given for a real regular quarrel—a more decent, a more *literary* one, so to speak. I had been treated like a fly. This officer was over six foot, while I was a spindly little fellow. But the quarrel was in my hands. I had only to protest and I certainly would have been thrown out of the window. But I changed my mind and preferred to beat a resentful retreat.

I went out of the tavern straight home, confused and troubled, and the next night I went out again with the same lewd intentions, still more furtively, abjectly and miserably than before, as it were, with tears in my eyes—but still I did go out again. Don't imagine, though, it was cowardice made me slink away from the officer; I never have been a coward at heart, though I have always been a coward in action. Don't be in a hurry to laugh—I assure you I can explain it all.

Oh, if only that officer had been one of the sort who would consent to fight a duel! But no, he was one of those gentlemen (alas, long extinct!) who preferred fighting with cues or, like Gogol's Lieutenant Pirogov, appealing to the police. They did not fight duels and would have thought a duel with a civilian like me an utterly unseemly procedure in any case—and they looked upon the duel altogether as something impossible, something free-thinking and French. But they were quite ready to bully, especially when they were over six foot.

I did not slink away through cowardice, but through an unbounded vanity. I was afraid not of his six foot, not of getting a sound thrashing and being thrown out of the window; I should have had physical courage enough, I assure you; but I had not the moral courage. What I was afraid of was that everyone present, from the insolent marker down to the lowest little stinking, pimply clerk in a greasy collar, would jeer at me and fail to understand when I began to protest and to address them in literary language. For of the point of honour—not of honour, but of the point of honour (*point d'honneur*)—one cannot speak among us except in literary language. You can't allude to the "point of honour" in ordinary language. I was fully convinced (the sense of reality, in spite of all my romanticism!) that they would all simply split their sides with laughter, and that the officer would not simply beat me, that is, without insulting me, but would certainly prod me in the back with his knee, kick me round the billiard-table, and only then perhaps have pity and drop me out of the window.

Of course, this trivial incident could not with me end in that. I often met that officer afterwards in the street and noticed him very carefully. I am not quite sure whether he recognised me, I imagine not; I judge from certain signs. But I—I stared at him with spite and hatred and so it went on . . . for several years! My resentment grew even deeper with years. At first I began making stealthy inquiries about this officer. It was difficult for me to do so, for I knew no one. But one day I heard someone shout his surname in the street as I was following him at a distance, as though I were tied to him—and so I learnt his surname. Another time I followed him to his flat, and for ten kopecks learned from the porter where he lived, on which storey, whether he lived alone or with others, and so on—in fact, everything one could learn from a porter. One morning, though I had never tried my hand with the pen, it suddenly occurred to me to write a satire on this officer in the form of a novel which would unmask his villainy. I wrote the novel with relish. I did unmask his villainy, I even exaggerated it; at first I so altered his surname that it could easily be recognised, but on second thoughts I changed it, and sent the story to the *Otetchestvenniya Zapiski.* But at that time such attacks were not the fashion and my story was not printed. That was a great vexation to me.

Sometimes I was positively choked with resentment. At last I determined to challenge my enemy to a duel. I composed a splendid, charming letter to him, imploring him to apologise to me, and hinting rather plainly at a duel in case of refusal. The letter was so composed that if the officer had had the least understanding of the sublime and the beautiful he would certainly have flung himself on my neck and have offered me his friendship. And how fine that would have been! How we should have got on together! "He could have shielded me with his higher rank, while I could have improved his mind with my culture, and, well . . . my ideas, and all sorts of things might have happened." Only fancy, this was two years after his insult to me, and my challenge would have been a ridiculous anachronism, in spite of all the ingenuity of my letter in disguising and explaining away the anachronism. But, thank God (to this day I thank the Almighty with tears in my eyes) I did not send the letter to him. Cold shivers run down my back when I think of what might have happened if I had sent it.

And all at once I revenged myself in the simplest way, by a stroke of genius! A brilliant thought suddenly dawned upon me. Sometimes on holidays I used to stroll along the sunny side of the Nevsky about four o'clock in the afternoon. Though it was hardly a stroll so much as a series of innumerable miseries, humiliations and resentments; but no doubt that was just what I wanted. I used to wriggle along in a most unseemly fashion, like an eel, continually moving aside to make way for generals, for officers of the guards and the hussars, or for ladies. At such minutes there used to be a convulsive twinge at my heart, and I used to feel hot all down my back at the mere thought of the wretchedness of my attire, of the wretchedness and abjectness of my little scurrying figure. This was a regular martyrdom, a continual, intolerable humiliation at the thought, which passed into an incessant and direct sensation, that I was a mere fly in the eyes of all this world, a nasty, disgusting fly—more intelligent, more highly developed, more refined in feeling than any of them, of course—but a fly that was continually making way for everyone, insulted and injured by everyone. Why I inflicted this torture upon myself, why I went to the Nevsky, I don't know. I felt simply drawn there at every possible opportunity.

Already then I began to experience a rush of the enjoyment of which I spoke in the first chapter. After my affair with the officer I felt even more drawn there than before: it was on the Nevsky that I met him most frequently, there I could admire him. He, too, went there chiefly on holidays, He, too, turned out of his path for generals and persons of high rank, and he too, wriggled between them like an eel; but people, like me, or even better dressed than me, he simply walked over; he made straight for them as though there was nothing but empty space before him, and never, under any circumstances, turned aside. I gloated over my resentment watching him and . . . always resentfully made way for him. It exasperated me that even in the street I could not be on an even footing with him.

"Why must you invariably be the first to move aside?" I kept asking myself in hysterical rage, waking up sometimes at three o'clock in the morning. "Why is it you and not he? There's no regulation about it; there's no written law. Let the making way be equal as it usually is when refined people meet; he moves half-way and you move half-way; you pass with mutual respect."

But that never happened, and I always moved aside, while he did not even notice my making way for him. And lo and behold a bright idea dawned upon me! "What," I thought, "if I meet him and don't move on one side? What if I don't move aside on purpose, even if I knock up against him? How would that be?" This audacious idea took such a hold on me that it gave me no peace. I was dreaming of it continually, horribly, and I purposely went more frequently to the Nevsky in order to picture more vividly how I should do it when I did do it. I was delighted. This intention seemed to me more and more practical and possible.

"Of course I shall not really push him," I thought, already more good-natured in my joy. "I will simply not turn aside, will run up against him, not very violently, but just shouldering each other—just as much as decency permits. I will push against him just as much as he pushes against me." At last I made up my mind completely. But my preparations took a great deal of time. To begin with, when I carried out my plan I should need to be looking rather more decent, and so I had to think of my get-up. "In case of emergency, if, for instance, there were any sort of public scandal (and the public there is of the most *recherché*: the Countess walks there; Prince D. walks there; all the literary world is there), I must be well dressed; that inspires respect and of itself puts us on an equal footing in the eyes of the society."

With this object I asked for some of my salary in advance, and bought at Tchurkin's a pair of black gloves and a decent hat. Black gloves seemed to me both more dignified and *bon ton* than the lemon-coloured ones which I had contemplated at first. "The colour is too gaudy, it looks as though one were trying to be conspicuous," and I did not take the lemon-coloured ones. I had got ready long beforehand a good shirt, with white bone studs; my overcoat was the only thing that held me back. The coat in itself was a very good one, it kept me warm; but it was wadded and it had a raccoon collar which was the height of vulgarity. I had to change the collar at any sacrifice, and to have a beaver one like an officer's. For this purpose I began visiting the Gostiny Dvor and after several attempts I pitched upon a piece of cheap German beaver. Though these German beavers soon grow shabby and look wretched, yet at first they look exceedingly well, and I only needed it for the occasion. I asked the price; even so, it was too expensive. After thinking it over thoroughly I decided to sell my raccoon collar. The rest of the money—a considerable sum for me, I decided to borrow from Anton Antonitch

Syetotchkin, my immediate superior, an unassuming person, though grave and judicious. He never lent money to anyone, but I had, on entering the service, been specially recommended to him by an important personage who had got me my berth. I was horribly worried. To borrow from Anton Antonitch seemed to me monstrous and shameful. I did not sleep for two or three nights. Indeed, I did not sleep well at that time, I was in a fever; I had a vague sinking at my heart or else a sudden throbbing, throbbing, throbbing! Anton Antonitch was surprised at first, then he frowned, then he reflected, and did after all lend me the money, receiving from me a written authorisation to take from my salary a fortnight later the sum that he had lent me.

In this way everything was at last ready. The handsome beaver replaced the mean-looking raccoon, and I began by degrees to get to work. It would never have done to act offhand, at random; the plan had to be carried out skilfully, by degrees. But I must confess that after many efforts I began to despair: we simply could not run into each other. I made every preparation, I was quite determined—it seemed as though we should run into one another directly—and before I knew what I was doing I had stepped aside for him again and he had passed without noticing me. I even prayed as I approached him that God would grant me determination. One time I had made up my mind thoroughly, but it ended in my stumbling and falling at his feet because at the very last instant when I was six inches from him my courage failed me. He very calmly stepped over me, while I flew on one side like a ball. That night I was ill again, feverish and delirious.

And suddenly it ended most happily. The night before I had made up my mind not to carry out my fatal plan and to abandon it all, and with that object I went to the Nevsky for the last time, just to see how I would abandon it all. Suddenly, three paces from my enemy, I unexpectedly made up my mind—I closed my eyes, and we ran full tilt, shoulder to shoulder, against one another! I did not budge an inch and passed him on a perfectly equal footing! He did not even look round and pretended not to notice it; but he was only pretending, I am convinced of that. I am convinced of that to this day! Of course, I got the worst of it—he was stronger, but that was not the point. The point was that I had attained my object, I had kept up my dignity, I had not yielded a step, and had put myself publicly on an equal social footing with him. I returned home feeling that I was fully avenged for everything. I was delighted. I was triumphant and sang Italian arias. Of course, I will not describe to you what happened to me three days later; if you have read my first chapter you can guess for yourself. The officer was afterwards transferred; I have not seen him now for fourteen years. What is the dear fellow doing now? Whom is he walking over?

II

But the period of my dissipation would end and I always felt very sick afterwards. It was followed by remorse—I tried to drive it away; I felt too sick. By degrees, however, I grew used to that too. I grew used to everything, or rather I voluntarily resigned myself to enduring it. But I had a means of escape that reconciled everything—that was to find refuge in "the sublime and the beautiful," in dreams, of course. I was a terrible dreamer, I would dream for three months on end, tucked away in my corner, and you may believe me that at those moments I had no resemblance to the gentleman who, in the perturbation of his chicken heart, put a collar of German beaver on his great-coat. I suddenly became a hero. I would not have admitted my six-foot lieutenant even if he had called on me. I could not even picture him before me then. What were my dreams and how I could satisfy myself with them—it is hard to say now, but at the time I was satisfied with them. Though, indeed, even now, I am to some extent satisfied with them. Dreams were particularly sweet and vivid after a spell of dissipation; they came with remorse and with tears, with curses and transports. There were moments of such positive intoxication, of such happiness, that there was not the faintest trace of irony within me, on my honour. I had faith, hope, love. I believed blindly at such times that by some miracle, by some external circumstance, all this would suddenly open out, expand; that suddenly a vista of suitable activity—beneficent, good, and, above all, *ready made* (what sort of activity I had no idea, but the great thing was that it should be all ready for me)—would rise up before me—and I should come out into the light of day, almost riding a white horse and crowned with laurel. Anything but the foremost place I could not conceive for myself, and for that very reason I quite contentedly occupied the lowest in reality. Either to be a hero or to grovel in the mud—there was nothing between. That was my ruin, for when I was in the mud I comforted myself with the thought that at other times I was a hero, and the hero was a cloak for the mud: for an ordinary man it was shameful to defile himself, but a hero was too lofty to be utterly defiled, and so he might defile himself. It is worth noting that these attacks of the "sublime and the beautiful" visited me even during the period of dissipation and just at the times when I was touching the bottom. They came in separate spurts, as though reminding me of themselves, but did not banish the dissipation by their appearance. On the contrary, they seemed to add a zest to it by contrast, and were only sufficiently present to serve as an appetising sauce. That sauce was made up of contradictions and sufferings, of agonising inward analysis, and all these pangs and pin-pricks gave a certain piquancy, even a significance to my dissipation—in fact, completely answered the purpose of an appetising sauce. There was a certain depth of meaning in it. And I could hardly have resigned myself to the simple, vulgar, direct debauchery of a clerk and have endured all the filthiness of it. What could have allured me about it then and have drawn me at night into the street? No, I had a lofty way of getting out of it all.

And what loving-kindness, oh Lord, what loving-kindness I felt at times in those dreams of mine! in those "flights into the sublime and the beautiful"; though it was fantastic love, though it was never applied to anything human in reality, yet there was so much of this love that one did not feel afterwards even the impulse to apply it in reality; that would have been superfluous. Everything, however, passed satisfactorily by a lazy and fascinating transition into the sphere of art, that is, into the beautiful forms of life, lying ready, largely stolen from the poets and novelists and adapted to all sorts of needs and uses. I, for instance, was triumphant over everyone; everyone, of course, was in dust and ashes, and was forced spontaneously to recognise my superiority, and I forgave them all. I was a poet and a grand gentleman, I fell in love; I came in for countless millions and immediately devoted them to humanity, and at the same time I confessed before all the people my shameful deeds, which, of course, were not merely shameful, but had in them much that was "sublime and beautiful" something in the Manfred style. Everyone would kiss me and weep (what idiots they would be if they did not), while I should go barefoot and hungry preaching new ideas and fighting a victorious Austerlitz against the obscurantists. Then the band would play a march, an amnesty would be declared, the Pope would agree to retire from Rome to Brazil; then there would be a ball for the whole of Italy at the Villa Borghese on the shores of Lake Como, Lake Como being for that purpose transferred to the neighbourhood of Rome; then would come a scene in the bushes, and so on, and so on—as though you did not know all about it? You will say that it is vulgar and contemptible to drag all this into public after all the tears and transports which I have myself confessed. But why is it contemptible? Can you imagine that I am ashamed of it all, and that it was stupider than anything in your life, gentlemen? And I can assure you that some of these fancies were by no means badly composed. . . . It did not all happen on the shores of Lake Como. And yet you are right—it really is vulgar and contemptible. And most contemptible of all it is that now I am attempting to justify myself to you. And even more contemptible than that is my making this remark now. But that's enough, or there will be no end to it; each step will be more contemptible than the last. . . .

I could never stand more than three months of dreaming at a time without feeling an irresistible desire to plunge into society. To plunge into society meant to visit my superior at the office, Anton Antonitch Syetotchkin. He was the only permanent acquaintance I have had in my life, and I wonder at the fact myself now. But I only went to see him when that phase came over me, and when my dreams had reached such a point of bliss that it became essential at once to embrace my fellows and all mankind; and for that purpose I needed, at least, one human being, actually existing. I had to call on Anton Antonitch, however, on Tuesday—his at-home day; so I had always to time my passionate desire to embrace humanity so that it might fall on a Tuesday.

This Anton Antonitch lived on the fourth storey in a house in Five Corners, in four low-pitched rooms, one smaller than the other, of a particularly frugal and sallow appearance. He had two daughters and their aunt, who used to pour out the tea. Of the daughters one was thirteen and another fourteen, they both had snub noses, and I was awfully shy of them because they were always whispering and giggling together. The master of the house usually sat in his study on a leather couch in front of the table with some grey-headed gentleman, usually a colleague from our office or some other department. I never saw more than two or three visitors there, always the same. They talked about the excise duty; about business in the senate, about salaries, about promotions, about His Excellency, and the best means of pleasing him, and so on. I had the patience to sit like a fool beside these people for four hours at a stretch, listening to them without knowing what to say to them or venturing to say a word. I became stupefied, several times I felt myself perspiring, I was overcome by a sort of paralysis; but this was pleasant and good for me. On returning home I deferred for a time my desire to embrace all mankind.

I had however one other acquaintance of a sort, Simonov, who was an old schoolfellow. I had a number of schoolfellows, indeed, in Petersburg, but I did not associate with them and had even given up nodding to them in the street. I believe I had transferred into the department I was in simply to avoid their company and to cut off all connection with my hateful childhood. Curses on that school and all those terrible years of penal servitude! In short, I parted from my schoolfellows as soon as I got out into the world. There were two or three left to whom I nodded in the street. One of them was Simonov, who had in no way been distinguished at school, was of a quiet and equable disposition; but I discovered in him a certain independence of character and even honesty I don't even suppose that he was particularly stupid. I had at one time spent some rather soulful moments with him, but these had not lasted long and had somehow been suddenly clouded over. He was evidently uncomfortable at these reminiscences, and was, I fancy, always afraid that I might take up the same tone again. I suspected that he had an aversion for me, but still I went on going to see him, not being quite certain of it.

And so on one occasion, unable to endure my solitude and knowing that as it was Thursday Anton Antonitch's door would be closed, I thought of Simonov. Climbing up to his fourth storey I was thinking that the man disliked me and that it was a mistake to go and see him. But as it always happened that such reflections impelled me, as though purposely, to put myself into a false position, I went in. It was almost a year since I had last seen Simonov.

III

I found two of my old schoolfellows with him. They seemed to be discussing an important matter. All of them took scarcely any notice of my entrance, which was strange, for I had not met them for years. Evidently they looked upon me as something on the level of a common fly. I had not been treated like that even at school, though they all hated me. I knew, of course, that they must despise me now for my lack of success in the service, and for my having let myself sink so low, going about badly dressed and so on—which seemed to them a sign of my incapacity and insignificance. But I had not expected such contempt. Simonov was positively surprised at my turning up. Even in old days he had always seemed surprised at my coming. All this disconcerted me: I sat down, feeling rather miserable, and began listening to what they were saying.

They were engaged in warm and earnest conversation about a farewell dinner which they wanted to arrange for the next day to a comrade of theirs called Zverkov, an officer in the army, who was going away to a distant province. This Zverkov had been all the time at school with me too. I had begun to hate him particularly in the upper forms. In the lower forms he had simply been a pretty, playful boy whom everybody liked. I had hated him, however, even in the lower forms, just because he was a pretty and playful boy. He was always bad at his lessons and got worse and worse as he went on; however, he left with a good certificate, as he had powerful interests. During his last year at school he came in for an estate of two hundred serfs, and as almost all of us were poor he took up a swaggering tone among us. He was vulgar in the extreme, but at the same time he was a good-natured fellow, even in his swaggering. In spite of superficial, fantastic and sham notions of honour and dignity, all but very few of us positively grovelled before Zverkov, and the more so the more he swaggered. And it was not from any interested motive that they grovelled, but simply because he had been favoured by the gifts of nature. Moreover, it was, as it were, an accepted idea among us that Zverkov was a specialist in regard to tact and the social graces. This last fact particularly infuriated me. I hated the abrupt self-confident tone of his voice, his admiration of his own witticisms, which were often frightfully stupid, though he was bold in his language; I hated his handsome, but stupid face (for which I would, however, have gladly exchanged my intelligent one), and the free-and-easy military manners in fashion in the "'forties." I hated the way in which he used to talk of his future conquests of women (he did not venture to begin his attack upon women until he had the epaulettes of an officer, and was looking forward to them with impatience), and boasted of the duels he would constantly be fighting. I remember how I, invariably so taciturn, suddenly fastened upon Zverkov, when one day talking at a leisure moment with his schoolfellows of his future relations with the fair sex, and growing as sportive as a puppy in the sun, he all at once declared that he would not leave a single village girl on his estate unnoticed, that that was his *droit de seigneur,* and that if the peasants dared to protest he would have them all flogged and double the tax on them, the bearded rascals. Our servile rabble applauded, but I attacked him, not from compassion for the girls and their fathers, but simply because they were applauding such an insect. I got the better of him on that occasion, but though Zverkov was stupid he was lively and impudent, and so laughed it off, and in such a way that my victory was not really complete; the laugh was on his side. He got the better of me on several occasions afterwards, but without malice, jestingly, casually. I remained angrily and contemptuously silent and would not answer him. When we left school he made advances to me; I did not rebuff them, for I was flattered, but we soon parted and quite naturally. Afterwards I heard of his barrack-room success as a lieutenant, and of the fast life he was leading. Then there came other rumours—of his successes in the service. By then he had taken to cutting me in the street, and I suspected that he was afraid of compromising himself by greeting a personage as insignificant as me. I saw him once in the theatre, in the third tier of boxes. By then he was wearing shoulder-straps. He was twisting and twirling about, ingratiating himself with the daughters of an ancient General. In three years he had gone off considerably, though he was still rather handsome and adroit. One could see that by the time he was thirty he would be corpulent. So it was to this Zverkov that my schoolfellows were going to give a dinner on his departure. They had kept up with him for those three years, though privately they did not consider themselves on an equal footing with him, I am convinced of that.

Of Simonov's two visitors, one was Ferfitchkin, a Russianised German—a little fellow with the face of a monkey, a blockhead who was always deriding everyone, a very bitter enemy of mine from our days in the lower forms—a vulgar, impudent, swaggering fellow, who affected a most sensitive feeling of personal honour, though, of course, he was a wretched little coward at heart. He was one of those worshippers of Zverkov who made up to the latter from interested motives, and often borrowed money from him. Simonov's other visitor, Trudolyubov, was a person in no way remarkable—a tall young fellow, in the army, with a cold face, fairly honest, though he worshipped success of every sort, and was only capable of thinking of promotion. He was some sort of distant relation of Zverkov's, and this, foolish as it seems, gave him a certain importance among us. He always thought me of no consequence whatever; his behaviour to me, though not quite courteous, was tolerable.

"Well, with seven roubles each," said Trudolyubov, "twenty-one roubles between the three of us, we ought to be able to get a good dinner. Zverkov, of course, won't pay."

"Of course not, since we are inviting him," Simonov decided.

"Can you imagine," Ferfitchkin interrupted hotly and conceitedly, like some insolent flunkey boasting of his master the General's decorations, "can you imagine that Zverkov will let us pay alone? He will accept from delicacy, but he will order half a dozen bottles of champagne."

"Do we want half a dozen for the four of us?" observed Trudolyubov, taking notice only of the half dozen.

"So the three of us, with Zverkov for the fourth, twenty-one roubles, at the Hotel de Paris at five o'clock tomorrow," Simonov, who had been asked to make the arrangements, concluded finally.

"How twenty-one roubles?" I asked in some agitation, with a show of being offended; "if you count me it will not be twenty-one, but twenty-eight roubles."

It seemed to me that to invite myself so suddenly and unexpectedly would be positively graceful, and that they would all be conquered at once and would look at me with respect.

"Do you want to join, too?" Simonov observed, with no appearance of pleasure, seeming to avoid looking at me. He knew me through and through.

It infuriated me that he knew me so thoroughly.

"Why not? I am an old schoolfellow of his, too, I believe, and I must own I feel hurt that you have left me out," I said, boiling over again.

"And where were we to find you?" Ferfitchkin put in roughly.

"You never were on good terms with Zverkov," Trudolyubov added, frowning.

But I had already clutched at the idea and would not give it up.

"It seems to me that no one has a right to form an opinion upon that," I retorted in a shaking voice, as though something tremendous had happened. "Perhaps that is just my reason for wishing it now, that I have not always been on good terms with him."

"Oh, there's no making you out . . . with these refinements," Trudolyubov jeered.

"We'll put your name down," Simonov decided, addressing me. "Tomorrow at five-o'clock at the Hotel de Paris."

"What about the money?" Ferfitchkin began in an undertone, indicating me to Simonov, but he broke off, for even Simonov was embarrassed.

"That will do," said Trudolyubov, getting up. "If he wants to come so much, let him."

"But it's a private thing, between us friends," Ferfitchkin said crossly, as he, too, picked up his hat. "It's not an official gathering."

"We do not want at all, perhaps . . ."

They went away. Ferfitchkin did not greet me in any way as he went out, Trudolyubov barely nodded. Simonov, with whom I was left *tête-à-tête,* was in a state of vexation and perplexity, and looked at me queerly. He did not sit down and did not ask me to.

"H'm . . . yes . . . tomorrow, then. Will you pay your subscription now? I just ask so as to know," he muttered in embarrassment.

I flushed crimson, as I did so I remembered that I had owed Simonov fifteen roubles for ages—which I had, indeed, never forgotten, though I had not paid it.

"You will understand, Simonov, that I could have no idea when I came here. . . . I am very much vexed that I have forgotten. . . ."

"All right, all right, that doesn't matter. You can pay tomorrow after the dinner. I simply wanted to know. . . . Please don't . . ."

He broke off and began pacing the room still more vexed. As he walked he began to stamp with his heels.

"Am I keeping you?" I asked, after two minutes of silence.

"Oh!" he said, starting, "that is—to be truthful—yes. I have to go and see someone . . . not far from here," he added in an apologetic voice, somewhat abashed.

"My goodness, why didn't you say so?" I cried, seizing my cap, with an astonishingly free-and-easy air, which was the last thing I should have expected of myself.

"It's close by . . . not two paces away," Simonov repeated, accompanying me to the front door with a fussy air which did not suit him at all. "So five o'clock, punctually, tomorrow," he called down the stairs after me. He was very glad to get rid of me. I was in a fury.

"What possessed me, what possessed me to force myself upon them?" I wondered, grinding my teeth as I strode along the street, "for a scoundrel, a pig like that Zverkov! Of course I had better not go; of course, I must just snap my fingers at them. I am not bound in any way. I'll send Simonov a note by tomorrow's post. . . ."

But what made me furious was that I knew for certain that I should go, that I should make a point of going; and the more tactless, the more unseemly my going would be, the more certainly I would go.

And there was a positive obstacle to my going: I had no money. All I had was nine roubles, I had to give seven of that to my servant, Apollon, for his monthly wages. That was all I paid him—he had to keep himself.

Not to pay him was impossible, considering his character. But I will talk about that fellow, about that plague of mine, another time.

However, I knew I should go and should not pay him his wages.

That night I had the most hideous dreams. No wonder; all the evening I had been oppressed by memories of my miserable days at school, and I could not shake them off. I was sent to the school by distant relations, upon whom I was dependent and of whom I have heard nothing since—they sent me there a forlorn, silent boy, already crushed by their reproaches, already troubled by doubt, and looking with savage distrust at everyone. My schoolfellows met me with spiteful and merciless jibes because I was not like any of them. But I could not endure their taunts; I could not give in to them with the ignoble readiness with which they gave in to one another. I hated them from the first, and shut myself away from everyone in timid, wounded and disproportionate pride. Their coarseness revolted me. They laughed cynically at my face, at my clumsy figure; and yet what stupid faces they had themselves. In our school the boys' faces seemed in a special way to degenerate and grow stupider. How many fine-looking boys came to us! In a few years they became repulsive. Even at sixteen I wondered at them morosely; even then I was struck by the pettiness of their thoughts, the stupidity of their pursuits, their games, their conversations. They had no understanding of such essential things, they took no interest in such striking, impressive subjects, that I could not help considering them inferior to myself. It was not wounded vanity that drove me to it, and for God's sake do not thrust upon me your hackneyed remarks, repeated to nausea, that "I was only a dreamer," while they even then had an understanding of life. They understood nothing, they had no idea of real life, and I swear that that was what made me most indignant with them. On the contrary, the most obvious, striking reality they accepted with fantastic stupidity and even at that time were accustomed to respect success. Everything that was just, but oppressed and looked down upon, they laughed at heartlessly and shamefully. They took rank for intelligence; even at sixteen they were already talking about a snug berth. Of course, a great deal of it was due to their stupidity, to the bad examples with which they had always been surrounded in their childhood and boyhood. They were monstrously depraved. Of course a great deal of that, too, was superficial and an assumption of cynicism; of course there were glimpses of youth and freshness even in their depravity; but even that freshness was not attractive, and showed itself in a certain rakishness. I hated them horribly, though perhaps I was worse than any of them. They repaid me in the same way, and did not conceal their aversion for me. But by then I did not desire their affection: on the contrary, I continually longed for their humiliation. To escape from their derision I purposely began to make all the progress I could with my studies and forced my way to the very top. This impressed them. Moreover, they all began by degrees to grasp that I had already read books none of them could read, and understood things (not forming part of our school curriculum) of which they had not even heard. They took a savage and sarcastic view of it, but were morally impressed, especially as the teachers began to notice me on those grounds. The mockery ceased, but the hostility remained, and cold and strained relations became permanent between us. In the end I could not put up with it: with years a craving for society, for friends, developed in me. I attempted to get on friendly terms with some of my schoolfellows; but somehow or other my intimacy with them was always strained and soon ended of itself. Once, indeed, I did have a friend. But I was already a tyrant at heart; I wanted to exercise unbounded sway over him; I tried to instil into him a contempt for his surroundings; I required of him a disdainful and complete break with those surroundings. I frightened him with my passionate affection; I reduced him to tears, to hysterics. He was a simple and devoted soul; but when he devoted himself to me entirely I began to hate him immediately and repulsed him—as though all I needed him for was to win a victory over him, to subjugate him and nothing else. But I could not subjugate all of them; my friend was not at all like them either, he was, in fact, a rare exception. The first thing I did on leaving school was to give up the special job for which I had been destined so as to break all ties, to curse my past and shake the dust from off my feet. . . . And goodness knows why, after all that, I should go trudging off to Simonov's!

Early next morning I roused myself and jumped out of bed with excitement, as though it were all about to happen at once. But I believed that some radical change in my life was coming, and would inevitably come that day. Owing to its rarity, perhaps, any external event, however trivial, always made me feel as though some radical change in my life were at hand. I went to the office, however, as usual, but sneaked away home two hours earlier to get ready. The great thing, I thought, is not to be the first to arrive, or they will think I am overjoyed at coming. But there were thousands of such great points to consider, and they all agitated and overwhelmed me. I polished my boots a second time with my own hands; nothing in the world would have induced Apollon to clean them twice a day, as he considered that it was more than his duties required of him. I stole the brushes to clean them from the passage, being careful he should not detect it, for fear of his contempt. Then I minutely examined my clothes and thought that everything looked old, worn and threadbare. I had let myself get too slovenly. My uniform, perhaps, was tidy, but I could not go out to dinner in my uniform. The worst of it was that on the knee of my trousers was a big yellow stain. I had a foreboding that that stain would deprive me of nine-tenths of my personal dignity. I knew, too, that it was very poor to think so. "But this is no time for thinking: now I am in for the real thing," I thought, and my heart sank. I knew, too, perfectly well even then, that I was monstrously exaggerating the facts. But how could I help it? I could not control myself and was already shaking with fever. With despair I pictured to myself how coldly and disdainfully that "scoundrel"

Zverkov would meet me; with what dull-witted, invincible contempt the blockhead Trudolyubov would look at me; with what impudent rudeness the insect Ferfitchkin would snigger at me in order to curry favour with Zverkov; how completely Simonov would take it all in, and how he would despise me for the abjectness of my vanity and lack of spirit—and, worst of all, how paltry, *unliterary*, commonplace it would all be. Of course, the best thing would be not to go at all. But that was most impossible of all: if I feel impelled to do anything, I seem to be pitchforked into it. I should have jeered at myself ever afterwards: "So you funked it, you funked it, you funked the *real thing*!" On the contrary, I passionately longed to show all that "rabble" that I was by no means such a spiritless creature as I seemed to myself. What is more, even in the acutest paroxysm of this cowardly fever, I dreamed of getting the upper hand, of dominating them, carrying them away, making them like me—if only for my "elevation of thought and unmistakable wit." They would abandon Zverkov, he would sit on one side, silent and ashamed, while I should crush him. Then, perhaps, we would be reconciled and drink to our everlasting friendship; but what was most bitter and humiliating for me was that I knew even then, knew fully and for certain, that I needed nothing of all this really, that I did not really want to crush, to subdue, to attract them, and that I did not care a straw really for the result, even if I did achieve it. Oh, how I prayed for the day to pass quickly! In unutterable anguish I went to the window, opened the movable pane and looked out into the troubled darkness of the thickly falling wet snow. At last my wretched little clock hissed out five. I seized my hat and, trying not to look at Apollon, who had been all day expecting his month's wages, but in his foolishness was unwilling to be the first to speak about it, I slipped between him and the door and, jumping into a high-class sledge, on which I spent my last half rouble, I drove up in grand style to the Hotel de Paris.

IV

I had been certain the day before that I should be the first to arrive. But it was not a question of being the first to arrive. Not only were they not there, but I had difficulty in finding our room. The table was not laid even. What did it mean? After a good many questions I elicited from the waiters that the dinner had been ordered not for five, but for six o'clock. This was confirmed at the buffet too. I felt really ashamed to go on questioning them. It was only twenty-five minutes past five. If they changed the dinner hour they ought at least to have let me know—that is what the post is for, and not to have put me in an absurd position in my own eyes and . . . and even before the waiters. I sat down; the servant began laying the table; I felt even more humiliated when he was present. Towards six o'clock they brought in candles, though there were lamps burning in the room. It had not occurred to the waiter, however, to bring them in at once when I arrived. In the next room two gloomy, angry-looking persons were eating their dinners in silence at two different tables. There was a great deal of noise, even shouting, in a room further away; one could hear the laughter of a crowd of people, and nasty little shrieks in French: there were ladies at the dinner. It was sickening, in fact. I rarely passed more unpleasant moments, so much so that when they did arrive all together punctually at six I was overjoyed to see them, as though they were my deliverers, and even forgot that it was incumbent upon me to show resentment.

Zverkov walked in at the head of them; evidently he was the leading spirit. He and all of them were laughing; but, seeing me, Zverkov drew himself up a little, walked up to me deliberately with a slight, rather jaunty bend from the waist. He shook hands with me in a friendly, but not over-friendly, fashion, with a sort of circumspect courtesy like that of a General, as though in giving me his hand he were warding off something. I had imagined, on the contrary, that on coming in he would at once break into his habitual thin, shrill laugh and fall to making his insipid jokes and witticisms. I had been preparing for them ever since the previous day, but I had not expected such condescension, such high-official courtesy. So, then, he felt himself ineffably superior to me in every respect! If he only meant to insult me by that high-official tone, it would not matter, I thought—I could pay him back for it one way or another. But what if, in reality, without the least desire to be offensive, that sheepshead had a notion in earnest that he was superior to me and could only look at me in a patronising way? The very supposition made me gasp.

"I was surprised to hear of your desire to join us," he began, lisping and drawling, which was something new. "You and I seem to have seen nothing of one another. You fight shy of us. You shouldn't. We are not such terrible people as you think. Well, anyway, I am glad to renew our acquaintance."

And he turned carelessly to put down his hat on the window.

"Have you been waiting long?" Trudolyubov inquired.

"I arrived at five o'clock as you told me yesterday," I answered aloud, with an irritability that threatened an explosion.

"Didn't you let him know that we had changed the hour?" said Trudolyubov to Simonov.

"No, I didn't. I forgot," the latter replied, with no sign of regret, and without even apologising to me he went off to order the *hors d'oeuvre*.

"So you've been here a whole hour? Oh, poor fellow!" Zverkov cried ironically, for to his notions this was bound to be extremely funny. That rascal Ferfitchkin followed with his nasty little snigger like a puppy yapping. My position struck him, too, as exquisitely ludicrous and embarrassing.

"It isn't funny at all!" I cried to Ferfitchkin, more and more irritated. "It wasn't my fault, but other people's. They neglected to let me know. It was . . . it was . . . it was simply absurd."

"It's not only absurd, but something else as well," muttered Trudolyubov, naively taking my part. "You are not hard enough upon it. It was simply rudeness—unintentional, of course. And how could Simonov . . . h'm!"

"If a trick like that had been played on me," observed Ferfitchkin, "I should . . ."

"But you should have ordered something for yourself," Zverkov interrupted, "or simply asked for dinner without waiting for us."

"You will allow that I might have done that without your permission," I rapped out. "If I waited, it was . . ."

"Let us sit down, gentlemen," cried Simonov, coming in. "Everything is ready; I can answer for the champagne; it is capitally frozen. . . . You see, I did not know your address, where was I to look for you?" he suddenly turned to me, but again he seemed to avoid looking at me. Evidently he had something against me. It must have been what happened yesterday.

All sat down; I did the same. It was a round table. Trudolyubov was on my left, Simonov on my right, Zverkov was sitting opposite, Ferfitchkin next to him, between him and Trudolyubov.

"Tell me, are you . . . in a government office?" Zverkov went on attending to me. Seeing that I was embarrassed he seriously thought that he ought to be friendly to me, and, so to speak, cheer me up.

"Does he want me to throw a bottle at his head?" I thought, in a fury. In my novel surroundings I was unnaturally ready to be irritated.

"In the N— office," I answered jerkily, with my eyes on my plate.

"And ha-ave you a go-od berth? I say, what ma-a-de you leave your original job?"

"What ma-a-de me was that I wanted to leave my original job," I drawled more than he, hardly able to control myself. Ferfitchkin went off into a guffaw. Simonov looked at me ironically. Trudolyubov left off eating and began looking at me with curiosity.

Zverkov winced, but he tried not to notice it.

"And the remuneration?"

"What remuneration?"

"I mean, your sa-a-lary?"

"Why are you cross-examining me?" However, I told him at once what my salary was. I turned horribly red.

"It is not very handsome," Zverkov observed majestically.

"Yes, you can't afford to dine at cafes on that," Ferfitchkin added insolently.

"To my thinking it's very poor," Trudolyubov observed gravely.

"And how thin you have grown! How you have changed!" added Zverkov, with a shade of venom in his voice, scanning me and my attire with a sort of insolent compassion.

"Oh, spare his blushes," cried Ferfitchkin, sniggering.

"My dear sir, allow me to tell you I am not blushing," I broke out at last; "do you hear? I am dining here, at this cafe, at my own expense, not at other people's—note that, Mr. Ferfitchkin."

"Wha-at? Isn't every one here dining at his own expense? You would seem to be . . ." Ferfitchkin flew out at me, turning as red as a lobster, and looking me in the face with fury. "Tha-at," I answered, feeling I had gone too far, "and I imagine it would be better to talk of something more intelligent."

"You intend to show off your intelligence, I suppose?"

"Don't disturb yourself, that would be quite out of place here."

"Why are you clacking away like that, my good sir, eh? Have you gone out of your wits in your office?"

"Enough, gentlemen, enough!" Zverkov cried, authoritatively.

"How stupid it is!" muttered Simonov.

"It really is stupid. We have met here, a company of friends, for a farewell dinner to a comrade and you carry on an altercation," said Trudolyubov, rudely addressing himself to me alone. "You invited yourself to join us, so don't disturb the general harmony."

"Enough, enough!" cried Zverkov. "Give over, gentlemen, it's out of place. Better let me tell you how I nearly got married the day before yesterday. . . ."

And then followed a burlesque narrative of how this gentleman had almost been married two days before. There was not a word about the marriage, however, but the story was adorned with generals, colonels and kammer-junkers, while Zverkov almost took the lead among them. It was greeted with approving laughter; Ferfitchkin positively squealed.

No one paid any attention to me, and I sat crushed and humiliated.

"Good Heavens, these are not the people for me!" I thought. "And what a fool I have made of myself before them! I let Ferfitchkin go too far, though. The brutes imagine they are doing me an honour in letting me sit down with them. They don't understand that it's an honour to them and not to me! I've grown thinner! My clothes! Oh, damn my trousers! Zverkov noticed the yellow stain on the knee as soon as he came in. . . . But what's the use! I must get up at once, this very minute, take my hat and simply go without a word . . . with contempt! And tomorrow I can send a challenge. The scoundrels! As though I cared about the seven roubles. They may think . . . Damn it! I don't care about the seven roubles. I'll go this minute!"

Of course I remained. I drank sherry and Lafitte by the glassful in my discomfiture. Being unaccustomed to it, I was quickly affected. My annoyance increased as the wine went to my head. I longed all at once to insult them all in a most flagrant manner and then go away. To seize the moment and show what I could do, so that they would say, "He's clever, though he is absurd," and . . . and . . . in fact, damn them all!

I scanned them all insolently with my drowsy eyes. But they seemed to have forgotten me altogether. They were noisy, vociferous, cheerful. Zverkov was talking all the time. I began listening. Zverkov was talking of some exuberant lady whom he had at last led on to declaring her love (of course, he was lying like a horse), and how he had been helped in this affair by an intimate friend of his, a Prince Kolya, an officer in the hussars, who had three thousand serfs.

"And yet this Kolya, who has three thousand serfs, has not put in an appearance here tonight to see you off," I cut in suddenly.

For one minute every one was silent. "You are drunk already." Trudolyubov deigned to notice me at last, glancing contemptuously in my direction. Zverkov, without a word, examined me as though I were an insect. I dropped my eyes. Simonov made haste to fill up the glasses with champagne.

Trudolyubov raised his glass, as did everyone else but me.

"Your health and good luck on the journey!" he cried to Zverkov. "To old times, to our future, hurrah!"

They all tossed off their glasses, and crowded round Zverkov to kiss him. I did not move; my full glass stood untouched before me.

"Why, aren't you going to drink it?" roared Trudolyubov, losing patience and turning menacingly to me.

"I want to make a speech separately, on my own account . . . and then I'll drink it, Mr. Trudolyubov."

"Spiteful brute!" muttered Simonov. I drew myself up in my chair and feverishly seized my glass, prepared for something extraordinary, though I did not know myself precisely what I was going to say.

"*Silence!*" cried Ferfitchkin. "Now for a display of wit!"

Zverkov waited very gravely, knowing what was coming.

"Mr. Lieutenant Zverkov," I began, "let me tell you that I hate phrases, phrasemongers and men in corsets . . . that's the first point, and there is a second one to follow it."

There was a general stir.

"The second point is: I hate ribaldry and ribald talkers. Especially ribald talkers! The third point: I love justice, truth and honesty." I went on almost mechanically, for I was beginning to shiver with horror myself and had no idea how I came to be talking like this. "I love thought, Monsieur Zverkov; I love true comradeship, on an equal footing and not . . . H'm . . . I love . . . But, however, why not? I will drink your health, too, Mr. Zverkov. Seduce the Circassian girls, shoot the enemies of the fatherland and . . . and . . . to your health, Monsieur Zverkov!"

Zverkov got up from his seat, bowed to me and said:

"I am very much obliged to you." He was frightfully offended and turned pale.

"Damn the fellow!" roared Trudolyubov, bringing his fist down on the table.

"Well, he wants a punch in the face for that," squealed Ferfitchkin.

"We ought to turn him out," muttered Simonov.

"Not a word, gentlemen, not a movement!" cried Zverkov solemnly, checking the general indignation. "I thank you all, but I can show him for myself how much value I attach to his words."

"Mr. Ferfitchkin, you will give me satisfaction tomorrow for your words just now!" I said aloud, turning with dignity to Ferfitchkin.

"A duel, you mean? Certainly," he answered. But probably I was so ridiculous as I challenged him and it was so out of keeping with my appearance that everyone including Ferfitchkin was prostrate with laughter.

"Yes, let him alone, of course! He is quite drunk," Trudolyubov said with disgust.

"I shall never forgive myself for letting him join us," Simonov muttered again.

"Now is the time to throw a bottle at their heads," I thought to myself. I picked up the bottle . . . and filled my glass. . . . "No, I'd better sit on to the end," I went on thinking; "you would be pleased, my friends, if I went away. Nothing will induce me to go. I'll go on sitting here and drinking to the end, on purpose, as a sign that I don't think you of the slightest consequence. I will go on sitting and drinking, because this is a public-house and I paid my entrance money. I'll sit here and drink, for I look upon you as so many pawns, as inanimate pawns. I'll sit here and drink . . . and sing if I want to, yes, sing, for I have the right to . . . to sing . . . H'm!"

But I did not sing. I simply tried not to look at any of them. I assumed most unconcerned attitudes and waited with impatience for them to speak *first*. But alas, they did not address me! And oh, how I wished, how I wished at that moment to be reconciled to them! It struck eight, at last nine. They moved from the table to the sofa. Zverkov stretched himself on a lounge and put one foot on a round table. Wine was brought there. He did, as a fact, order three bottles on his own account. I, of course, was not invited to join them. They all sat round him on the sofa. They listened to him, almost with reverence. It was evident that they were fond of him. "What for? What for?" I wondered. From time to time they were moved to drunken enthusiasm and kissed each other. They talked of the Caucasus, of the nature of true passion, of snug berths in the service, of the income of an hussar called Podharzhevsky, whom none of them knew personally, and rejoiced in the largeness of it, of the extraordinary grace and beauty of a Princess D., whom none of them had ever seen; then it came to Shakespeare's being immortal.

I smiled contemptuously and walked up and down the other side of the room, opposite the sofa, from the table to the stove and back again. I tried my very utmost to show them that I could do without them, and yet I purposely made a noise with my boots, thumping with my heels. But it was all in vain. They paid no attention. I had the patience to walk up and down in front of them from eight o'clock till eleven, in the same place, from the table to the stove and back again. "I walk up and down to please myself and no one can prevent me." The waiter who came into the room stopped, from time to time, to look at me. I was somewhat giddy from turning round so often; at moments it seemed to me that I was in delirium. During those three hours I was three times soaked with sweat and dry again. At times, with an intense, acute pang I was stabbed to the heart by the thought that ten years, twenty years, forty years would pass, and that even in forty years I would remember with loathing and humiliation those filthiest, most ludicrous, and most awful moments of my life. No one could have gone out of his way to degrade himself more shamelessly, and I fully realised it, fully, and yet I went on pacing up and down from the table to the stove. "Oh, if you only knew what thoughts and feelings I am capable of, how cultured I am!" I thought at moments, mentally addressing the sofa on which my enemies were sitting. But my enemies behaved as though I were not in the room. Once—only once—they turned towards me, just when Zverkov was talking about Shakespeare, and I suddenly gave a contemptuous laugh. I laughed in such an affected and disgusting way that they all at once broke off their conversation, and silently and gravely for two minutes watched me walking up and down from the table to the stove, *taking no notice of them.* But nothing came of it: they said nothing, and two minutes later they ceased to notice me again. It struck eleven.

"Friends," cried Zverkov getting up from the sofa, "let us all be off now, *there*!"

"Of course, of course," the others assented. I turned sharply to Zverkov. I was so harassed, so exhausted, that I would have cut my throat to put an end to it. I was in a fever; my hair, soaked with perspiration, stuck to my forehead and temples.

"Zverkov, I beg your pardon," I said abruptly and resolutely. "Ferfitchkin, yours too, and everyone's, everyone's: I have insulted you all!"

"Aha! A duel is not in your line, old man," Ferfitchkin hissed venomously.

It sent a sharp pang to my heart.

"No, it's not the duel I am afraid of, Ferfitchkin! I am ready to fight you tomorrow, after we are reconciled. I insist upon it, in fact, and you cannot refuse. I want to show you that I am not afraid of a duel. You shall fire first and I shall fire into the air."

"He is comforting himself," said Simonov.

"He's simply raving," said Trudolyubov.

"But let us pass. Why are you barring our way? What do you want?" Zverkov answered disdainfully. They were all flushed, their eyes were bright: they had been drinking heavily.

"I ask for your friendship, Zverkov; I insulted you, but . . ."

"Insulted? *You* insulted *me*? Understand, sir, that you never, under any circumstances, could possibly insult *me*."

"And that's enough for you. Out of the way!" concluded Trudolyubov.

"Olympia is mine, friends, that's agreed!" cried Zverkov.

"We won't dispute your right, we won't dispute your right," the others answered, laughing.

I stood as though spat upon. The party went noisily out of the room. Trudolyubov struck up some stupid song. Simonov remained behind for a moment to tip the waiters. I suddenly went up to him.

"Simonov! give me six roubles!" I said, with desperate resolution.

He looked at me in extreme amazement, with vacant eyes. He, too, was drunk.

"You don't mean you are coming with us?"

"Yes."

"I've no money," he snapped out, and with a scornful laugh he went out of the room.

I clutched at his overcoat. It was a nightmare.

"Simonov, I saw you had money. Why do you refuse me? Am I a scoundrel? Beware of refusing me: if you knew, if you knew why I am asking! My whole future, my whole plans depend upon it!"

Simonov pulled out the money and almost flung it at me.

"Take it, if you have no sense of shame!" he pronounced pitilessly, and ran to overtake them.

I was left for a moment alone. Disorder, the remains of dinner, a broken wine-glass on the floor, spilt wine, cigarette ends, fumes of drink and delirium in my brain, an agonising misery in my heart and finally the waiter, who had seen and heard all and was looking inquisitively into my face.

"I am going there!" I cried. "Either they shall all go down on their knees to beg for my friendship, or I will give Zverkov a slap in the face!"

V

"So this is it, this is it at last—contact with real life," I muttered as I ran headlong downstairs. "This is very different from the Pope's leaving Rome and going to Brazil, very different from the ball on Lake Como!"

"You are a scoundrel," a thought flashed through my mind, "if you laugh at this now."

"No matter!" I cried, answering myself. "Now everything is lost!"

There was no trace to be seen of them, but that made no difference—I knew where they had gone.

At the steps was standing a solitary night sledge-driver in a rough peasant coat, powdered over with the still falling, wet, and as it were warm, snow. It was hot and steamy. The little shaggy piebald horse was also covered with snow and coughing, I remember that very well. I made a rush for the roughly made sledge; but as soon as I raised my foot to get into it, the recollection of how Simonov had just given me six roubles seemed to double me up and I tumbled into the sledge like a sack.

"No, I must do a great deal to make up for all that," I cried. "But I will make up for it or perish on the spot this very night. Start!"

We set off. There was a perfect whirl in my head.

"They won't go down on their knees to beg for my friendship. That is a mirage, cheap mirage, revolting, romantic and fantastical—that's another ball on Lake Como. And so I am bound to slap Zverkov's face! It is my duty to. And so it is settled; I am flying to give him a slap in the face. Hurry up!"

The driver tugged at the reins.

"As soon as I go in I'll give it him. Ought I before giving him the slap to say a few words by way of preface? No. I'll simply go in and give it him. They will all be sitting in the drawing-room, and he with Olympia on the sofa. That damned Olympia! She laughed at my looks on one occasion and refused me. I'll pull Olympia's hair, pull Zverkov's ears! No, better one ear, and pull him by it round the room. Maybe they will all begin beating me and will kick me out. That's most likely, indeed. No matter! Anyway, I shall first slap him; the initiative will be mine; and by the laws of honour that is everything: he will be branded and cannot wipe off the slap by any blows, by nothing but a duel. He will be forced to fight. And let them beat me now. Let them, the ungrateful wretches! Trudolyubov will beat me hardest, he is so strong; Ferfitchkin will be sure to catch hold sideways and tug at my hair. But no matter, no matter! That's what I am going for. The blockheads will be forced at last to see the tragedy of it all! When they drag me to the door I shall call out to them that in reality they are not worth my little finger. Get on, driver, get on!" I cried to the driver. He started and flicked his whip, I shouted so savagely.

"We shall fight at daybreak, that's a settled thing. I've done with the office. Ferfitchkin made a joke about it just now. But where can I get pistols? Nonsense! I'll get my salary in advance and buy them. And powder, and bullets? That's the second's business. And how can it all be done by daybreak? and where am I to get a second? I have no friends. Nonsense!" I cried, lashing myself up more and more. "It's of no consequence! The first person I meet in the street is bound to be my second, just as he would be bound to pull a drowning man out of water. The most eccentric things may happen. Even if I were to ask the director himself to be my second tomorrow, he would be bound to consent, if only from a feeling of chivalry, and to keep the secret! Anton Antonitch. . . ."

The fact is, that at that very minute the disgusting absurdity of my plan and the other side of the question was clearer and more vivid to my imagination than it could be to anyone on earth. But . . .

"Get on, driver, get on, you rascal, get on!"

"Ugh, sir!" said the son of toil.

Cold shivers suddenly ran down me. Wouldn't it be better . . . to go straight home? My God, my God! Why did I invite myself to this dinner yesterday? But no, it's impossible. And my walking up and down for three hours from the table to the stove? No, they, they and no one else must pay for my walking up and down! They must wipe out this dishonour! Drive on!

And what if they give me into custody? They won't dare! They'll be afraid of the scandal. And what if Zverkov is so contemptuous that he refuses to fight a duel? He is sure to; but in that case I'll show them . . . I will turn up at the posting station when he's setting off tomorrow, I'll catch him by the leg, I'll pull off his coat when he gets into the carriage. I'll get my teeth into his hand, I'll bite him. "See what lengths you can drive a desperate man to!" He may hit me on the head and they may belabour me from behind. I will shout to the assembled multitude: "Look at this young puppy who is driving off to captivate the Circassian girls after letting me spit in his face!"

Of course, after that everything will be over! The office will have vanished off the face of the earth. I shall be arrested, I shall be tried, I shall be dismissed from the service, thrown in prison, sent to Siberia. Never mind! In fifteen years when they let me out of prison I will trudge off to him, a beggar, in rags. I shall find him in some provincial town. He will be married and happy. He will have a grown-up daughter. . . . I shall say to him: "Look, monster, at my hollow cheeks and my rags! I've lost everything—my career, my happiness, art, science, *the woman I loved,* and all through you. Here are pistols. I have come to discharge my pistol and . . . and I . . . forgive you. Then I shall fire into the air and he will hear nothing more of me. . . ."

I was actually on the point of tears, though I knew perfectly well at that moment that all this was out of Pushkin's *Silvio* and Lermontov's *Masquerade*. And all at once I felt horribly ashamed, so ashamed that I stopped the horse, got out of the sledge, and stood still in the snow in the middle of the street. The driver gazed at me, sighing and astonished.

What was I to do? I could not go on there—it was evidently stupid, and I could not leave things as they were, because that would seem as though . . . Heavens, how could I leave things! And after such insults! "No!" I cried, throwing myself into the sledge again. "It is ordained! It is fate! Drive on, drive on!"

And in my impatience I punched the sledge-driver on the back of the neck.

"What are you up to? What are you hitting me for?" the peasant shouted, but he whipped up his nag so that it began kicking.

The wet snow was falling in big flakes; I unbuttoned myself, regardless of it. I forgot everything else, for I had finally decided on the slap, and felt with horror that it was going to happen *now, at once,* and that *no force could stop it.* The deserted street lamps gleamed sullenly in the snowy darkness like torches at a funeral. The snow drifted under my great-coat, under my coat, under my cravat, and melted there. I did not wrap myself up—all was lost, anyway.

At last we arrived. I jumped out, almost unconscious, ran up the steps and began knocking and kicking at the door. I felt fearfully weak, particularly in my legs and knees. The door was opened quickly as though they knew I was coming. As a fact, Simonov had warned them that perhaps another gentleman would arrive, and this was a place in which one had to give notice and to observe certain precautions. It was one of those "millinery establishments" which were abolished by the police a good time ago. By day it really was a shop; but at night, if one had an introduction, one might visit it for other purposes.

I walked rapidly through the dark shop into the familiar drawing-room, where there was only one candle burning, and stood still in amazement: there was no one there. "Where are they?" I asked somebody. But by now, of course, they had separated. Before me was standing a person with a stupid smile, the "madam" herself, who had seen me before. A minute later a door opened and another person came in.

Taking no notice of anything I strode about the room, and, I believe, I talked to myself. I felt as though I had been saved from death and was conscious of this, joyfully, all over: I should have given that slap, I should certainly, certainly have given it! But now they were not here and . . . everything had vanished and changed! I looked round. I could not realise my condition yet. I looked mechanically at the girl who had come in: and had a glimpse of a fresh, young, rather pale face, with straight, dark eyebrows, and with grave, as it were wondering, eyes that attracted me at once; I should have hated her if she had been smiling. I began looking at her more intently and, as it were, with effort. I had not fully collected my thoughts. There was something simple and good-natured in her face, but something strangely grave. I am sure that this stood in her way here, and no one of those fools had noticed her. She could not, however, have been called a beauty, though she was tall, strong-looking, and well built. She was very simply dressed. Something loathsome stirred within me. I went straight up to her.

I chanced to look into the glass. My harassed face struck me as revolting in the extreme, pale, angry, abject, with dishevelled hair. "No matter, I am glad of it," I thought; "I am glad that I shall seem repulsive to her; I like that."

VI

. . . Somewhere behind a screen a clock began wheezing, as though oppressed by something, as though someone were strangling it. After an unnaturally prolonged wheezing there followed a shrill, nasty, and as it were unexpectedly rapid, chime—as though someone were suddenly jumping forward. It struck two. I woke up, though I had indeed not been asleep but lying half-conscious.

It was almost completely dark in the narrow, cramped, low-pitched room, cumbered up with an enormous wardrobe and piles of cardboard boxes and all sorts of frippery and litter. The candle end that had been burning on the table was going out and gave a faint flicker from time to time. In a few minutes there would be complete darkness.

I was not long in coming to myself; everything came back to my mind at once, without an effort, as though it had been in ambush to pounce upon me again. And, indeed, even while I was unconscious a point seemed continually to remain in my memory unforgotten, and round it my dreams moved drearily. But strange to say, everything that had happened to me in that day seemed to me now, on waking, to be in the far, far away past, as though I had long, long ago lived all that down.

My head was full of fumes. Something seemed to be hovering over me, rousing me, exciting me, and making me restless. Misery and spite seemed surging up in me again and seeking an outlet. Suddenly I saw beside me two wide open eyes scrutinising me curiously and persistently. The look in those eyes was coldly detached, sullen, as it were utterly remote; it weighed upon me.

A grim idea came into my brain and passed all over my body, as a horrible sensation, such as one feels when one goes into a damp and mouldy cellar. There was something unnatural in those two eyes, beginning to look at me only now. I recalled, too, that during those two hours I had not said a single word to this creature, and had, in fact, considered it utterly superfluous; in fact, the silence had for some reason gratified me. Now I suddenly realised vividly the hideous idea—revolting as a spider—of vice, which, without love, grossly and shamelessly begins with that in which true love finds its consummation. For a long time we gazed at each other like that, but she did not drop her eyes before mine and her expression did not change, so that at last I felt uncomfortable.

"What is your name?" I asked abruptly, to put an end to it.

"Liza," she answered almost in a whisper, but somehow far from graciously, and she turned her eyes away.

I was silent.

"What weather! The snow . . . it's disgusting!" I said, almost to myself, putting my arm under my head despondently, and gazing at the ceiling.

She made no answer. This was horrible.

"Have you always lived in Petersburg?" I asked a minute later, almost angrily, turning my head slightly towards her.

"No."

"Where do you come from?"

"From Riga," she answered reluctantly.

"Are you a German?"

"No, Russian."

"Have you been here long?"

"Where?"

"In this house?"

"A fortnight."

She spoke more and more jerkily. The candle went out; I could no longer distinguish her face.

"Have you a father and mother?"

"Yes . . . no . . . I have."

"Where are they?"

"There . . . in Riga."

"What are they?"

"Oh, nothing."

"Nothing? Why, what class are they?"

"Tradespeople."

"Have you always lived with them?"

"Yes."

"How old are you?"

"Twenty." "Why did you leave them?"

"Oh, for no reason."

That answer meant "Let me alone; I feel sick, sad."

We were silent.

God knows why I did not go away. I felt myself more and more sick and dreary. The images of the previous day began of themselves, apart from my will, flitting through my memory in confusion. I suddenly recalled something I had seen that morning when, full of anxious thoughts, I was hurrying to the office.

"I saw them carrying a coffin out yesterday and they nearly dropped it," I suddenly said aloud, not that I desired to open the conversation, but as it were by accident.

"A coffin?"

"Yes, in the Haymarket; they were bringing it up out of a cellar."

"From a cellar?"

"Not from a cellar, but a basement. Oh, you know . . . down below . . . from a house of ill-fame. It was filthy all round . . . Egg-shells, litter . . . a stench. It was loathsome."

Silence.

"A nasty day to be buried," I began, simply to avoid being silent.

"Nasty, in what way?"

"The snow, the wet." (I yawned.)

"It makes no difference," she said suddenly, after a brief silence.

"No, it's horrid." (I yawned again). "The gravediggers must have sworn at getting drenched by the snow. And there must have been water in the grave."

"Why water in the grave?" she asked, with a sort of curiosity, but speaking even more harshly and abruptly than before.

I suddenly began to feel provoked.

"Why, there must have been water at the bottom a foot deep. You can't dig a dry grave in Volkovo Cemetery."

"Why?"

"Why? Why, the place is waterlogged. It's a regular marsh. So they bury them in water. I've seen it myself . . . many times."

(I had never seen it once, indeed I had never been in Volkovo, and had only heard stories of it.)

"Do you mean to say, you don't mind how you die?"

"But why should I die?" she answered, as though defending herself.

"Why, some day you will die, and you will die just the same as that dead woman. She was . . . a girl like you. She died of consumption."

"A wench would have died in hospital . . ." (She knows all about it already: she said "wench," not "girl.")

"She was in debt to her madam," I retorted, more and more provoked by the discussion; "and went on earning money for her up to the end, though she was in consumption. Some sledge-drivers standing by were talking about her to some soldiers and telling them so. No doubt they knew her. They were laughing. They were going to meet in a pot-house to drink to her memory."

A great deal of this was my invention. Silence followed, profound silence. She did not stir.

"And is it better to die in a hospital?"

"Isn't it just the same? Besides, why should I die?" she added irritably.

"If not now, a little later."

"Why a little later?"

"Why, indeed? Now you are young, pretty, fresh, you fetch a high price. But after another year of this life you will be very different—you will go off."

"In a year?"

"Anyway, in a year you will be worth less," I continued malignantly. "You will go from here to something lower, another house; a year later—to a third, lower and lower, and in seven years you will come to a basement in the Haymarket. That will be if you were lucky.

But it would be much worse if you got some disease, consumption, say . . . and caught a chill, or something or other. It's not easy to get over an illness in your way of life. If you catch anything you may not get rid of it. And so you would die."

"Oh, well, then I shall die," she answered, quite vindictively, and she made a quick movement.

"But one is sorry."

"Sorry for whom?"

"Sorry for life." Silence.

"Have you been engaged to be married? Eh?"

"What's that to you?"

"Oh, I am not cross-examining you. It's nothing to me. Why are you so cross? Of course you may have had your own troubles. What is it to me? It's simply that I felt sorry."

"Sorry for whom?"

"Sorry for you."

"No need," she whispered hardly audibly, and again made a faint movement.

That incensed me at once. What! I was so gentle with her, and she . . .

"Why, do you think that you are on the right path?"

"I don't think anything."

"That's what's wrong, that you don't think. Realise it while there is still time. There still is time. You are still young, good-looking; you might love, be married, be happy. . . ."

"Not all married women are happy," she snapped out in the rude abrupt tone she had used at first.

"Not all, of course, but anyway it is much better than the life here. Infinitely better. Besides, with love one can live even without happiness. Even in sorrow life is sweet; life is sweet, however one lives. But here what is there but . . . foulness? Phew!"

I turned away with disgust; I was no longer reasoning coldly. I began to feel myself what I was saying and warmed to the subject. I was already longing to expound the cherished ideas I had brooded over in my corner. Something suddenly flared up in me. An object had appeared before me.

"Never mind my being here, I am not an example for you. I am, perhaps, worse than you are. I was drunk when I came here, though," I hastened, however, to say in self-defence. "Besides, a man is no example for a woman. It's a different thing. I may degrade and defile myself, but I am not anyone's slave. I come and go, and that's an end of it. I shake it off, and I am a different man. But you are a slave from the start. Yes, a slave! You give up everything, your whole freedom. If you want to break your chains afterwards, you won't be able to; you will be more and more fast in the snares. It is an accursed bondage. I know it. I won't speak of anything else, maybe you won't understand, but tell me: no doubt you are in debt to your madam? There, you see," I added, though she made no answer, but only listened in silence, entirely absorbed, "that's a bondage for you! You will never buy your freedom. They will see to that. It's like selling your soul to the devil. . . . And besides . . . perhaps, I too, am just as unlucky—how do you know—and wallow in the mud on purpose, out of misery? You know, men take to drink from grief; well, maybe I am here from grief. Come, tell me, what is there good here? Here you and I . . . came together . . . just now and did not say one word to one another all the time, and it was only afterwards you began staring at me like a wild creature, and I at you. Is that loving? Is that how one human being should meet another? It's hideous, that's what it is!"

"Yes!" she assented sharply and hurriedly.

I was positively astounded by the promptitude of this "Yes." So the same thought may have been straying through her mind when she was staring at me just before. So she, too, was capable of certain thoughts? "Damn it all, this was interesting, this was a point of likeness!" I thought, almost rubbing my hands. And indeed it's easy to turn a young soul like that!

It was the exercise of my power that attracted me most.

She turned her head nearer to me, and it seemed to me in the darkness that she propped herself on her arm. Perhaps she was scrutinising me. How I regretted that I could not see her eyes. I heard her deep breathing.

"Why have you come here?" I asked her, with a note of authority already in my voice.

"Oh, I don't know."

"But how nice it would be to be living in your father's house! It's warm and free; you have a home of your own."

"But what if it's worse than this?"

"I must take the right tone," flashed through my mind. "I may not get far with sentimentality." But it was only a momentary thought. I swear she really did interest me. Besides, I was exhausted and moody. And cunning so easily goes hand-in-hand with feeling.

"Who denies it!" I hastened to answer. "Anything may happen. I am convinced that someone has wronged you, and that you are more sinned against than sinning. Of course, I know nothing of your story, but it's not likely a girl like you has come here of her own inclination. . . ."

"A girl like me?" she whispered, hardly audibly; but I heard it.

Damn it all, I was flattering her. That was horrid. But perhaps it was a good thing. . . . She was silent.

"See, Liza, I will tell you about myself. If I had had a home from childhood, I shouldn't be what I am now. I often think that. However bad it may be at home, anyway they are your father and mother, and not enemies, strangers. Once a year at least, they'll show their love of you. Anyway, you know you are at home. I grew up without a home; and perhaps that's why I've turned so . . . unfeeling."

I waited again. "Perhaps she doesn't understand," I thought, "and, indeed, it is absurd—it's moralising."

"If I were a father and had a daughter, I believe I should love my daughter more than my sons, really," I began indirectly, as though talking of something else, to distract her attention. I must confess I blushed.

"Why so?" she asked.

Ah! so she was listening!

"I don't know, Liza. I knew a father who was a stern, austere man, but used to go down on his knees to his daughter, used to kiss her hands, her feet, he couldn't make enough of her, really. When she danced at parties he used to stand for five hours at a stretch, gazing at her. He was mad over her: I understand that! She would fall asleep tired at night, and he would wake to kiss her in her sleep and make the sign of the cross over her. He would go about in a dirty old coat, he was stingy to everyone else, but would spend his last penny for her, giving her expensive presents, and it was his greatest delight when she was pleased with what he gave her. Fathers always love their daughters more than the mothers do. Some girls live happily at home! And I believe I should never let my daughters marry."

"What next?" she said, with a faint smile.

"I should be jealous, I really should. To think that she should kiss anyone else! That she should love a stranger more than her father! It's painful to imagine it. Of course, that's all nonsense, of course every father would be reasonable at last. But I believe before I should let her marry, I should worry myself to death; I should find fault with all her suitors. But I should end by letting her marry whom she herself loved. The one whom the daughter loves always seems the worst to the father, you know. That is always so. So many family troubles come from that."

"Some are glad to sell their daughters, rather than marrying them honourably."

Ah, so that was it!

"Such a thing, Liza, happens in those accursed families in which there is neither love nor God," I retorted warmly, "and where there is no love, there is no sense either. There are such families, it's true, but I am not speaking of them. You must have seen wickedness in your own family, if you talk like that. Truly, you must have been unlucky. H'm! . . . that sort of thing mostly comes about through poverty."

"And is it any better with the gentry? Even among the poor, honest people who live happily?"

"H'm . . . yes. Perhaps. Another thing, Liza, man is fond of reckoning up his troubles, but does not count his joys. If he counted them up as he ought, he would see that every lot has enough happiness provided for it. And what if all goes well with the family, if the blessing of God is upon it, if the husband is a good one, loves you, cherishes you, never leaves you! There is happiness in such a family! Even sometimes there is happiness in the midst of sorrow;

and indeed sorrow is everywhere. If you marry *you will find out for yourself*. But think of the first years of married life with one you love: what happiness, what happiness there sometimes is in it! And indeed it's the ordinary thing. In those early days even quarrels with one's husband end happily. Some women get up quarrels with their husbands just because they love them. Indeed, I knew a woman like that: she seemed to say that because she loved him, she would torment him and make him feel it. You know that you may torment a man on purpose through love. Women are particularly given to that, thinking to themselves 'I will love him so, I will make so much of him afterwards, that it's no sin to torment him a little now.' And all in the house rejoice in the sight of you, and you are happy and gay and peaceful and honourable. . . . Then there are some women who are jealous. If he went off anywhere—I knew one such woman, she couldn't restrain herself, but would jump up at night and run off on the sly to find out where he was, whether he was with some other woman. That's a pity. And the woman knows herself it's wrong, and her heart fails her and she suffers, but she loves—it's all through love. And how sweet it is to make up after quarrels, to own herself in the wrong or to forgive him! And they both are so happy all at once—as though they had met anew, been married over again; as though their love had begun afresh. And no one, no one should know what passes between husband and wife if they love one another. And whatever quarrels there may be between them they ought not to call in their own mother to judge between them and tell tales of one another. They are their own judges. Love is a holy mystery and ought to be hidden from all other eyes, whatever happens. That makes it holier and better. They respect one another more, and much is built on respect. And if once there has been love, if they have been married for love, why should love pass away? Surely one can keep it! It is rare that one cannot keep it. And if the husband is kind and straightforward, why should not love last? The first phase of married love will pass, it is true, but then there will come a love that is better still. Then there will be the union of souls, they will have everything in common, there will be no secrets between them. And once they have children, the most difficult times will seem to them happy, so long as there is love and courage. Even toil will be a joy, you may deny yourself bread for your children and even that will be a joy, They will love you for it afterwards; so you are laying by for your future. As the children grow up you feel that you are an example, a support for them; that even after you die your children will always keep your thoughts and feelings, because they have received them from you, they will take on your semblance and likeness. So you see this is a great duty. How can it fail to draw the father and mother nearer? People say it's a trial to have children. Who says that? It is heavenly happiness! Are you fond of little children, Liza? I am awfully fond of them. You know—a little rosy baby boy at your bosom, and what husband's heart is not touched, seeing his wife nursing his child! A plump little rosy baby, sprawling and snuggling, chubby little hands and feet, clean tiny little nails, so tiny that it makes one laugh to look at them; eyes that look as if they understand everything. And while it sucks it clutches at your bosom with its little hand, plays. When its father comes up, the child tears itself away from the bosom, flings itself back, looks at its father, laughs, as though it were fearfully funny, and falls to sucking again. Or it will bite its mother's breast when its little teeth are coming, while it looks sideways at her with its little eyes as though to say, 'Look, I am biting!' Is not all that happiness when they are the three together, husband, wife and child? One can forgive a great deal for the sake of such moments. Yes, Liza, one must first learn to live oneself before one blames others!"

"It's by pictures, pictures like that one must get at you," I thought to myself, though I did speak with real feeling, and all at once I flushed crimson. "What if she were suddenly to burst out laughing, what should I do then?" That idea drove me to fury. Towards the end of my speech I really was excited, and now my vanity was somehow wounded. The silence continued. I almost nudged her.

"Why are you—" she began and stopped. But I understood: there was a quiver of something different in her voice, not abrupt, harsh and unyielding as before, but something soft and shamefaced, so shamefaced that I suddenly felt ashamed and guilty.

"What?" I asked, with tender curiosity.

"Why, you . . ."

"What?"

"Why, you . . . speak somehow like a book," she said, and again there was a note of irony in her voice.

That remark sent a pang to my heart. It was not what I was expecting.

I did not understand that she was hiding her feelings under irony, that this is usually the last refuge of modest and chaste-souled people when the privacy of their soul is coarsely and intrusively invaded, and that their pride makes them refuse to surrender till the last moment and shrink from giving expression to their feelings before you. I ought to have guessed the truth from the timidity with which she had repeatedly approached her sarcasm, only bringing herself to utter it at last with an effort. But I did not guess, and an evil feeling took possession of me.

"Wait a bit!" I thought.

VII

"Oh, hush, Liza! How can you talk about being like a book, when it makes even me, an outsider, feel sick? Though I don't look at it as an outsider, for, indeed, it touches me to the heart. . . . Is it possible, is it possible that you do not feel sick at being here yourself? Evidently habit does wonders! God knows what habit can do with anyone. Can you seriously think that you will never grow old, that you will always be good-looking, and that they will keep you here for ever and ever? I say nothing of the loathsomeness of the life here. . . . Though let me tell you this about it—about your present life, I mean; here though you are young now, attractive, nice, with soul and feeling, yet you know as soon as I came to myself just now I felt at once sick at being here with you! One can only come here when one is drunk. But if you were anywhere else, living as good people live, I should perhaps be more than attracted by you, should fall in love with you, should be glad of a look from you, let alone a word; I should hang about your door, should go down on my knees to you, should look upon you as my betrothed and think it an honour to be allowed to. I should not dare to have an impure thought about you. But here, you see, I know that I have only to whistle and you have to come with me whether you like it or not. I don't consult your wishes, but you mine. The lowest labourer hires himself as a workman, but he doesn't make a slave of himself altogether; besides, he knows that he will be free again presently. But when are you free? Only think what you are giving up here? What is it you are making a slave of? It is your soul, together with your body; you are selling your soul which you have no right to dispose of! You give your love to be outraged by every drunkard! Love! But that's everything, you know, it's a priceless diamond, it's a maiden's treasure, love—why, a man would be ready to give his soul, to face death to gain that love. But how much is your love worth now? You are sold, all of you, body and soul, and there is no need to strive for love when you can have everything without love. And you know there is no greater insult to a girl than that, do you understand? To be sure, I have heard that they comfort you, poor fools, they let you have lovers of your own here. But you know that's simply a farce, that's simply a sham, it's just laughing at you, and you are taken in by it! Why, do you suppose he really loves you, that lover of yours? I don't believe it. How can he love you when he knows you may be called away from him any minute? He would be a low fellow if he did! Will he have a grain of respect for you? What have you in common with him? He laughs at you and robs you—that is all his love amounts to! You are lucky if he does not beat you. Very likely he does beat you, too. Ask him, if you have got one, whether he will marry you. He will laugh in your face, if he doesn't spit in it or give you a blow—though maybe he is not worth a bad halfpenny himself. And for what have you ruined your life, if you come to think of it? For the coffee they give you to drink and the plentiful meals? But with what object are they feeding you up? An honest girl couldn't swallow the food, for she would know what she was being fed for. You are in debt here, and, of course, you will always be in debt, and you will go on in debt to the end, till the visitors here begin to scorn you. And that will soon happen, don't rely upon your youth—all that flies by express train here, you know. You will be kicked out. And not simply kicked out; long before that she'll begin nagging at you, scolding you, abusing you, as though you had not sacrificed your health for her, had not thrown away your youth and your soul for her benefit, but as though you had ruined her, beggared her, robbed her. And don't expect anyone to take your part: the others, your companions, will attack you, too, win her favour, for all are in slavery here, and have lost all conscience and pity here long ago. They have become utterly vile, and nothing on earth is viler, more loathsome, and more insulting than their abuse. And you are laying down everything here, unconditionally, youth and health and beauty and hope, and at twenty-two you will look like a woman of five-and-thirty, and you will be lucky if you are not diseased, pray to God for that! No doubt you are thinking now that you have a gay time and no work to do! Yet there is no work harder or more dreadful in the world or ever has been. One would think that the heart alone would be worn out with tears. And you won't dare to say a word, not half a word when they drive you away from here; you will go away as though you were to blame. You will change to another house, then to a third, then somewhere else, till you come down at last to the Haymarket. There you will be beaten at every turn; that is good manners there, the visitors don't know how to be friendly without beating you. You don't believe that it is so hateful there? Go and look for yourself some time, you can see with your own eyes. Once, one New Year's Day, I saw a woman at a door. They had turned her out as a joke, to give her a taste of the frost because she had been crying so much, and they shut the door behind her. At nine o'clock in the morning she was already quite drunk, dishevelled, half-naked, covered with bruises, her face was powdered, but she had a black-eye, blood was trickling from her nose and her teeth; some cabman had just given her a drubbing. She was sitting on the stone steps, a salt fish of some sort was in her hand; she was crying, wailing something about her luck and beating with the fish on the steps, and cabmen and drunken soldiers were crowding in the doorway taunting her. You don't believe that you will ever be like that? I should be sorry to believe it, too, but how do you know; maybe ten years, eight years ago that very woman with the salt fish came here fresh as a cherub, innocent, pure, knowing no evil, blushing at every word. Perhaps she was like you, proud, ready to take offence, not like the others; perhaps she looked like a queen, and knew what happiness was in store for the man who should love her and whom she should love. Do you see how it ended? And what if at that very minute when she was beating on the filthy steps with that fish, drunken and dishevelled—what if at that very minute she recalled the pure early days in her father's house, when she used to go to school and the neighbour's son watched for her on the way, declaring that he would love her as long as he lived, that he would devote his life to her, and when they vowed to love one another for ever and be married as soon as they were grown up! No, Liza, it would be happy for you if you were to die soon of consumption in some corner, in some cellar like that woman just now. In the hospital, do you say? You will be lucky if they take you, but what if you are still of use to the madam here? Consumption is a queer disease, it is not like fever. The patient goes on hoping till the last minute and says he is all right. He deludes himself And that just suits your madam. Don't doubt it, that's how it is; you have sold your soul, and what is more you owe money, so you daren't say a word. But when you are dying, all will abandon you, all will turn away from you, for then there will be nothing to get from you. What's more, they will reproach you for cumbering the place, for being so long over dying. However you beg you won't get a drink of water without abuse: 'Whenever are you going off, you nasty hussy, you won't let us sleep with your moaning, you make the gentlemen sick.' That's true, I have heard such things said myself. They will thrust you dying into the filthiest corner in the cellar—in the damp and darkness; what will your thoughts be, lying there alone? When you die, strange hands will lay you out, with grumbling and impatience; no one will bless you, no one will sigh for you, they only want to get rid of you as soon as may be; they will buy a coffin, take you to the grave as they did that poor woman today, and celebrate your memory at the tavern. In the grave, sleet, filth, wet snow—no need to put themselves out for you—'Let her down, Vanuha; it's just like her luck—even here, she is head-foremost, the hussy. Shorten the cord, you rascal.' 'It's all right as it is.' 'All right, is it? Why, she's on her side! She was a fellow-creature, after all! But, never mind, throw the earth on her.' And they won't care to waste much time quarrelling over you. They will scatter the wet blue clay as quick as they can and go off to the tavern . . . and there your memory on earth will end; other women have children to go to their graves, fathers, husbands. While for you neither tear, nor sigh, nor remembrance; no one in the whole world will ever come to you, your name will vanish from the face of the earth—as though you had never existed, never been born at all! Nothing but filth and mud, however you knock at your coffin lid at night, when the dead arise, however you cry: 'Let me out, kind people, to live in the light of day! My life was no life at all; my life has been thrown away like a dish-clout; it was drunk away in the tavern at the Haymarket; let me out, kind people, to live in the world again.'"

And I worked myself up to such a pitch that I began to have a lump in my throat myself, and . . . and all at once I stopped, sat up in dismay and, bending over apprehensively, began to listen with a beating heart. I had reason to be troubled.

I had felt for some time that I was turning her soul upside down and rending her heart, and—and the more I was convinced of it, the more eagerly I desired to gain my object as quickly and as effectually as possible. It was the exercise of my skill that carried me away; yet it was not merely sport. . . .

I knew I was speaking stiffly, artificially, even bookishly, in fact, I could not speak except "like a book." But that did not trouble me: I knew, I felt that I should be understood and that this very bookishness might be an assistance. But now, having attained my effect, I was suddenly panic-stricken. Never before had I witnessed such despair! She was lying on her face, thrusting her face into the pillow and clutching it in both hands. Her heart was being torn. Her youthful body was shuddering all over as though in convulsions. Suppressed sobs rent her bosom and suddenly burst out in weeping and wailing, then she pressed closer into the pillow: she did not want anyone here, not a living soul, to know of her anguish and her tears. She bit the pillow, bit her hand till it bled (I saw that afterwards), or, thrusting her fingers into her dishevelled hair, seemed rigid with the effort of restraint, holding her breath and clenching her teeth. I began saying something, begging her to calm herself, but felt that I did not dare; and all at once, in a sort of cold shiver, almost in terror, began fumbling in the dark, trying hurriedly to get dressed to go. It was dark; though I tried my best I could not finish dressing quickly. Suddenly I felt a box of matches and a candlestick with a whole candle in it. As soon as the room was lighted up, Liza sprang up, sat up in bed, and with a contorted face, with a half insane smile, looked at me almost senselessly. I sat down beside her and took her hands; she came to herself, made an impulsive movement towards me, would have caught hold of me, but did not dare, and slowly bowed her head before me.

"Liza, my dear, I was wrong . . . forgive me, my dear," I began, but she squeezed my hand in her fingers so tightly that I felt I was saying the wrong thing and stopped.

"This is my address, Liza, come to me."

"I will come," she answered resolutely, her head still bowed.

"But now I am going, good-bye . . . till we meet again."

I got up; she, too, stood up and suddenly flushed all over, gave a shudder, snatched up a shawl that was lying on a chair and muffled herself in it to her chin. As she did this she gave another sickly smile, blushed and looked at me strangely. I felt wretched; I was in haste to get away—to disappear.

"Wait a minute," she said suddenly, in the passage just at the doorway, stopping me with her hand on my overcoat. She put down the candle in hot haste and ran off; evidently she had thought of something or wanted to show me something. As she ran away she flushed, her eyes shone, and there was a smile on her lips—what was the meaning of it? Against my will I waited: she came back a minute later with an expression that seemed to ask forgiveness for something. In fact, it was not the same face, not the same look as the evening before: sullen, mistrustful and obstinate. Her eyes now were imploring, soft, and at the same time trustful, caressing, timid. The expression with which children look at people they are very fond of, of whom they are asking a favour. Her eyes were a light hazel, they were lovely eyes, full of life, and capable of expressing love as well as sullen hatred.

Making no explanation, as though I, as a sort of higher being, must understand everything without explanations, she held out a piece of paper to me. Her whole face was positively beaming at that instant with naive, almost childish, triumph. I unfolded it. It was a letter to her from a medical student or someone of that sort—a very high-flown and flowery, but extremely respectful, love-letter. I don't recall the words now, but I remember well that through the high-flown phrases there was apparent a genuine feeling, which cannot be feigned. When I had finished reading it I met her glowing, questioning, and childishly impatient eyes fixed upon me. She fastened her eyes upon my face and waited impatiently for what I should say. In a few words, hurriedly, but with a sort of joy and pride, she explained to me that she had been to a dance somewhere in a private house, a family of "very nice people, *who knew nothing,* absolutely nothing, for she had only come here so lately and it had all happened . . . and she hadn't made up her mind to stay and was certainly going away as soon as she had paid her debt. . ." and at that party there had been the student who had danced with her all the evening. He had talked to her, and it turned out that he had known her in old days at Riga when he was a child, they had played together, but a very long time ago—and he knew her parents, but *about this* he knew nothing, nothing whatever, and had no suspicion! And the day after the dance (three days ago) he had sent her that letter through the friend with whom she had gone to the party . . . and . . . well, that was all."

She dropped her shining eyes with a sort of bashfulness as she finished.

The poor girl was keeping that student's letter as a precious treasure, and had run to fetch it, her only treasure, because she did not want me to go away without knowing that she, too, was honestly and genuinely loved; that she, too, was addressed respectfully. No doubt that letter was destined to lie in her box and lead to nothing. But none the less, I am certain that she would keep it all her life as a precious treasure, as her pride and justification, and now at such a minute she had thought of that letter and brought it with naive pride to raise herself in my eyes that I might see, that I, too, might think well of her. I said nothing, pressed her hand and went out. I so longed to get away . . . I walked all the way home, in spite of the fact that the melting snow was still falling in heavy flakes. I was exhausted, shattered, in bewilderment. But behind the bewilderment the truth was already gleaming. The loathsome truth.

VIII

It was some time, however, before I consented to recognise that truth. Waking up in the morning after some hours of heavy, leaden sleep, and immediately realising all that had happened on the previous day, I was positively amazed at my last night's *sentimentality* with Liza, at all those "outcries of horror and pity." "To think of having such an attack of womanish hysteria, pah!" I concluded. And what did I thrust my address upon her for? What if she comes? Let her come, though; it doesn't matter. . . . But *obviously*, that was not now the chief and the most important matter: I had to make haste and at all costs save my reputation in the eyes of Zverkov and Simonov as quickly as possible; that was the chief business. And I was so taken up that morning that I actually forgot all about Liza.

First of all I had at once to repay what I had borrowed the day before from Simonov. I resolved on a desperate measure: to borrow fifteen roubles straight off from Anton Antonitch. As luck would have it he was in the best of humours that morning, and gave it to me at once, on the first asking. I was so delighted at this that, as I signed the IOU with a swaggering air, I told him casually that the night before "I had been keeping it up with some friends at the Hotel de Paris; we were giving a farewell party to a comrade, in fact, I might say a friend of my childhood, and you know—a desperate rake, fearfully spoilt—of course, he belongs to a good family, and has considerable means, a brilliant career; he is witty, charming, a regular Lovelace, you understand; we drank an extra 'half-dozen' and . . ."

And it went off all right; all this was uttered very easily, unconstrainedly and complacently.

On reaching home I promptly wrote to Simonov.

To this hour I am lost in admiration when I recall the truly gentlemanly, good-humoured, candid tone of my letter. With tact and good-breeding, and, above all, entirely without superfluous words, I blamed myself for all that had happened. I defended myself, "if I really may be allowed to defend myself," by alleging that being utterly unaccustomed to wine, I had been intoxicated with the first glass, which I said, I had drunk before they arrived, while I was waiting for them at the Hotel de Paris between five and six o'clock. I begged Simonov's pardon especially; I asked him to convey my explanations to all the others, especially to Zverkov, whom "I seemed to remember as though in a dream" I had insulted. I added that I would have called upon all of them myself, but my head ached, and besides I had not the face to. I was particularly pleased with a certain lightness, almost carelessness (strictly within the bounds of politeness, however), which was apparent in my style, and better than any possible arguments, gave them at once to understand that I took rather an independent view of "all that unpleasantness last night"; that I was by no means so utterly crushed as you, my friends, probably imagine; but on the contrary, looked upon it as a gentleman serenely respecting himself should look upon it. "On a young hero's past no censure is cast!"

"There is actually an aristocratic playfulness about it!" I thought admiringly, as I read over the letter. "And it's all because I am an intellectual and cultivated man! Another man in my place would not have known how to extricate himself, but here I have got out of it and am as jolly as ever again, and all because I am 'a cultivated and educated man of our day.' And, indeed, perhaps, everything was due to the wine yesterday. H'm!" . . . No, it was not the wine. I did not drink anything at all between five and six when I was waiting for them. I had lied to Simonov; I had lied shamelessly; and indeed I wasn't ashamed now. . . . Hang it all though, the great thing was that I was rid of it.

I put six roubles in the letter, sealed it up, and asked Apollon to take it to Simonov. When he learned that there was money in the letter, Apollon became more respectful and agreed to take it. Towards evening I went out for a walk. My head was still aching and giddy after yesterday. But as evening came on and the twilight grew denser, my impressions and, following them, my thoughts, grew more and more different and confused. Something was not dead within me, in the depths of my heart and conscience it would not die, and it showed itself in acute depression. For the most part I jostled my way through the most crowded business streets, along Myeshtchansky Street, along Sadovy Street and in Yusupov Garden. I always liked particularly sauntering along these streets in the dusk, just when there were crowds of working people of all sorts going home from their daily work, with faces looking cross with anxiety. What I liked was just that cheap bustle, that bare prose. On this occasion the jostling of the streets irritated me more than ever, I could not make out what was wrong with me, I could not find the clue, something seemed rising up continually in my soul, painfully, and refusing to be appeased. I returned home completely upset, it was just as though some crime were lying on my conscience.

The thought that Liza was coming worried me continually. It seemed queer to me that of all my recollections of yesterday this tormented me, as it were, especially, as it were, quite separately. Everything else I had quite succeeded in forgetting by the evening; I dismissed it all and was still perfectly satisfied with my letter to Simonov. But on this point I was not satisfied at all. It was as though I were worried only by Liza. "What if she comes," I thought incessantly, "well, it doesn't matter, let her come! H'm! it's horrid that she should see, for instance, how I live. Yesterday I seemed such a hero to her, while now, h'm! It's horrid, though, that I have let myself go so, the room looks like a beggar's. And I brought myself to go out to dinner in such a suit! And my American leather sofa with the stuffing sticking out. And my dressing-gown, which will not cover me, such tatters, and she will see all this and she will see Apollon. That beast is certain to insult her. He will fasten upon her in order to be rude to me. And I, of course, shall be panic-stricken as usual, I shall begin bowing and scraping before her and pulling my dressing-gown round me, I shall begin smiling, telling lies. Oh, the beastliness! And it isn't the beastliness of it that matters most! There is something more important, more loathsome, viler! Yes, viler! And to put on that dishonest lying mask again! . . ."

When I reached that thought I fired up all at once.

"Why dishonest? How dishonest? I was speaking sincerely last night. I remember there was real feeling in me, too. What I wanted was to excite an honourable feeling in her. . . . Her crying was a good thing, it will have a good effect."

Yet I could not feel at ease. All that evening, even when I had come back home, even after nine o'clock, when I calculated that Liza could not possibly come, still she haunted me, and what was worse, she came back to my mind always in the same position. One moment out of all that had happened last night stood vividly before my imagination; the moment when I struck a match and saw her pale, distorted face, with its look of torture. And what a pitiful, what an unnatural, what a distorted smile she had at that moment! But I did not know then, that fifteen years later I should still in my imagination see Liza, always with the pitiful, distorted, inappropriate smile which was on her face at that minute.

Next day I was ready again to look upon it all as nonsense, due to over-excited nerves, and, above all, as *exaggerated*. I was always conscious of that weak point of mine, and sometimes very much afraid of it. "I exaggerate everything, that is where I go wrong," I repeated to myself every hour. But, however, "Liza will very likely come all the same," was the refrain with which all my reflections ended. I was so uneasy that I sometimes flew into a fury: "She'll come, she is certain to come!" I cried, running about the room, "if not today, she will come tomorrow; she'll find me out! The damnable romanticism of these pure hearts! Oh, the vileness—oh, the silliness—oh, the stupidity of these 'wretched sentimental souls!' Why, how fail to understand? How could one fail to understand? . . ."

But at this point I stopped short, and in great confusion, indeed.

And how few, how few words, I thought, in passing, were needed; how little of the idyllic (and affectedly, bookishly, artificially idyllic too) had sufficed to turn a whole human life at once according to my will. That's virginity, to be sure! Freshness of soil!

At times a thought occurred to me, to go to her, "to tell her all," and beg her not to come to me. But this thought stirred such wrath in me that I believed I should have crushed that "damned" Liza if she had chanced to be near me at the time. I should have insulted her, have spat at her, have turned her out, have struck her!

One day passed, however, another and another; she did not come and I began to grow calmer. I felt particularly bold and cheerful after nine o'clock, I even sometimes began dreaming, and rather sweetly: I, for instance, became the salvation of Liza, simply through her coming to me and my talking to her. . . . I develop her, educate her. Finally, I notice that she loves me, loves me passionately. I pretend not to understand (I don't know, however, why I pretend, just for effect, perhaps). At last all confusion, transfigured, trembling and sobbing, she flings herself at my feet and says that I am her saviour, and that she loves me better than anything in the world. I am amazed, but. . . . "Liza," I say, "can you imagine that I have not noticed your love? I saw it all, I divined it, but I did not dare to approach you first, because I had an influence over you and was afraid that you would force yourself, from gratitude, to respond to my love, would try to rouse in your heart a feeling which was perhaps absent, and I did not wish that . . . because it would be tyranny . . . it would be indelicate (in short, I launch off at that point into European, inexplicably lofty subtleties a la George Sand), but now, now you are mine, you are my creation, you are pure, you are good, you are my noble wife.

"Into my house come bold and free,
Its rightful mistress there to be."

Then we begin living together, go abroad and so on, and so on. In fact, in the end it seemed vulgar to me myself, and I began putting out my tongue at myself.

Besides, they won't let her out, "the hussy!" I thought. They don't let them go out very readily, especially in the evening (for some reason I fancied she would come in the evening, and at seven o'clock precisely). Though she did say she was not altogether a slave there yet, and had certain rights; so, h'm! Damn it all, she will come, she is sure to come!

It was a good thing, in fact, that Apollon distracted my attention at that time by his rudeness. He drove me beyond all patience! He was the bane of my life, the curse laid upon me by Providence. We had been squabbling continually for years, and I hated him. My God, how I hated him! I believe I had never hated anyone in my life as I hated him, especially at some moments. He was an elderly, dignified man, who worked part of his time as a tailor. But for some unknown reason he despised me beyond all measure, and looked down upon me insufferably. Though, indeed, he looked down upon everyone. Simply to glance at that flaxen, smoothly brushed head, at the tuft of hair he combed up on his forehead and oiled with sunflower oil, at that dignified mouth, compressed into the shape of the letter V, made one feel one was confronting a man who never doubted of himself. He was a pedant, to the most extreme point, the greatest pedant I had met on earth, and with that had a vanity only befitting Alexander of Macedon. He was in love with every button on his coat, every nail on his fingers—absolutely in love with them, and he looked it! In his behaviour to me he was a perfect tyrant, he spoke very little to me, and if he chanced to glance at me he gave me a firm, majestically self-confident and invariably ironical look that drove me sometimes to fury. He did his work with the air of doing me the greatest favour, though he did scarcely anything for me, and did not, indeed, consider himself bound to do anything. There could be no doubt that he looked upon me as the greatest fool on earth, and that "he did not get rid of me" was simply that he could get wages from me every month. He consented to do nothing for me for seven roubles a month. Many sins should be forgiven me for what I suffered from him. My hatred reached such a point that sometimes his very step almost threw me into convulsions. What I loathed particularly was his lisp. His tongue must have been a little too long or something of that sort, for he continually lisped, and seemed to be very proud of it, imagining that it greatly added to his dignity. He spoke in a slow, measured tone, with his hands behind his back and his eyes fixed on the ground. He maddened me particularly when he read aloud the psalms to himself behind his partition. Many a battle I waged over that reading! But he was awfully fond of reading aloud in the evenings, in a slow, even, sing-song voice, as though over the dead. It is interesting that that is how he has ended: he hires himself out to read the psalms over the dead, and at the same time he kills rats and makes blacking. But at that time I could not get rid of him, it was as though he were chemically combined with my existence. Besides, nothing would have induced him to consent to leave me. I could not live in furnished lodgings: my lodging was my private solitude, my shell, my cave, in which I concealed myself from all mankind, and Apollon seemed to me, for some reason, an integral part of that flat, and for seven years I could not turn him away.

To be two or three days behind with his wages, for instance, was impossible. He would have made such a fuss, I should not have known where to hide my head. But I was so exasperated with everyone during those days, that I made up my mind for some reason and with some object to *punish* Apollon and not to pay him for a fortnight the wages that were owing him. I had for a long time—for the last two years—been intending to do this, simply in order to teach him not to give himself airs with me, and to show him that if I liked I could withhold his wages. I purposed to say nothing to him about it, and was purposely silent indeed, in order to score off his pride and force him to be the first to speak of his wages. Then I would take the seven roubles out of a drawer, show him I have the money put aside on purpose, but that I won't, I won't, I simply won't pay him his wages, I won't just because that is "what I wish," because "I am master, and it is for me to decide," because he has been disrespectful, because he has been rude; but if he were to ask respectfully I might be softened and give it to him, otherwise he might wait another fortnight, another three weeks, a whole month. . . .

But angry as I was, yet he got the better of me. I could not hold out for four days. He began as he always did begin in such cases, for there had been such cases already, there had been attempts (and it may be observed I knew all this beforehand, I knew his nasty tactics by heart). He would begin by fixing upon me an exceedingly severe stare, keeping it up for several minutes at a time, particularly on meeting me or seeing me out of the house. If I held out and pretended not to notice these stares, he would, still in silence, proceed to further tortures. All at once, *à propos* of nothing, he would walk softly and smoothly into my room, when I was pacing up and down or reading, stand at the door, one hand behind his back and one foot behind the other, and fix upon me a stare more than severe, utterly contemptuous. If I suddenly asked him what he wanted, he would make me no answer, but continue staring at me persistently for some seconds, then, with a peculiar compression of his lips and a most significant air, deliberately turn round and deliberately go back to his room. Two hours later he would come out again and again present himself before me in the same way. It had happened that in my fury I did not even ask him what he wanted, but simply raised my head sharply and imperiously and began staring back at him. So we stared at one another for two minutes; at last he turned with deliberation and dignity and went back again for two hours.

If I were still not brought to reason by all this, but persisted in my revolt, he would suddenly begin sighing while he looked at me, long, deep sighs as though measuring by them the depths of my moral degradation, and, of course, it ended at last by his triumphing completely: I raged and shouted, but still was forced to do what he wanted.

This time the usual staring manoeuvres had scarcely begun when I lost my temper and flew at him in a fury. I was irritated beyond endurance apart from him.

"Stay," I cried, in a frenzy, as he was slowly and silently turning, with one hand behind his back, to go to his room. "Stay! Come back, come back, I tell you!" and I must have bawled so unnaturally, that he turned round and even looked at me with some wonder. However, he persisted in saying nothing, and that infuriated me.

"How dare you come and look at me like that without being sent for? Answer!"

After looking at me calmly for half a minute, he began turning round again.

"Stay!" I roared, running up to him, "don't stir! There. Answer, now: what did you come in to look at?"

"If you have any order to give me it's my duty to carry it out," he answered, after another silent pause, with a slow, measured lisp, raising his eyebrows and calmly twisting his head from one side to another, all this with exasperating composure.

"That's not what I am asking you about, you torturer!" I shouted, turning crimson with anger. "I'll tell you why you came here myself: you see, I don't give you your wages, you are so proud you don't want to bow down and ask for it, and so you come to punish me with your stupid stares, to worry me and you have no sus-pic-ion how stupid it is—stupid, stupid, stupid, stupid! . . ."

He would have turned round again without a word, but I seized him.

"Listen," I shouted to him. "Here's the money, do you see, here it is," (I took it out of the table drawer); "here's the seven roubles complete, but you are not going to have it, you . . . are . . . not . . . going . . . to . . . have it until you come respectfully with bowed head to beg my pardon. Do you hear?"

"That cannot be," he answered, with the most unnatural self-confidence.

"It shall be so," I said, "I give you my word of honour, it shall be!"

"And there's nothing for me to beg your pardon for," he went on, as though he had not noticed my exclamations at all. "Why, besides, you called me a 'torturer,' for which I can summon you at the police-station at any time for insulting behaviour."

"Go, summon me," I roared, "go at once, this very minute, this very second! You are a torturer all the same! a torturer!"

But he merely looked at me, then turned, and regardless of my loud calls to him, he walked to his room with an even step and without looking round.

"If it had not been for Liza nothing of this would have happened," I decided inwardly. Then, after waiting a minute, I went myself behind his screen with a dignified and solemn air, though my heart was beating slowly and violently.

"Apollon," I said quietly and emphatically, though I was breathless, "go at once without a minute's delay and fetch the police-officer."

He had meanwhile settled himself at his table, put on his spectacles and taken up some sewing. But, hearing my order, he burst into a guffaw.

"At once, go this minute! Go on, or else you can't imagine what will happen."

"You are certainly out of your mind," he observed, without even raising his head, lisping as deliberately as ever and threading his needle. "Whoever heard of a man sending for the police against himself? And as for being frightened—you are upsetting yourself about nothing, for nothing will come of it."

"Go!" I shrieked, clutching him by the shoulder. I felt I should strike him in a minute.

But I did not notice the door from the passage softly and slowly open at that instant and a figure come in, stop short, and begin staring at us in perplexity I glanced, nearly swooned with shame, and rushed back to my room. There, clutching at my hair with both hands, I leaned my head against the wall and stood motionless in that position.

Two minutes later I heard Apollon's deliberate footsteps. "There is some woman asking for you," he said, looking at me with peculiar severity. Then he stood aside and let in Liza. He would not go away, but stared at us sarcastically.

"Go away, go away," I commanded in desperation. At that moment my clock began whirring and wheezing and struck seven.

IX

"Into my house come bold and free,
Its rightful mistress there to be."

I stood before her crushed, crestfallen, revoltingly confused, and I believe I smiled as I did my utmost to wrap myself in the skirts of my ragged wadded dressing-gown—exactly as I had imagined the scene not long before in a fit of depression. After standing over us for a couple of minutes Apollon went away, but that did not make me more at ease. What made it worse was that she, too, was overwhelmed with confusion, more so, in fact, than I should have expected. At the sight of me, of course.

"Sit down," I said mechanically, moving a chair up to the table, and I sat down on the sofa. She obediently sat down at once and gazed at me open-eyed, evidently expecting something from me at once. This naivete of expectation drove me to fury, but I restrained myself.

She ought to have tried not to notice, as though everything had been as usual, while instead of that, she . . . and I dimly felt that I should make her pay dearly for *all this*.

"You have found me in a strange position, Liza," I began, stammering and knowing that this was the wrong way to begin. "No, no, don't imagine anything," I cried, seeing that she had suddenly flushed. "I am not ashamed of my poverty. . . . On the contrary, I look with pride on my poverty. I am poor but honourable. . . . One can be poor and honourable," I muttered. "However . . . would you like tea?. . . ."

"No," she was beginning.

"Wait a minute."

I leapt up and ran to Apollon. I had to get out of the room somehow.

"Apollon," I whispered in feverish haste, flinging down before him the seven roubles which had remained all the time in my clenched fist, "here are your wages, you see I give them to you; but for that you must come to my rescue: bring me tea and a dozen rusks from the restaurant. If you won't go, you'll make me a miserable man! You don't know what this woman is. . . . This is—everything! You may be imagining something. . . . But you don't know what that woman is! . . ."

Apollon, who had already sat down to his work and put on his spectacles again, at first glanced askance at the money without speaking or putting down his needle; then, without paying the slightest attention to me or making any answer, he went on busying himself with his needle, which he had not yet threaded. I waited before him for three minutes with my arms crossed *à la Napoléon*. My temples were moist with sweat. I was pale, I felt it. But, thank God, he must have been moved to pity, looking at me. Having threaded his needle he deliberately got up from his seat, deliberately moved back his chair, deliberately took off his spectacles, deliberately counted the money, and finally asking me over his shoulder: "Shall I get a whole portion?" deliberately walked out of the room. As I was going back to Liza, the thought occurred to me on the way: shouldn't I run away just as I was in my dressing-gown, no matter where, and then let happen what would?

I sat down again. She looked at me uneasily. For some minutes we were silent.

"I will kill him," I shouted suddenly, striking the table with my fist so that the ink spurted out of the inkstand.

"What are you saying!" she cried, starting.

"I will kill him! kill him!" I shrieked, suddenly striking the table in absolute frenzy, and at the same time fully understanding how stupid it was to be in such a frenzy. "You don't know, Liza, what that torturer is to me. He is my torturer. . . . He has gone now to fetch some rusks; he . . ."

And suddenly I burst into tears. It was an hysterical attack. How ashamed I felt in the midst of my sobs; but still I could not restrain them.

She was frightened.

"What is the matter? What is wrong?" she cried, fussing about me.

"Water, give me water, over there!" I muttered in a faint voice, though I was inwardly conscious that I could have got on very well without water and without muttering in a faint voice. But I was, what is called, *putting it on,* to save appearances, though the attack was a genuine one.

She gave me water, looking at me in bewilderment. At that moment Apollon brought in the tea. It suddenly seemed to me that this commonplace, prosaic tea was horribly undignified and paltry after all that had happened, and I blushed crimson. Liza looked at Apollon with positive alarm. He went out without a glance at either of us.

"Liza, do you despise me?" I asked, looking at her fixedly, trembling with impatience to know what she was thinking.

She was confused, and did not know what to answer.

"Drink your tea," I said to her angrily. I was angry with myself, but, of course, it was she who would have to pay for it. A horrible spite against her suddenly surged up in my heart; I believe I could have killed her. To revenge myself on her I swore inwardly not to say a word to her all the time. "She is the cause of it all," I thought.

Our silence lasted for five minutes. The tea stood on the table; we did not touch it. I had got to the point of purposely refraining from beginning in order to embarrass her further; it was awkward for her to begin alone. Several times she glanced at me with mournful perplexity. I was obstinately silent. I was, of course, myself the chief sufferer, because I was fully conscious of the disgusting meanness of my spiteful stupidity, and yet at the same time I could not restrain myself.

"I want to. . . get away . . . from there altogether," she began, to break the silence in some way, but, poor girl, that was just what she ought not to have spoken about at such a stupid moment to a man so stupid as I was. My heart positively ached with pity for her tactless and unnecessary straightforwardness. But something hideous at once stifled all compassion in me; it even provoked me to greater venom. I did not care what happened. Another five minutes passed.

"Perhaps I am in your way," she began timidly, hardly audibly, and was getting up.

But as soon as I saw this first impulse of wounded dignity I positively trembled with spite, and at once burst out.

"Why have you come to me, tell me that, please?" I began, gasping for breath and regardless of logical connection in my words. I longed to have it all out at once, at one burst; I did not even trouble how to begin. "Why have you come? Answer, answer," I cried, hardly knowing what I was doing. "I'll tell you, my good girl, why you have come. You've come because I talked sentimental stuff to you then. So now you are soft as butter and longing for fine sentiments again. So you may as well know that I was laughing at you then. And I am laughing at you now. Why are you shuddering? Yes, I was laughing at you! I had been insulted just before, at dinner, by the fellows who came that evening before me. I came to you, meaning to thrash one of them, an officer; but I didn't succeed, I didn't find him; I had to avenge the insult on someone to get back my own again; you turned up, I vented my spleen on you and laughed at you. I had been humiliated, so I wanted to humiliate; I had been treated like a rag, so I wanted to show my power. . . . That's what it was, and you imagined I had come there on purpose to save you. Yes? You imagined that? You imagined that?"

I knew that she would perhaps be muddled and not take it all in exactly, but I knew, too, that she would grasp the gist of it, very well indeed. And so, indeed, she did. She turned white as a handkerchief, tried to say something, and her lips worked painfully; but she sank on a chair as though she had been felled by an axe. And all the time afterwards she listened to me with her lips parted and her eyes wide open, shuddering with awful terror. The cynicism, the cynicism of my words overwhelmed her. . . .

"Save you!" I went on, jumping up from my chair and running up and down the room before her. "Save you from what? But perhaps I am worse than you myself. Why didn't you throw it in my teeth when I was giving you that sermon: 'But what did you come here yourself for? was it to read us a sermon?' Power, power was what I wanted then, sport was what I wanted, I wanted to wring out your tears, your humiliation, your hysteria—that was what I wanted then! Of course, I couldn't keep it up then, because I am a wretched creature, I was frightened, and, the devil knows why, gave you my address in my folly. Afterwards, before I got home, I was cursing and swearing at you because of that address, I hated you already because of the lies I had told you. Because I only like playing with words, only dreaming, but, do you know, what I really want is that you should all go to hell. That is what I want. I want peace; yes, I'd sell the whole world for a farthing, straight off, so long as I was left in peace. Is the world to go to pot, or am I to go without my tea? I say that the world may go to pot for me so long as I always get my tea. Did you know that, or not? Well, anyway, I know that I am a blackguard, a scoundrel, an egoist, a sluggard. Here I have been shuddering for the last three days at the thought of your coming. And do you know what has worried me particularly for these three days? That I posed as such a hero to you, and now you would see me in a wretched torn dressing-gown, beggarly, loathsome. I told you just now that I was not ashamed of my poverty; so you may as well know that I am ashamed of it; I am more ashamed of it than of anything, more afraid of it than of being found out if I were a thief, because I am as vain as though I had been skinned and the very air blowing on me hurt. Surely by now you must realise that I shall never forgive you for having found me in this wretched dressing-gown, just as I was flying at Apollon like a spiteful cur. The saviour, the former hero, was flying like a mangy, unkempt sheep-dog at his lackey, and the lackey was jeering at him! And I shall never forgive you for the tears I could not help shedding before you just now, like some silly woman put to shame! And for what I am confessing to you now, I shall never forgive you either! Yes—you must answer for it all because you turned up like this, because I am a blackguard, because I am the nastiest, stupidest, absurdest and most envious of all the worms on earth, who are not a bit better than I am, but, the devil knows why, are never put to confusion; while I shall always be insulted by every louse, that is my doom! And what is it to me that you don't understand a word of this! And what do I care, what do I care about you, and whether you go to ruin there or not? Do you understand? How I shall hate you now after saying this, for having been here and listening. Why, it's not once in a lifetime a man speaks out like this, and then it is in hysterics! . . . What more do you want? Why do you still stand confronting me, after all this? Why are you worrying me? Why don't you go?"

But at this point a strange thing happened. I was so accustomed to think and imagine everything from books, and to picture everything in the world to myself just as I had made it up in my dreams beforehand, that I could not all at once take in this strange circumstance. What happened was this: Liza, insulted and crushed by me, understood a great deal more than I imagined. She understood from all this what a woman understands first of all, if she feels genuine love, that is, that I was myself unhappy.

The frightened and wounded expression on her face was followed first by a look of sorrowful perplexity. When I began calling myself a scoundrel and a blackguard and my tears flowed (the tirade was accompanied throughout by tears) her whole face worked convulsively. She was on the point of getting up and stopping me; when I finished she took no notice of my shouting: "Why are you here, why don't you go away?" but realised only that it must have been very bitter to me to say all this. Besides, she was so crushed, poor girl; she considered herself infinitely beneath me; how could she feel anger or resentment? She suddenly leapt up from her chair with an irresistible impulse and held out her hands, yearning towards me, though still timid and not daring to stir. . . . At this point there was a revulsion in my heart too. Then she suddenly rushed to me, threw her arms round me and burst into tears. I, too, could not restrain myself, and sobbed as I never had before.

"They won't let me . . . I can't be good!" I managed to articulate; then I went to the sofa, fell on it face downwards, and sobbed on it for a quarter of an hour in genuine hysterics. She came close to me, put her arms round me and stayed motionless in that position. But the trouble was that the hysterics could not go on for ever, and (I am writing the loathsome truth) lying face downwards on the sofa with my face thrust into my nasty leather pillow, I began by degrees to be aware of a far-away, involuntary but irresistible feeling that it would be awkward now for me to raise my head and look Liza straight in the face. Why was I ashamed? I don't know, but I was ashamed. The thought, too, came into my overwrought brain that our parts now were completely changed, that she was now the heroine, while I was just a crushed and humiliated creature as she had been before me that night—four days before. . . . And all this came into my mind during the minutes I was lying on my face on the sofa.

My God! surely I was not envious of her then.

I don't know, to this day I cannot decide, and at the time, of course, I was still less able to understand what I was feeling than now. I cannot get on without domineering and tyrannising over someone, but . . . there is no explaining anything by reasoning and so it is useless to reason.

I conquered myself, however, and raised my head; I had to do so sooner or later . . . and I am convinced to this day that it was just because I was ashamed to look at her that another feeling was suddenly kindled and flamed up in my heart . . . a feeling of mastery and possession. My eyes gleamed with passion, and I gripped her hands tightly. How I hated her and how I was drawn to her at that minute! The one feeling intensified the other. It was almost like an act of vengeance. At first there was a look of amazement, even of terror on her face, but only for one instant. She warmly and rapturously embraced me.

X

A quarter of an hour later I was rushing up and down the room in frenzied impatience, from minute to minute I went up to the screen and peeped through the crack at Liza. She was sitting on the ground with her head leaning against the bed, and must have been crying. But she did not go away, and that irritated me. This time she understood it all. I had insulted her finally, but . . . there's no need to describe it. She realised that my outburst of passion had been simply revenge, a fresh humiliation, and that to my earlier, almost causeless hatred was added now a *personal hatred*, born of envy. . . . Though I do not maintain positively that she understood all this distinctly; but she certainly did fully understand that I was a despicable man, and what was worse, incapable of loving her. I know I shall be told that this is incredible—but it is incredible to be as spiteful and stupid as I was; it may be added that it was strange I should not love her, or at any rate, appreciate her love. Why is it strange? In the first place, by then I was incapable of love, for I repeat, with me loving meant tyrannising and showing my moral superiority. I have never in my life been able to imagine any other sort of love, and have nowadays come to the point of sometimes thinking that love really consists in the right—freely given by the beloved object—to tyrannise over her.

Even in my underground dreams I did not imagine love except as a struggle. I began it always with hatred and ended it with moral subjugation, and afterwards I never knew what to do with the subjugated object. And what is there to wonder at in that, since I had succeeded in so corrupting myself, since I was so out of touch with "real life," as to have actually thought of reproaching her, and putting her to shame for having come to me to hear "fine sentiments"; and did not even guess that she had come not to hear fine sentiments, but to love me, because to a woman all reformation, all salvation from any sort of ruin, and all moral renewal is included in love and can only show itself in that form.

I did not hate her so much, however, when I was running about the room and peeping through the crack in the screen. I was only insufferably oppressed by her being here. I wanted her to disappear. I wanted "peace," to be left alone in my underground world. Real life oppressed me with its novelty so much that I could hardly breathe.

But several minutes passed and she still remained, without stirring, as though she were unconscious. I had the shamelessness to tap softly at the screen as though to remind her. . . . She started, sprang up, and flew to seek her kerchief, her hat, her coat, as though making her escape from me. . . . Two minutes later she came from behind the screen and looked with heavy eyes at me. I gave a spiteful grin, which was forced, however, to *keep up appearances,* and I turned away from her eyes.

"Good-bye," she said, going towards the door.

I ran up to her, seized her hand, opened it, thrust something in it and closed it again. Then I turned at once and dashed away in haste to the other corner of the room to avoid seeing, anyway . . . .

I did mean a moment since to tell a lie—to write that I did this accidentally, not knowing what I was doing through foolishness, through losing my head. But I don't want to lie, and so I will say straight out that I opened her hand and put the money in it . . . from spite. It came into my head to do this while I was running up and down the room and she was sitting behind the screen. But this I can say for certain: though I did that cruel thing purposely, it was not an impulse from the heart, but came from my evil brain. This cruelty was so affected, so purposely made up, so completely a product of the brain, of books, that I could not even keep it up a minute—first I dashed away to avoid seeing her, and then in shame and despair rushed after Liza. I opened the door in the passage and began listening.

"Liza! Liza!" I cried on the stairs, but in a low voice, not boldly. There was no answer, but I fancied I heard her footsteps, lower down on the stairs.

"Liza!" I cried, more loudly.

No answer. But at that minute I heard the stiff outer glass door open heavily with a creak and slam violently; the sound echoed up the stairs.

She had gone. I went back to my room in hesitation. I felt horribly oppressed.

I stood still at the table, beside the chair on which she had sat and looked aimlessly before me. A minute passed, suddenly I started; straight before me on the table I saw. . . . In short, I saw a crumpled blue five-rouble note, the one I had thrust into her hand a minute before. It was the same note; it could be no other, there was no other in the flat. So she had managed to fling it from her hand on the table at the moment when I had dashed into the further corner.

Well! I might have expected that she would do that. Might I have expected it? No, I was such an egoist, I was so lacking in respect for my fellow-creatures that I could not even imagine she would do so. I could not endure it. A minute later I flew like a madman to dress, flinging on what I could at random and ran headlong after her. She could not have got two hundred paces away when I ran out into the street.

It was a still night and the snow was coming down in masses and falling almost perpendicularly, covering the pavement and the empty street as though with a pillow. There was no one in the street, no sound was to be heard. The street lamps gave a disconsolate and useless glimmer. I ran two hundred paces to the cross-roads and stopped short.

Where had she gone? And why was I running after her?

Why? To fall down before her, to sob with remorse, to kiss her feet, to entreat her forgiveness! I longed for that, my whole breast was being rent to pieces, and never, never shall I recall that minute with indifference. But—what for? I thought. Should I not begin to hate her, perhaps, even tomorrow, just because I had kissed her feet today? Should I give her happiness? Had I not recognised that day, for the hundredth time, what I was worth? Should I not torture her?

I stood in the snow, gazing into the troubled darkness and pondered this.

"And will it not be better?" I mused fantastically, afterwards at home, stifling the living pang of my heart with fantastic dreams. "Will it not be better that she should keep the resentment of the insult for ever? Resentment—why, it is purification; it is a most stinging and painful consciousness! Tomorrow I should have defiled her soul and have exhausted her heart, while now the feeling of insult will never die in her heart, and however loathsome the filth awaiting her—the feeling of insult will elevate and purify her . . . by hatred . . . h'm! . . . perhaps, too, by forgiveness. . . . Will all that make things easier for her though? . . ."

And, indeed, I will ask on my own account here, an idle question: which is better—cheap happiness or exalted sufferings? Well, which is better?

So I dreamed as I sat at home that evening, almost dead with the pain in my soul. Never had I endured such suffering and remorse, yet could there have been the faintest doubt when I ran out from my lodging that I should turn back half-way? I never met Liza again and I have heard nothing of her. I will add, too, that I remained for a long time afterwards pleased with the phrase about the benefit from resentment and hatred in spite of the fact that I almost fell ill from misery.

***

Even now, so many years later, all this is somehow a very evil memory. I have many evil memories now, but . . . hadn't I better end my "Notes" here? I believe I made a mistake in beginning to write them, anyway I have felt ashamed all the time I've been writing this story; so it's hardly literature so much as a corrective punishment. Why, to tell long stories, showing how I have spoiled my life through morally rotting in my corner, through lack of fitting environment, through divorce from real life, and rankling spite in my underground world, would certainly not be interesting; a novel needs a hero, and all the traits for an anti-hero are *expressly* gathered together here, and what matters most, it all produces an unpleasant impression, for we are all divorced from life, we are all cripples, every one of us, more or less. We are so divorced from it that we feel at once a sort of loathing for real life, and so cannot bear to be reminded of it. Why, we have come almost to looking upon real life as an effort, almost as hard work, and we are all privately agreed that it is better in books. And why do we fuss and fume sometimes? Why are we perverse and ask for something else? We don't know what ourselves. It would be the worse for us if our petulant prayers were answered. Come, try, give any one of us, for instance, a little more independence, untie our hands, widen the spheres of our activity, relax the control and we . . . yes, I assure you . . . we should be begging to be under control again at once. I know that you will very likely be angry with me for that, and will begin shouting and stamping. Speak for yourself, you will say, and for your miseries in your underground holes, and don't dare to say all of us—excuse me, gentlemen, I am not justifying myself with that "all of us." As for what concerns me in particular I have only in my life carried to an extreme what you have not dared to carry halfway, and what's more, you have taken your cowardice for good sense, and have found comfort in deceiving yourselves. So that perhaps, after all, there is more life in me than in you. Look into it more carefully! Why, we don't even know what living means now, what it is, and what it is called? Leave us alone without books and we shall be lost and in confusion at once. We shall not know what to join on to, what to cling to, what to love and what to hate, what to respect and what to despise. We are oppressed at being men—men with a real individual body and blood, we are ashamed of it, we think it a disgrace and try to contrive to be some sort of impossible generalised man. We are stillborn, and for generations past have been begotten, not by living fathers, and that suits us better and better. We are developing a taste for it. Soon we shall contrive to be born somehow from an idea. But enough; I don't want to write more from "Underground."

[The notes of this paradoxalist do not end here, however. He could not refrain from going on with them, but it seems to us that we may stop here.]

A Gentle Spirit

A Fantastic Story

Translated by Constance Garnett

Part I

I

Who I Was and Who She Was

Oh, while she is still here, it is still all right; I go up and look at her every minute; but tomorrow they will take her away—and how shall I be left alone? Now she is on the table in the drawing-room, they put two card tables together, the coffin will be here tomorrow—white, pure white "gros de Naples"—but that's not it . . .

I keep walking about, trying to explain it to myself. I have been trying for the last six hours to get it clear, but still I can't think of it all as a whole.

The fact is I walk to and fro, and to and fro.

This is how it was. I will simply tell it in order. (Order!)

Gentlemen, I am far from being a literary man and you will see that; but no matter, I'll tell it as I understand it myself. The horror of it for me is that I understand it all!

It was, if you care to know, that is to take it from the beginning, that she used to come to me simply to pawn things, to pay for advertising in the *voice* to the effect that a governess was quite willing to travel, to give lessons at home, and so on, and so on. That was at the very beginning, and I, of course, made no difference between her and the others: "She comes," I thought, "like any one else," and so on.

But afterwards I began to see a difference. She was such a slender, fair little thing, rather tall, always a little awkward with me, as though embarrassed (I fancy she was the same with all strangers, and in her eyes, of course, I was exactly like anybody else—that is, not as a pawnbroker but as a man).

As soon as she received the money she would turn round at once and go away. And always in silence. Other women argue so, entreat, haggle for me to give them more; this one did not ask for more. . . .

I believe I am muddling it up.

Yes; I was struck first of all by the things she brought: poor little silver gilt earrings, a trashy little locket, things not worth sixpence. She knew herself that they were worth next to nothing, but I could see from her face that they were treasures to her, and I found out afterwards as a fact that they were all that was left her belonging to her father and mother.

Only once I allowed myself to scoff at her things. You see I never allow myself to behave like that. I keep up a gentlemanly tone with my clients: few words, politeness and severity. "Severity, severity!"

But once she ventured to bring her last rag, that is, literally the remains of an old hareskin jacket, and I could not resist saying something by way of a joke. My goodness! how she flared up! Her eyes were large, blue and dreamy but—how they blazed. But she did not drop one word; picking up her "rags" she walked out.

It was then for the first time I noticed her particularly, and thought something of the kind about her—that it, something of a particular kind. Yes, I remember another impression—that is, if you will have it, perhaps the chief impression, that summed up everything. It was that she was terribly young, so young that she looked just fourteen. And yet she was within three months of sixteen. I didn't mean that, though, that wasn't what summed it all up. Next day she came again. I found out later that she had been to Dobranravov's and to Mozer's with that jacket, but they take nothing but gold and would have nothing to say to it. I once took some stones from her (rubbishy little ones) and, thinking it over afterwards, I wondered: I, too, only lend on gold and silver, yet from her I accepted stones. That was my second thought about her then; that I remember. That time, that is when she came from Mozer's, she brought an amber cigar-holder. It was a connoisseur's article, not bad, but again, of no value to us, because we only deal in gold. As it was the day after her "mutiny," I received her sternly. Sternness with me takes the form of dryness. As I gave her two roubles, however, I could not resist saying, with a certain irritation, "I only do it for you, of course; Mozer wouldn't take such a thing."

The word "for you" I emphasised particularly, and with a particular implication.

I was spiteful. She flushed up again when she heard that "for you," but she did not say a word, she did not refuse the money, she took it—that is poverty! But how hotly she flushed! I saw I had stung her. And when she had gone out, I suddenly asked myself whether my triumph over her was worth two roubles. He! He!! He!!! I remember I put that question to myself twice over, "Was is worth it? was it worth it?"

And, laughing, I inwardly answered it in the affirmative. And I felt very much elated. But that was not an evil feeling; I said it with design, with a motive; I wanted to test her, because certain ideas with regard to her had suddenly come into my mind. That was the third thing I thought particularly about her. . . . Well, it was from that time it all began. Of course, I tried at once to find out all her circumstances indirectly, and awaited her coming with a special impatience. I had a presentiment that she would come soon. When she came, I entered into affable conversation with her, speaking with unusual politeness. I have not been badly brought up and have manners. H'm. It was then I guessed that she was soft-hearted and gentle.

The gentle and soft-hearted do not resist long, and though they are by no means very ready to reveal themselves, they do not know how to escape from a conversation; they are niggardly in their answers, but they do answer, and the more readily the longer you go on. Only, on your side you must not flag, if you want them to talk. I need hardly say that she did not explain anything to me then. About the Voice and all that I found out afterwards. She was at that time spending her last farthing on advertising, haughtily at first, of course. "A governess prepared to travel and will send terms on application," but, later on: "willing to do anything, to teach, to be a companion, to be a housekeeper, to wait on an invalid, plain sewing, and so on, and so on," the usual thing! Of course, all this was added to the advertisement a bit at a time and finally, when she was reduced to despair, it came to: "without salary in return for board." No, she could not find a situation. I made up my mind then to test her for the last time. I suddenly took up the Voice of the day and showed her an advertisement. "A young person, without friends and relations, seeks a situation as a governess to young children, preferably in the family of a middle-aged widower. Might be a comfort in the home."

"Look here how this lady has advertised this morning, and by the evening she will certainly have found a situation. That's the way to advertise."

Again she flushed crimson and her eyes blazed, she turned round and went straight out. I was very much pleased, though by that time I felt sure of everything and had no apprehensions; nobody will take her cigar-holders, I thought. Besides, she has got rid of them all. And so it was, two days later, she came in again, such a pale little creature, all agitation—I saw that something had happened to her at home, and something really had. I will explain directly what had happened, but now I only want to recall how I did something chic, and rose in her opinion. I suddenly decided to do it. The fact is she was pawning the ikon (she had brought herself to pawn it!). . . . Ah! listen! listen! This is the beginning now, I've been in a muddle. You see I want to recall all this, every detail, every little point. I want to bring them all together and look at them as a whole and—I cannot . . . It's these little things, these little things. . . . It was an ikon of the Madonna. A Madonna with the Babe, and old-fashioned, homely one, and the setting was silver gilt, worth—well, six roubles perhaps. I could see the ikon was precious to her; she was pawning it whole, not taking it out of the setting. I said to her—

"You had better take it out of the setting, and take the ikon home; for it's not the thing to pawn."

"Why, are you forbidden to take them?"

"No, it's not that we are forbidden, but you might, perhaps, yourself . . ."

"Well, take it out."

"I tell you what. I will not take it out, but I'll set it here in the shrine with the other ikons," I said, on reflection. "Under the little lamp" (I always had the lamp burning as soon as the shop was opened), "and you simply take ten roubles."

"Don't give me ten roubles. I only want five; I shall certainly redeem it."

"You don't want ten? The ikon's worth it," I added noticing that her eyes flashed again.

She was silent. I brought out five roubles.

"Don't despise any one; I've been in such straits myself; and worse too, and that you see me here in this business . . . is owing to what I've been through in the past. . . ."

"You're revenging yourself on the world? Yes?" she interrupted suddenly with rather sarcastic mockery, which, however, was to a great extent innocent (that is, it was general, because certainly at that time she did not distinguish me from others, so that she said it almost without malice).

"Aha," thought I; "so that's what you're like. You've got character; you belong to the new movement."

"You see!" I remarked at once, half-jestingly, half-mysteriously, "I am part of that part of the Whole that seeks to do ill, but does good. . . ."

Quickly and with great curiosity, in which, however, there was something very childlike, she looked at me.

"Stay . . . what's that idea? Where does it come from? I've heard it somewhere . . ."

"Don't rack your brains. In those words Mephistopheles introduces himself to Faust. Have you read Faust?"

"Not . . . not attentively."

"That is, you have not read it at all. You must read it. But I see an ironical look in your face again. Please don't imagine that I've so little taste as to try to use Mephistopheles to commend myself to you and grace the role of pawnbroker. A pawnbroker will still be a pawnbroker. We know."

"You're so strange . . . I didn't mean to say anything of that sort."

She meant to say: "I didn't expect to find you were an educated man"; but she didn't say it; I knew, though, that she thought that. I had pleased her very much.

"You see," I observed, "One may do good in any calling—I'm not speaking of myself, of course. Let us grant that I'm doing nothing but harm, yet . . ."

"Of course, one can do good in every position," she said, glancing at me with a rapid, profound look. "Yes, in any position," she added suddenly.

Oh, I remember, I remember all those moments! And I want to add, too, that when such young creatures, such sweet young creatures want to say something so clever and profound, they show at once so truthfully and naively in their faces, "Here I am saying something clever and profound now"—and that is not from vanity, as it is with any one like me, but one sees that she appreciates it awfully herself, and believes in it, and thinks a lot of it, and imagines that you think a lot of all that, just as she does. Oh, truthfulness! it's by that they conquer us. How exquisite it was in her!

I remember it, I have forgotten nothing! As soon as she had gone, I made up my mind. That same day I made my last investigations and found out every detail of her position at the moment; every detail of her past I had learned already from Lukerya, at that time a servant in the family, whom I had bribed a few days before. This position was so awful that I can't understand how she could laugh as she had done that day and feel interest in the words of Mephistopheles, when she was in such horrible straits. But—that's youth! That is just what I thought about her at the time with pride and joy; for, you know, there's a greatness of soul in it—to be able to say, "Though I am on the edge of the abyss, yet Goethe's grand words are radiant with light." Youth always has some greatness of soul, if its only a spark and that distorted. Though it's of her I am speaking, of her alone. And, above all, I looked upon her then as mine and did not doubt of my power. You know, that's a voluptuous idea when you feel no doubt of it.

But what is the matter with me? If I go on like this, when shall I put it all together and look at it as a whole. I must make haste, make haste—that is not what matters, oh, my God!

II

The Offer of Marriage

The "details" I learned about her I will tell in one word: her father and mother were dead, they had died three years before, and she had been left with two disreputable aunts: though it is saying too little to call them disreputable. One aunt was a widow with a large family (six children, one smaller than another), the other a horrid old maid. Both were horrid. Her father was in the service, but only as a copying clerk, and was only a gentleman by courtesy; in fact, everything was in my favour. I came as though from a higher world; I was anyway a retired lieutenant of a brilliant regiment, a gentleman by birth, independent and all the rest of it, and as for my pawnbroker's shop, her aunts could only have looked on that with respect. She had been living in slavery at her aunts' for those three years: yet she had managed to pass an examination somewhere—she managed to pass it, she wrung the time for it, weighed down as a she was by the pitiless burden of daily drudgery, and that proved something in the way of striving for what was higher and better on her part! Why, what made me want to marry her? Never mind me, though; of that later on . . . As though that mattered!—She taught her aunt's children; she made their clothes; and towards the end not only washed the clothes, but with her weak chest even scrubbed the floors. To put it plainly, they used to beat her, and taunt her with eating their bread. It ended by their scheming to sell her. Tfoo! I omit the filthy details. She told me all about it afterwards.

All this had been watched for a whole year by a neighbour, a fat shopkeeper, and not a humble one but the owner of two grocer's shops. He had ill-treated two wives and now he was looking for a third, and so he cast his eye on her. "She's a quiet one," he thought; "she's grown up in poverty, and I am marrying for the sake of my motherless children."

He really had children. He began trying to make the match and negotiating with the aunts. He was fifty years old, besides. She was aghast with horror. It was then she began coming so often to me to advertise in the Voice. At last she began begging the aunts to give her just a little time to think it over. They granted her that little time, but would not let her have more; they were always at her: "We don't know where to turn to find food for ourselves, without an extra mouth to feed."

I had found all this out already, and the same day, after what had happened in the morning, I made up my mind. That evening the shopkeeper came, bringing with him a pound of sweets from the shop; she was sitting with him, and I called Lukerya out of the kitchen and told her to go and whisper to her that I was at the gate and wanted to say something to her without delay. I felt pleased with myself. And altogether I felt awfully pleased all that day.

On the spot, at the gate, in the presence of Lukerya, before she had recovered from her amazement at my sending for her, I informed her that I should look upon it as an honour and happiness . . . telling her, in the next place, not to be surprised at the manner of my declaration and at my speaking at the gate, saying that I was a straightforward man and had learned the position of affairs. And I was not lying when I said I was straightforward. Well, hang it all. I did not only speak with propriety—that is, showing I was a man of decent breeding, but I spoke with originality and that was the chief thing. After all, is there any harm in admitting it? I want to judge myself and am judging myself. I must speak pro and contra, and I do. I remembered afterwards with enjoyment, though it was stupid, that I frankly declared, without the least embarrassment, that, in the first place, I was not particularly talented, not particularly intelligent, not particularly good-natured, rather a cheap egoist (I remember that expression, I thought of it on the way and was pleased with it) and that very probably there was a great deal that was disagreeable in me in other respects. All this was said with a special sort of pride—we all know how that sort of thing is said. Of course, I had good taste enough not to proceed to enlarge on my virtues after honourably enumerating my defects, not to say "to make up for that I have this and that and the other." I saw that she was still horrible frightened I purposely exaggerated. I told her straight out that she would have enough to eat, but that fine clothes, theatres, balls—she would have none of, at any rate not till later on, when I had attained my object. This severe tone was a positive delight to me. I added as cursorily as possible, that in adopting such a calling—that is, in keeping a pawnbroker's shop, I had one object, hinting there was a special circumstance . . . but I really had a right to say so: I really had such an aim and there really was such a circumstance. Wait a minute, gentlemen; I have always been the first to hate this pawnbroking business, but in reality, though it is absurd to talk about oneself in such mysterious phrases, yet, you know, I was "revenging myself on society," I really was, I was, I was! So that her gibe that morning at the idea of my revenging myself was unjust. That is, do you see, if I had said to her straight out in words: "yes, I am revenging myself on society," she would have laughed as she did that morning, and it would, in fact have been absurd. But by indirect hints, but dropping mysterious phrases, it appeared that it was possible to work upon her imagination. Besides, I had no fears then: I knew that the fat shopkeeper was anyway more repulsive to her than I was, and that I, standing at the gate, had appeared as a deliverer. I understood that, of course. Oh, what is base a man understands particularly well! But was it base? How can a man judge? Didn't I love her even then?

Wait a bit: of course, I didn't breathe a word to her of doing her a benefit; the opposite, oh, quite the opposite; I made out that it was I that would be under an obligation to her, not she to me. Indeed, I said as much—I couldn't resist saying it—and it sounded stupid, perhaps, for I noticed a shade flit across her face. But altogether I won the day completely. Wait a bit, if I am to recall all that vileness, then I will tell of that worst beastliness. As I stood there what was stirring in my mind was, "You are tall, a good figure, educated and—speaking without conceit—good-looking." That is what was at work in my mind. I need hardly say that, on the spot, out there at the gate she said "yes." But . . . but I ought to add: that out there by the gate she thought a long time before she said "yes." She pondered for so long that I said to her, "Well?"—and could not even refrain from asking it with a certain swagger.

"Wait a little. I'm thinking."

And her little face was so serious, so serious that even then I might have read it! And I was mortified: "Can she be choosing between me and the grocer!" I thought. Oh, I did not understand then! I did not understand anything, anything, then! I did not understand till today! I remember Lukerya ran after me as I was going away, stopped me on the road and said, breathlessly: "God will reward you, sir, for taking our dear young lady; only don't speak of that to her—she's proud."

Proud, is she! "I like proud people," I thought. Proud people are particularly nice when . . . well, when one has no doubt of one's power over them, eh? Oh, base, tactless man! Oh, how pleased I was! You know, when she was standing there at the gate, hesitating whether to say "yes" to me, and I was wondering at it, you know, she may have had some such thought as this: "If it is to be misery either way, isn't it best to choose the very worst"—that is, let the fat grocer beat her to death when he was drunk! Eh! what do you think, could there have been a thought like that?

And, indeed, I don't understand it now, I don't understand it at all, even now. I have only just said that she may have had that thought: of two evils choose the worst—that is the grocer. But which was the worst for her then—the grocer or I? The grocer or the pawnbroker who quoted Goethe? That's another question! What a question! And even that you don't understand: the answer is lying on the table and you call it a question! Never mind me, though. It's not a question of me at all . . . and, by the way, what is there left for me now—whether it's a question of me or whether it is not? That's what I am utterly unable to answer. I had better go to bed. My head aches. . . .

III

The Noblest of Men, Though I Don't Believe It Myself

I could not sleep. And how should I? There is a pulse throbbing in my head. One longs to master it all, all that degradation. Oh, the degradation! Oh, what degradation I dragged her out of then! Of course, she must have realized that, she must have appreciated my action! I was pleased, too, by various thoughts—for instance, the reflection that I was forty-one and she was only sixteen. That fascinated me, that feeling of inequality was very sweet, was very sweet.

I wanted, for instance, to have a wedding a l'anglaise, that is only the two of us, with just the two necessary witnesses, one of them Lukerya, and from the wedding straight to the train to Moscow (I happened to have business there, by the way), and then a fortnight at the hotel. She opposed it, she would not have it, and I had to visit her aunts and treat them with respect as though they were relations from whom I was taking her. I gave way, and all befitting respect was paid the aunts. I even made the creatures a present of a hundred roubles each and promised them more—not telling her anything about it, of course, that I might not make her feel humiliated by the lowness of her surroundings. The aunts were as soft as silk at once. There was a wrangle about the trousseau too; she had nothing, almost literally, but she did not want to have anything. I succeeded in proving to her, though, that she must have something, and I made up the trousseau, for who would have given her anything? But there, enough of me. I did, however, succeed in communicating some of my ideas to her then, so that she knew them anyway. I was in too great a hurry, perhaps. The best of it was that, from the very beginning, she rushed to meet me with love, greeted me with rapture, when I went to see her in the evening, told me in her chatter (the enchanting chatter of innocence) all about her childhood and girlhood, her old home, her father and mother. But I poured cold water upon all that at once. That was my idea. I met her enthusiasm with silence, friendly silence, of course . . . but, all the same, she could quickly see that we were different and that I was—an enigma. And being an enigma was what I made a point of most of all! Why, it was just for the sake of being an enigma, perhaps—that I have been guilty of all this stupidity. The first thing was sternness—it was with an air of sternness that I took her into my house. In fact, as I went about then feeling satisfied, I framed a complete system. Oh, it came of itself without any effort. And it could not have been otherwise. I was bound to create that system owing to one inevitable fact—why should I libel myself indeed! The system was a genuine one. Yes, listen; if you must judge a man, better judge him knowing all about it . . . listen.

How am I to begin this, for it is very difficult. When you begin to justify yourself—then it is difficult. You see, for instance, young people despise money—I made money of importance at once; I laid special stress on money. And laid such stress on it that she became more and more silent. She opened her eyes wide, listened, gazed and said nothing. You see, the young are heroic, that is the good among them are heroic and impulsive, but they have little tolerance; if the least thing is not quite right they are full of contempt. And I wanted breadth, I wanted to instil breadth into her very heart, to make it part of her inmost feeling, did I not? I'll take a trivial example: how should I explain my pawnbroker's shop to a character like that? Of course, I did not speak of it directly, or it would have appeared that I was apologizing, and I, so to speak, worked it through with pride, I almost spoke without words, and I am masterly at speaking without words. All my life I have spoken without words, and I have passed through whole tragedies on my own account without words. Why, I, too, have been unhappy! I was abandoned by every one, abandoned and forgotten, and no one, no one knew it! And all at once this sixteen-year-old girl picked up details about me from vulgar people and thought she knew all about me, and, meanwhile, what was precious remained hidden in this heart! I went on being silent, with her especially I was silent, with her especially, right up to yesterday—why was I silent? Because I was proud. I wanted her to find out for herself, without my help, and not from the tales of low people; I wanted her to divine of herself what manner of man I was and to understand me! Taking her into my house I wanted all her respect, I wanted her to be standing before me in homage for the sake of my sufferings—and I deserved it. Oh, I have always been proud, I always wanted all or nothing! You see it was just because I am not one who will accept half a happiness, but always wanted all, that I was forced to act like that then: it was a much as to say, "See into me for yourself and appreciate me!" For you must see that if I had begun explaining myself to her and prompting her, ingratiating myself and asking for her respect—it would have been as good as asking for charity . . . But . . . but why am I talking of that!

Stupid, stupid, stupid, stupid! I explained to her than, in two words, directly, ruthlessly (and I emphasize the fact that it was ruthlessly) that the heroism of youth was charming, but—not worth a farthing. Why not? Because it costs them so little, because it is not gained through life; it is, so to say, merely "first impressions of existence," but just let us see you at work! Cheap heroism is always easy, and even to sacrifice life is easy too; because it is only a case of hot blood and an overflow of energy, and there is such a longing for what is beautiful! No, take the deed of heroism that is labourious, obscure, without noise or flourish, slandered, in which there is a great deal of sacrifice and not one grain of glory—in which you, a splendid man, are made to look like a scoundrel before every one, though you might be the most honest man in the world—you try that sort of heroism and you'll soon give it up! While I—have been bearing the burden of that all my life. At first she argued—ough, how she argued—but afterwards she began to be silent, completely silent, in fact, only opened her eyes wide as she listened, such big, big eyes, so attentive. And . . . and what is more, I suddenly saw a smile, mistrustful, silent, an evil smile. Well, it was with that smile on her face I brought her into my house. It is true that she had nowhere to go.

IV

Plans and Plans

Which of us began it first?

Neither. It began of itself from the very first. I have said that with sternness i brought her into the house. From the first step, however, I softened it. Before she was married it was explained to her that she would have to take pledges and pay out money, and she said nothing at the time (note that). What is more, she set to work with positive zeal. Well, of course, my lodging, my furniture all remained as before. My lodging consisted of two rooms, a large room from which the shop was partitioned off, and a second one, also large, our living room and bedroom. My furniture is scanty: even her aunts had better things. My shrine of ikons with the lamp was in the outer room where the shop is; in the inner room my bookcase with a few books in and a trunk of which I keep the key; married I told her that one rouble a day and not more, was to be spent on our board—that is, on food for me, her and Lukerya whom I had enticed to come to us. "I must have thirty thousand in three years," said I, "and we can't save the money if we spend more." She fell in with this, but I raised the sum by thirty kopecks a day. It was the same with the theatre. I told her before marriage that she would not go to the theatre, and yet I decided once a month to go to he theatre, and in a decent way, to the stalls. We went together. We went three times and saw The Hunt after Happiness, and Singing Birds, I believe. (Oh, what does it matter!) We went in silence and in silence we returned. Why, why, from the very beginning, did we take to being silent? From the very first, you know, we had no quarrels, but always the same silence. She was always, I remember, watching me stealthily in those days; as soon as I noticed it I became more silent that before. It is true that it was I insisted on the silence, not she. On her part there were one or two outbursts, she rushed to embrace me; but as these outbursts were hysterical, painful, and I wanted secure happiness, with respect from her, I received them coldly. And indeed, I was right; each time the outburst was followed next day by a quarrel.

Though, again, there were no quarrels, but there was silence and—and on her side a more and more defiant air. "Rebellion and independence," that's what it was, only she didn't know how to show it. Yes, that gentle creature was becoming more and more defiant. Would you believe it, I was becoming revolting to her? I learned that.

And there could be no doubt that she was moved to frenzy at times. Think, for instance, of her beginning to sniff at our poverty, after her coming from such sordidness and destitution—from scrubbing the floors! you see, there was no poverty; there was frugality, but there was abundance of what was necessary, of linen, for instance, and the greatest cleanliness. I always used to dream that cleanliness in a husband attracts a wife. It was not our poverty she was scornful of, but my supposed miserliness in the housekeeping: "He has his objects," she seemed to say, "he is showing his strength of will." She suddenly refused to go to the theatre. And more and more often an ironical look. . . . And I was more silent, more and more silent.

I could not begin justifying myself, could I? What was at the bottom of all this was the pawnbroking business. Allow me, I knew that a woman, above all at sixteen, must be in complete subordination to a man. Women have no originality. That—that is an axiom; even now, even now, for me it is an axiom! What does it prove that she is lying there in the outer room? Truth is truth, and even Mill is no use against it! And a woman who loves, oh, a woman who loves idealizes even the vices, even the villainies of the man she loves. He would not himself even succeed in finding such justification for his villainies as she will find for him. That is generous but not original. It is the lack of originality alone that has been the ruin of women. And, I repeat, what is the use of your point to that table? Why, what is there original in her being on that table? O—O—Oh!

Listen. I was convinced of her love at that time. Why, she used to throw herself on my neck in those days. She loved me; that is, more accurately, she wanted to love. Yes, that's just what it was, she wanted to love; she was trying to love. And the point was that in this case there were no villainies for which she had to find justification. You will say, I'm a pawnbroker; and every one says the same. But what if I am a pawnbroker? It follows that there must be reasons since the most generous of men had become a pawnbroker. You see, gentlemen, there are ideas . . . that is, if one expresses some ideas, utters them in words, the effect is very stupid. The effect is to make one ashamed. For what reason? For no reason. Because we are all wretched creatures and cannot hear the truth, or I do not know why.

I said just now, "the most generous of men"—that is absurd, and yet that is how it was. It's the truth, that is, the absolute, absolute truth! Yes, I had the right to want to make myself secure and open that pawnbroker's shop: "You have rejected me, you—people, I mean—you have cast me out with contemptuous silence. My passionate yearning towards you you have met with insult all my life. Now I have the right to put up a wall against you, to save up that thirty thousand roubles and end my life somewhere in the Crimea, on the south coast, among the mountains and vineyards, on my own estate bought with that thirty thousand, and above everything, far away from you all, living without malice against you, with an ideal in my soul, with a beloved woman at my heart, and a family, if God sends one, and—helping the inhabitants all around."

Of course, it is quite right that I say this to myself now, but what could have been more stupid than describing all that aloud to her? That was the cause of my proud silence, that's why we sat in silence. For what could she have understood? Sixteen years old, the earliest youth—yes, what could she have understood of my justification, of my sufferings? Undeviating straightness, ignorance of life, the cheap convictions of youth, the hen-like blindness of those "noble hearts," and what stood for most was—the pawnbroker's shop and—enough! (And was I a villain in the pawnbroker's shop? Did not she see how I acted? Did I extort too much?)

Oh, how awful is truth on earth! That exquisite creature, that gentle spirit, that heaven—she was a tyrant, she was the insufferable tyrant and torture of my soul! I should be unfair to myself if I didn't say so! You imagine I didn't love her? Who can say that I did not love her! Do you see, it was a case of irony, the malignant irony of fate and nature! We were under a curse, the life of men in general is under a curse! (mine in particular). Of course, I understand now that I made some mistake! Something went wrong. Everything was clear, my plan was clear as daylight: "Austere and proud, asking for no moral comfort, but suffering in silence." And that was how it was. I was not lying, I was not lying! "She will see for herself, later on, that it was heroic, only that she had not known how to see it, and when, some day, she divines, it she will prize me ten times more and will abase herself in the dust and fold her hands in homage"—that was my plan. But I forgot something or lost sight of it. There was something I failed to manage. But, enough, enough! And whose forgiveness am I to ask now? What is done is done. By bolder, man, and have some pride! It is not your fault! . . .

Well, I will tell the truth, I am not afraid to face the truth; it was her fault, her fault!

V

A Gentle Spirit in Revolt

Quarrels began from her suddenly beginning to pay out loans on her own account, to price things above their worth, and even, on two occasions, she deigned to enter into a dispute about it with me. I did not agree. But then the captain's widow turned up.

This old widow brought a medallion—a present from her dead husband, a souvenir, of course. I lent her thirty roubles on it. She fell to complaining, begged me to keep the thing for her—of course we do keep things. Well, in short, she came again to exchange it for a bracelet that was not worth eight roubles; I, of course, refused. She must have guessed something from my wife's eyes, anyway she came again when I was not there and my wife changed it for the medallion.

Discovering it the same day, I spoke mildly but firmly and reasonably. She was sitting on the bed, looking at the ground and tapping with her right foot on the carpet (her characteristic movement); there was an ugly smile on her lips. Then, without raising my voice in the least, I explained calmly that the money was mine, that I had a right to look at life with my own eyes and—and that when I had offered to take her into my house, I had hidden nothing from her.

She suddenly leapt up, suddenly began shaking all over and—what do you think—she suddenly stamped her foot at me; it was a wild animal, it was a frenzy, it was the frenzy of a wild animal. I was petrified with astonishment; I had never expected such an outburst. But I did not lose my head. I made no movement even, and again, in the same calm voice, I announced plainly that from that time forth I should deprive her of the part she took in my work. She laughed in my face, and walked out of the house.

The fact is, she had not the right to walk out of the house. Nowhere without me, such was the agreement before she was married. In the evening she returned; I did not utter a word.

The next day, too, she went out in the morning, and the day after again. I shut the shop and went off to her aunts. I had cut off all relations with them from the time of the wedding—I would not have them to see me, and I would not go to see them. But it turned out that she had not been with them. They listened to me with curiosity and laughed in my face: "It serves you right," they said. But I expected their laughter. At that point, then I bought over the younger aunt, the unmarried one, for a hundred roubles, giving her twenty-five in advance. Two days later she came to me: "There's an officer called Efimovitch mixed up in this," she said; "a lieutenant who was a comrade of yours in the regiment."

I was greatly amazed. That Efimovitch had done me more harm than any one in the regiment, and about a month ago, being a shameless fellow, he once or twice came into the shop with a pretence of pawning something, and I remember, began laughing with my wife. I went up at the time and told him not to dare to come to me, recalling our relations; but there was no thought of anything in my head, I simply thought that he was insolent. Now the aunt suddenly informed me that she had already appointed to see him and that the whole business had been arranged by a former friend of the aunt's, the widow of a colonel, called Yulia Samsonovna. "It's to her," she said, "your wife goes now."

I will cut the story short. The business cost me three hundred roubles, but in a couple of days it had been arranged that I should stand in an adjoining room, behind closed doors, and listen to the first rendezvous between my wife and Efimovitch, tete-a-tete. Meanwhile, the evening before, a scene, brief but very memorable for me, took place between us.

She returned towards evening, sat down on the bed, looked at me sarcastically, and tapped on the carpet with her foot. Looking at her, the idea suddenly came into my mind that for the whole of the last month, or rather, the last fortnight, her character had not been her own; one might even say that it had been the opposite of her own; she had suddenly shown herself a mutinous, aggressive creature; I cannot say shameless, but regardless of decorum and eager for trouble. She went out of her way to stir up trouble. Her gentleness hindered her, though. When a girl like that rebels, however outrageously she may behave, one can always see that she is forcing herself to do it, that she is driving herself to do it, and that it is impossible for her to master and overcome her own modesty and shamefacedness. That is why such people go such lengths at times, so that one can hardly believe one's eyes. One who is accustomed to depravity, on the contrary, always softens things, acts more disgustingly, but with a show of decorum and seemliness by which she claims to be superior to you.

"Is it true that you were turned out of the regiment because you were afraid to fight a duel?" she asked suddenly, apropos of nothing—and her eyes flashed.

"It is true that by the sentence of the officers I was asked to give up my commission, though, as a fact, I had sent in my papers before that."

"You were turned out as a coward?"

"Yes, they sentenced me as a coward. But I refused to fight a duel, not from cowardice, but because I would not submit to their tyrannical decision and send a challenge when I did not consider myself insulted. You know," I could not refrain from adding, "that to resist such tyranny and to accept the consequences meant showing far more manliness than fighting any kind of duel."

I could not resist it. I dropped the phrase, as it were, in self-defence, and that was all she wanted, this fresh humiliation for me.

She laughed maliciously.

"And is it true that for three years afterwards you wandered about the streets of Petersburg like a tramp, begging for coppers and spending your nights in billiard-rooms?"

"I even spent the night in Vyazemsky's House in the Haymarket. Yes, it is true; there was much disgrace and degradation in my life after I left the regiment, but not moral degradation, because even at the time I hated what I did more than any one. It was only the degradation of my will and my mind, and it was only caused by the desperateness of my position. But that is over. . . ."

"Oh, now you are a personage—a financier!"

A hint at the pawnbroker's shop. But by then I had succeeded in recovering my mastery of myself. I saw that she was thirsting for explanations that be humiliating to me and—I did not give them. A customer rang the bell very opportunely, and I went out into the shop. An hour later, when she was dressed to go out, she stood still, facing me, and said -

"You didn't tell me anything about that, though, before our marriage?"

I made no answer and she went away.

And so next day I was standing in that room, the other side of the door, listening to hear how my fate was being decided, and in my pocket I had a revolver. She was dressed better than usual and sitting at a the table, and Efimovitch was showing off before her. And after all, it turned out exactly (I say it to my credit) as I had foreseen and had assumed it would, though I was not conscious of having foreseen and assumed it. I do not know whether I express myself intelligibly.

This is what happened.

I listened for a whole hour. For a whole hour I was present at a duel between a noble, lofty woman and a worldly, corrupt, dense man with a crawling soul. And how, I wondered in amazement, how could that naive, gentle, silent girl have come to know all that? The wittiest author of a society comedy could not have created such a scene of mockery, of naive laughter, and of the holy contempt of virtue for vice. And how brilliant her sayings, her little phrases were: what wit there was in her rapid answers, what truths in her condemnation. And, at the same time, what almost girlish simplicity. She laughed in his face at his declarations of love, at his gestures, at his proposals. Coming coarsely to the point at once, and not expecting to meet with opposition, he was utterly nonplussed. At first I might have imagined that it was simply coquetry on her part—"the coquetry of a witty, though depraved creature to enhance her own value." But no, the truth shone out like the sun, and to doubt was impossible. It was only an exaggerated and impulsive hatred for me that had led her, in her inexperience, to arrange this interview, but, when it came off—her eyes were opened at once. She was simply in desperate haste to mortify me, come what might, but though she had brought herself to do something so low she could not endure unseemliness. And could she, so pure and sinless, with an ideal in her heart, have been seduced by Efimovitch or any worthless snob? On the contrary, she was only moved to laughter by him. All her goodness rose up from her soul and her indignation roused her to sarcasm. I repeat, the buffoon was completely nonplussed at last and sat frowning, scarcely answering, so much so that I began to be afraid that he might insult her, from a mean desire for revenge. And I repeat again: to my credit, I listened to that scene almost without surprise. I met, as it were, nothing but what I knew well. I had gone, as it were, on purpose to meet it, believing not a word of it, not a word said against her, though I did take the revolver in my pocket—that is the truth. And could I have imagined her different? For what did I love her, for what did I prize her, for what had I married her? Oh, of course, I was quite convinced of her hate for me, but at the same time I was quite convinced of her sinlessness. I suddenly cut short the scene by opening the door. Efimovitch leapt up. I took her by the hand and suggested she should go home with me. Efimovitch recovered himself and suddenly burst into loud peals of laughter.

"Oh, to sacred conjugal rights I offer no opposition; take her away, take her away! And you know," he shouted after me, "though no decent man could fight you, yet from respect to your lady I am at your service . . . If you are ready to risk yourself."

"Do you hear?" I said, stopping her for a second in the doorway.

After which not a word was said all the way home. I led her by the arm and she did not resist. On the contrary, she was greatly impressed, and this lasted after she got home. On reaching home she sat down in a chair and fixed her eyes upon me. She was extremely pale; though her lips were compressed ironically yet she looked at me with solemn and austere defiance and seemed convinced in earnest, for the minute, that I should kill her with the revolver. But I took the revolver from my pocket without a word and laid it on the table! She looked at me and at the revolver (note that the revolver was already an object familiar to her. I had kept one loaded ever since I opened the shop. I made up my mind when I set up the shop that I would not keep a huge dog or a strong manservant, as Mozer does, for instance. My cook opens the doors to my visitors. But in our trade it is impossible to be without means of self-defence in case of emergency, and I kept a loaded revolver. In early days, when first she was living in my house, she took great interest in that revolver, and asked questions about it, and I even explained its construction and working; I even persuaded her once to fire at a target. Note all that). Taking no notice of her frightened eyes, I lay down on the bed, half-undressed. I felt very much exhausted; it was by then about eleven o'clock. She went on sitting in the same place, not stirring, for another hour. Then she put out the candle and she, too, without undressing, lay down on the sofa near the wall. For the first time she did not sleep with me—note that too. . . .

VI

A Terrible Reminiscence

Now for a terrible reminiscence. . . .

I woke up, I believe, before eight o'clock, and it was very nearly broad daylight. I woke up completely to full consciousness and opened my eyes. She was standing at the table holding the revolver in her hand. She did not see that I had woken up and was looking at her. And suddenly I saw that she had begun moving towards me with the revolver in her hand. I quickly closed my eyes and pretended to be still asleep.

She came up to the bed and stood over me. I heard everything; though a dead silence had fallen I heard that silence. All at once there was a convulsive movement and, irresistibly, against my will, I suddenly opened my eyes. She was looking straight at me, straight into my eyes, and the revolver was at my temple. Our eyes met. But we looked at each other for no more than a moment. With an effort I shut my eyes again, and at the same instant I resolved that I would not stir and would not open my eyes, whatever might be awaiting me.

It does sometimes happen that people who are sound asleep suddenly open their eyes, even raise their heads for a second and look about the room, then, a moment later, they lay their heads again on the pillow unconscious, and fall asleep without understanding anything. When meeting her eyes and feeling the revolver on my forehead, I closed my eyes and remained motionless, as though in a deep sleep—she certainly might have supposed that I really was asleep, and that I had seen nothing, especially as it was utterly improbable that, after seeing what I had seen, I should shut my eyes again at such a moment.

Yes, it was improbable. But she might guess the truth all the same—that thought flashed upon my mind at once, all at the same instant. Oh, what a whirl of thoughts and sensations rushed into my mind in less than a minute. Hurrah for the electric speed of thought! In that case (so I felt), if she guessed the truth and knew that I was awake, I should crush her by my readiness to accept death, and her hand might tremble. Her determination might be shaken by a new, overwhelming impression. They say that people standing on a height have an impulse to throw themselves down. I imagine that many suicides and murders have been committed simply because the revolver has been in the hand. It is like a precipice, with an incline of an angle of forty-five degrees, down which you cannot help sliding, and something impels you irresistibly to pull the trigger. But the knowledge that I had seen, that I knew it all, and was waiting for death at her hands without a word—might hold her back on the incline.

The stillness was prolonged, and all at once I felt on my temple, on my hair, the cold contact of iron. You will ask: did I confidently expect to escape? I will answer you as God is my judge: I had no hope of it, except one chance in a hundred. Why did I accept death? But I will ask, what use was life to me after that revolver had been raised against me by the being I adored? Besides, I knew with the whole strength of my being that there was a struggle going on between us, a fearful duel for life and death, the duel fought be the coward of yesterday, rejected by his comrades for cowardice. I knew that and she knew it, if only she guessed the truth that I was not asleep.

Perhaps that was not so, perhaps I did not think that then, but yet it must have been so, even without conscious thought, because I've done nothing but think of it every hour of my life since.

But you will ask me again: why did you not save her from such wickedness? Oh! I've asked myself that question a thousand times since—every time that, with a shiver down my back, I recall that second. But at that moment my soul was plunged in dark despair! I was lost, I myself was lost—how could I save any one? And how do you know whether I wanted to save any one then? How can one tell what I could be feeling then?

My mind was in a ferment, though; the seconds passed; she still stood over me—and suddenly I shuddered with hope! I quickly opened my eyes. She was no longer in the room: I got out of bed: I had conquered—and she was conquered for ever!

I went to the samovar. We always had the samovar brought into the outer room and she always poured out the tea. I sat down at the table without a word and took a glass of tea from her. Five minutes later I looked at her. She was fearfully pale, even paler than the day before, and she looked at me. And suddenly . . . and suddenly, seeing that I was looking at her, she gave a pale smile with her pale lips, with a timid question in her eyes. "So she still doubts and is asking herself: does he know or doesn't he know; did he see or didn't he?" I turned my eyes away indifferently. After tea I close the shop, went to the market and bought an iron bedstead and a screen. Returning home, I directed that the bed should be put in the front room and shut off with a screen. It was a bed for her, but I did not say a word to her. She understood without words, through that bedstead, that I "had seen and knew all," and that all doubt was over. At night I left the revolver on the table, as I always did. At night she got into her new bed without a word: our marriage bond was broken, "she was conquered but not forgiven." At night she began to be delirious, and in the morning she had brain-fever. She was in bed for six weeks.

Part II

I

The Dream of Pride

Lukerya has just announced that she can't go on living here and that she is going away as soon as her lady is buried. I knelt down and prayed for five minutes. I wanted to pray for an hour, but I keep thinking and thinking, and always sick thoughts, and my head aches—what is the use of praying?—it's only a sin! It is strange, too, that I am not sleepy: in great, too great sorrow, after the first outbursts one is always sleepy. Men condemned to death, they say, sleep very soundly on the last night. And so it must be, it is the law of nature, otherwise their strength would not hold out . . . I lay down on the sofa but I did not sleep. . . .

. . . For the six weeks of her illness we were looking after her day and night—Lukerya and I together with a trained nurse whom I had engaged from the hospital. I spared no expense—in fact, I was eager to spend my money for her. I called in Dr. Shreder and paid him ten roubles a visit. When she began to get better I did not show myself so much. But why am I describing it? When she got up again, she sat quietly and silently in my room at a special table, which I had bought for her, too, about that time. . . . Yes, that's the truth, we were absolutely silent; that is, we began talking afterwards, but only of the daily routine. I purposely avoided expressing myself, but I noticed that she, too, was glad not to have to say a word more than was necessary. It seemed to me that this was perfectly normal on her part: "She is too much shattered, too completely conquered," I thought, "and I must let her forget and grow used to it." In this way we were silent, but every minute I was preparing myself for the future. I thought that she was too, and it was fearfully interesting to me to guess what she was thinking about to herself then. I will say more: oh! of course, no one knows what I went through, moaning over her in her illness. But I stifled my moans in my own heart, even from Lukerya. I could not imagine, could not even conceive of her dying without knowing the whole truth. When she was out of danger and began to regain her health, I very quickly and completely, I remember, recovered my tranquillity. What is more, I made up my mind to defer out future as long as possible, and meanwhile to leave things just as they were. Yes, something strange and peculiar happened to me then, I cannot call it anything else: I had triumphed, and the mere consciousness of that was enough for me. So the whole winter passes. Oh! I was satisfied as I had never been before, and it lasted the whole winter.

You see, there had been a terrible external circumstance in my life which, up till then—that is, up to the catastrophe with my wife—had weighed upon me every day and every hour. I mean the loss of my reputation and my leaving the regiment. In two words, I was treated with tyrannical injustice. It is true my comrades did not love me because of my difficult character, and perhaps because of my absurd character, though it often happens that what is exalted, precious and of value to one, for some reason amuses the herd of one's companions. Oh, I was never liked, not even at school! I was always and everywhere disliked. Even Lukerya cannot like me. What happened in the regiment, though it was the result of their dislike to me, was in a sense accidental. I mention this because nothing is more mortifying and insufferable than to be ruined by an accident, which might have happened or not have happened, from an unfortunate accumulation of circumstances which might have passed over like a cloud. For an intelligent being it is humiliating. This is what happened.

In an interval, at a theatre, I went out to the refreshment bar. A hussar called A——— came in and began, before all the officers present and the public, loudly talking to two other hussars, telling them that Captain Bezumtsev, of our regiment, was making a disgraceful scene in the passage and was, "he believed, drunk." The conversation did not go further and, indeed, it was a mistake, for Captain Bezumtsev was not drunk and the "disgraceful scene" was not really disgraceful. The hussars began talking of something else, and the matter ended there, but the next day the story reached our regiment, and then they began saying at once that I was the only officer of our regiment in the refreshment bar at the time, and that when

A——— the hussar, had spoken insolently of Captain Bezumtsev, I had not gone up to A——— and stopped him by remonstrating. But on what grounds could I have done so? If he had a grudge against Bezumtsev, it was their personal affair and why should I interfere? Meanwhile, the officers began to declare that it was not a personal affair, but that it concerned the regiment, and as I was the only officer of the regiment present I had thereby shown all the officers and other people in the refreshment bar that there could be officers in our regiment who were not over-sensitive on the score of their own honour and the honour of their regiment. I could not agree with this view. They let me know that I could set everything right if I were willing, even now, late as it was, to demand a formal explanation from A———. I was not willing to do this, and as I was irritated I refused with pride. And thereupon I forthwith resigned my commission—that is the whole story. I left the regiment, proud but crushed in spirit. I was depressed in will and mind. Just then it was that my sister's husband in Moscow squandered all our little property and my portion of it, which was tiny enough, but the loss of it left me homeless, without a farthing. I might have taken a job in a private business, but I did not. After wearing a distinguished uniform I could not take work in a railway office. And so—if it must be shame, let it be shame; if it must be disgrace, let it be disgrace; if it must be degradation, let it be degradation—(the worse it is, the better) that was my choice. Then followed three years of gloomy memories, and even Vyazemsky's House. A year and a half ago my godmother, a wealthy old lady, died in Moscow, and to my surprise left me three thousand in her will. I thought a little and immediately decided on my course of action. I determined on setting up as a pawnbroker, without apologizing to any one: money, then a home, as far as possible from memories of the past, that was my plan. Nevertheless, the gloomy past and my ruined reputation fretted me every day, every hour. But then I married. Whether it was by chance or not I don't know. But when I brought her into my home I thought I was bringing a friend, and I needed a friend so much. But I saw clearly that the friend must be trained, schooled, even conquered. Could I have explained myself straight off to a girl of sixteen with her prejudices?

How, for instance, could I, without the chance help of the horrible incident with the revolver, have made her believe I was not a coward, and that I had been unjustly accused of cowardice in the regiment? But that terrible incident came just in the nick of time. Standing the test of the revolver, I scored off all my gloomy past. And though no one knew about it, she knew, and for me that was everything, because she was everything for me, all the hope of the future that I cherished in my dreams! She was the one person I had prepared for myself, and I needed no one else—and here she knew everything; she knew, at any rate, that she had been in haste to join my enemies against me unjustly. That thought enchanted me. In her eyes I could not be a scoundrel now, but at most a strange person, and that thought after all that had happened was by no means displeasing to me; strangeness is not a vice—on the contrary, it sometimes attracts the feminine heart. In fact, I purposely deferred the climax: what had happened was meanwhile, enough for my peace of mind and provided a great number of pictures and materials for my dreams. That is what is wrong, that I am a dreamer: I had enough material for my dreams, and about her, I thought she could wait.

So the whole winter passed in a sort of expectation. I liked looking at her on the sly, when she was sitting at her little table. She was busy at her needlework, and sometimes in the evening she read books taken from my bookcase. The choice of books in the bookcase must have had an influence in my favour too. She hardly ever went out. Just before dusk, after dinner, I used to take her out every day for a walk. We took a constitutional, but we were not absolutely silent, as we used to be. I tried, in fact, to make a show of our not being silent, but talking harmoniously, but as I have said already, we both avoided letting ourselves go. I did it purposely, I thought it was essential to "give her time." Of course, it was strange that almost till the end of the winter it did not once strike me that, though I love to watch her stealthily, I had never once, all the winter, caught her glancing at me! I thought it was timidity in her. Besides, she had an air of such timid gentleness, such weakness after her illness. Yes, better to wait and—"she will come to you all at once of herself. . . ."

That thought fascinated me beyond all words. I will add one thing; sometimes, as it were purposely, I worked myself up and brought my mind and spirit to the point of believing she had injured me. And so it went on for some time. But my anger could never be very real or violent. And I felt myself as though it were only acting. And though I had broken off out marriage by buying that bedstead and screen, I could never, never look upon her as a criminal. And not that I took a frivolous view of her crime, but because I had the sense to forgive her completely, from the very first day, even before I bought the bedstead. In fact, it is strange on my part, for I am strict in moral questions. On the contrary, in my eyes, she was so conquered, so humiliated, so crushed, that sometimes I felt agonies of pity for her, though sometimes the thought of her humiliation was actually pleasing to me. The thought of our inequality pleased me. . . .

I intentionally performed several acts of kindness that winter. I excused two debts, I have one poor woman money without any pledge. And I said nothing to my wife about it, and I didn't do it in order that she should know; but the woman came to thank me, almost on her knees. And in that way it became public property; it seemed to me that she heard about the woman with pleasure.

But spring was coming, it was mid-April, we took out the double windows and the sun began lighting up our silent room with its bright beams. But there was, as it were, a veil before my eyes and a blindness over my mind. A fatal, terrible veil! How did it happen that the scales suddenly fell from my eyes, and I suddenly saw and understood? Was it a chance, or had the hour come, or did the ray of sunshine kindle a thought, a conjecture, in my dull mind? No, it was not a thought, not a conjecture. But a chord suddenly vibrated, a feeling that had long been dead was stirred and came to life, flooding all my darkened soul and devilish pride with light. It was as though I had suddenly leaped up from my place. And, indeed, it happened suddenly and abruptly. It happened towards evening, at five o'clock, after dinner. . . .

II

The Veil Suddenly Falls

Two words first. A month ago I noticed a strange melancholy in her, not simply silence, but melancholy. That, too, I noticed suddenly. She was sitting at her work, her head bent over her sewing, and she did not see that I was looking at her. And it suddenly struck me that she had grown so delicate-looking, so thin, that her face was pale, her lips were white. All this, together with her melancholy, struck me all at once. I had already heard a little dry cough, especially at night. I got up at once and went off to ask Shreder to come, saying nothing to her.

Shreder came next day. She was very much surprised and looked first at Shreder and then at me.

"But I am well," she said, with an uncertain smile.

Shreder did not examine her very carefully (these doctors are sometimes superciliously careless), he only said to me in the other room, that it was just the result of her illness, and that it wouldn't be amiss to go for a trip to the sea in the spring, or, if that were impossible to take a cottage out of town for the summer. In fact, he said nothing except that there was weakness, or something of that sort. When Shreder had gone, she said again, looking at me very earnestly -

"I am quite well, quite well."

But as she said this she suddenly flushed, apparently from shame. Apparently it was shame. Oh! now I understand: she was ashamed that I was still her husband, that I was looking after her still as though I were a real husband. But at the time I did not understand and put down her blush to humility (the veil!).

And so, a month later, in April, at five o'clock on a bright sunny day, I was sitting in the shop making up my accounts. Suddenly I heard her, sitting in our room, at work at her table, begin softly, softly . . . singing. This novelty made an overwhelming impression upon me, and to this day I don't understand it. Till then I had hardly ever heard her sing, unless, perhaps, in those first days, when we were still able to be playful and practise shooting at a target. Then her voice was rather strong, resonant; though not quit true it was very sweet and healthy. Now her little song was so faint—it was not that it was melancholy (it was some sort of ballad), but in her voice there was something jangled, broken, as though her voice were not equal to it, as though the song itself were sick. She sang in an undertone, and suddenly, as her voice rose, it broke—such a poor little voice, it broke so pitifully; she cleared her throat and again began softly, softly singing. . . .

My emotions will be ridiculed, but no one will understand why I was so moved! No, I was still not sorry for her, it was still something quite different. At the beginning, for the first minute, at any rate, I was filled with sudden perplexity and terrible amazement—a terrible and strange, painful and almost vindictive amazement: "She is singing, and before me; has she forgotten about me?"

Completely overwhelmed, I remained where I was, then I suddenly got up, took my hat and went out, as it were, without thinking. At least I don't know why or where I was going. Lukerya began giving me my overcoat.

"She is singing?" I said to Lukerya involuntarily. She did not understand, and looked at me still without understanding; and, indeed, I was really unintelligible.

"Is it the first time she is singing?"

"No, she sometimes does sing when you are out," answered Lukerya.

I remember everything. I went downstairs, went out into the street and walked along at random. I walked to the corner and began looking into the distance. People were passing by, the pushed against me. I did not feel it. I called a cab and told the man, I don't know why, to drive to Politseysky Bridge. Then suddenly changed my mind and gave him twenty kopecks.

"That's for my having troubled you," I said, with a meaningless laugh, but a sort of ecstasy was suddenly shining within me.

I returned home, quickening my steps. The poor little jangled, broken note was ringing in my heart again. My breath failed me. The veil was falling, was falling from my eyes! Since she sang before me, she had forgotten me—that is what was clear and terrible. My heart felt it. But rapture was glowing in my soul and it overcame my terror.

Oh! the irony of fate! Why, there had been nothing else, and could have been nothing else but that rapture in my soul all the winter, but where had I been myself all the winter? Had I been there together with my soul? I ran up the stairs in great haste, I don't know whether I went in timidly. I only remember that the whole floor seemed to be rocking and I felt as though I were floating on a river. I went into the room. She was sitting in the same place as before, with her head cursorily and without interest at me; it was hardly a look but just a habitual and indifferent movement upon somebody's coming into the room.

I went straight up and sat down beside her in a chair abruptly, as though I were mad. She looked at me quickly, seeming frightened; I took her hand and I don't remember what I said to her—that is, tried to say, for I could not even speak properly. My voice broke and would not obey me and I did not know what to say. I could only gasp for breath.

"Let us talk . . . you know . . . tell me something!" I muttered something stupid. Oh! how could I help being stupid? She started again and drew back in great alarm, looking at my face, but suddenly there was an expression of stern surprise in her eyes. Yes, surprise and stern. She looked at me with wide-open eyes. That sternness, that stern surprise shattered me at once: "So you still expect love? Love?" that surprise seemed to be asking, though she said nothing. But I read it all, I read it all. Everything within me seemed quivering, and I simply fell down at her feet. Yes, I grovelled at her feet. She jumped up quickly, but I held her forcibly by both hands.

And I fully understood my despair—I understood it! But, would you believe it? Ecstasy was surging up in my head so violently that I thought I should die. I kissed her feet in delirium and rapture. Yes, in immense, infinite rapture, and that, in spite of understanding all the hopelessness of my despair. I wept, said something, but could not speak. Her alarm and amazement were followed by some uneasy misgiving, some grave question, and she looked at me strangely, wildly even; she wanted to understand something quickly and she smiled. She was horribly ashamed at my kissing her feet and she drew them back. But I kissed the place on the floor where her foot had rested. She saw it and suddenly began laughing with shame (you know how it is when people laugh with shame). She became hysterical, I saw that her hands trembled—I did not think about that but went on muttering that I loved her, that I would not get up. "Let me kiss your dress . . . and worship you like this all my life." . . . I don't know, I don't remember—but suddenly she broke into sobs and trembled all over. A terrible fit of hysterics followed. I had frightened her.

I carried her to the bed. When the attack had passed off, sitting on the edge of the bed, with a terribly exhausted look, she took my two hands and begged me to calm myself: "Come, come, don't distress yourself, be calm!" and she began crying again. All that evening I did not leave her side. I kept telling her I should take her to Boulogne to bathe in the sea now, at once, in a fortnight, that she had such a broken voice, I had heard it that afternoon, that I would shut up the shop, that I would sell it Dobronravov, that everything should begin afresh and, above all, Boulogne, Boulogne! She listened and was still afraid. She grew more and more afraid. But that was not what mattered most for me: what mattered most to me was the more and more irresistible longing to fall at her feet again, and again to kiss and kiss the spot where her foot had rested, and to worship her; and—"I ask nothing, nothing more of you," I kept repeating, "do not answer me, take no notice of me, only let me watch you from my corner, treat me as your dog, your thing. . . ." She was crying.

"I thought you would let me go on like that," suddenly broke from her unconsciously, so unconsciously that, perhaps, she did not notice what she had said, and yet—oh, that was the most significant, momentous phrase she uttered that evening, the easiest for me to understand, and it stabbed my heart as though with a knife! It explained everything to me, everything, but while she was beside me, before my eyes, I could not help hoping and was fearfully happy. Oh, I exhausted her fearfully that evening. I understood that, but I kept thinking that I should alter everything directly. At last, towards night, she utterly exhausted. I persuaded her to go to sleep and she fell sound asleep at once. I expected her to be delirious, she was a little delirious, but very slightly. I kept getting up every minute in the night and going softly in my slippers to look at her. I wrung my hands over her, looking at that frail creature in that wretched little iron bedstead which I had bought for three roubles. I knelt down, but did not dare to kiss her feet in her sleep (without her consent). I began praying but leapt up again. Lukerya kept watch over me and came in and out from the kitchen. I went in to her, and told her to go to bed, and that to-morrow "things would be quite different."

And I believed in this, blindly, madly.

Oh, I was brimming over with rapture, rapture! I was eager for the next day. Above all, I did not believe that anything could go wrong, in spite of the symptoms. Reason had not altogether come back to me, though the veil had fallen from my eyes, and for a long, long time it did not come back—not till today, not till this very day! Yes, and how could it have come back then: why, she was still alive then; why, she was here before my eyes, and I was before her eyes: "To-morrow she will wake up and I will tell her all this, and she will see it all." That was how I reasoned then, simply and clearly, because I was in an ecstasy! My great idea was the trip to Boulogne. I kept thinking for some reason that Boulogne would be everything, that there was something final and decisive about Boulogne. "To Boulogne, to Boulogne!" . . . I waited frantically for the morning.

III

I Understand Too Well

But you know that was only a few days ago, five days, only five days ago, last Tuesday! Yes, yes, if there had only been a little longer, if she had only waited a little—and I would have dissipated the darkness!—It was not as though she had not recovered her calmness. The very next day she listened to me with a smile, in spite of her confusion. . . . All this time, all these five days, she was either confused or ashamed. She was afraid, too, very much afraid. I don't dispute it, I am not so mad as to deny it. It was terror, but how could she help being frightened? We had so long been strangers to one another, had grown so alienated from one another, and suddenly all this. . . . But I did not look at her terror. I was dazzled by the new life beginning! . . . It is true, it is undoubtedly true that I made a mistake. There were even, perhaps, many mistakes. When I woke up next day, the first thing in the morning (that was on Wednesday), I made a mistake: I suddenly made her my friend. I was in too great a hurry, but a confession was necessary, inevitable—more than a confession! I did not even hide what I had hidden from myself all my life. I told her straight out that the whole winter I had been doing nothing but brood over the certainty of her love. I made clear to her that my money-lending had been simply the degradation of my will and my mind, my personal idea of self-castigation and self-exaltation. I explained to her that I really had been cowardly that time in the refreshment bar, that it was owing to my temperament, to my self-consciousness. I was impressed by the surroundings, by the theatre: I was doubtful how I should succeed and whether it would be stupid. I was not afraid of a duel, but of its being stupid . . . and afterwards I would not own it and tormented every one and had tormented her for it, and had married her so as to torment her for it. In fact, for the most part I talked as though in delirium. She herself took my hands and made me leave off. "You are exaggerating . . . you are distressing yourself," and again there were tears, again almost hysterics! She kept begging me not to say all this, not to recall it.

I took no notice of her entreaties, or hardly noticed them: "Spring, Boulogne! There there would be sunshine, there our new sunshine," I kept saying that! I shut up the shop and transferred it to Dobronravov. I suddenly suggested to her giving all our money to the poor except the three thousand left me by my godmother, which we would spend on going to Boulogne, and then we would come back and begin a new life of real work. So we decided, for she said nothing. . . . She only smiled. And I believe she smiled chiefly from delicacy, for fear of disappointing me. I saw, of course, that I was burdensome to her, don't imagine I was so stupid or egoistic as not to see it. I saw it all, all, to the smallest detail, I saw better than any one; all the hopelessness of my position stood revealed.

I told her everything about myself and about her. And about Lukerya. I told her that I had wept. . . . Oh, of course, I changed the conversation. I tried, too, not to say a word more about certain things. And, indeed, she did revive once or twice—I remember it, I remember it! Why do you say I looked at her and saw nothing? And if only this had not happened, everything would have come to life again. Why, only the day before yesterday, when we were talking of reading and what she had been reading that winter, she told me something herself, and laughed as she told me, recalling the scene of Gil Blas and the Archbishop of Granada. And with that sweet, childish laughter, just as in old days when we were eager (one instant! one instant!); how glad I was! I was awfully struck, though, by the story of the Archbishop; so she had found peace of mind and happiness enough to laugh at that literary masterpiece while she was sitting there in the winter. So then she had begun to be fully at rest, had begun to believe confidently "that I should leave her like that. I thought you would leave me like that," those were the word she uttered then on Tuesday! Oh! the thought of a child of ten! And you know she believed it, she believed that really everything would remain like that: she at her table and I at mine, and we both should go on like that till we were sixty. And all at once—I come forward, her husband, and the husband wants love! Oh, the delusion! Oh, my blindness!

It was a mistake, too, that I looked at her with rapture; I ought to have controlled myself, as it was my rapture frightened her. But, indeed, I did control myself, I did not kiss her feet again. I never made a sign of . . . well, that I was her husband—oh, there was no thought of that in my mind, I only worshipped her! But, you know, I couldn't be quite silent, I could not refrain from speaking altogether! I suddenly said to her frankly, that I enjoyed her conversation and that I thought her incomparably more cultured and developed than I. She flushed crimson and said in confusion that I exaggerated. Then, like a fool, I could not resist telling her how delighted I had been when I had stood behind the door listening to her duel, the duel of innocence with that low cad, and how I had enjoyed her cleverness, the brilliance of her wit, and, at the same time, her childlike simplicity. She seemed to shudder all over, was murmuring again that I exaggerated, but suddenly her whole face darkened, she hit it in her hands and broke into sobs. . . . Then I could not restrain myself: again I fell at her feet, again I began kissing her feet, and again it ended in a fit of hysterics, just as on Tuesday. That was yesterday evening—and—in the morning. . . .

In the morning! Madman! why, that morning was today, just now, only just now!

Listen and try to understand: why, when we met by the samovar (it was after yesterday's hysterics), I was actually struck by her calmness, that is the actual fact! And all night I had been trembling with terror over what happened yesterday. But suddenly she came up to me and, clasping her hands (this morning, this morning!) began telling me that she was a criminal, that she knew it, that her crime had been torturing her all the winter, was torturing her now. . . . That she appreciated my generosity. . . . "I will be your faithful wife, I will respect you . . ."

Then I leapt up and embraced her like a madman. I kissed her, kissed her face, kissed her lips like a husband for the first time after a long separation. And why did I go out this morning, only two hours . . . our passports for abroad. . . . Oh, God! if only I had come back five minutes, only five minutes earlier! . . . That crowd at our gates, those eyes all fixed upon me. Oh, God!

Lukerya says (oh! I will not let Lukerya go now for anything. She knows all about it, she has been here all the winter, she will tell me everything!), she says that when I had gone out of the house and only about twenty minutes before I came back—she suddenly went into our room to her mistress to ask her something, I don't remember what, and saw that her ikon (that same ikon of the Mother of God) had been taken down and was standing before her on the table, and her mistress seemed to have only just been praying before it. "What are you doing, mistress?" "Nothing, Lukerya, run along." "Wait a minute, Lukerya." "She came up and kissed me." "Are you happy, mistress?" I said. "Yes, Lukerya," and she smiled, but so strangely. So strangely that Lukerya went back ten minutes later to have a look at her.

"She was standing by the wall, close to the window, she had laid her arm against the wall, and her head was pressed on her arm, she was standing like that thinking. And she was standing so deep in thought that she did not hear me come and look at her from the other room. She seemed to be smiling—standing, thinking and smiling. I looked at her, turned softly and went out wondering to myself, and suddenly I heard the window opened. I went in at once to say: 'It's fresh, mistress; mind you don't catch cold,' and suddenly I saw she had got on the window and was standing there, her full height, in the open window, with her back to me, holding the ikon in her hand. My heart sank on the spot. I cried, 'Mistress, mistress.' She heard, made a movement to turn back to me, but, instead of turning back, took a step forward, pressed the ikon to her bosom, and flung herself out of window."

I only remember that when I went in at the gate she was still warm. The worst of it was they were all looking at me. At first they shouted and then suddenly they were silent, and then all of them moved away from me . . . and she was lying there with the ikon. I remember, as it were, in a darkness, that I went up to her in silence and looked at her a long while. But all came round me and said something to me. Lukerya was there too, but I did not see her. She says she said something to me. I only remember that workman. He kept shouting to me that, "Only a handful of blood came from her mouth, a handful, a handful!" and he pointed to the blood on a stone. I believe I touched the blood with my finger, I smeared my finger, I looked at my finger (that I remember), and he kept repeating: "a handful, a handful!"

"What do you mean by a handful?" I yelled with all my might, I am told, and I lifted up my hands and rushed at him.

Oh, wild! wild! Delusion! Monstrous! Impossible!

IV

I Was Only Five Minutes Too Late

Is it not so? Is it likely? Can one really say it was possible? What for, why did this woman die?

Oh, believe me, I understand, but why she dies is still a question. She was frightened of my love, asked herself seriously whether to accept it or not, could not bear the question and preferred to die. I know, I know, no need to rack my brains: she had made too many promises, she was afraid she could not keep them—it is clear. There are circumstances about it quite awful.

For why did she die? That is still a question, after all. The question hammers, hammers at my brain. I would have left her like that if she had wanted to remain like that. She did not believe it, that's what it was! No—no. I am talking nonsense, it was not that at all. It was simply because with me she had to be honest—if she loved me, she would have had to love me altogether, and not as she would have loved the grocer. And as she was too chaste, too pure, to consent to such love as the grocer wanted she did not want to deceive me. Did not want to deceive me with half love, counterfeiting love, or a quarter love. They are honest, too honest, that is what it is! I wanted to instil breadth of heart in her, in those days, do you remember? A strange idea.

It is awfully interesting to know: did she respect me or not? I don't know whether she despised me or not. I don't believe she did despise me. It is awfully strange: why did it never once enter my head all the winter that she despised me? I was absolutely convinced of the contrary up to that moment when she looked at me with stern surprise. Stern it was. I understood once for all, for ever! Ah, let her, let her despise me all her life even, only let her be living! Only yesterday she was walking about, talking. I simply can't understand how she threw herself out of window! And how could I have imagined it five minutes before? I have called Lukerya. I won't let Lukerya go now for anything!

Oh, we might still have understood each other! We had simply become terribly estranged from one another during the winter, but couldn't we have grown used to each other again? Why, why, couldn't we have come together again and begun a new life again? I am generous, she was too—that was a point in common! Only a few more words, another two days—no more, and she would have understood everything.

What is most mortifying of all is that it is chance—simply a barbarous, lagging chance. That is what is mortifying! Five minutes, only five minutes too late! Had I come five minutes earlier, the moment would have passed away like a cloud, and it would never have entered her head again. And it would have ended by her understanding it all. But now again empty rooms, and me alone. Here the pendulum is ticking; it does not care, it has no pity. . . . There is no one—that's the misery of it!

I keep walking about, I keep walking about. I know, I know, you need not tell me; it amuses you, you think it absurd that I complain of chance and those five minutes. But it is evident. Consider one thing: she did not even leave a note, to say, "Blame no one for my death," as people always do. Might she not have thought that Lukerya might get into trouble. "She was alone with her," might have been said, "and pushed her out." In any case she would have been taken up by the police if it had not happened that four people, from the windows, from the lodge, and from the yard, had seen her stand with the ikon in her hands and jump out of herself. But that, too, was a chance, that the people were standing there and saw her. No, it was all a moment, only an irresponsible moment. A sudden impulse, a fantasy! What if she did pray before the ikon? It does not follow that she was facing death. The whole impulse lasted, perhaps, only some ten minutes; it was all decided, perhaps, while she stood against the wall with her head on her arm, smiling. The idea darted into her brain, she turned giddy and—and could not resist it.

Say what you will, it was clearly misunderstanding. It could have been possible to live with me. And what if it were anaemia? Was it simply from poorness of blood, from the flagging of vital energy? She had grown tired during the winter, that was what it was. . . .

I was too late ! ! !

How thin she is in her coffin, how sharp her nose has grown! Her eyelashes lie straight as arrows. And, you know, when she fell, nothing was crushed, nothing was broken! Nothing but that "handful of blood." A dessertspoonful, that is. From internal injury. A strange thought: if only it were possible not to bury her? For if they take her away, then . . . oh, no, it is almost incredible that they take her away! I am not mad and I am not raving—on the contrary, my mind was never so lucid—but what shall I do when again there is no one, only the two rooms, and me alone with the pledges? Madness, madness, madness! I worried her to death, that is what it is!

What are your laws to me now? What do I car for your customs, your morals, your life, your state, your faith! Let your judge judge me, let me be brought before your court, let me be tried by jury, and I shall say that I admit nothing. The judge will shout, "Be silent, officer." And I will shout to him, "What power have you now that I will obey? Why did blind, inert force destroy that which was dearest of all? What are your laws to me now? They are nothing to me." Oh, I don't care!

She was blind, blind! She is dead, she does not hear! You do not know with what paradise I would have surrounded you. There was paradise in my soul, I would have made it blossom around you! Well, you wouldn't have loved me—so be it, what of it? Things should still have been like that, everything should have remained like that. You should only have talked to me as a friend—we could have rejoiced and laughed with joy looking at one another. And so we should have lived. And if you had loved another—well, so be it, so be it! You should have walked with him laughing, and I should have watched you from the other side of the street. . . . Oh, anything, anything, if only she would open her eyes just once! For one instant, only one! If she would look at me as she did this morning, when she stood before me and made a vow to be a faithful wife! Oh, in one look she would have understood it all!

Oh, blind force! Oh, nature! Men are alone on earth—that is what is dreadful! "Is there a living man in the country?" cried the Russian hero. I cry the same, though I am not a hero, and no one answers my cry. They say the sun gives life to the universe. The sun is rising and—look at it, is it not dead? Everything is dead and everywhere there are dead. Men are alone—around them is silence—that is the earth! "Men, love one another"—who said that? Whose commandment is that? The pendulum ticks callously, heartlessly. Two o'clock at night. Her little shoes are standing by the little bed, as though waiting for her. . . . No, seriously, when they take her away tomorrow, what will become of me?

The Honest Thief

One morning, just as I was about to leave for my place of employment, Agrafena (my cook, laundress, and housekeeper all in one person) entered my room, and, to my great astonishment, started a conversation.

She was a quiet, simple-minded woman, who during the whole six years of her stay with me had never spoken more than two or three words daily, and that in reference to my dinner—at least, I had never heard her.

"I have come to you, sir," she suddenly began, "about the renting out of the little spare room."

"What spare room?"

"The one that is near the kitchen, of course; which should it be?"

"Why?"

"Why do people generally take lodgers? Because."

"But who will take it?"

"Who will take it! A lodger, of course! Who should take it?"

"But there is hardly room in there, mother mine, for a bed; it will be too cramped. How can one live in it?"

"But why live in it! He only wants a place to sleep in; he will live on the window-seat."

"What window-seat?"

"How is that? What window-seat? As if you did not know! The one in the hall. He will sit on it and sew, or do something else. But maybe he will sit on a chair; he has a chair of his own—and a table also, and everything."

"But who is he?"

"A nice, worldly-wise man. I will cook for him and will charge him only three rubles in silver a month for room and board—"

At last, after long endeavor, I found out that some elderly man had talked Agrafena into taking him into the kitchen as lodger. When Agrafena once got a thing into her head that thing had to be; otherwise I knew I would have no peace. On those occasions when things did go against her wishes, she immediately fell into a sort of brooding, became exceedingly melancholy, and continued in that state for two or three weeks. During this time the food was invariably spoiled, the linen was missing, the floors unscrubbed; in a word, a lot of unpleasant things happened. I had long ago become aware of the fact that this woman of very few words was incapable of forming a decision, or of coming to any conclusion based on her own thoughts; and yet when it happened that by some means there had formed in her weak brain a sort of idea or wish to undertake a thing, to refuse her permission to carry out this idea or wish meant simply to kill her morally for some time. And so, acting in the sole interest of my peace of mind, I immediately agreed to this new proposition of hers.

"Has he at least the necessary papers, a passport, or anything of the kind?"

"How then? Of course he has. A fine man like him—who has seen the world—He promised to pay three rubles a month."

On the very next day the new lodger appeared in my modest bachelor quarters; but I did not feel annoyed in the least—on the contrary, in a way I was glad of it. I live a very solitary, hermit-like life. I have almost no acquaintance and seldom go out. Having led the existence of a moor-cock for ten years, I was naturally used to solitude. But ten, fifteen years or more of the same seclusion in company with a person like Agrafena, and in the same bachelor dwelling, was indeed a joyless prospect. Therefore, the presence of another quiet, unobtrusive man in the house was, under these circumstances, a real blessing.

Agrafena had spoken the truth: the lodger was a man who had seen much in his life. From his passport it appeared that he was a retired soldier, which I noticed even before I looked at the passport.

As soon as I glanced at him, in fact.

Astafi Ivanich, my lodger, belonged to the better sort of soldiers, another thing I noticed as soon as I saw him. We liked each other from the first, and our life flowed on peacefully and comfortably. The best thing was that Astafi Ivanich could at times tell a good story, incidents of his own life. In the general tediousness of my humdrum existence, such a narrator was a veritable treasure. Once he told me a story which has made a lasting impression upon me; but first the incident which led to the story.

Once I happened to be left alone in the house, Astafi and Agrafena having gone out on business. Suddenly I heard some one enter, and I felt that it must be a stranger; I went out into the corridor and found a man of short stature, and notwithstanding the cold weather, dressed very thinly and without an overcoat.

"What is it you want?"

"The Government clerk Alexandrov? Does he live here?"

"There is no one here by that name, little brother; good day."

"The porter told me he lived here," said the visitor, cautiously retreating toward the door.

"Go on, go on, little brother; be off!"

Soon after dinner the next day, when Astafi brought in my coat, which he had repaired for me, I once more heard a strange step in the corridor. I opened the door.

The visitor of the day before, calmly and before my very eyes, took my short coat from the rack, put it under his arm, and ran out.

Agrafena, who had all the time been looking at him in open-mouthed surprise through the kitchen door, was seemingly unable to stir from her place and rescue the coat. But Astafi Ivanich rushed after the rascal, and, out of breath and panting, returned empty-handed. The man had vanished as if the earth had swallowed him.

"It is too bad, really, Astafi Ivanich," I said. "It is well that I have my cloak left. Otherwise the scoundrel would have put me out of service altogether."

But Astafi seemed so much affected by what had happened that as I gazed at him I forgot all about the theft. He could not regain his composure, and every once in a while threw down the work which occupied him, and began once more to recount how it had all happened, where he had been standing, while only two steps away my coat had been stolen before his very eyes, and how he could not even catch the thief. Then once more he resumed his work, only to throw it away again, and I saw him go down to the porter, tell him what had happened, and reproach him with not taking sufficient care of the house, that such a theft could be perpetrated in it. When he returned he began to upbraid Agrafena. Then he again resumed his work, muttering to himself for a long time—how this is the way it all was—how he stood here, and I there, and how before our very eyes, no farther than two steps away, the coat was taken off its hanger, and so on. In a word, Astafi Ivanich, though he knew how to do certain things, worried a great deal over trifles.

"We have been fooled, Astafi Ivanich," I said to him that evening, handing him a glass of tea, and hoping from sheer ennui to call forth the story of the lost coat again, which by dint of much repetition had begun to sound extremely comical.

"Yes, we were fooled, sir. It angers me very much. Though the loss is not mine, and I think there is nothing so despicably low in this world as a thief. They steal what you buy by working in the sweat of your brow—Your time and labor—The loathsome creature! It sickens me to talk of it—pfui! It makes me angry to think of it. How is it, sir, that you do not seem to be at all sorry about it?"

"To be sure, Astafi Ivanich, one would much sooner see his things burn up than see a thief take them. It is exasperating!"

"Yes, it is annoying to have anything stolen from you. But of course there are thieves and thieves—I, for instance, met an honest thief through an accident."

"How is that? An honest thief? How can a thief be honest, Astafi Ivanich?"

"You speak truth, sir. A thief cannot be an honest man. There never was such. I only wanted to say that he was an honest man, it seems to me, even though he stole. I was very sorry for him."

"And how did it happen, Astafi Ivanich?"

"It happened just two years ago. I was serving as house steward at the time, and the baron whom I served expected shortly to leave for his estate, so that I knew I would soon be out of a job, and then God only knew how I would be able to get along; and just then it was that I happened to meet in a tavern a poor forlorn creature, Emelian by name. Once upon a time he had served somewhere or other, but had been driven out of service on account of tippling. Such an unworthy creature as he was! He wore whatever came along. At times I even wondered if he wore a shirt under his shabby cloak; everything he could put his hands on was sold for drink. But he was not a rowdy. Oh, no; he was of a sweet, gentle nature, very kind and tender to everyone; he never asked for anything, was, if anything, too conscientious—Well, you could see without asking when the poor fellow was dying for a drink, and of course you treated him to one. Well, we became friendly, that is, he attached himself to me like a little dog—you go this way, he follows—and all this after our very first meeting.

"Of course, he remained with me that night; his passport was in order and the man seemed all right. On the second night also. On the third he did not leave the house, sitting on the window-seat of the corridor the whole day, and of course he remained over that night too. Well, I thought, just see how he has forced himself upon you. You have to give him to eat and to drink and to shelter him. All a poor man needs is some one to sponge upon him. I soon found out that once before he had attached himself to a man just as he had now attached himself to me; they drank together, but the other one soon died of some deep-seated sorrow. I thought and thought: What shall I do with him? Drive him out—my conscience would not allow it—I felt very sorry for him: he was such a wretched, forlorn creature, terrible! And so dumb he did not ask for anything, only sat quietly and looked you straight in the eyes, just like a faithful little dog. That is how drink can ruin a man. And I thought to myself: Well, suppose I say to him: 'Get out of here, Emelian; you have nothing to do in here, you come to the wrong person; I will soon have nothing to eat myself, so how do you expect me to feed you?' And I tried to imagine what he would do after I'd told him all this. And I could see how he would look at me for a long time after he had heard me, without understanding a word; how at last he would understand what I was driving at, and, rising from the window-seat, take his little bundle—I see it before me now—a red-checked little bundle full of holes, in which he kept God knows what, and which he carted along with him wherever he went; how he would brush and fix up his worn cloak a little, so that it would look a bit more decent and not show so much the holes and patches—he was a man of very fine feelings! How he would have opened the door afterward and would have gone forth with tears in his eyes.

"Well, should a man be allowed to perish altogether? I all at once felt heartily sorry for him; but at the same time I thought: And what about me? Am I any better off? And I said to myself: Well, Emelian, you will not feast overlong at my expense; soon I shall have to move from here myself, and then you will not find me again. Well, sir, my baron soon left for his estate with all his household, telling me before he went that he was very well satisfied with my services, and would gladly employ me again on his return to the capital. A fine man my baron was, but he died the same year.

"Well, after I had escorted my baron and his family a little way, I took my things and the little money I had saved up, and went to live with an old woman I knew, who rented out a corner of the room she occupied by herself. She used to be a nurse in some well-to-do family, and now, in her old age, they had pensioned her off. Well, I thought to myself, now it is good-by to you, Emelian, dear man, you will not find me now! And what do you think, sir? When I returned in the evening—I had paid a visit to an acquaintance of mine—whom should I see but Emelian sitting quietly upon my trunk with his red-checked bundle by his side. He was wrapped up in his poor little cloak, and was awaiting my home-coming. He must have been quite lonesome, because he had borrowed a prayer-book of the old woman and held it upside down. He had found me after all! My hands fell helplessly at my sides. Well, I thought, there is nothing to be done. Why did I not drive him away first off? And I only asked him: 'Have you taken your passport along, Emelian?' Then I sat down, sir, and began to turn the matter over in my mind: Well, could he, a roving man, be much in my way? And after I had considered it well, I decided that he would not, and besides, he would be of very little expense to me. Of course, he would have to be fed, but what does that amount to? Some bread in the morning and, to make it a little more appetizing, a little onion or so. For the midday meal again some bread and onion, and for the evening again onion and bread, and some kvass, and, if some cabbage-soup should happen to come our way, then we could both fill up to the throat. I ate little, and Emelian, who was a drinking man, surely ate almost nothing: all he wanted was vodka. He would be the undoing of me with his drinking; but at the same time I felt a curious feeling creep over me. It seemed as if life would be a burden to me if Emelian went away. And so I decided then and there to be his father-benefactor. I would put him on his legs, I thought, save him from perishing, and gradually wean him from drink. Just you wait, I thought. Stay with me, Emelian, but stand pat now. Obey the word of command!

"Well, I thought to myself, I will begin by teaching him some work, but not at once; let him first enjoy himself a bit, and I will in the meanwhile look around and discover what he finds easiest, and would be capable of doing, because you must know, sir, a man must have a calling and a capacity for a certain work to be able to do it properly. And I began stealthily to observe him. And a hard subject he was, that Emelian! At first I tried to get at him with a kind word. Thus and thus I would speak to him: 'Emelian, you had better take more care of yourself and try to fix yourself up a little.

"'Give up drinking. Just look at yourself, man, you are all ragged, your cloak looks more like a sieve than anything else. It is not nice. It is about time for you to come to your senses and know when you have had enough.'

"He listened to me, my Emelian did, with lowered head; he had already reached that state, poor fellow, when the drink affected his tongue and he could not utter a sensible word. You talk to him about cucumbers, and he answers beans. He listened, listened to me for a long time, and then he would sigh deeply.

"'What are you sighing for, Emelian?' I ask him.

"'Oh, it is nothing, Astafi Ivanich, do not worry. Only what I saw to-day, Astafi Ivanich—two women fighting about a basket of huckleberries that one of them had upset by accident.

"'Well, what of that?'

"'And the woman whose berries were scattered snatched a like basket of huckleberries from the other woman's hand, and not only threw them on the ground, but stamped all over them.'

"'Well, but what of that, Emelian?'

"'Ech!' I think to myself, 'Emelian! You have lost your poor wits through the cursed drink!'

"'And again,' Emelian says, 'a baron lost a bill on the Gorokhova Street—or was it on the Sadova? A muzhik saw him drop it, and says, "My luck," but here another one interfered and says, "No, it is my luck! I saw it first. . . ."'

"'Well, Emelian?'

"'And the two muzhiks started a fight, Astafi Ivanich, and the upshot was that a policeman came, picked up the money, handed it back to the baron, and threatened to put the muzhiks under lock for raising a disturbance.'

"'But what of that? What is there wonderful or edifying in that, Emelian?'

"'Well, nothing, but the people laughed, Astafi Ivanich.'

"'E-ch, Emelian! What have the people to do with it?' I said. 'You have sold your immortal soul for a copper. But do you know what I will tell you, Emelian?'

"'What, Astafi Ivanich?'

"'You'd better take up some work, really you should. I am telling you for the hundredth time that you should have pity on yourself!'

"'But what shall I do, Astafi Ivanich? I do not know where to begin and no one would employ me, Astafi Ivanich.'

"'That is why they drove you out of service, Emelian; it is all on account of drink!'

"'And to-day,' said Emelian, 'they called Vlass the barkeeper into the office.'

"'What did they call him for, Emelian?' I asked.

"'I don't know why, Astafi Ivanich. I suppose it was needed, so they called him.'

"'Ech,' I thought to myself, 'no good will come of either of us, Emelian! It is for our sins that God is punishing us!'

"Well, what could a body do with such a man, sir!

"But he was sly, the fellow was, I tell you! He listened to me, listened, and at last it seems it began to tire him, and as quick as he would notice that I was growing angry he would take his cloak and slip out—and that was the last to be seen of him! He would not show up the whole day, and only in the evening would he return, as drunk as a lord. Who treated him to drinks, or where he got the money for it, God only knows; not from me, surely! . . .

"'Well,' I say to him, 'Emelian, you will have to give up drink, do you hear? you will have to give it up! The next time you return tipsy, you will have to sleep on the stairs. I'll not let you in!'

"After this Emelian kept to the house for two days; on the third he once more sneaked out. I wait and wait for him; he does not come! I must confess that I was kind of frightened; besides, I felt terribly sorry for him. What had I done to the poor devil! I thought. I must have frightened him off. Where could he have gone to now, the wretched creature? Great God, he may perish yet! The night passed and he did not return. In the morning I went out into the hall, and he was lying there with his head on the lower step, almost stiff with cold.

"'What is the matter with you, Emelian? The Lord save you! Why are you here?'

"'But you know, Astafi Ivanich,' he replied, 'you were angry with me the other day; I irritated you, and you promised to make me sleep in the hall, and I—so I—did not dare—to come in—and lay down here.'

"'It would be better for you, Emelian,' I said, filled with anger and pity, 'to find a better employment than needlessly watching the stairs!'

"'But what other employment, Astafi Ivanich?'

"'Well, wretched creature that you are,' here anger had flamed up in me, 'if you would try to learn the tailoring art. Just look at the cloak you are wearing! Not only is it full of holes, but you are sweeping the stairs with it! You should at least take a needle and mend it a little, so it would look more decent. E-ch, a wretched tippler you are, and nothing more!'

"Well, sir! What do you think! He did take the needle—I had told him only for fun, and there he got scared and actually took the needle. He threw off his cloak and began to put the thread through; well, it is easy to see what would come of it; his eyes began to fill and reddened, his hands trembled! He pushed and pushed the thread—could not get it through: he wetted it, rolled it between his fingers, smoothed it out, but it would not—go! He flung it from him and looked at me.

"'Well, Emelian!' I said, 'you served me right! If people had seen it I would have died with shame! I only told you all this for fun, and because I was angry with you. Never mind sewing; may the Lord keep you from sin! You need not do anything, only keep out of mischief, and do not sleep on the stairs and put me to shame thereby!'

"'But what shall I do, Astafi Ivanich; I know myself that I am always tipsy and unfit for anything! I only make you, my be—benefactor, angry for nothing.'

"And suddenly his bluish lips began to tremble, and a tear rolled down his unshaven, pale cheek, then another and another one, and he broke into a very flood of tears, my Emelian. Father in Heaven! I felt as if some one had cut me over the heart with a knife.

"'E-ch, you sensitive man; why, I never thought! And who could have thought such a thing! No, I'd better give you up altogether, Emelian; do as you please.'

"Well, sir, what else is there to tell! But the whole thing is so insignificant and unimportant, it is really not worth while wasting words about it; for instance, you, sir, would not give two broken groschen for it; but I, I would give much, if I had much, that this thing had never happened! I owned, sir, a pair of breeches, blue, in checks, a first-class article, the devil take them—a rich landowner who came here on business ordered them from me, but refused afterward to take them, saying that they were too tight, and left them with me.

"Well, I thought, the cloth is of first-rate quality! I can get five rubles for them in the old clothes market place, and, if not, I can cut a fine pair of pantaloons out of them for some St. Petersburg gent, and have a piece left over for a vest for myself. Everything counts with a poor man! And Emelian was at that time in sore straits. I saw that he had given up drinking, first one day, then a second, and a third, and looked so downhearted and sad.

"Well, I thought, it is either that the poor fellow lacks the necessary coin or maybe he has entered on the right path, and has at last listened to good sense.

"Well, to make a long story short, an important holiday came just at that time, and I went to vespers. When I came back I saw Emelian sitting on the window-seat as drunk as a lord. Eh! I thought, so that is what you are about! And I go to my trunk to get out something I needed. I look! The breeches are not there. I rummage about in this place and that place: gone! Well, after I had searched all over and saw that they were missing for fair, I felt as if something had gone through me! I went after the old woman—as to Emelian, though there was evidence against him in his being drunk, I somehow never thought of him!

"'No,' says my old woman; 'the good Lord keep you, gentleman, what do I need breeches for! can I wear them? I myself missed a skirt the other day. I know nothing at all about it.'

"'Well,' I asked, 'has anyone called here?'

"'No one called,' she said. 'I was in all the time; your friend here went out for a short while and then came back; here he sits! Why don't you ask him?'

"'Did you happen, for some reason or other, Emelian, to take the breeches out of the trunk? The ones, you remember, which were made for the landowner?'

"'No,' he says, 'I have not taken them, Astafi Ivanich.'

"'What could have happened to them?' Again I began to search, but nothing came of it! And Emelian sat and swayed to and fro on the window-seat.

"I was on my knees before the open trunk, just in front of him. Suddenly I threw a sidelong glance at him. Ech, I thought, and felt very hot round the heart, and my face grew very red. Suddenly my eyes encountered Emelian's.

"'No,' he says, 'Astafi Ivanich. You perhaps think that I—you know what I mean—but I have not taken them.'

"'But where have they gone, Emelian?'

"'No,' he says, 'Astafi Ivanich, I have not seen them at all.'

"'Well, then, you think they simply went and got lost by themselves, Emelian?'

"'Maybe they did, Astafi Ivanich.'

"After this I would not waste another word on him. I rose from my knees, locked the trunk, and after I had lighted the lamp I sat down to work. I was remaking a vest for a government clerk, who lived on the floor below. But I was terribly rattled, just the same. It would have been much easier to bear, I thought, if all my wardrobe had burned to ashes. Emelian, it seems, felt that I was deeply angered. It is always so, sir, when a man is guilty; he always feels beforehand when trouble approaches, as a bird feels the coming storm.

"'And do you know, Astafi Ivanich,' he suddenly began, 'the leech married the coachman's widow today.'

"I just looked at him; but, it seems, looked at him so angrily that he understood: I saw him rise from his seat, approach the bed, and begin to rummage in it, continually repeating: 'Where could they have gone? Vanished, as if the devil had taken them!'

"I waited to see what was coming; I saw that my Emelian had crawled under the bed. I could contain myself no longer.

"'Look here,' I said. 'What makes you crawl under the bed?'

"'I am looking for the breeches, Astafi Ivanich,' said Emelian from under the bed. 'Maybe they got here somehow or other.'

"'But what makes you, sir (in my anger I addressed him as if he was—somebody), what makes you trouble yourself on account of such a plain man as I am; dirtying your knees for nothing!'

"'But, Astafi Ivanich—I did not mean anything—I only thought maybe if we look for them here we may find them yet.'

"'Mm! Just listen to me a moment, Emelian!'

"'What, Astafi Ivanich?'

"'Have you not simply stolen them from me like a rascally thief, serving me so for my bread and salt?' I said to him, beside myself with wrath at the sight of him crawling under the bed for something he knew was not there.

"'No, Astafi Ivanich.' For a long time he remained lying flat under the bed. Suddenly he crawled out and stood before me—I seem to see him even now—as terrible a sight as sin itself.

"'No,' he says to me in a trembling voice, shivering through all his body and pointing to his breast with his finger, so that all at once I became scared and could not move from my seat on the window. 'I have not taken your breeches, Astafi Ivanich.'

"'Well,' I answered, 'Emelian, forgive me if in my foolishness I have accused you wrongfully. As to the breeches, let them go hang; we will get along without them. We have our hands, thank God, we will not have to steal, and now, too, we will not have to sponge on another poor man; we will earn our living.'

"Emelian listened to me and remained standing before me for some time, then he sat down and sat motionless the whole evening; when I lay down to sleep, he was still sitting in the same place.

"In the morning, when I awoke, I found him sleeping on the bare floor, wrapped up in his cloak; he felt his humiliation so strongly that he had no heart to go and lie down on the bed.

"Well, sir, from that day on I conceived a terrible dislike for the man; that is, rather, I hated him the first few days, feeling as if, for instance, my own son had robbed me and given me deadly offense. Ech, I thought, Emelian, Emelian! And Emelian, my dear sir, had gone on a two weeks' spree. Drunk to bestiality from morning till night. And during the whole two weeks he had not uttered a word. I suppose he was consumed the whole time by a deep-seated grief, or else he was trying in this way to make an end to himself. At last he gave up drinking. I suppose he had no longer the wherewithal to buy vodka—had drunk up every copeck—and he once more took up his old place on the window-seat. I remember that he sat there for three whole days without a word; suddenly I see him weep; sits there and cries, but what crying! The tears come from his eyes in showers, drip, drip, as if he did not know that he was shedding them. It is very painful, sir, to see a grown man weep, all the more when the man is of advanced years, like Emelian, and cries from grief and a sorrowful heart.

"'What ails you, Emelian?' I say to him.

"He starts and shivers. This was the first time I had spoken to him since that eventful day.

"'It is nothing—Astafi Ivanich.'

"'God keep you, Emelian; never you mind it all. Let bygones be bygones. Don't take it to heart so, man!' I felt very sorry for him.

"'It is only that—that I would like to do something—some kind of work, Astafi Ivanich.'

"'But what kind of work, Emelian?'

"'Oh, any kind. Maybe I will go into some kind of service, as before. I have already been at my former employer's, asking. It will not do for me, Astafi Ivanich, to use you any longer. I, Astafi Ivanich, will perhaps obtain some employment, and then I will pay you for everything, food and all.'

"'Don't, Emelian, don't. Well, let us say you committed a sin; well, it is all over! The devil take it all! Let us live as before—as if nothing had happened!'

"'You, Astafi Ivanich, you are probably hinting about that . But I have not taken your breeches.'

"'Well, just as you please, Emelian!'

"'No, Astafi Ivanich, evidently I cannot live with you longer. You will excuse me, Astafi Ivanich.'

"'But God be with you, Emelian,' I said to him; 'who is it that is offending you or driving you out of the house? Is it I who am doing it?'

"'No, but it is unseemly for me to misuse your hospitality any longer, Astafi Ivanich; 'twill be better to go.'

"I saw that he had in truth risen from his place and donned his ragged cloak—he felt offended, the man did, and had gotten it into his head to leave, and—basta .

"'But where are you going, Emelian? Listen to sense: what are you? Where will you go?'

"'No, it is best so, Astafi Ivanich, do not try to keep me back,' and he once more broke into tears; 'let me be, Astafi Ivanich, you are no longer what you used to be.'

"'Why am I not? I am just the same. But you will perish when left alone—like a foolish little child, Emelian.'

"'No, Astafi Ivanich. Lately, before you leave the house, you have taken to locking your trunk, and I, Astafi Ivanich, see it and weep—No, it is better you should let me go, Astafi Ivanich, and forgive me if I have offended you in any way during the time we have lived together.'

"Well, sir! And so he did go away. I waited a day and thought: Oh, he will be back toward evening. But a day passes, then another, and he does not return. On the third—he does not return. I grew frightened, and a terrible sadness gripped at my heart. I stopped eating and drinking, and lay whole nights without closing my eyes. The man had wholly disarmed me! On the fourth day I went to look for him; I looked in all the taverns and pot-houses in the vicinity, and asked if anyone had seen him. No, Emelian had wholly disappeared! Maybe he has done away with his miserable existence, I thought. Maybe, when in his cups, he has perished like a dog, somewhere under a fence. I came home half dead with fatigue and despair, and decided to go out the next day again to look for him, cursing myself bitterly for letting the foolish, helpless man go away from me. But at dawn of the fifth day (it was a holiday) I heard the door creak. And whom should I see but Emelian! But in what a state! His face was bluish and his hair was full of mud, as if he had slept in the street; and he had grown thin, the poor fellow had, as thin as a rail. He took off his poor cloak, sat down on my trunk, and began to look at me. Well, sir, I was overjoyed, but at the same time felt a greater sadness than ever pulling at my heart-strings. This is how it was, sir: I felt that if a thing like that had happened to me, that is—I would sooner have perished like a dog, but would not have returned. And Emelian did. Well, naturally, it is hard to see a man in such a state. I began to coddle and comfort him in every way.

"'Well,' I said, 'Emelian, I am very glad you have returned; if you had not come so soon, you would not have found me in, as I intended to go hunting for you. Have you had anything to eat?'

"'I have eaten, Astafi Ivanich.'

"'I doubt it. Well, here is some cabbage soup—left over from yesterday; a nice soup with some meat in it—not the meagre kind. And here you have some bread and a little onion. Go ahead and eat; it will do you good.'

"I served it to him; and immediately realized that he must have been starving for the last three days—such an appetite as he showed! So it was hunger that had driven him back to me. Looking at the poor fellow, I was deeply touched, and decided to run into the nearby dram-shop. I will get him some vodka, I thought, to liven him up a bit and make peace with him. It is enough. I have nothing against the poor devil any longer. And so I brought the vodka and said to him: 'Here, Emelian, let us drink to each other's health in honor of the holiday. Come, take a drink. It will do you good.'

"He stretched out his hand, greedily stretched it out, you know, and stopped; then, after a while, he lifted the glass, carried it to his mouth, spilling the liquor on his sleeve; at last he did carry it to his mouth, but immediately put it back on the table.

"'Well, why don't you drink, Emelian?'

"'But no, I'll not, Astafi Ivanich.'

"'You'll not drink it!'

"'But I, Astafi Ivanich, I think—I'll not drink any more, Astafi Ivanich.'

"'Is it for good you have decided to give it up, Emelian, or only for to-day?'

"He did not reply, and after a while I saw him lean his head on his hand, and I asked him: 'Are you not feeling well, Emelian?'

"'Yes, pretty well, Astafi Ivanich.'

"I made him go to bed, and saw that he was truly in a bad way. His head was burning hot and he was shivering with ague. I sat by him the whole day; toward evening he grew worse. I prepared a meal for him of kvass, butter, and some onion, and threw in it a few bits of bread, and said to him: "Go ahead and take some food; maybe you will feel better!'

"But he only shook his head: 'No, Astafi Ivanich, I shall not have any dinner to-day.'

"I had some tea prepared for him, giving a lot of trouble to the poor old woman with whom I rented a part of the room—but he would not take even a little tea.

"Well, I thought to myself, it is a bad case. On the third morning I went to see the doctor, an acquaintance of mine, Dr. Kostopravov, who had treated me when I still lived in my last place. The doctor came, examined the poor fellow, and only said: 'There was no need of sending for me; he is already too far gone; but you can give him some powders which I will prescribe.'

"Well, I didn't give him the powders at all, as I understood that the doctor was only doing it for form's sake; and in the meanwhile came the fifth day.

"He lay dying before me, sir. I sat on the window-seat with some work I had on hand lying on my lap. The old woman was raking the stove. We were all silent, and my heart was breaking over this poor, shiftless creature, as if he were my own son whom I was losing. I knew that Emelian was gazing at me all the time: I noticed from the earliest morning that he longed to tell me something, but seemingly dared not. At last I looked at him, and saw that he did not take his eyes from me, but that whenever his eyes met mine, he immediately lowered his own.

"'Astafi Ivanich!'

"'What, Emelian?'

"'What if my cloak should be carried over to the old clothes market, would they give much for it, Astafi Ivanich?'

"'Well,' I said, 'I do not know for certain, but three rubles they would probably give for it, Emelian.' I said it only to comfort the simple-minded creature; in reality they would have laughed in my face for even thinking to sell such a miserable, ragged thing.

"'And I thought that they might give a little more, Astafi Ivanich. It is made of cloth, so how is it that they would not wish to pay more than three rubles for it?'

"'Well, Emelian, if you wish to sell it, then of course you may ask more for it at first.'

"Emelian was silent for a moment, then he once more called to me.

"'Astafi Ivanich!'

"'What is it, Emelian?'

"'You will sell the cloak after I am gone; no need of burying me in it; I can well get along without it; it is worth something, and may come handy to you.'

"Here I felt such a painful gripping at my heart as I cannot even express, sir. I saw that the sadness of approaching death had already come upon the man. Again we were silent for some time. About an hour passed in this way. I looked at him again and saw that he was still gazing at me, and when his eyes met mine he immediately lowered his.

"'Would you like a drink of cold water?' I asked him.

"'Give me some, and may God repay you, Astafi Ivanich.'

"'Would you like anything else, Emelian?'

"'No, Astafi Ivanich, I do not want anything, but I—'

"'What?'

"'You know that—'

"'What is it you want, Emelian?'

"'The breeches—You know—It was I who took them—Astafi Ivanich.'

"'Well,' I said, 'the great God will forgive you, Emelian, poor, unfortunate fellow that you are! Depart in peace.'

"And I had to turn away my head for a moment because grief for the poor devil took my breath away and the tears came in torrents from my eyes.

"'Astafi Ivanich!—'

"I looked at him, saw that he wished to tell me something more, tried to raise himself, and was moving his lips—He reddened and looked at me—Suddenly I saw that he began to grow paler and paler; in a moment he fell with his head thrown back, breathed once, and gave his soul into God's keeping."

Made in the USA